A Shadowed I

By
Frederick Merrick White

I. — HARD UP.

Nothing from the hot languid street below but a grumbling, whining voice or two. A mean London street off the river in August. How men who know the country and have the scent of the sap in their nostrils can toil and moil under such conditions is known only to themselves and their God.

High up a cheap low-flash lamp added to the heat of a third-floor room, and gave a spice of danger to the occupant's more sordid condition. The man, bending over a penny exercise book, rose as there came from below a succession of knocks growing gradually louder. The dull double thud came presently far down below. A small servant came presently and laid a letter by the writer's elbow.

It was no manuscript returned or stereo-typed note of acceptance, nothing more than a curt intimation that unless the rent of the third floor of No. 19, Pant-street, was paid before twelve o'clock to-morrow a distress would be levied. These things are not idle threats in Pant-street.

"What is it, Dick?" a pleasant voice asked from the outer darkness.

"Rent," Dick Stevenson said between his teeth. "Midday to-morrow. Our last anchor gone—'a poor thing, but mine own.'"

Molly Stevenson groaned. It seemed dreadfully disloyal, but she had been wondering lately if Dick was the genius that they had both fondly imagined.

They all used to be under this delusion in the old vicarage.
Molly was to be a great artist, and Dick to combine Scott and Dickens and a few great lights of fiction. The streets of London were paved with gold, and so those noble-hearted, simple young folks walked into it hand in hand two years ago, since which time—
But that is an old story, and has been told time out of mind. The prosaic fact was three pounds twelve shillings were due for rent, and that, if the sum was not paid by high noon to-morrow, two struggling geniuses would be turned into the street.
"Could you possibly get that money from 'The Record?'" Molly asked.
Dick shook his head. 'The Record' only paid on Fridays, it was nearly ten o'clock, and the business manager of the morning journal in question would have gone home before now. Moreover, he was a member of the firm who left a great deal to his well-trained subordinates.
"It is nearly six pounds, Molly," Dick said, "a little stroke of luck that came just in the nick of time between ourselves and the workhouse. Still I'll try it."
They were busy enough in the office of "The Record." A score of pale-faced clerks were slaving away under the brilliant bands of light thrown by the electrics. Without looking up, a cashier asked Stevenson's business.
"Mr. Spencer gone for the day," was the quick reply. "Won't be back till Friday, anyway. Account? Let me see. There was an account passed for you—six pounds odd. Get it on Friday in due course."
"If I could only have it now?"
"Rubbish. We don't do business like that, as you ought to know by this time. If I paid that I should get myself into trouble."
Dick turned heavily away. The cashier was not to blame, he was a mere machine in the office. As Dick passed into the street somebody followed him.
"I'm awfully sorry," he stammered, "but you see I recognised you, Mr. Stevenson. My father was head gardener at Stanmere, and many a kindness we used to get from the rector and your mother. Are you—er, are you—"
The bright eyed lad hesitated in confusion.
"Hard up," Dick said, grimly. "I recognise you now, young Williams. How about those Ribstone Pippins that his lordship—"
"Please don't jest with me," the other said, imploringly. "I came out to tell you that Mr. Spencer has gone home. His address is 117 Cambria Square—he has one of those big flats there. If you go and see Mr. Spencer and tell him exactly how you stand, he will give you an order on the counting-house at once. Mr. Spencer will do anything for anybody."
"That's very good of you," Dick said, gratefully. "As it happens, I have never seen Mr. Spencer. What is he like?"
"Tall and spare, with a long grey beard. He's an enormously rich man, and practically our paper belongs to him. He never goes out in the daytime because

he has something queer the matter with his eyes. During the year I have been in the office I have never seen him in the daytime."

Apparently Mr. Spencer of 'The Record' was a difficult person to find. It was a long time before the porter motioned Dick into the lift. Eventually a sombre-looking man in black livery conveyed him into a sitting-room, the solitary light of which was so shaded down that the intruder could see nothing but dim shadows. Presently out of these shadows loomed a tall figure, with the suggestion of a beard on his face.

"You wished to see me," he said. His voice was kindly, but there was a strange note of agitation in it. There was no reason why this rich and powerful man should be frightened, but undoubtedly he was. "Your name is strange to me."

Dick explained more or less incoherently. As he stumbled on nervously his almost unseen companion seemed to gain courage.

"It's a dreadful liberty," Dick mumbled. "But my little home is all I have, and —and the money is owing to me, and—"

"And you most assuredly shall have it," Mr. Spencer interrupted. "My secretary has unfortunately gone out, or I could give you a cheque now. But my card and a line or two on it will produce the money at the office. And if you call and see me there after nine to-morrow night I'll see what I can do for you."

Dick murmured his thanks.

The sudden kindness, the prospect of something beyond this terrible hand-to-mouth kind of existence, had thoroughly unhinged him. As he stood there, a little white-haired terrier trotted along the passage and sniffed at him with an eye to friendship. Dick stooped with a kindly pat, and the dog licked his hand.

"Your coat is coming off, sir," Dick said, huskily. "Look at my trousers, the best pair I have, and between ourselves, doggie, the only pair. And all smothered with white hairs. And if the editor of 'The Times' sent for me suddenly, why—"

Dick paused, conscious that he was talking pure nonsense. He was also conscious of the sudden opening of a door at the end of the corridor, a brilliant bath of light, and the figure of the most beautiful girl Dick had ever seen in his life. He was destined never to forget the perfect symmetry of that lovely face and the deep pathos of those dark blue eyes. A man came out, half turning to kiss the face of the girl, evidently previous to his departure.

"Exquisite!" Dick muttered. "At the same time it strikes me that I am more or less playing the spy. There's an air of mystery about them that appeals to the novelist's imagination. Good-night, doggie!"

He stooped down, gave the terrier a friendly pat, and was gone.

II. — AN ADVENTURE IN THE SQUARE.

"You'll get on," the cashier said with grim admiration, as he glanced at Mr. Spencer's card with its few pencilled lines. "There's your money."
"Thanks," Dick replied. "Would you mind giving me that card back? It's sentimental, of course, but I should like to keep it. And if I can do anything for you—"
"Well, you can, as it happens. There's your card. There's a letter come for the governor which is marked urgent. I've got nobody I can send without inconvenience, and if it is not too much out of your way perhaps you will take it?"
It was a little cooler now, a few drops of rain had fallen, but not more than sufficient to lay the dust. Cambria Square was getting dark, a brooding silence lay over the gardens. Dick delivered his letter to the surly hall porter, and then turned his face eastwards. A few drops of the late rain pattered from leaf to leaf; there was a pleasant smell of moist earth in the air. By shutting his eyes Dick could conjure up visions of Stanmere.
The sound of hurried footsteps brought him to earth again. As he re-crossed to the pavement a tall figure, with streaming beard and white agitated face came round the corner almost into his arms. On the impulse of the moment Dick shot out a strong arm and detained him.
"I hope there is nothing wrong, sir?" he asked, meaningly.
The tall man with the beard paused and rubbed his eyes. He had every appearance of one who flies in his sleep from some terror.
"Did you see anybody?" he whispered. "A man who had—but of course you didn't, the thing is utterly absurd. Sir, are you a man of imagination?"
Dick replied that unless he possessed imagination, he had cruelty mistaken his vocation in life. The strange man with the wild air was utterly unknown to him, and yet there was something in his voice that was familiar. The terror was gradually dying from his face; he was growing sane and quiet again. It was a fine, broad, kindly face, but there was the shadow of some great trouble haunting the deep-set grey eyes.
"I must have astonished you just now," he said. "As a matter or fact, I have had a great many years abroad. Sunstroke, you understand; since when I have never been quite the same. I can manage my property as well as anybody; for months I am quite myself, and then these attacks come suddenly. Always at night when I am alone in the dark; I come out to try and cure myself. At the same time, are you quite sure that you met nobody?"
"If you would like," Dick suggested, "I shall be glad to walk a little way—"
The stranger replied somewhat curtly to the effect that there was no occasion for anything of the kind. He passed on with a steady step, leaving Dick to his more or less amused thoughts. Such a character might be useful to him in fiction. The whole facts of the case appealed to the young novelist's imagination. Here was a rich and prosperous man, envied and flattered and

admired, who was constantly pursued by some haunting terror. Perhaps in the early days he had committed some great crime; perhaps some dreadful vengeance was hanging over his head.
But the noble, kindly face belied all that. No doubt the explanation given was no more than the truth. The poor fellow suffered in that peculiar form, and he was doing his best to shame himself out of it.
"I'll take another turn round the square," Dick said to himself. "It's foolish, but I am too restless to go home quite yet."
It was very still there. Most of the lights were out in the staid houses by this time, a policeman clanked along and disappeared. Then a murmur of voices arose, the distant sound of laboured breathing, a shout and a strangled cry. It was all strange and dreamy for a moment, then the reality of tragedy flashed upon the listener. He might be in time to prevent outrage or worse.
He turned the corner quickly. As he did so, his tall friend with the beard came along. He was running fast, with the free and easy stride of the athlete, running with an ease surprising in one of his time of life, his beard streaming in the breeze caused by his own swift motion. He was without a hat; there was a certain ferocious furtiveness in his eyes, but the broad, noble face had not changed. It was not the face of a man in terror now, but the face of one who flies from some crime.
He dodged Dick, who stood to bar his progress, with the greatest ease. The smile on his face was of contempt. There was not the slightest sign of recognition on it. And Dick could have sworn that his late companion had worn a black tie, yet there he was again with a vivid red one.
Meanwhile the groans were still going on. Dick sped rapidly round the corner. The whole thing had happened so quickly that no time had been lost. Just by one of the pillars of the stout, square railings, was a patch of blood. From somewhere close by moaning could be heard.
"Where are you?" Dick whispered.
"Inside," came the reply. "When he struck me down I saw that there was somebody behind him. Then I turned and lifted up the second rail from the stone capital and crept inside here. It comes up from the bottom. You can get through that way."
Dick staggered back. The voice was quite familiar to him. It sounded just like the voice of the dangerous lunatic he had encountered half an hour ago. But that could not be, seeing that the madman in question had just passed him, flying apparently for his life, in another direction.
"I'll come to you," Dick Stammered. "It's quite safe."
"You are quite sure that he has gone?"
"Certain. He passed me running his best. Did you say the second rail? Yes, here it is. Now then."
The railing slid back in its socket, leaving a space large enough to admit a

human body. Dick squeezed through, until presently he could see the dim outline of a figure prostrate on the grass.
"Are you very much hurt?" he asked.
"No," said the strangely familiar voice. "A mere flesh wound. What's that?"
"So far as I can judge, a belated policeman hurrying to the spot. Shall I call him?"
Dick's arm was grasped with passionate force.
"Not for worlds!" came a hoarse reply. "If you have any regard for more than one pure and innocent life you will be silent. Let the man search; he will find nothing. I found that loose rail by accident, and by this means I often come here late at night. Hush! that man is coming close."
The flashing zones of light ceased, the beat of footsteps died away. All was still and quiet once again.
"We can't stay here all night," Dick suggested.
His companion staggered to his feet, Dick helping him into the roadway. He stood under the lamplight the most astonished young man in London, for his companion was the man with the grey beard and the kindly face.
"You seem to be my guardian spirit to-night," he said, faintly.
Dick had no reply. He was too dazed to think as yet

III. — A VANISHED MEMORY.

"Tell me all about sir," he suggested.
"I can tell you nothing whatever," said the other, still slinking with terror. "My mind has gone again, I only know that I have had a great shock, which is none the less terrible because I have been expecting it for years. I heard his step and ran. Put me in a crowd with a million people and I could pick out his step without hesitation."
The speaker wiped the blood from his face. He was not very much hurt, only frightened to the verge of insanity. He was quivering all over like a reed shaken by the wind.
"Why does this man pursue you?" Stevenson asked.
"I don't know. I have entirely forgotten. But I never forget his step and that I must fly when I hear it coming. You are a gentleman?"
Dick modestly hoped so. The knowledge was one of the few consolations that remained to him. The old man looked long and earnestly into his pleasant, open face. It was some time before he spoke.
"At present I know nothing," he said at length. "The terror has deprived me of my wits for the time being. To-morrow I shall be doing my business again as if nothing had happened. I ask you to leave me now, sir, and think no more of what you have seen and heard. Let it be a secret between us."
"Provided that you let me see you home," said Dick.

"No; I am going to walk about a little longer. Then it may come back to me. At present I could not tell you my address or even—"

He broke off abruptly, and regarded his companion with troubled eyes. The man had actually forgotten his name and address. It was utterly impossible for him to be left like this.

"We'll speak to a policeman," Dick said, promptly.

The terror shut down again, the deep-set eyes dilated.

"No, no," he whispered; "anything but that. The police must not know. Do you want to ruin me utterly?"

"Then I am going to take you home," Dick said, firmly. "Yours may be an exceedingly valuable life for all I know. Where do you live?"

"As I hope for salvation I cannot tell you. It will come back to me presently, perhaps in a few minutes, two hours. But it will come back."

"But surely your own name, sir—"

"I have no more cognisance of it than I have of your own."

The man spoke in evident sincerity. It was clear that he concealed nothing. All the time Dick wondered why his voice was so strangely familiar. But he had other things to occupy his attention. He must respect the old man's earnest prayer to keep the story from the police. At the same time, in his present demented condition, it was impossible to leave him to the mercy of the streets. It was a pretty puzzle for the young novelist. If this thing were a story, how would he have got out of the difficulty?

"How long have you been out to-night?" he asked, tentatively.

"I don't know. At present I don't know anything. There is only a vague impression that a beautiful girl with blue eyes is waiting for me anxiously. If you ask me who she is, I fancy it is my daughter."

"Then the beautiful girl with the blue eyes shall not be disappointed," said Stevenson, cheerfully. "I shall find a way out."

He rubbed his coat sleeve thoughtfully. There was a little dampness on it from the effects of the recent spurt of rain, and Dick noticed that the clothing of his companion was perfectly dry. The rain had been over for nearly half an hour, therefore it was manifest the old man had quite recently left the house. He was not a fast walker, therefore he could not be far from home. The deduction was quite logical.

"You came out after the rain?" Dick asked.

"Yes, I went back, fearing that it would be heavy. It is too hot a night for one to wear an overcoat. Therefore I waited for the rain to stop."

Something had been gained, at any rate. Stevenson studied his companion latently. On his dark coat he could see a number of short white hairs.

"You keep a small fox-terrier dog?" he asked, with sudden inspiration.

The other nodded. His memory seemed to be curiously patchy. The little things seemed with him, the great ones were gone. "A little fox-terrier called

Ben," he said.
With that Dick was fain to be content. Here he was saddled with a lunatic old gentleman in the streets of midnight London, and the only clue to the local habitation of his companion was that he possessed a dog called Ben. That master and dog were good friends Stevenson deduced from the hairs on his companion's clothing. What the novelist had to do now was to look for a house within a radius of a mile or so where there was a dog called Ben.
It seemed slightly ridiculous, but Stevenson could think of no better plan than getting his companion to whistle and call the dog at intervals. If the worst came to the worst he could take his demented friend to his own humble abode and keep him there till morning. For some time it had been painfully apparent to Dick that he was faint for want of food. If he collapsed now there would be nothing for it but the nearest police station.
"Whistle again," he said, dreamily. "Try once more."
They were in Cambria Square now, near the large block of flats. The flats appeared to have several doors, for this one was not even on the same side as Stevenson entered an hour or two before. The old gentleman whistled softly, and called Ben by name for about the fiftieth time. There was a yelping and scratching behind the door, and a dog whining in joyful recognition.
"Shades of the immortal Dupurin," Dick cried, "success at last. It is very certain that we have found your house, sir."
With no fear of surly porter before his eyes, Dick opened the door.
A little dog came bounding out and gyrated wildly. A hall porter appeared, and with the surly insolence of his kind demanded to know what was the matter.
"This gentleman lives here, I think," Dick said. "He has had a nasty fall—"
"Second floor," the porter growled. "Lift's off for the night. Better take him up, sir. Telephone on next floor if you want a doctor."
With a certain pardonable curiosity Dick led the way upstairs. So far as he could see there was only two sets of flats on the second floor, and one of them was obviously in the hands of the decorators. Therefore, there was only one alternative. Dick pushed into a corridor that seemed familiar to him, and boldly led the way into a drawing-room, where a girl was seated at the piano playing soft dreamy music.
The room was bathed in electric light; there were wonderful works of art there —silver of Cellini, engravings after Romney and Reynolds, a Hopper or two, some marvellous old French furniture. But the most striking thing about the room were the marvellous masses of flowers everywhere. The whole place was a veritable bower of them, roses and lilies and violets. The mere arrangement of them was in itself a work of art.
But Dick forgot the flowers a moment later as the girl turned her face towards him. It was the beautiful girl with the pathetic blue eyes he had seen two hours before. The intruder had not the least doubt about this, that face and those eyes

were too indelibly printed on his mind for that.
The girl came forward without hesitation.
"I have been anxious about you," she cried. "Father, you have had one of your bad turns, I could hear that by your step as you came upstairs. And this gentleman has brought you home, though he is tired and utterly worn out himself."
"It is good of you to think of me," Dick stammered; "but how could you possibly know that I am—"
Starving, he was about to say, but stopped in time. The girl laughed with a rippling music that filled the room.
"I have the gift of second sight," she said. Though her face was wreathed in smiles, the great blue eyes never laughed, but ever remained so strangely pathetic. "Only a man utterly worn out would walk as you do. And you are quite young, too. You must have something to eat at once."
She crossed the room and rang the bell. Dick watched her graceful motions with a pleasure that was almost akin to pain.

IV. — "I KNOW HER."

A servant or two came and went as if an order for a midnight supper was a matter of course, then there came a stolid looking man with a Teutonic face, who took the host away like a prisoner in custody.
"My father will be better presently," the girl said. "He is subject to strange lapses of memory. Kant's system of treatment never fails to benefit him. Now, will you please to have some supper, Mr.—"
"My name is Richard Stevenson," Dick said. "I was in the building some time ago, and I had the pleasure of seeing you before, Miss—"
"Call me Miss Mary. That is the only name I have. As I have no friends and never see anybody, my name cannot matter. Also, as I have the strongest possible reasons for disliking my own, I am always Miss Mary. Now, will you please eat your supper without further delay?"
It was delicious, especially to a man who had long been a stranger to daintily-served, well-cooked food. The chicken and ham were perfect, the lettuce crisp and cool, and the claret soft and velvety to the taste. It was a different man who rose from the table presently.
"You must finish the claret," Mary said. "You have only had one glass. Are there not some cigarettes on the table there?"
Dick could not see any. Mary advanced to find them. Her long, slim fingers seemed to caress everything that she touched.
"Surely they are on the far corner by your left hand," Dick suggested.
For some reason the girl blushed deeply.
"Then they have been moved," she said. "I cannot find them. I don't like things

to be moved. It upsets all my scheme of memory. I always boast that I can see anything in the room, and when the servants—"
"Is your eye-sight deficient?" Dick asked.
"I have no eye-sight," came the quiet reply. "I am stone-blind."
Dick was utterly shocked. This was the last thing in the world that he had expected. Those great blue eyes were very pathetic and sorrowful; but they looked so pure and clear and liquid. He stammered an apology.
"I am so deeply sorry," he said. "But you see I could not possibly know. And you seemed to see me when I came in, you moved so freely, and you actually knew that I had taken only one glass of claret."
"That is because my hearing is so good," Mary replied. "One instinctively trains one sense to take the place of the missing one. I can deduce a great deal by the way people walk. And I have lived almost entirely in this and my bedroom for many years. Really, so far as this room is concerned, I can see. I know where everything is, I can tell you what flowers there are in this and that vase, though there are scores of them. I was not always blind."
Dick lingered on, feeling that he ought to go. The feeling became more absolute when the Teutonic servant came in with the information that his master was much better, and had gone to bed. He hinted that under the circumstances his kind young friend would excuse him. The dismissal was polite enough, but it was none the less complete and final. There was even no excuse left for calling.
"We are very quiet people," Mary said, as if she could actually read the thoughts of her visitor. "Believe me, I am more than grateful for your kindness to-night. You are a gentleman, and you will understand."
She came forward and held out her hand. Dick held it with a certain longing at his heart. The pathetic beauty of that sightless face stirred him strangely. It was not Mary's beauty alone, but her helplessness, that moved him. And she seemed to be utterly lonely.
"Good-night," he said; "there need be no obligation on your side. Good-night."
"Good-night, and a thousand thanks. Do you like flowers as well as I do? Let me give you a few of my favorite violets."
She walked rapidly to a vase and took out a fragrant mass of purple bloom. Without the slightest hesitation she picked up an envelope—one of the transparent grease-proof kind that proofs of photographs are sent in—and placed the blossoms in it.
It seemed hard to credit the fact that she was sightless.
"There!" she said, quite gaily. "A little trifle to remember me by. Good-night."
Dick was well out into the square before he could think of a suitable reply. Truly it had been a night of strange adventures. Not the least strange thing was that the scene of these happenings had been all in the Cambria Square flats. Stevenson felt strangely alert and wide awake as he put his latchkey in the

door.

Molly was awaiting him anxiously. She looked almost pitifully into his cheerful face.

"I began to imagine all sorts of dreadful things," she said. "You have never been out so late before without letting me know. When you have had your supper—"

Dick stooped and kissed the pretty speaker. Really, Molly was a very pretty girl with her delicate coloring and high-bred face.

"Thoughtful girl," he said. "Always thinking of others first. My dear Molly, I have supped on superb chicken and salad and claret, such as Ouida's guardsmen would not disdain to drink. I partook of it in a perfect bower of bliss filled with flowers and priceless works of art, and in the company of the most lovely girl I have ever seen in all my life. I walked into the prosaic streets of London and suddenly found myself plunged into the Arabian Nights."

"Always in good spirits," Molly murmured. "But to be more practical. There is nothing of the Haroun al Raschid about our landlord."

"The landlord will be paid, Molly. I took my courage in both hands and went to see Mr. Spencer. He gave me an order for the money, which is at present in my pocket, and, what is more, he asked me to call upon him to-morrow night, when he as good as promised me regular work to do. Think of it, Molly; a cottage in the country where we can breathe the pure air and grow our own flowers."

Molly began to cry quietly. Not even good kind old Dick knew what she had suffered here. She wiped her eyes presently and called herself a goose.

"I suppose I'm run down," she said, in extenuation. "And now tell me all about those wonderful adventures of yours."

Dick launched out into a graphic account of all that he had seen or heard. Molly's pretty face was aglow with interest. She had never heard anything like it before out of the pages of a book. She took the packet of violets presently and quietly removed them from the envelope.

"Why, there is something inside here!" she cried.

It was the proof of a photograph still unmounted. A pretty girl with great pathetic eyes, taken with a background of palms and flowers.

"Why, it's Miss Mary herself," Dick cried. "The photo must have been taken in the Cambria square drawing-room, and this odd proof must have escaped attention in the envelope. Now tell me candidly, Molly, did you ever see a more lovely face in all your life?"

Molly looked up with a dazed expression.

"Why, I know her," she whispered. "I recognised her in a moment. You have heard me speak of my old schoolfellow, Mary Gay."

V. — THE MOTH CATCHER.

Dick Stevenson nodded approvingly.

"I shall make a capital story out of this," he said. "One smiles at this kind of thing in books, and yet more remarkable events are chronicled in the papers every day. But isn't she lovely, Molly?"

Molly laid the photograph carefully on the table. The more she looked at it the more she was drawn and fascinated.

"It is a pretty episode," she said, "but only an episode, after all. I don't see how you are going to follow up the acquaintance, Dick. The poor girl is blind, and never goes out; the way you were dismissed was a pretty strong hint not to call again. And yet I should like to see Mary once more."

In his heart of hearts Dick was telling himself that this thing should be done. What was the use of being an author with all a novelist's imagination if one could not scheme some ingenious plan or other? He lighted a cigarette over the evil-smelling lamp with a thoughtful air. Somebody was knocking at the door.

"Come in," Molly said; "it can be nobody but Herr Greigstein."

A small, stout man, with close-cut hair and enormous moustache came into the room. He had a high, broad forehead and a magnificent pair of flashing eyes that seemed to be marred by spectacles. There was a suggestion of power about this man of strong intellectual force and determination. For the most part he was smiling and loquacious; he possessed a boyish flow of animal spirits, belied now and again by a quick-flashing glance, and a gathering of deep-set eyebrows. For the rest, Max Greigstein was a lodger on the top floor of the Pant-street house, and he was generally supposed to be a German master in a North London school.

"I am late," he said, breezily, "but I come with news of the best. You remember, Herr Dick, I give you certain information about German anarchists in London. You put him in the form of some articles for a friend of mine, who has a paper in Berlin. My friend, he sends me eleven pounds for those pen pictures and asks, like Oliver Twist, for more, therefore, we divide the money as arranged, and when landlord he come to-morrow he grovel and eat dust before you. Behold, the little fairies that make sad hearts light!"

With something of the air of a conjurer and something of his swiftness, Greigstein laid some gold coins on the little table. His tongue had no pause, his restless dark eyes seemed as if seeking for something. For all his friendship and his many little kindnesses, Dick rather disliked Greigstein. He admitted the fact with shame, but there it was. He knew the little German scientist to be miserably poor; still he had played the good fairy like this often before.

"Here is the beginning of fame and fortune," he cried. "You grow rich, you marry a beautiful and talented young lady, and in the course of time—Gott in Himmel, what is this? where did it come from?"

The man's whole manner changed, there was quick command in his tone. He laid a strong brown finger on the photograph lying upwards on the table. He might have been a general who finds a fault in some strategic scheme, a lawyer who at length finds the weak spot in the witness's armor. His eyes flashed with strange brilliancy behind his glasses.

"I cannot tell you," Dick said coldly. "That proof came into my hands by the merest accident. It is no business of mine—or yours."

Greigstein waved the whole thing aside with a quick motion of his hand. The next moment he was chatting gaily of moths and butterflies. It was his own great hobby—that and science. There was a new moth that Dick must see, a new moth captured in the gardens of a London square.

"I catch him in a square," he cried excitedly. "I make friends with all the square keepers for miles around, and they let me go into the gardens when the world is dark and quiet. And I get my new moth. I take him to South Kensington, and they say he is but, Callimorpha Lecontei. Ach, the fools!"

Dick listened more or less vaguely. He had heard all about those nocturnal rambles before.

"Some day you listen to my theories," Greigstein rabbled on. It seemed to Dick that he was keeping his eyes too scrupulously averted from the table and the photograph. "Again there was the new clouded moth which I found at Stanmere. Some day, if I am lucky, I retire to Stanmere. It is the paradise of the entomologist. Herr Dick, do you know that I was at Stanmere last week?"

"You were lucky," Dick said, with a sigh.

"Even so, I was on the lake. The family were away from home. Strange that I should come and take rooms under the very roof of young people who had been born and bred at Stanmere. There are no dragon-flies like those on the lake yonder. I should never tire of Stanmere."

"I may never see the dear old place again," Dick said, regretfully. "I'd give a great deal to have a month there now, to lie in the bracken under the old park oaks, or to drift amongst the water-lilies in a punt. Fancy having a day with those trout once more! My good friend, if you don't stop talking about Stanmere at once, I shall be constrained to throw a book at you."

Greigstein would take himself off at once. It was getting very late, and he had some work to do before he went to bed. Meanwhile, would Herr Dick do some more of those brilliant articles? In a whirl of words the German departed, leaving his spectacles behind him. Dick noticed them presently.

"I don't believe he wants glasses at all," he said. "He is a Socialist. Meanwhile, I'll take his glasses, lest he should come back again. I'm too tired to swim in another sea of words to-night."

Dick slipped quietly up the stairs of the quiet house. Greigstein's bedroom was slightly open, and Dick looked in. The gas was lighted by the dressing-table. The German stood there in immaculate evening dress, his moustaches waxed.

To Dick's utter astonishment he saw that across the broad glistening expanse of shirtfront was a riband, and round the powerful throat a jewelled order was suspended. A silk-lined evening cloak lay across a chair.
Dick softly retired with the spectacles in his pocket. He heard the front door close presently, and footsteps going down the street. And on the table lay the photograph of the girl with the sad blue eyes!

VI. — THE RESTORED PHOTOGRAPH.

When Dick came down to breakfast Greigstein had departed, ostensibly on his scholastic duties. He had come in for the missing spectacles, Molly said. He had professed himself to be quite lost without them.
"That's all rubbish," Dick said, unfeelingly. "The fellow has no need for glasses. You may shake your head, Molly, but I will prove it to you."
In a few words Dick told the story of his discovery. Molly scented romance. They had evidently made the acquaintance of a disguised German nobleman.
"More likely a police spy," Dick laughed. "You need not go, Molly; I couldn't possibly do any work this morning. With that fateful interview with Mr. Spencer, of 'The Record,' before my eyes, I couldn't do a stroke."
He presently wandered out aimlessly. Though he had risen very late, the day seemed to drag on. It was hot, and the streets shimmered in the sunshine. Dick took a very frugal lunch at a cheap restaurant, and then turned for distraction to the early edition of the evening papers. The 'St. James's Gazette' and 'Pall Mall' and 'Globe' seemed to have nothing in them that he had not seen before. Over his cigarette he fell back on the advertisements.
There was something interesting at last. Dick recognised with a thrill that it concerned himself. It was in the agony column of 'The Globe.'
"Will the gentleman who took from 117 Cambria Square, last night, the proof of a photograph accidentally left in an envelope containing violets, kindly return the same to the above address without delay?"
Here was something to do at any rate. And, better than that, here was a good chance of seeing the girl with the pathetic eyes again. It would be a wrench to give up the photograph, but that would have to be done in any case. The precious picture was carefully stowed away in Dick's pocket-book.
He hurried off in the direction of Cambria Square. Not till he found himself confronted by the hall porter did he recollect that he had not the faintest idea whom to ask for.
"There is an advertisement in an evening paper," he stammered. "I was here last night; I had the good fortune to—"
"That's alright," the porter cut Dick short. "One of the servants told me in case anybody called. If you've got the photo, sir, I'll take it up."
Dick hesitated. He had looked forward to something more romantic than this.

He might be allowed to go up, he suggested, but the porter cut him short again by touching a bell and growling something hoarsely up a tube. In response the broad-faced, Teutonic-looking man who had acted as a kind of nurse to Dick's strange acquaintance of the night before, came down in the lift and touched his forehead respectfully.

"My mistress expected you, sir," he said. "You have the photograph?"

Dick could not deny it. He produced the picture grudgingly. It was absurd, of course, but it was a wrench to hand it over.

"My mistress has been in great distress," the German said. "I will not disguise from you, sir, that my employer has moods when he is not quite responsible for his actions. You found him last night in one of them. He has outbreaks over other things. For instance, my young lady thought she would like to surprise her father by having her photograph taken. There was but one proof, and only one plate exposed. I have rarely seen my employer so terribly upset over anything, which was strange, considering that the photograph was actually taken in the house. My young lady promised to destroy the proof, but by mistake she left it in the photographer's envelope. She found that out early this morning. She is greatly desirous that you will say nothing of what has happened."

"Of course not," Dick replied.

The mystery was getting deeper.

"If I may take the liberty of seeing her for a few moments—"

"No," the other said, with a cold curtness that brought the blood into Dick's face. "It is absolutely impossible. You must not come here again. I do not wish to be rude, sir, only I would urge you, both for your own sake and the sake of others, not to come here again."

Mr. Spencer had not yet arrived when he reached the counting-house. His young friend of the previous night gave him an encouraging smile. Presently Dick found himself waiting nervously in an outer office, where the lad who had previously given him Mr. Spencer's address had ushered him.

"Just a moment," Dick said, hurriedly. "Can you tell me anything about your chief? I only saw him in the dark last night."

"That is a peculiarity of his," the young clerk replied. "He often does that when he sees strangers here. It is some fad of his of judging people by their voices. But as he has met you once he won't do that again. Another peculiarity is that he never comes here till dusk. Not one of us ever saw Mr. Spencer here in the daytime."

"But you find him a good and kind employer?"

"Oh, very. He is the right class of philanthropist. He never appears to, and yet he does a tremendous deal of good. If he takes a fancy to you it is your own fault if you don't succeed here. He never spoke to me for months, and then I found that he knew all my affairs, and what my father was, and all about my

home at Stanmere, and everything. There's his bell."
The speaker turned away, to return a moment later with the information that Mr. Spencer was ready to see his visitor. It was a small, dark-papered room, with one brilliant light gleaming on a little table covered with paper. A man sat there who looked up and smiled at Dick genially, then he looked down again, as if giving his visitor time to recover himself.
It was as well that he did, well that he failed to see the blank amazement on the face of Dick Stevenson. He placed his hands on the back of his chair to steady himself from falling. For there, seated opposite him, as if utterly unconscious that anything out of the common had happened, was the very man whose life Dick had saved in Cambria Square last night.
Could it be acting? No, it was impossible. The man by the table evidently had not the faintest idea that he and Dick met before. This kindly noble-looking face was calm and placid. Evidently the events of last night had been absolutely and entirely wiped from his memory.
"Are you unwell?" he asked, in a considerate tone. "I am afraid you are in trouble. If you will only make a friend of me—"
"A passing faintness," Dick stammered. "A queer lapse of memory."
Mr. Spencer looked up, a feeling expression dimmed his eyes.
"I understand," he said. "Nobody better. I am occasionally troubled by the same thing myself. My dear boy, pray sit down and let us get to business."

VII. — GREIGSTEIN.

The keen eye of a detective would have noticed certain anomalies in Herr Max Greigstein's modest sitting-room. For instance, the table linen was very fine, the cutlery and plate, which the German preferred to clean himself, were of silver and fine steel mounted on ivory. These are things not unusually found in obscure bed-sitting rooms at nine shillings a week, and though the once exclusive cigarette is now given over to the multitude, they do not usually smoke a 'Nestor' at eleven shillings a hundred, such as Greigstein had between his lips at present.
The modest breakfast things were pushed away, and Greigstein was frowning over his ruminative cigarette. There was an excuse for his laziness this morning, as he had no scholastic engagement on Saturday. Greigstein was thinking aloud—a favorite habit of his—but the door was closed.
"You are a fool," he told himself, "you think you have yourself well in hand, but that is where you make the mistake. Come, why did you let Dick Stevenson see that you were interested in that photograph?"
Greigstein frowned at himself in a little mirror opposite.
"That is a clever boy," he went on, "he has intuition. Only he has the bad taste not to like Herr Greigstein. He will tell me nothing about the original of that

fascinating photo. With a lad of meaner instincts I should try bribery. But I shall find out, yes, I shall find out."
There was a gleam in Greigstein's eyes as he spoke. A moment later he was deeply engrossed in his cases of moths and butterflies as if they were of all-absorbing interest. Then he put his breakfast things outside the door and locked it after him. He carried a net and a specimen case with the simple air of a man who is going on an innocent holiday. The door of Stevenson's sitting-room was open.
"May I come in?" Greigstein asked, and entered the room without waiting for a reply. "What is the news, my young hero? Good, I imagine, by the expression of your face. That interview with the newspaper magnate, for instance. In my mind's eye I can see Dick Stevenson, editor of 'The Times.'"
Greigstein's glasses twinkled as he spoke, and Dick was disarmed. He was in a mood to be charmed with all the world this morning. The stuffy, evil-smelling rooms in Pant-street would soon be a thing of the past. Already there were visions of a charming house in the country presided over by a sweet-faced, blue-eyed girl who was none the less beloved because she was blind.
"Three hundred a year," Dick said, with a poor assumption of indifference; "I have got an appointment on the literary staff of 'The Record.' And I shall have plenty of time for my fiction writing besides. It isn't very often that one gets a good appointment and an excellent plot of a strong novel in one week."
Greigstein's congratulations were obviously sincere. At the same time there was a strange gleam behind his spectacles. There was a story here that the German was anxious to know, otherwise Dick would have said nothing about the plot of a novel. Greigstein passed his cigarette case across the table.
"I should like to hear more of your good fortune," he said, quietly. "I am glad for your sake and the sake of your charming and most courageous sister. So your good fortune was the result of an adventure?"
"Who told you so?" Dick asked with a smile.
"Why, you did yourself. You say it is not often one gets a good appointment and a good plot in the same week. Obviously, the good fortune in your case follows the good plot—the adventure, that is. That is the way, my good friend, to write a good novel. Personal experience, nothing like personal experience. I should like very much to hear all about those personal experiences. Now my butterflies—"
"Never mind the butterflies," Dick said, hastily; falling into the trap that Greigstein had laid for him. "But I'll tell you my adventure if you like."
Not all of it, Greigstein told himself. For instance, he knew perfectly well that he would hear nothing as to the photograph and its charming original, and in this the German was perfectly right, for Mary Gay was not mentioned.
"I think I have really interested you," Dick said, presently.
Greigstein nodded. Dick would have been fairly startled to know how deeply

his companion was interested. All the same, he had wisely said nothing as to the identity between Mr. Spencer and the excited stranger in Cambria Square. It was this half-truth that so sorely puzzled Greigstein and led him into so wide a labyrinth later on.
"And where did all this happen?" Greigstein asked, vaguely. "Cambria Square? Ah, I got a magnificent specimen of the silver-haired moth there a week or two ago. Your friend was a friend of Mr. Spencer, then, and thus your new appointment?"
"You may put it that way with truth," Dick replied, with a feeling that he had better have kept the whole story to himself. At any rate, he had concealed the fact that his benefactor was one of the actors in the strange drama. "Now, you can give me a clue to the real situation? For the purpose of fiction, I want to know why two men should act in so strange a manner."
Greigstein laughed, and professed the matter to be entirely beyond him. His face expressed a pleased and amiable curiosity. Yet he passed a hand over his face to conceal the strange, quick quivering of his lips.
"Alas! I am no novelist," he cried. "That you must work out for yourself, young Dick. And now I must be going. To-day is a holiday for me; I get away from those dreadful boys and forget that I am a mere drudge who imparts a mother tongue for a mere pittance."
He slipped out of the room with a thoughtful expression on his face. He saw nothing of the crowded streets; he pushed along mechanically.
"So they are both close at hand," he said to himself; "the one fleeing from a phantom the other pursuing an empty vengeance! And my young friend blunders into them and he finds the girl as well! Well, everything comes to the man who can afford to wait. On the whole, I can do no better than go down to Stanmere."

VIII. — ONE OF THE STATELY HOMES OF ENGLAND.

There are some fine houses in the Thames Valley between Oxford and Windsor, but none of greater beauty than Stanmere. It is not large, but it is pure Tudor, with never so much as a stone or window restored; its grey gables are softened and beautified by the hand of time; the velvet lawns have been rolled and shaven and shaven and rolled for three centuries. But the beauty of the place lies in its grounds.
There are green terraces slipping to a lake which is fed by a strong stream. The lake is dotted with islands and surrounded by woods at the far end, which renders it dark and gloomy. There is a summer-house with steps leading down to the water, and here Lady Stanmere spends a deal of her time in the warm weather.
The great green woods are wonderfully cool and silent; the great dragon flies

hover over the still water, covered here and there by sheets of white water-lilies; the paths all around are of grass, and behind them are yews cut into fantastic shapes like a stone cloister turned into living green. Withal the peace and silence is very mournful, as if some tragedy brooded here.

And in sooth there had been trouble enough and to spare at Stanmere. Lady Stanmere had lived to see her husband taken out of the placid lake where the dragon flies were brooding, and laid in what was no better than a suicide's grave; she had lived to see one son an outlaw and the other a nameless wanderer, until she could do no more than marvel at the amount of suffering she could endure and yet retain her reason. And here she was now, white-haired, broken, gentle, yet with some gleams of the once haughty spirit that had sustained her in the dark years of her life.

But this was not all the mystery. Whom the property would go to when Lady Stanmere no longer needed it nobody knew, save, perhaps, Mr. Martlett, the family lawyer, who was never yet known to tell anything to a soul. For all Lady Stanmere knew, both her sons were dead, and they might or might not have left a son behind them. And the mystery was rendered deeper by the fact that the last of the reigning Stanmeres had left his property hopelessly encumbered and had died heavily in debt. It was not an extravagant household, for Lady Stanmere's wants were simple; but the grounds were superb, and a small army of gardeners were required to keep them trim in the beautiful order for which they had always been famous.

Yet, despite debt and difficulty, everything was going on just the same as usual. The orchard houses and the vineries poured out their purple and golden harvest, the green lawns and the luxurious gardens were as trim and riotous as ever, not a single boy was discharged. And from time to time the thin, dried-up little Martlett presented certain papers for Lady Stanmere to sign, and with a cough that defied question, stated that this or that further mortgage had been paid off. A wonderful manager, Martlett, people said. But Martlett was dumb as an oyster.

Lady Stanmere sat in the summer-house overlooking the lake, her long slim hands engaged in some pretty silk meshwork upon which she was constantly engaged. Those long slim hands were never still for long together.

She had been tall and straight once, now she was bent and broken. Yet the dark eyes in the pale face could flash at times, and the old imperious ring came back into the gentle voice. For a long space the hands with their flashing rings went in and out of the silken web. A gorgeous butterfly hovered round the honeysuckle over the porch.

"Ah, my beauty," a deep voice said. "So I've got you now!"

At the sound of that voice the black netting fell a tangled heap into Lady Stanmere's lap. A queer little cry escaped her. There was something like fear in her eyes, and yet not so much fear as agonised expectation. With a great effort she composed herself and walked to the entrance of the summer-house.

"Von Wrangel," she said, firmly, "I'm surprised, I am ashamed of you. Put that net down and come and tell me what you want here."

Greigstein dropped his net instantly, not without a passing look of regret for the great purple butterfly still hovering over the honeysuckle. His manner changed so utterly that his friends would hardly have recognised him. Plainly as he was dressed, there was no suggestion of the suburban schoolmaster about him now. His English had become singularly good and clearly enunciated.

"I am exceedingly sorry, dear Lady Stanmere; I had not the remotest idea that you were here. I came down to see you to-day, though I have been here for years on and off without any attempt to do so. I was trying to think out some way of seeing you without coming up to the house, but the sight of that superb cassiopa—"

"Still the same strange contradiction," Lady Stanmere cried. "Still turned from great ends by the trivialities of life. But you may come in; there is no chance of our being interrupted here. Have you any news for me?"

Greigstein followed into the grateful coolness of the summer-house. All the hardness had died out of his eyes, his manner was gentle, almost subservient.

"I believe you have forgiven me," he said.

"I believe that I have forgiven everybody," Lady Stanmere replied, "even a Hungarian patriot like yourself. My husband ruined himself and died for your wild scheme; my son Stephen is an outcast in fear of his life—if indeed he still lives—for the same cause."

"Stephen was bound to have an outlet for his tremendous energies," Greigstein said, coolly. "If he had not taken up the cause he would have given way to drink and gambling and such like evils, and I never countenanced violence. Remember that I am a disgraced and broken man because I stood between Stephen and the grip of the law."

There was just a flash in the speaker's eyes for a moment, the glance that one might see on the face of a great general in the hour of misfortune. Lady Stanmere laid her hand with a pretty gesture on his arm.

"I did not mean to wound you," she said gently. "And I must not hold you responsible for the wild blood of the Gays. It is only because I am so utterly lonely, because I have none of my own kith and kin to love that I find myself regretting that you ever came to remind me that my mother was a Von Wrangel. You recall our last meeting?"

"'Shall I ever forget it?" Greigstein asked, in a low voice.

"Well, we need not go into that, it is three years ago. My boys I never hoped to see again. But Mary was another matter. You were to find her for me, you were not to come again until you did so. And when I heard your voice just now my heart—"

"I know, I know," Greigstein murmured sympathetically, "that was the promise. Now tell me the story of the girl's disappearance."
"A mystery," Lady Stanmere cried, "like everything connected with this house. She came mysteriously, late at night, with a brief note to the effect that her father's life was in danger and that I was to give her shelter. I can see her now, as she stood in the hall with those beautiful sightless blue eyes turned on me intuitively. She knew nothing, she could tell me nothing except that her father was alive. And I took her to my starved heart; and for two years I was quite happy."
A tear or two stood in Lady Stanmere's eyes. Greigstein lifted her hand to his lips and kissed it.
"Then, I understand she disappeared again," he said.
"As mysteriously as she came. She went for a walk in the park, a walk that she had learnt by heart. She never came back again, but an hour or two afterwards a stranger left a card for me, saying Mary had gone, and that as I valued the peace and future of our house I was to do nothing."
"And you consulted old Martlett, of course?"
"I did. His advice to me was to do just as I was told. What could a helpless old woman like myself, strangled in these mysteries, do? But if you know anything—"
"I know something, but not much. Accident has placed a clue in my hands. For reasons which will be obvious to you, I am in humble guise in London at present. My single room is in Pant-street, from which charming locality I go to teach German in a school. Beneath me lodge a charming young couple, by name Stevenson. They are the son and daughter of the late vicar here."
"This is very interesting," Lady Stanmere murmured.
"So it occurred to me. I have made friends with these young people. I have even put money in their way, for they are very poor. Now, tell me, did these Stevensons know your niece by any chance?"
"I don't see how they possibly could," Lady Stanmere said, thoughtfully, "seeing that they left the vicarage some time before Mary first arrived here."
"Which only serves to heighten the mystery and make it more interesting," Greigstein replied. "Now, a few nights ago, young Stevenson had a queer sort of adventure. There can be no doubt that he was in close contact with both your—but we need not go into that."
Greigstein paused in some confusion. There was just a gleam of suspicion and anger in the glance that Lady Stanmere gave him.
"You are concealing something from me," she said.
"Well, I am," Greigstein replied, coolly. "With your gracious permission I propose to go on doing so for the present. Now, young Stevenson told me part of the adventure. He little guessed what a mine of information he had tapped for me. Mixed up in that adventure was a photograph. I saw that photograph

with my own eyes. And it was a photography quite recently taken of your niece Mary."
The silken mesh fell from Lady Stanmere's hands. The agitation of those long, slim fingers told a tale of silent suffering. But there was a hope in her eyes now that made the white face beautiful.
"You are certain," she asked. "But you could not make a mistake. Strange that Mary should have made friends with people from our own parish. Then you really have solved the mystery?"
"Not yet. You must have patience. Your niece was no friend of these young people. By a judicious question or two I elicited the fact that the photograph in question had come quite by accident into Dick Stevenson's hands. The boy knows very little, but his sympathies have been enlisted on the side of those whose interest it is to keep the matter secret."
"Then he declined to tell you?"
"Absolutely. For the present we must leave things as they are. Your niece is safe and happy. Later on I may bring her back to you. But you must have patience. Lady Stanmere, you are attached to this place?"
Lady Stanmere looked across the lake to the silence of the green woods beyond. Her eyes filled with tears.
"God knows I am," she said. "It's all that remains to me, my dear old home and the recollection of the early days."
"And yet there is mystery here. Even you dare not inquire whence comes the mysterious prosperity that has built up the future of the family again. And in that strange hidden fortune the disappearance of your niece plays its part. Mind you, I don't know for certain, I can only surmise. Therefore we must proceed slowly. Of course, I could force the truth, but at the same time I might bring about an explosion that would lay Stanmere in ruins."
Lady Stanmere threw up her hands in a helpless gesture.
"As you please," she said. "I am utterly helpless. Only bring Mary back to me, give me something to love and care for. This place is very dear to me, but there are times when I am utterly lonely."
Greigstein kissed the slim fingers once more. A little while later, and he had forgotten everything of his mission and his own stormy past, in the heart-whole pursuit of a saffron-hued butterfly. It was characteristic of the man that he could give himself over, heart and soul, to those gentle pursuits.
The butterfly was captured presently on the terrace before the house. A horrified footman demanded to know if the intruder was aware of the fact that he was trespassing. Greigstein meekly admitted the fact.
"Then you'd better be off, my man," the footman said loftily. "And mind as I don't ketch you 'ere again."
Greigstein went off meekly enough, and filled with a proper awe of the gorgeous footman. Relieved of that inspiring presence he could afford to

laugh.
"Not a bad day's work," he said. "She has forgiven me, which is much. And, really, that is a very fine specimen of the 'clouded yellow.'"

IX. — "THE TIGER MOTH."

"And so I am going to be left to the beauties of Pant-street and my butterflies," said Greigstein, pulling meditatively at his cigarette. "Miss Molly, I shall be desolate. Herr Dick, do not forget your old friend when you are famous."
Dick replied that it would be a long process. It was the last night he and Molly would be in Pant-street, a hot, airless night that brought the moisture shining on the faces of them all. To-morrow they would be in a pretty, sweet-smelling place of their own.
"And do you give us an occasional thought from your butterflies," Molly laughed. "You pretend to bewail our loss, and you have been out every night this week after your specimens. Again this evening."
"I must," Greigstein protested. "I go as I have done constantly of late, to Cambria Square. Positively I am on the track of a new specimen. In the gardens I shall capture him. An ugly, cruel, treacherous moth, but absolutely essential to my collection."
Two little sparks gleamed in Greigstein's eyes. At the same time he leaned back smiling in his chair, watching the blue smoke drift upwards. A collecting case was on the table by his side. Molly opened it playfully.
"But there is a revolver in here," she cried. "Surely you don't collect even the most dangerous of moths with a revolver?"
Greigstein smiled. Dick regarded him fixedly.
"A penny for your thoughts, Herr Dick," he exclaimed.
"They were professional," Dick replied. "I was wishing that I knew your life's history. It is a fascinating discovery for a novelist to make, that a harmless collector of fera-natura goes out hunting in London squares with a revolver."
Again the steely points in Greigstein's eyes flashed.
"And I," he cried, "would give much to wipe out the past and stand as you do. Good-night, my dear young friends. I invite myself to breakfast with you to-morrow. Meanwhile, my moth may be waiting."
He went off coolly enough, whistling an air as he went. Through the dark streets he took his way to Cambria Square. As he crossed over to the gardens a clock somewhere struck the hour of midnight. A policeman passing by touched his hat to the German. Evidently the two had met before. Then Greigstein sat down on the edge of the pavement, and proceeded to pull a pair of galoshes over his boots. He took a key from his pocket and proceeded to open the big iron gates leading into the gardens. The hinges slipped back noiselessly as if they had been oiled lately.

Once inside, there was no occasion for further secrecy. The big trees and the closely planted shrubs made a perfect screen. Yet Greigstein crept along noiselessly, as if fearful lest the breaking of a twig should scare away his quarry.
He crept along in the same cat-like manner until he reached the railings near the spot of Dick Stevenson's adventure. Then he lay at full length behind a laurel bush and waited patiently. He fumbled intuitively for his cigarette case, but abandoned the longing for tobacco with a sigh.
He waited patiently for an hour or more, listening intently to any passing sound. Then a shadow hovered before the railings and another figure crept through into the gardens by means of the railing that moved.
"Ah," Greigstein muttered, "so I have got my tiger moth!"
The figure came along, actually stepping on the back of the German's hand as he passed. The latter was on his feet in a moment. His arms shot out and the cold blue rim of a revolver barrel was pressed against the intruder's neck.
"Don't stir," Greigstein whispered. "As you value your precious and estimable existence, don't stir an inch. Oh, yes, it is a revolver you feel against you right enough. Go down on your knees."
The stranger obeyed. He seemed absolutely overcome by fear or surprise.
"Well, now I proceed to place these spectacles over your eyes. They fit tight by means of extra springs. For the purpose of ocular display they are not a success, seeing that the lenses are of ground glass. Now permit me to take your arm and lead you from here. If you try to give an alarm—"
The pause was ominous. The other man gave no sign, though Greigstein could feel his arm quivering. Presently they were walking rapidly along the deserted streets, stopping and turning and crossing the road as danger threatened. At length Greigstein dexterously piloted his capture into his own room, locking the door behind him.
"Now, my tiger moth," he said, jubilantly, and speaking for the first time in his natural voice, "now my scorpion, take off those glasses."
The glasses were snatched off and flung violently across the room. A tall man with a fine face and noble presence stood confessed. But the thin lips and shifty eyes detracted from the first favorable impression; there was a nasty red shade in the eyes, a certain restless movement of the hawk-like fingers.
"Von Wrangel," he exclaimed, "I might have guessed it. Always florid, always theatrical. If you had taken the trouble to send for me—"
"You would not have come, Stephen," Greigstein said quietly. "Besides, I did not know your address. By accident I heard that you were to be found some of these nights near Cambria Square, therefore I waited for you. Only force could have compelled your presence."
"But no force can compel me to speak."
"You will tell me everything that I desire to know," Greigstein said. "Bah, I

have only to hold up my hand and you are no more than an empty husk of corn by the wayside. A word or a sign and you are a dead body floating on the Thames. For the sake of your good name and the noble race you belong so, I am here in London little better than an outcast. You betrayed us, and you betrayed those who were against the cause. And because of that your father drowned himself in the lake at Stanmere. You nearly killed your mother—she would be dead now if she only shared our knowledge. Bah, you will tell me all that I desire to learn, and you know it."

The other man muttered something. He was palpably ill at ease.

"Go on," he said, "and get it over. I don't suppose my society is any more congenial to you than yours is to me. Speak out."

"I am coming to it. Sit down and smoke. I shall not detain you long; I shall say nothing of your search, which is doomed to be unsuccessful. It is of the past that I desire knowledge. What have you done with the girl?"

"What girl? If you are alluding to Mary—"

"Of course I am. How a pure white soul like hers ever came—But I need not touch that. And when your mother came to love her you took her away cruelly without a word. Of all the cruel, dastardly things you ever did—"

"Stop!" the other cried. His voice rang clear and loud. "With all my faults I loved that child. She was everything to me. In her presence I was another man; of my past she guessed nothing. When the time came that I could have her back with me, I sought her. And she had vanished."

"Vanished?" Greigstein said, hoarsely. "Dog! if you dare lie to me—"

"Before God I am telling the truth, Von Wrangel. I can look you in the face and say it again and again. I know not where the child has gone. I have laid my cherished vengeance aside to find her. Aye, I would go down on my knees to you if you would tell me where Mary is now."

Greigstein had no reply. The cigarette fell from his fingers, and smouldered unheeded on the floor. The man spoke no more than the truth.

"For once in my life," Greigstein said, slowly, "I am utterly and hopelessly beaten."

X. — POLICY OF SILENCE.

Dick Stephenson, face to face with Mr. Spencer in the 'Record' office, could say nothing for a time. Surely his new-found friend must recognise him for the man who had done him a single service so short a time ago. But there was absolutely no sign of recognition in Spencer's eyes.

Well, it did not much matter. Dick's plain policy was to be discreet. He would hold the secret of the adventure close, and some day it could be turned to account. He waited now for Spencer to speak.

"Tell me about yourself," the latter said, presently. "Do not be afraid. I, too,

have known what it is to be poor."
Dick spoke freely enough. Spencer might have been a mystery, there might be something terribly wrong about his past, but his was a face that most men would trust. And as Dick told his history he felt that his companion was following him with the deepest interest and attention.
"The old story," he said, kindly. "All you want is a start. It is good work that you have done for us, but, unfortunately, there are so many journalists nowadays who can do good general work. I am going to send you into the assistant editor's office, there to make yourself useful. I can give you £300 a year, and as to the rest, why, that is in your hands."
Dick tried to say something and failed. He had not expected anything like this. The realisation of a score of fond dreams was possible now. He could get Molly away from Pant-street without delay. For the present they would rent a furnished cottage. They might even get back to Stanmere again. Manby Junction was only a mile from the village, and there were plenty of trains.
Dick came out of his reveries to the knowledge that his benefactor was speaking. As he looked about the room his eyes caught sight of a large photograph of Stanmere House. Spencer followed the glance.
"Do you know that place?" he asked.
"I was born there," Dick said, with a shaky voice. "My father was rector of the parish for twenty years. Ah, if I could only get back there!"
"Bless my soul," Spencer cried. "You are the son of my old—"
"Then you, too, know Stanmere!" Dick interrupted eagerly.
"I never said so," Spencer responded coldly. There was something furtive in his eyes now, a suggestion of fear, of having said too much. "I—I was nearly buying the place once. You must excuse me, but I am on the verge of one of my forgetful fits again."
He passed his hand across his eyes wearily. The next moment he seemed to be trying to look into Dick's very soul.
"I was trying to recall what I know of Stanmere," he said. "I knew the district well as a boy; in fact, I used to go there in my schooldays and look for white heather on the uplands behind the Warren. An old friend of mine had a cottage there, called 'Shepherd's Spring.'"
Dick gave an exclamation of delight. Just for the moment he had forgotten that he was talking business in a great newspaper office. The beauties of the rolling landscape were before his eyes now, he could see the fertile valley and the great sheets of purple heather with the sombre pines and the no-man's-land beyond.
"I know the country blindfold," Dick said. "I could take you right through those bogs and soft spots at midnight. I could hide there and baffle my pursuers for a month. I could—"
Dick paused, for Spencer's eyes were blazing. His face was working with an

excitement that was almost painful.
"Ah, to be sure," he said hoarsely. He was pacing up and down the office now. "One would like to be there, of course. One could double and twist and turn and none be any the wiser. Boy, can I really honestly trust you?"
"I try to be like my father," Dick said, simply.
"And he was a good man. Mind you, I didn't say that I knew him. I dare say that you could manage it. There are plenty of trains and a good road from the junction. I could get Fisher to see that you were not kept late."
All this with more or less incoherent words and excited gestures. Heaven alone knew what strong emotions were passing through the man's mind. Presently he grew more calm and dropped into his seat with the air of one physically exhausted.
"I see what you are longing for," he said. "You want to get away from the miserable street where you are and into the country. I will arrange with Mr. Fisher that you can leave the office pretty early. You shall take your sister away for the summer at any rate, and I will place Shepherd's Spring at your disposal. As a matter of fact, it belongs to me. I bought it for the sake of quietness after a long illness."
Dick said something, he hardly knew what. He seemed suddenly to have blundered into a country of fairy surprises. And yet at the same time he could not rid himself of the feeling that he was playing a part in a drama, he was a subordinate piece on a chessboard where a tremendous game was going on.
"The place is small, but well furnished," Spencer said. He was quite cool and matter-of-fact now. "You will find everything you want there, and should easily manage with one servant. No, you must not thank me, because some day you may be able to repay me."
He glanced at his watch, an indication that the interview was finished and that the man of money had greater interests in hand.
"I will," Dick said, passionately. "Anything I can do for you, sir, I will. You have taken a great weight from my heart, and I will serve you as man was never served before. I can be discreet and silent, I can—"
He paused, a little ashamed of himself. Spencer smiled.
"You can't buy friends," he said. "Yes, I think I can trust you. I will arrange for your duties with my editor, Mr. Fisher. If you go around to Mr. Marlett's, 66 Lincoln's Inn, to-morrow, and say you came from me, he will give you the key of Shepherd's Spring. And now I must ask you to say good-night."
Spencer touched the bell, his face grew keen and alert; he was the rigorous man of business once more before Dick had time to leave the office.

XI. — WHITE HEATHER.

"I shall wake up presently and find it is all a dream," Molly said, with her face

turned to the blue sky. "Dick, to think that a week should make all the difference to our fortunes! Already Pant-street has become a vague memory."
Dick was lying on his back on a patch of purple heather and listening to the hum of the bees. The air was crisp and pure. Down below lay the valley with its golden patches of cornland. In a belt or trees Stanmere nestled. High up were the great woods and the stretches of heather, and behind again a desolate land of ravine and rock and bog and larch, where no man ventured after dark unless he was born to the soil. But Dick had had the benefit of twenty years' personal acquaintance with the place, and it was no idle boast of his that he could find his way over the moor blindfold.
Down in a little hollow in the centre of a shady garden lay Shepherd's Spring. Dick had the key in his pocket, but they had not entered yet. But all their belongings lay outside the gate, and a freshly engaged maidservant mounted guard over it. It was quite impossible to think about the house yet, for Dick and Molly had a thousand sweet old associations to renew.
They stayed there on the heath pointing this and that spot out to one another till Molly's eyes grew dim, and she had to use her handkerchief. When Dick produced a lunch basket, a hearty meal was partaken of in spite of the wasps. There was zeal about that luncheon that neither of them ever forgot.
"I want to dance and shout and sing," Molly cried. "And I shall have you here from now till Monday morning. And there is a sprig of white heather!"
She darted on it, and placed it in her hat. The cream white coralled bloom was all that was needed to make her happiness complete. Dick was more sober. Perhaps he was a little frightened at his sudden good fortune.
"Let us go into the house," he said. "I'm just a trifle fay, as the Scotch say. I don't know, Molly, but we are on the verge of tremendous events, and I am chosen for one of the puppets in the drama. Let us see the cottage."
The garden was trim and tidy, for it had been seen to regularly. Inside the rooms were small, and Spencer's estimate that they were well furnished was a modest statement, for the place was luxuriously appointed. There were fine carpets and pictures and statues, old china and Empire furniture, oak and Chippendale, and Adam and the like. Dick gasped as he looked at the drawing-room.
"Have you seen a ghost?" Molly asked.
"Well, something like it," Dick admitted. "This room has given me quite a turn. It is smaller, but it is furnished exactly like the drawing-room in Cambria Square where I first met my dear little blind girl."
"Something resembling, you mean?"
"Absolutely the same. The same small tables and the vases and glasses for flowers. When you have filled them all with blossoms the likeness will be marvellous. Molly, what does all this mean?"
No lucid explanation came to the bewildered Molly. The two seemed to have

blundered into the heart of a mystery like a dark, unfamiliar landscape that from time to time was illuminated by a flash of lightning. Every day seemed to bring some fresh surprise.
"It maddens me," Dick cried. "Just think of the extraordinary patchwork of adventures that I have had lately, and how inexplicable they are, and how they fit together. If that man has deliberately led us into trouble—"
"But it does not seem possible," Molly urged. "Mr. Spencer has a great reputation. He has been very kind to you, and you say he has a noble face."
"So he has," Dick admitted, "but—"
"But me no buts, sir. It was by the purest accident that you became of service to Mr. Spencer. And see how kind he has been to you."
"And yet I am certain he had some deep design when he offered me this place. If you had only seen how his eyes lighted up and how he talked to himself! I tell you, it was a sudden inspiration."
"And a very good one for us," Molly laughed. "Oh, I admit the mystery, which, my dear boy, is no business of ours. Mr. Spencer chooses to keep his daughter to himself, and you are warned to keep clear and think no more about the matter."
"I shall never forget that pathetic, beautiful face and those blue eyes," Dick said. "And I am glad to think she has been here."
"My dear Dick, what do you mean?"
"Sherlock Holmes," Dick smiled. "She has told me that she needed no eyes so far as her own room was concerned. This room would not be a replica of the one in Cambria Square unless blind Mary had been here. Here is the foundation of a novel, if I could only get to the bottom of it."
"Meanwhile I have something more practical to do," said Molly. "Give a hand, Dick, so that we can have a walk after tea with a clear conscience."
It was a glorious ramble after tea through that lovely familiar country, down through the leafy silence of the warren, where every step held some precious association, and back again by way of the Stanmere woods and through the breast-high bracken home. Then they rested for a moment, silent for the time being.
The silence was broken presently by a sharp voice, followed by one pitched in a rusty key like the creaking of a door. Down the drive under the beeches towards Stanmere two men were walking, apparently discussing some point of the deepest interest. They passed Dick and his sister quite unconscious of their presence.
"Herr Greigstein," Molly exclaimed. "Greigstein in Harris tweeds, looking like a large landed proprietor. It is quite apparent that he is not down here for the pleasure of our society. Who is the little man with the face of dried parchment. He looks like Mr. Tulkinghorn—the traditional receptacle for family secrets."
Dick nodded approvingly.

"You have got it," he said. "That is Mr. Martlett, of Lincoln's Inn, the old lawyer from whom I got the keys of our cottage. The drama progresses, Molly. I wonder what part I am cut for—the fool or the hero?"

XII. — MR. MARTLETT.

A little way down the road Greigstein stopped and said something to his rusty-looking companion, then he turned aside from the main road and disappeared into the woods. The small man with the parchment face and the inscrutable expression sauntered on thoughtfully till he reached the lodge gates of Stanmere. With his hands behind him he strolled along very much with the air of one who possesses the place. The butler who answered the ring fell into an attitude of deference before the little man in the rusty black, for this was Mr. James Martlett, the family lawyer, and a power in the land.

Nobody knew anything about Mr. Martlett, who he was or whence he came, but most people knew that he was an exceedingly rich lawyer, who for the last thirty years had lived dingily in Lincoln's Inn.

A close, secretive, furtive man, who said very little, but that little to the point. Many a family secret reposed in that unemotional breast, many a great house on the verge of ruin had found safety in Martlett's capable hands. But he would always have his own way, and nothing would deviate him from his course. His clear grey eyes seemed to read everything. There was a sense of power about the man. The Stanmere butler was a great personage, but even he deemed it best to be deferential to Mr. James Martlett.

"I've come down to dine and sleep, Goss," he said, calmly. "See that my things are put out in my bedroom, and let her ladyship know that I have arrived. I don't suppose that I shall be in to tea."

Goss intimated that all these things should be done. He hoped that Mr. Martlett had had a pleasant journey from town. Dinner was at eight as usual. Her ladyship was at present in her room. Martlett strolled away with his hands still behind him. He inspected the lawns and the gravelled walks carefully, even the Scotch head gardener was polite to him. Then he went on, as if aimlessly, across the park and up the slopes of purple heather until he came at length to Shepherd's Spring. With the same air of possession upon him he walked into the house. In the hall Molly was arranging some flowers, and Dick was watching her approvingly.

"So you young people have found your way here," Martlett said in a voice that sounded like the creaking of a rusty hinge. "How are you both? Dick Stevenson, I am very much displeased with you. When your father died I wound up his affairs for him. Contrary to my usual custom, I made no charge for so doing. Why didn't you come and see me in London?"

"Because he is too proud," Molly laughed. "Like most people, Dick is a little afraid of you. On the contrary, I am not in the least afraid, though it happens I have never seen you before. There! What do you think of that, sir?"

She stooped and laid her fresh cool lips to the lawyer's crackled face. Martlett came as near to a smile as he permitted himself.

"Dick called for the keys," he said, "actually called for the keys of this house, and never asked to see me. He never told my friend Spencer that we were old acquaintances. Now, there's pride for you! And yet you would never have had the offer of Shepherd's Spring if it had not been for me."

"That's very kind of you," Dick said, gratefully. "But we didn't want anybody to know—"

"That you were not the great genius that you took yourself to be, therefore you preferred to starve in London. I had my eye on you. And if there is one thing I admire more than another it is grit and determination. But you are all right; you should get on now."

Dick had not the slightest doubt about it. The little man with his hands behind his back eyed him critically. He was pulling the strings of all the puppets in the drama. He chose his figures deliberately, and the specimen before him pleased the old lawyer exceedingly.

"It is a charming little house, and I trust you will be happy here," he said. "Only you must be careful not to lose yourself in those bogs over yonder. They tell me there are some horrible places in the woods beyond the Warren."

"And I know every inch of it," Dick cried. "Give me a supply of provisions and I could defy a regiment of detectives for a month there. I don't suppose anybody knows the lower moorland paths besides myself, now."

Mr. Martlett was deeply interested. There was something subtle about Dick's suggestion. He insisted upon having it all explained to him outside.

"It appeals to me," he cried. His eyes gleamed with an unusual fire. "Now, suppose you had to hide somebody here, somebody in peril of the law. The police are hot on his track. You mean to say you could baffle them?"

Dick responded eagerly. He proceeded to draw a map like the web of a spider on the garden path. He knew a hut at a certain part where nobody had been for years, a hut low down in a ferny hollow. There was no known pathway to it, its existence was forgotten.

"I know every blade of grass by the way," Dick said. "I learnt the moorland by heart from the last of the old shepherds. Sheep are not kept here now, because people are afraid of losing them. When I was young and longed to be a pirate the old hut beyond the moss bog used to be my ship, you see."

But Martlett was no longer listening. The fire had died out of his eyes, his mind seemed to be fixed on other problems. He came to himself with an uneasy kind of laugh as he met Dick's injured gaze.

"I am more interested than you imagine," he said. "My dear boy, you fancy that you are here by the accident, of a happy circumstance. Nothing of the kind. There are great interests at stake, and I am the general directing them. But I am old, and my nerves are not what they were, and I may want strength and courage and audacity to rely upon. Our conversation may seem trivial to you now, but the time may come when you will recall it vividly. Are you sure you can do what you say?"

Martlett's voice sank to a hoarse whisper. His hand had fallen on Dick's arm and crooked upon it with a nervous grip.

"I spoke no more than the truth, sir," Dick said, quietly.

"Good boy, good boy! Permit me to take a pinch of snuff. Nothing is so soothing to the nerves. If you serve those who would be your friends, there is a fine fortune before you. And don't be too curious as to our friend Greigstein."

Martlett passed down the garden path, leaving Dick to his own bewildered thoughts. The little shuffling man in the rusty black seemed to know everything. Certainly he was on the best terms with himself as he tied his old fashioned cravat and donned his quaint dress clothes an hour or so later.

He passed down the wide old staircase into the drawing-room in time to open the door for Lady Stanmere. There was quite a bouquet in the flavor of his manners—courtly, chivalrous, but ever with the suggestion of power. He had it now as he bent over Lady Stanmere's hand. He never lost it as he stood there chatting over a variety of general topics. The place was looking charming; Goss had informed him that the trout fishing had been good—to all of which Lady Stanmere replied timidly with her eyes on the clock.

Dinner was served at length—a long, elaborate meal, with a fine show of old silver and Venetian glass, the artistic beauty of which appealed to Martlett much, as if it had been Dutch delf. A simple chop and a glass of port would have sufficed him. The oaken wall, with their pictures and armor, the pools of light from shaded lamps, and the banks of flowers, passed unheeded. Dessert was over at length, and then Goss handed the lawyer a box of cigars and a cedar-spill.

"Have I your permission, my lady?" Martlett asked.

Lady Stanmere bowed. The little ceremony lost none of its flavour by lapse of years. A faint blue cloud drifted across the banks of flowers. Lady Stanmere played nervously with her wineglass, empty as it was.

"I received your most amazing letter," she said. "We are under a great debt to you, a very great debt indeed, sir, that—"

"But your ladyship imagines that I am going too far. That is a perfectly natural idea. When I made the suggestion that—"

"Suggestion! It was a positive command."

Martlett bowed. Nothing seemed to disturb his equanimity.

"Hardly that," he said. "You wrote to me that you had made a discovery. You were aware to a certain extent what had become of a certain young lady. Von Wrangel, otherwise Greigstein, had seen her photograph in the hands of a young man who had lodged under the same roof as our valuable German friend. I am sorry that you received Von Wrangel at all. Surely your family has suffered enough at his hands. Not that I doubt his good intentions. There was your son Stephen, for instance. I have my own suspicions as to Stephen's character."

"Which are not very favorable," Lady Stanmere said, bitterly.

"Well, madam, they are not. Truth compels me to state that I know no more unmitigated scoundrel than Stephen. But all this is beside the point. If I had seen Von Wrangel a day or two sooner you would never have heard about that photograph. I wish I could tell you everything, but the secret is not entirely mine. It may seem strange, perhaps dramatic, but the greatest misfortune that could overtake your house now would be to have your niece back under your roof again."

The words fell with cold and clear distinctness from Martlett's lips. Lady Stanmere regarded him with astonished eyes. Above all things Martlett was practical. He spoke now like the stage lawyer of melodrama.

"You are playing with me," Lady Stanmere cried. The long slim hands were trembling, her rings streamed like unsteady fire. "What harm could it do?"

"I repeat, I cannot tell you," Martlett replied. "Be advised by me, think what I have done for you. Only a few years since and the house was on the verge of ruin. And look at it now. I pledge you my word that the child shall come back some day. If you defy me in the matter you will never cease to regret it. If you elect to do so the work of years will be lost."

Martlett's voice sank to a hoarse, whisper. The stem of a wineglass snapped in his fingers, but he did not heed. Evidently the man was terribly in earnest. It seemed strange, almost incredible, that the presence or absence of a blind girl should make all this terrible difference to the family fortunes.

"The girl is the heart of the mystery," Martlett went on. "She came to you mysteriously, she vanished in the same way. The girl is pure and good and an angel, and she knows as little of the intrigues about her. And now your ladyship will be good enough to promise me that you will take no further steps in the matter."

Lady Stanmere bowed. She did not care to trust herself to words. Martlett rose and offered his arm with old-fashioned courtesy. His manner was deferential, he might have been overcome with a sense of the honour conferred upon him. There was a queer, dry smile on his lips as he returned to the dining-room. He drew up an easy chair by the fireplace and rang the bell.

"You were pleased to want something, sir," Goss asked.

"I was," Martlett said. "Within a few minutes there will be a man here asking to see Lady Stanmere. He looks like a gentleman, Goss, but in these matters appearances are apt to be terribly deceptive. When this man comes show him in here without a word of explanation. And then—"

"Yes, sir," Goss murmured, as Martlett paused. "And then, sir?"
"Well, then you can close the door carefully behind you and keep an eye on the place."

XIII. — BLACKMAIL.

Martlett lay back dreamily contemplating the loves of the angels as depicted on the ceiling of the dining room, as if that fine artistic effort had been the crowning work of his career. In a way he had built up the fortunes of Stanmere, and yet this dry practical lawyer was one of the central figures in one of the strangest romances ever known.
And the work was not finished yet, though Stanmere was once more a fine, almost free property. Martlett and another had built it up step by step, and the fascinating process was no less fragrant because the house of cards might be knocked down at any moment. Resolution and tact were required, and the exercise of that delicate finesse which the soul of the lawyer loved.
He did not look very much as if he were waiting for an antagonist who might at moment ruin the whole beautiful scheme. It was a dangerous antagonist, but that did not prevent Martlett from getting the full flavour of his tobacco. He smiled grimly as he heard the clang of the door bell. Almost immediately Goss entered the dining room stiff and dignified, with his nose in the air, as if he smelt something unpleasant.
"The person you spoke of, sir," he said. "Party of the name of Venner."
"A gentleman named Venner, confound you," a swaggering voice said. "But when your ladyship has had as much to do with—"
The door closed with more force than the immaculate Goss generally employed, and the new-comer came to an abrupt pause. His easy swagger vanished, he stood with an uneasy grin on his face.
A handsome, cunning brutal face; a face lighted by shifty grey eyes, a face coarsened and hardened by dissipation. The man was tall and well set up, but his swaggering air was a veneer: he had bully written all over him. His dress, too, was fashionable, with a touch of caricature in it. A certain staginess clung like scent to the man.
"Well, Venner," Martlett said, in his dry way. He looked up with the end of his cigar between his fingers. "So you came to see Lady Stanmere? As matter of fact you are not going to see Lady Stanmere."
"Oh, indeed," Vernier sneered. "We shall see about that."
"We shall indeed. What are you going to do with that chair?"
"What does a man generally do with a chair? Sit on it, of course."
"You are not going to sit down. I do not choose to be a vis-a-vis with a scoundrel of a valet who has just served a term of imprisonment. If you try that on again I'll have you flung from the house by a footman."

All very quietly spoken and in a low voice. But the lawyer's face was hard and his eyes steely. The other man laughed uneasily. But during the rest of the interview he stood, moving restlessly from one foot to the other.

"My wife put you up to this," he growled. "My angel wife, my dove-eyed partner who calls herself Nurse Cecilia. When I—I came back to London—"

"By the way of Portland and Wormwood Scrubbs?"

"Never mind that. I hastened back to the partner of my joys and sorrows. You can imagine my anxiety to see her—"

"With a view to something—strictly temporary—in the way of a loan."

Venner stepped from one leg to the other again.

"I didn't got it," he muttered, "not a penny. She said that I was the cross she had to bear. She offered me food and shelter till I could find some honest living, but on the currency question she was firm. Then I lost my temper and was fool enough to tell Cecily that down here there were chances. You couldn't have got to know my game in any other way."

"All the same I did," Martlett replied. "Now listen to me. For over five years we have been free of you. In five years many things have happened."

"Ay, ay. The house of Stanmere has got prosperous for one thing."

"It has. Exceedingly prosperous. We have money to spare now, money to go into your pocket if necessary. You smile. Oh, I know your power. It is possible for a dirty, cowardly scoundrel like you to bring disgrace upon this house. If our penal laws were not so unhappily strict I should know how to act. In Corsica, for instance, I should give some bravo twenty pounds to put a knife between your ribs. In so doing I should look confidently for the applause of society. In this effete country one has to buy off men like you."

Venner's grey eyes gleamed. Martlett was coming to business at last.

"The question is," the lawyer went on, "what do you know?"

"And a fair question too. I know that my master, Mr. Paul, is hiding away somewhere in London."

Martlett nodded and glanced critically at his cigar. The fencing was beginning in earnest now. The keen intellect was aroused.

"I hate Mr. Paul," Venner went on. "I should never have known the inside of a gaol but for him. He put me aside when he could have told a lie or two to save me, and he started on what he called a new life. And when I came out of an American prison I started to hunt for him. There is still that warrant out for him across the water for murder. It would be a nice thing to see a Stanmere hanged for a crime like that. Revenge I wanted, revenge I craved for. But what is revenge compared with money!"

"What, indeed?" Martlett asked, sententiously. "Go on."

"Well, I got into trouble again, and my wife put me off the scent once. She can never forget that her father had a small farm on this Stanmere Estate."

"Your wife is a good and true woman, Venner."

"Oh, of course," Vernier sneered. "But I am on the track of my man now, and when I have hunted him down I shall state my terms. If I asked you, I should be told that Mr. Paul in dead, which would be a lie, my old fox. When I am sure of my game I shall want ten thousand pounds."

"You will never have so many pence, Venner."

"Oh, yes I shall. Mr. Stephen will be good for something for the credit of my family. Mr. Stephen has turned respectable. Mr. Stephen lives in Cambria Square with his daughter in a style that isn't done for nothing; Mr. Stephen lies low and takes his walks abroad at night, as gentlemen frequently have to do who dabble too much in shady European politics."

Mr. Martlett smiled approvingly at the end of his cigar. He had every scrap of information that the bully had to offer him. Like most of his class, the man talked too fast. He had said more in the last few minutes than Martlett could have hoped to pump out of him in an hour. His face hardened.

"Now listen to me," he said. "For the present you can do nothing; for the present you are perfectly harmless. When you find your man it will be time enough to come here with your threats. But I warn you that you stand on dangerous ground. There are tremendous interests at stake here with which you cannot be allowed to interfere. Perhaps you may compel me to purchase your silence later on, ay, but the proof must be clear. I know your past life like an open book. There are three charges upon which I could have you arrested at any moment. And if you dare to write one line or one word to Lady Stanmere I'll lay you by the heels before a day is over your head."

Venner would have threatened, only his courage failed. For the present, at any rate, he was going to get nothing here. And, quite imprudently, he had laid out his last five shillings in his return journey to Stanmere. It was very hard, so hard that the tears of self-pity were very near the surface.

"If you would not mind advancing me a few pounds," he said, with a servile manner that caused Martlett to smile. "Say five pounds, sir. I've got a little scheme on hand that in the course of a few days—"

"Not a farthing," said Martlett. "If you are penniless, so much the better." He had his hand on the bell, and Goss, with his nose still suspicious of unsavoury odours, appeared. "Goss, show this fellow out. And if he comes again bang the door in his face. If that does not suffice, duck him in the lake. You need not be in the least afraid of the consequences."

The door closed again, and Martlett carefully selected another cigar. It was a piece of reckless dissipation on his part.

"So the deception works," he said to himself. "It was the only way of keeping that fellow in the dark. Did ever such tremendous interests before rest on the shoulders of a poor blind girl!"

XIV. — A DISCOVERY.

Turned out into a cold and heartless world, Venner made his way from Victoria Station in an easterly direction. He had nothing in his pockets, the accommodating establishments under the three golden balls were all closed for the night, and his land lady was of a harsh and suspicious nature. Even the bright genius of Horace Venner could see no way out of the difficulty—-but one.

He would go and see his wife. Hunger and thirst—especially the latter—had sharpened his wits, and before he had come to the end of his journey a dozen brilliant lies and plausible excuses for the loan of a sovereign occurred to him. It was cruelly hard work, for he had counted upon seeing Lady Stanmere, who might have been 'good for anything' up to three figures. And now that was entirely a thing of the past. He knew and feared Mr. Martlett too well to disregard his instructions.

He reached his destination at length, a fairly large house at the back of Southampton square, let out into rooms and suites of rooms. On the second floor he paused, and then passed into a pleasantly furnished little sitting room, which was empty. There was a bedroom beyond, and into this Venner peeped. It was empty, but the gas was not turned down, so the occupant of the rooms could not be far off. Venner knew his wife's careful, thrifty ways.

He could afford to wait patiently, for the simple reason that he had nowhere else to go, unless good luck were on his side. His predatory eye glanced round the room disapprovingly. There was none of that class of portable property here such as the soul of Mr. Wemmick loved—no watch, no spoons or rings or anything of that kind. A gold watch, now, might have saved a useless discussion.

Perhaps they were in the bedroom. Women often keep trifles of that kind on their dressing-tables. Venner strolled casually into the bedroom, whistling an air. His heart glowed within him. There was a gold watch there with an inscription upon it, a present from a grateful patient.

Venner conveyed it to his pocket. The air on his lips grew more gay, and then suddenly stopped altogether. For there were voices in the sitting room, low and hurried voices; a man's, hard and defiant; a woman's, urging and persuading. There was some familiar suggestion about the man, as to the woman, there was no mistake whatever. It was Venner's wife.

Well, he would wait for developments. If he was caught he would slip the watch back again, and make some excuse for his appearance there. He was listening intently now, for experience told him that though listeners seldom heard any good of themselves they frequently heard ill of other people, and knowledge of human weaknesses is something remunerative.

"I fancy I managed it all right," the man said. "It was a stroke of genius using your cloak and bonnet in the dark. And of course you passed unmolested. I fancy it quite safe to go now."

"Not just yet," the woman's voice urged. "Stay a little longer, sir. For the sake of the old days, and Stanmere, don't run into needless danger."
The listener started joyfully. Here was a piece of amazing luck, luck so stupendous that he could hardly contain himself. He stumbled quite by accident upon the very man out of all the world that he most desired to see. In his own wife's lodgings he had found him.
Yet there was nothing so wonderful about it, seeing that Cecilia Venner had ever been devoted to the family of Stanmere.
"But I can't stay," the man said. "I am pretty sure that we baffled them and that the coast is clear. My dear soul, you need not be alarmed."
"All the same, I am going down into the roadway to see, sir," Nurse Cecilia said. "You can wait at the top of the stairs. It is quite dark there. But, whatever you do, don't go downstairs till I come back."
"Well, then, I won't. What a loyal little thing you are, to be sure. If all the people about Stanmere had been like you, I might have turned out differently."
The listener peeped through the crack of the door. He saw his wife creep out, he could make out the outline of the man's figure. There was no mistake about it, the passing years had made changes on hair and features and carriage, but there was the man that Venner longed to see. As the man followed impatiently into the darkness of the landing Venner crept after him. On second thoughts he decided to retain possession of the watch for the present.
He was safe now, he was quite sure that his quarry had not seen him emerge on the landing. He had only to wait now and to follow, and the £10,000 would be in his grip. The mere thought of it turned him dizzy. There was a footstep on the stairs and a few whispered words. It was all safe evidently. The stranger was in the street at length and Venner close behind him. He could swear to that walk and the swing of those shoulders anywhere. The man in front came presently into Gordon square, silent and deserted now, and then Venner ranged up alongside the figure in front.
His discoloured teeth showed in a broad grin, he reached out his hand playfully and smote the other on the shoulder.
"So I've got you at last," he said. "I've had some bits of good luck in my time, but never anything quite so fine as this. Say that you are glad to see me, say that the sight of my rugged, honest face—"
Venner paused. The man turned and faced him with a cool smile and a face as unbroken as that of an amused child. Venner had expected him to stagger back and cry out, to turn white and stammer for mercy.
There was nothing of this in the programme. The man with the cool smile flashed out an arm with the suddenness of lightning; there was a sickening sound, and Venner went down headlong to the ground with blood trickling from a cut lip. Only the instinct that it might spoil the game kept him from howling for mercy.

"Now, don't you try that on with me again," the stranger said with perfect equanimity. "Get up, you rascal. If this had happened in San Francisco—"
"You are a bold hand, Mr. Paul," Venner said, as he struggled to his feet. "But you shall pay for this a hundred-fold."
The cool smile faded from the other man's face.
"Well, I almost fancied that I recognised you," he said. "But my good man, you have made a great mistake. I am not Paul, but the other man. And you are Paul's valet, Horace Venner. There is no mistaking that half-cringing, half-bullying manner of yours. I have known a good many scoundrels in my time, but never a worse than you. And your father was an honest man."
"So was your father for that matter," Venner said, sullenly.
The other man laughed silently, as if the joke amused him.
"You are looking for your master," he said. "Strange to say, I am also looking for your late master. I have been looking for him for years. And when I do meet him there will be an account that will take some wiping out. Where is he?"
Venner gave a gesture of despair.
"Goodness knows," he muttered. "I thought I had him here to-night. When I was in—but never mind that. I followed the wrong man. Trust a Stanmere to do queer things. I should prefer Cambria Square; but there is no accounting for tastes."
"What has Cambria Square got to do with it?"
Venner executed an ingenious wink expressive of deep cunning.
"Knowledge is power," he said. "I've seen you coming out of that handsome flat in Cambria Square more than once. You must have had a good stroke of luck lately to be able to afford a place like that. Only it can't be pleasant to have to creep out after dark, like the bats and the cats—what's up?"
The other man gave a cry, a cry of pain. He staggered back with his hand to his side, his face was ghastly white.
"An old wound," he said, "I got in New Orleans. The pain is dreadful. You are an excellent scout, Venner, and have a way of nosing out secrets that is marvelous. But I wouldn't say too much about Cambria Square if I were you. Sometimes I am there and sometimes I have missions that take me elsewhere. Good-night."
"Half a minute sir," Venner said, eagerly. "If you've got a sovereign or two about you—"
"I haven't got five shillings; I am as poor as you are. And even if circumstances were otherwise I shouldn't help you. You are a pestilential scoundrel, Venner, and I would gladly come to your execution to-morrow. Good-night Venner, I am going back to Cambria Square."
The speaker turned on his heel and strode rapidly into the darkness. His face was white and set, his eyes gleamed like sullen fire.

"So I have got it at last," he muttered. "Almost! Confound my impetuosity! I might have got Venner to tell me the number of my flat in Cambria Square."

XV. — A LIGHTED MATCH.

Dick was disposed to make fun of the mystery as he and Molly walked back to Shepherd's Spring, after seeing Mr. Martlett and Greigstein together. The strong, clear air had got into his veins; the knowledge that all this wide, silent beauty was his to share thrilled him. After the weary struggle and the sordid horror of Pant-street, Stanmere was delicious.

Molly and Dick loitered along till the grey shadows began to creep over the moor, and and the tangled woods faded to a dark mass. The cottage door was open, and the lamplight streamed hospitably out.

"I am really hungry," Dick cried; "a real healthy hunger; not the dreadful feeling we had in Pant-street. New bread and butter and fresh eggs and tea. Nothing like Arcadia! But that tobacco does not smell Arcadia at all."

The air of the house was heavy with cigarette smoke. Greigstein was seated in the in the dining room. He was looking wistfully at the table.

"My young friends, I am delighted," he he cried. "Positively it is useless for you to try and get rid of me. The loneliness of Pant-street is appalling. I could not resist the temptation to run down here."

Dick looked at Molly and smiled. In the light of recent discoveries they could not take much of a compliment to themselves. And Greigstein looked different —more spruce and far better groomed than usual. Nobody but a West-End tailor could have made the clothes that he was wearing. He did not look in the least like the little German schoolmaster with the taste for butterflies.

"I have been been on the hunt, of course," he said, "but with poor results. An intelligent labourer tells me there are wondrous winged things of amazing beauty in the bogs over behind the Warren. But as nobody dare venture there, the information is all the more disappointing. I ask for a guide, and and behold! there is none. The last was a boy who used to live here. I demand his name; and do you suppose they told me his name was? Why, Master Dick Stevenson."

"Behold the man!" Dick laughed. "Come and have some tea."

Greigstein ate sparingly. He was full of the moorland and its mysterious paths and deep morasses. Would Dick take him there and teach him the paths? He was wildly enthusiastic, but there was something in his eyes that told of a strange earnestness in the matter. Strange that nearly everybody who came along wanted to know something about that mysterious moorland. Was there some treasure hidden there or some crime beyond solution?

"Oh, we shall see," Dick said. "I'm bored over the moor. My employer is always talking about it, and so is Mr. Martlett. Do you know him?

"The name seems familiar," Greigstein said, coolly, as he cracked an egg. "Solicitor to the Stanmere estates, I fancy."
Greigstein's expression was bland and childlike, his glasses twinkled benevolently. He changed the conversation in his light and airy way. He was going to stay till the last train. He had no intention of going away empty handed. If his good friends could give him some supper he would go out afterwards moth-hunting. There was no reason why they should not all go out moth-hunting.
The moon was a thin crescent in the sky, a long bank of mist lay like a blanket over the Stanmere Woods. They came presently to the avenue leading up to the house with the great forest trees hanging over to the right, past the lake, sleeping now like a great mirror in the dim light.
Greigstein had abandoned himself entirely to the work of the moment. He was no longer a mysterious German with a fancy for hiding himself in a dingy London purlieu, but an enthusiast. He took from his pocket a bottle containing a slimy-looking liquid.
"Treacle," he explained. "We smear the trees thus and thus. Nothing draws the moths like that. And presently we shall come back again and collect our prey. I will show you something then!"
They had grown more silent now, Dick had caught the spirit of the sport. Greigstein produced a lantern from his pocket.
"I'll push back the slide of this presently," he said. "Then you will see a pretty sight. But here is somebody coming, and we are on private property. I have no wish to be expelled by a zealous menial. We will obliterate ourselves."
The strange figure came swaggering along up the avenue. He paused for a moment before the tree against which the little party were pressing, and lighted a cigarette. The match illuminated his features with a dull red glow. An almost inarticulate cry came from Molly as the stranger passed.
"Why did you pinch me like that?" she asked.
"It was that man's face," Greigstein whispered, hoarsely. "Did you see his features? Of all the cruel nighthawks on the wing now there is none more false or cruel than he."
Molly shuddered. There was something ominous in Greigstein's words. She and Dick had both seen that face in the red halo of the vesta. A handsome, cruel, shifty face, a face not to be forgotten.
"It was far better if they had trusted me," Greigstein whispered. Obviously, he was talking to himself, he had entirely forgotten his companions. "Headstrong and rash I may be, but I could have saved this. He was going to the house."
"A friend of one of the servants, perhaps," Molly suggested.
"Friend to nobody but himself," Greigstein cried, coming to himself with a start. "He is going to the house. He must not go to the house."
Greigstein darted away and was lost in the darkness. Molly crept near to Dick,

as if fearful of something evil.
"I shall know that face again," Dick muttered. "I shall never forget it anymore."

XVI. — A COUNTERFEIT PRESENTMENT.

Molly held Dick tightly by the arm. She was not exactly frightened, but recent events were getting on her nerves. She and Dick seemed to have drifted into the heart of a great mystery from whence there appeared to be no avenue of escape. The air was full of a suggestion of tragedy, at every turn the grim phantom loomed. If there had been anything definite to go upon, Molly would have cared less. She was like a young soldier pressing on the enemy in the dark, with the danger all about her and no point at which to strike.
"I shall dream about that face," she said.
"Perhaps the sudden glare illuminated its bad points," Dick said. "And no doubt you would have thought less of it had not Greigstein gone off in so mysterious a manner. I'd give sixpence to know who that chap really is."
"But he was greatly upset," Molly urged. "He was almost frightened. Dick, I think we had better go home."
Dick hesitated. The artistic temperament is never without its strong leaven of curiosity, and he was anxious to know more. At any rate, they might finish their walk by way of the shrubbery. It was a private path, but they had always been allowed to use it in the days of the late rector. Molly caught Dick's arm again and hastened him on.
They were almost under the shadow of the house by now. The house loomed above them, the windows were filled with lights. It was hot and still, and the casements were wide open to catch the breeze. Dick lingered, pleased with the artistic beauties of the picture. There was the dining-room with its oak and silver and artistic confusion of dessert upon the table, the shaded lamps flooding the banks of flowers, the glow of red wine in cut-glass vessels.
"It's all a picture," Dick murmured. "There is nothing in the world more artistic and refined than a well-appointed English home. Look how those paintings—"
He paused as Molly gripped his arm.
"Look at the end of the table," the girl said. "Who stands there talking to somebody who is smoking a cigar and reclining in an armchair? His face is in the shadow just for a moment. Ah! now he has moved."
Dick looked attentively for a moment, then he caught some of Molly's excitement.
"I can guess," she said, "my instinct tells me. Dick, who was that we saw this afternoon talking to our German friend?"
"Why, Martlett, of course," Dick replied.

"Well, it is Mr. Martlett who is in that armchair. I can only see his hands, but I feel quite certain that I am right. Depend upon it, Mr. Martlett is down here to meet that man who seems to be so little at his ease. I should not wonder if he came to see Lady Stanmere and found the family lawyer instead. I wonder if the cloud of mystery and misery will ever lift from this unhappy family?"
Dick said nothing, he was taking in the scene before him with all his eyes. It was quite wrong, of course, but it suggested many possibilities in the way of a story. Dick looked along the whole facade of the house, past the blank spaces to the drawing-room, the windows of which were open, but nobody appeared to be there.
"You are quite right, Molly," he said. "It looks perfect, a place to be envied, a place to dream about; but, in our quiet way we are much happier than the poor people here. The larger the house the greater the skeleton. No wonder Lady Stanmere is fond of the quiet harbor by the lake."
"I am sorry for Lady Stanmere," said Molly. "If I could help her—"
She paused and started as a figure came apparently out of nowhere. It was impossible to distinguish the outline for a moment after gazing at the lights ahead.
"No occasion for alarm," Greigstein said. "I have made an absurd mistake. The man we saw was not coming here at all; in fact—"
"You are wrong," Dick said, coolly. "The fellow is at present in the dining-room yonder, and unless I am greatly mistaken, is having a bad quarter of an hour at the hands of our friend Mr. Martlett."
"Oh!" the discomfited Greigstein replied. "Bless me, is that so? Under the circumstances of the case we cannot do better than to leave him there. It is no concern of ours."
"Certainly not of mine!" Dick retorted. "But as to yourself, that seems to be quite another matter. There is too much mystery for my taste here—too much of a suggestion that I am being made use of. You have been a good friend of mine, and I am not ungrateful. But if there is anything wrong—"
"I swear to you that there is nothing wrong," Greigstein cried. "I swear that I am doing my best for a good and honorable family. I would speak if I only dared, but the secret is not my own. More I can't say."
"Not even to enlighten us as to your own past?"
"My past is my own, and I am not ashamed of it," Greigstein said, stiffly. "My dear boy, do not let us quarrel; it would be a great grief to me if there was any coldness between us. You may not believe me, you don't believe in me, but your opinion is not shared by Miss Molly."
"I am sure you are our good friend," Molly said, sweetly.
Greigstein bowed. He was silent for a moment, but not for long. There were some trees by the lake that he must positively visit. Then they would go home to supper and spend a pleasant evening. It was impossible to resist Greigstein's

good humor and to refuse a laugh over his enthusiasm.
"But there is far too much noise," the professor said. "We will collect our spoil and examine it in the summer-house by the lake. I love these expeditions; they make one feel like a poacher. Most people have sympathy with poachers."
Greigstein grabbed the spoil from the trees dexterously. There was one large white moth that moved him to a high degree of excitement. No specimen of that kind had been taken to England for eleven years. Greigstein was diffuse, and dwelt on the subject as the trio moved to the summer-house.
"Now to give you a lesson," the little German cried. "Hand over the lantern. Dick, will you kindly throw those rays this—Lady Stanmere!"
The great white moth dropped to the floor, fluttered its wings, and was gone. The light of the lantern fell on the white face and grey hair of Lady Stanmere. She had been sitting there in the darkness all alone. The sorrowful features were a little hard and set just now; the eyes had a haughty look in them.
"Von Wrangel," she said. There was a painful confusion on Greigstein's face. "Why do you come here? Am I never to be left alone?"
"I assure you," Greigstein stammered, "I assure you that it was the merest accident. I did not dream anyone would be here to-night. I merely came here to have a look at my specimens. We will go at once—with the deepest of apologies we will retire without delay."
There was a scarlet flush on the speaker's face; he turned abruptly with a suggestion of bustling his young friends out of the summer-house. Even to a less astute mind than Lady Stanmere's the intention was painfully obvious.
"Stay a moment," she said. There was a ring of command in her voice. "I am quite certain that nobody is to blame. I was startled and angry for the moment. It is one of my whims to come here on a fine evening—my husband was fond of the place. But I am not quite the recluse you take me for; for instance, I am not so shut up that I fail to recognise these young people as old acquaintances of mine. And we have met before. My dear child, come here."
Greigstein groaned, and Dick heard him with a certain cynical amusement. The German's confusion and his wild attempt to get them away had not been lost on the astute young man. Molly crossed over to Lady Stanmere, who kissed her tenderly.
"You have a sweet face," she said, "beautiful and amiable like your mother's, and a certain firmness that suggests your father. I lost a good friend the day he died. So you have come back again here?"
Molly explained. Dick was now in a position to live in the country again; a thing they had always regretted was dear old Stanmere.
"You must come and see me," Lady Stanmere said. "I am a lonely old woman, and it will be a pleasure to have somebody young about me again. I am glad you came here to-night. To me it seems like Providence."
As she spoke she glanced at Greigstein. He looked down quietly at the moths

that seemed no longer to interest him. Lady Stanmere rose and placed her arm in that of Molly.
"It is getting quite chilly," she said. "My dear, you are going to help me as far as the house. I may keep you there for a little chat for half an hour or so, because I go to bed very early. When I am asleep I can forget. Your brother can wait for you by the laurel gate."
The two disappeared together. By the light of the lantern Dick studied his companion's face. A schoolboy caught stealing apples, a fisherman with a broken line, something of that sort Greigstein might have sat for.
"A penny for your thoughts," said Dick, dryly.
"Extravagant!" Greigstein growled. "Young man, I am in a dangerous mood, as most people are when they take themselves to be wise and find themselves dolts instead. You chaff me any more and I take that handsome curly head of yours and bang him against the wall. I have lost my big moth, I have lost—no, there he is. Give me the lantern quick. You come this way. So."
"I give you up," Dick laughed. "You are too strange a mixture for any man to properly understand. And yet at the same time," he concluded, sotto voce, "I am not going to forget that Lady Stanmere called you Von Wrangel."
But Greigstein was ahead and in hot pursuit of the white moth. There was a gurgle of satisfaction as the specimen was captured. For the next half hour Greigstein talked a scientific jargon that Dick made no pretence of understanding. It seemed to him that Greigstein was talking for the sake of making speech, as if he dreaded questions on quite another topic. It might have been a sigh of relief or a sigh of pleasure that he gave when Molly's white dress loomed in sight.
"You found her ladyship charming?" he asked.
"As ever," Molly replied. "You seem to forget that I have been at Stanmere before. Lady Stanmere used to spoil me dreadfully when I was a child. Now, let us get along to supper—it's past ten o'clock."
But Greigstein regretted that he must change his plans. He had meant to stay till the last train, but he had forgotten an important letter he had to write. If he hurried to the station he would catch the 11.15. He was desolate; but there was no help for it, he must go at once.
He started hard down the road for a little way, then stopped, listening intently. A moment later he was back in the park again with his face in the direction of the house.
Molly was a little silent on her homeward walk.
"You are very quiet," Dick said at length.
"Am I?" Molly asked. "Dick, I have made a discovery. Do you remember the photograph of Mary Gay you brought home that night?"
"I am not likely to forget it," Dick said, quietly.
"Well, it's a strange thing, but a large portrait of Mary hangs in Lady

Stanmere's drawing-room."

XVII. — A FRIEND IN NEED.

Dick heard what Molly had to say with no feeling of surprise. Had the blind Mary risen from the roadside before him he would have felt no astonishment. His life was in some way bound up with that of the girl who had so fascinated him; that they would come together sooner or later he felt certain.

"I can't forget her," he said, "and indeed I would not if I could. So sweet and pathetic, so lonely and mysterious. And there is something like a great tragedy revolving round the poor girl. Did Lady Stanmere mention her?"

"Not directly," Molly replied. "But more than once she looked from the photograph to myself, and seemed on the point of asking a question. Oh, if we could only get at the bottom of it!"

Dick walked on in silence. Before the door of the cottage a boy stood with an orange-hued envelope in his hand.

"Telegram for you, sir," he said. "Special messenger from Formby, and a shilling to pay."

With a feeling that something was going to happen, Dick tore open the envelope. It was a message from the Record office. There was an extra pressure of work, and Stevenson was to come up at once, if possible. There was just a chance to catch the last train up from Stanmere.

"No supper," Dick said, briefly. "This is one of the joys of being a journalist. But anyway, it's better than Pant-street."

He caught up his hat and coat and shot off into the darkness. Five-and-twenty minutes later he was in the noise and glare of Fleet street. It was a strange contrast to the sylvan quietness of Stanmere. The Record office was humming like a hive; down below the machines were rattling and roaring. The only quiet spot appeared to be the office of the editor. The place looked prim and green and subdued, under its shaded lights.

"I came up as soon as I got your telegram, sir," Dick remarked to the figure under the green shade. "If there is anything that I could do—"

"Got no telegram from me," the editor said, curtly. "Try Mr. Spencer, who is here unusually late to-night. I'm busy."

The hint was plain and Dick took it promptly. The owner of the record was in his office drawing abstractedly on a sheet of 'copy' paper. He looked terribly pale and agitated, as disturbed as he had been when Dick had first met him in Cambria square.

"I had a telegram, sir," Dick began. "Mr. Fisher—"

Mr. Spencer looked up abstractedly. He seemed to see nothing but the shadow of despair out of those sombre eyes of his. Then it was borne in upon him that he was no longer alone.

"Yes, yes," he said. He breathed as if he had run hard and fast. "I sent for you —the business has nothing to do with the office. The man I could best trust is not in London to-night. Can I trust you?"
Dick met the troubled eyes firmly. It was impossible not to feel sorry for the speaker. Here was a millionaire philanthropist, a man of good name and widely respected, who carried about with him a trouble that his obscure companion would not have borne for all Golconda.
"Yes, yes, I see I can," Spencer went on; "you are very like your father. I lied to you when I said I did not know him, because I knew him very well indeed. My boy, I am in trouble, such a trouble as few men dream of. And all for one passing indiscretion. God knows, I have expiated that crime in remorse and sorrow. But it will be with me always. And, like most crimes, mine affects the happiness of others. If I am found out now, one of the most delicate fabrics falls to the ground. Two or three years hence and it would not matter. Anyone is welcome to drag my sin into the light of day then. Do you understand—this thing must be concealed?"
"I am very sorry," Dick stammered. "You have been very good to me, and I will serve you with my whole heart and soul. You are in danger—"
"Imminent danger. The blow may fall now for all I know. Dick, you are strong and resolute. You must help me to avert it."
Spencer's voice sunk to a half-pleading, piteous whisper. In the lamplight his face was shining as the great beads rolled down his cheeks.
"I will do anything you ask me," Dick cried.
"Ah, I was sure you would. Not that I am going to tell you my secret, the secret of my life. It is for my daughter that I require your aid."
Dick thrilled. Here was his chance at last. From the very first he was destined to see Mary again; he had felt that in his heart, and it had been no idle dream. His face flushed with sheer delight.
"I stumbled on my danger near my house as I came from my walk to-night," Spencer went on. "My danger was watching the house, so that I dared not return. I came here scarcely knowing what to do. To return home was impossible until the coast was clear. Then I sent for you."
"You could have found no more faithful servant, sir."
"I am sure of it. You have resolution and courage, and you are a gentleman besides. Your sister is as good and true as yourself. . . . . It would be a splendid thing to hide at Stanmere. . . . To double on one's tracks like a thief near the scene of his crime . . . And then there are the trackless moors where one could hide. . . . . ." The speaker was talking to himself. Evidently he had forgotten all about Dick. His lips were moving, but no further sound came. The quick purr of a telephone bell in the room startled him.
"Go and answer it," he said, hoarsely, to Dick. "I dare not do it myself. It is my private wire from Cambria square. If I could only think! God grant that I do

not get one of my brain attacks to-night."
Dick crossed the room and took down the receiver. He felt spurred on and braced up with the knowledge that he had been approved and chosen. He felt very near to the blind girl now.
"Are you there?" he asked. "Who is it? Who am I? Richard Stevenson, who speaks to you from Mr. Spencer's private room. He has asked me to speak for him."
"I'm glad of it, sir," came a strange voice. "If my master had taken my advice you would have been impressed into the service before. I'm Kant, sir."
Dick knew the voice now; it was Spencer's mysterious servant, the man who had taken Mary's photograph from him and advised him not to come near Cambria square again. He listened impatiently.
"The danger is still here," Kent went on, "outside waiting. Tell Mr. Spencer that I will do anything he likes, but I can't think of a way out. I can guard and watch with anybody, but I cannot scheme. If the young lady was only out of the way—"
"Stop a minute," Dick exclaimed. "I'll call you again presently." He hung up the receiver, and turned to his employer. He had fallen back in his chair a picture of abject despair. A shake of the shoulder failed to move him. And Dick felt that moments were precious.
"For Heaven's sake, arouse yourself," he said. "You say that everything depends upon the next few hours. You may save the situation yet. Your man Kant tells me that everything depends upon getting your your daughter away. Your daughter! Mary, Mary!"
The name moved Spencer. He nodded feebly.
"That is true," he groaned. "But how is it going to be done?"
"I am thinking of a way; in fact, I have practically done so. Dear sir, I do not seek to pry into your secrets, but I must know a little more if I am to be successful. Some danger menaces your daughter, some spy is watching outside. That spy has guessed something."
"Yes, yes," Spencer said, eagerly. "That is it."
"So far, so good. What we have to do now is to get your daughter away from under the very eyes of the spy. A little boldness and audacity may succeed. Tell me, does Miss Spencer know anything of this danger?"
"To a certain extent, yes. I have told her that I have a remorseless enemy. Once in Paris and again in San Francisco we had to steal away. If you go to Mary with a message to that effect from me she will follow you."
Dick thrilled again. The idea of having the blind girl under his care set his pulses drumming. And he was going to succeed.
"I will do it," he said. "You can trust your child to me?"
"I will trust my child to you implicitly."
"You will never have cause to repent it, sir," Dick said, as steadily as possible.

"She shall go down with me to Stanmere, and Molly shall look after her."
"That is it," Spencer cried. "That is the idea. . . . And you know all those woodland paths, where nobody else dare go. Take her and shield her as you would the most precious thing in your possession. If you only knew the tremendous interests that revolve round that poor blind girl! Now go."
Dick stepped across to the telephone. He had hardly got the receiver to his ear before Kant responded from the other end.
"Is the danger still there?" Dick asked.
"Ay, ay," came the startling reply; "the danger is in the house. Nothing has happened yet, but at any moment the explosion may occur. For goodness' sake, sir, tell me what to do."
Dick thought it out for a moment. His scheme was getting pretty clear.
"Does the danger take the form of a man who is the alter ego—I mean the second self of your master?" he asked. "It does? You have prevaricated, of course. Tell me what you have said."
"I am a servant of a gentleman who has this flat. My own master I am supposed to have left long ago. Heaven forgive all these lies."
"I am afraid they are necessary," Dick replied. "But we need have as few as possible. You are expecting your master, and he is coming. Do not express any astonishment, try and follow the lead that I shall give you. Fortunately, I recollect the way into Mr. Spencer's flat. Where is your visitor?"
"He is in the morning-room smoking a cigar. Make haste, sir. I dare not stay so far away as the telephone is any longer. When I think of the peril that a wall a few inches thick divides, I feel cold all over. Come at once, sir; take a cab and let us get to work. This is terribly trying to the nerves."
Dick turned away from the telephone, blessing it as he did so. It seemed to him that he had conveyed quite as much to Kant as was necessary.
"I am ready to go now," he said.
"Youth and a clear conscience!" Spencer cried. "What precious possessions they are! What would I not give to have them again!"
Meanwhile Dick had reached the street and hailed a hansom. A few minutes later and he was in Cambria square. His heart was beating a little faster now, but he was cool and resolute. He reached the flat at length, and stood listening for voices. He heard that of Kant at length behind a door, the handle of which he turned and walked in with the air of a master.
"What does this mean, Kant?" he demanded. "Where was the brougham? And James puts the blame upon you. I shall be glad of an explanation."

XVIII. — A VISITOR.

Released from his polite attentions to the startled Venner, the man called Stephen walked thoughtfully away. He looked like one who had some sudden

shock, as if a trouble had been chastened by some unexpected joy.
He began to pick his steps more cautiously presently, for ever glancing over his shoulder, fearful of seeing something undesirable behind. It was not exactly the action of a criminal, and yes the man was afraid of something that threatened his life.
He was by no means a bad-looking man if his face had been less reckless. Here was a man who would go any length if the spirit moved him, a man who could hate well and love well, and give no heed to the future once his passions ran with a loose rein. Presently he ceased to look over his shoulder and his eyes grew introspective.
"This is a fine piece of luck," he muttered. "If that scoundrel told the truth—and I see no reason why he should not—I have found the object of my search. Fancy blundering on the scent in this fashion after all these years! What shall I do with him? Kill him? That would be a poor kind of vengeance and gives the victim little pain. Hand him over to the tender mercies of Horace Venner perhaps. If ever I saw blackmail and the knowledge that it was going to be successful I saw it on Venner's face to-night. . . . But I have to find my quarry first. After all Cambria square is a trifle vague."
The speaker came to his destination at length. For some time he lingered under a lamp until the suspicious glance of a policeman moved him on. In the hope that he was sure of his ground, the man had been hanging about here for days. Now he was certain. But it was no use to hide in the square gardens as he had done before. He twisted a cigarette and prepared to wait. His luck was in to-night, and he was going to follow it up. His patience was not to be unduly tried.
A man in a quiet undress livery came slowly down the road. He was smoking a cigar and looked exactly what he was—a good-class servant enjoying his hour or so off duty. The watcher slackened his pace a little so that the other man might go by him. There was a furtive look and a sudden gleam in the eyes of the loiterer.
"Kant," he said to himself. "The astute, faithful, inestimable Kant! As the jackal is so near, the lion is not far off. It would seem as if things were prosperous with my dear, affectionate relative. I will follow Kant, and when he has finished his cigar he will go back to the house again. Where does all this prosperity come from?"
The cigar was finished at length, and Kant retraced his steps. He disappeared into the vestibule of a palatial pile of flats, and then the other man followed. It might be a little difficult if Kant availed himself of the lift, but fortunately the lift had just started for an upper floor, so that Kant walked up the stone stairs.
"Isn't going very far up then," the tracker muttered. "Evidently my esteemed friend has one of the best of the suites here. Well, before long, he will be ready to exchange it for a hovel in Shoreditch. Ah, here we are!"

Kant passed down a corridor into a morning-room, the other man following close behind. In an instant the door was shut and locked. Kant turned in some surprise to see a tall, gaunt figure standing before him. There was a mocking smile on the stranger's face. Just for an instant Kant turned pale; just for the fraction of a second there was a startled expression on his face. It was as if a fine fencer had been taken off his guard. But it was only just for an instant.
"You have been expecting me, Kant?" the new-comer said.
Kant bowed his head, the very model of a well-trained servant. It was impossible to associate him with disreputable secrets. He might have gone bail for the respectability of the household. He moved so as to get before the other door leading from the room.
"I am glad to see you, Mr. Stephen," he said. He was absolutely cold now, not at all like a man who has rehearsed this scene many times over. "I am glad to see that you—"
"Pshaw!—that I have not been hanged yet, Kant. You have some very snug quarters here. Your master is evidently doing a good thing for himself. Where is he?"
"At present he is out, sir. Do you happen to know him, sir?"
"Know him! Of all the audacious rascals! Why, you will tell me next that you are not a factotum, ally, fellow-conspirator, all the rest of it!"
"My master's name, sir, is Spencer. I had to look to myself, sir. There are others depending upon me."
"You lying rascal, where is your master?"
"My master is out, sir," Kant went on in the same bland tones. "And I beg to remark, Mr. Stephen, that, even a servant has his feelings. You would have been more popular at home had you remembered that fact, sir. Your late father would never have spoken like that."
The reproof was dignified and in the best possible taste. Stephen Stanmere shot a keen glance at Kant, but it was impossible to penetrate that armour again. The man's nerve was perfect, he was absolutely on his guard; behind that dull mask his brain was working rapidly.
"I apologise," the intruder said. "I have been far beyond schools of manners lately. All the same, I am going to stay here till your master returns."
Kant bowed. From somewhere a little way off a clear voice was singing, a sweet and well-trained voice, to the accompaniment of a piano.
"That is your mistress, I presume?" Stanmere sneered.
"If you would like to see her—"
"Not I! I am still sufficiently civilised not to venture into the company of a lady in this sorry garb. Still there is something in the voice—but that is impossible. Still I shall find that all out when I see your master."
There was a grim earnestness about the last few words, but they seemed to make no impression on Kant.

"Very well, sir," he said. "If you know my master, well and good. If you don't care to go into the drawing-room, can I get you anything here? A cigar, sir, or a glass of whisky and soda-water?"
Stephen Stanmere nodded. He was not feeling quite so sure of his ground now. The voice of the singer at the piano charmed him.
"Whisky and soda," he said, "and a cigar if it is a good one. It is just possible that I am a victim of a singular coincidence—'Thou art so near and yet so far,' and all that kind of thing. But I am going to leave nothing to chance."
"Very good, sir. I will get you what you require, Mr. Stephen."
Kant walked away in his own cool, deliberate fashion. But as he quietly closed the door behind him he turned the well-oiled key in the lock noiselessly. His mask-like face was instantly covered with a fine perspiration. He flew to the telephone in the closet at the end of the passage and stood there quivering with expectation.
So far so good. He had only to wait now for developments. Help was at hand, he would have an ally that he could depend upon. All he had to do now was to keep his eyes open and take up the cue that the new-comer would give him. There was no trace of agitation about him as he came back presently with the refreshments.
"I ought not to have let you go," Stanmere said, suspiciously. "Still you could not do much harm seeing that I am in possession. Your master—"
"Will be home in a few minutes, sir, now," Kant said, coolly. "He is here now."
The door flew open and a handsome young man came in. In his tweed suit and with a long coat over his arm he had evidently come off a journey. He seemed to be in a fine temper, he had eyes for Kant alone.
"What does this mean?" he demanded. "Where is the brougham? James put the blame on to you. If this happens again Kant—"
Kant spread out his hands helplessly. His face was downcast, but his heart beat with fierce delight.

XIX. — FENCING.

There was no reason to repeat the question, no cause so much as to raise an eyeglass. Kant had taken up his cue perfectly.
"I am very sorry, Mr. Spencer, sir," Kant said, humbly, and Dick knew that it would be wise of him to respond to the name of Spencer, which meant nothing after all. "James muddled up the order, sir. If there is anything that I can do, sir —"
"Nothing, only to see that my evening dress is all laid out for me at once. I presume that your mistress is ready. I don't want to keep her waiting."
"My mistress is in the drawing-room, sir."
The stranger followed with a feeling that something was slipping away from

him. Just for a moment it occurred to him that here was part of some subtle scheme for throwing dust in his eyes. He thought it all over in the quickness of a flash. And yet it could be hardly possible. Only just for the fraction of a second had Kant been taken by surprise, and that might have been caused by finding himself suddenly face to face with an old acquaintance. And this young man had come in with a sudden air of possession, he looked well and prosperous, and, again, there was the voice in the drawing-room. Mr. Spencer was a young man of the upper middle class, and the singer was his wife. And they were going out presently to some late function. The outsider was growing uncomfortable.

"Well, don't let it occur again," Dick cried. "And I shall be glad if you will find some other place to entertain your friends, Kant."

"Gentleman no friend of mine, sir," Kant responded. "Says he knows you, sir."

Kant disappeared discreetly with a comfortable assurance that he was leaving matters in capable hands.

"Glad they sent him," he muttered. "There's grit and pluck and brains there. We are going to pull through this time, but it has been touch and go."

Dick turned to the intruder somewhat haughtily.

"I am afraid there has been a mistake, sir," he said. "I do not know you."

"The advantage is quite mutual," Stanmere replied. "I—I came here under a misapprehension. I am looking for somebody who I am certain lives close here, possibly under this very roof. I don't suppose you have ever seen me before, but—"

Dick took a pace or two forward. The game was entirely in his own hands now if he only played it boldly. The man was the enemy of his benefactor, the strange man with the amazing likeness to the individual who called himself Mr. Spencer.

"I do know you," Dick cried. "By accident I was passing through Cambria square a few nights ago and I saw you make a murderous attack upon a gentleman there. If I had not come up in time you would have killed him. By sheer good luck you escaped from my hands, or you would have been fitly adorning a gaol by this time. What are you doing here, you cowardly ruffian?"

Stanmere muttered something. He was taken utterly by surprise. He had not expected this, and it was so overpoweringly true. He no longer swaggered with the certainty that he was on the right scent. There was a possibility of the police being called and he being given into custody.

"You know too much and too little," he said, hoarsely. "Rest assured of the fact that the man you speak of would never come forward to charge me. If he were here at this moment you would see him here at my feet pleading for mercy."

There was a sincerity about this speech that struck Dick forcibly. And from his own knowledge of the complicated mystery he knew it was true. Otherwise, why Mr. Spencer's pitiable fear of meeting this man?

"I have no more than your word for that," Dick said, coldly. "Nor have you satisfactorily explained why you are here at this moment."
"Well, I followed Kant in here," Stanmere said, lamely.
"I know you did. But why?"
"Because Kant was ever the devoted servant of my—of the man I am looking for. And I did not believe Kant when he told me he had changed situations. I did not believe him till you came into the room, and then I saw my mistake. All I can do is to tender you my most sincere apologies and leave the house without delay."
Dick bowed coldly. Stanmere took up his seedy hat and made for the door, with what dignity he could assume under the circumstances. He passed out into the corridor, where he paused for a moment with his nose in the air.
"Strange, very strange," he muttered. "The voice was familiar, and yet it could not be. And here is the scent of the violets that that she loved so well. One might say that there are other women who are fond of the smell of violets, but —Well, I'll wait. If those two people are going out presently, I'll not go till I am certain."
Dick breathed a little easier to find himself alone. Directly the outer door closed Kant came in. His features glowed with satisfaction.
"You did that splendidly, sir," he said; "but it was a very near thing."
"The danger is by no means over," Dick replied. "I forced that man to go away —indeed under the circumstances he could not stay. But if I could judge anything from the expression of his face, he was far from satisfied. He did not come here to-night without some good ground for doing so. He has only been choked off for the moment. Kant, that man must be satisfied, we must make him feel that he is wrong. I am ready to forfeit my whole scheme if you don't find him still looking about the square."
"Better go and see, sir?" Kant suggested.
Dick nodded. Kant was some little time away. When he came back his face was grave.
"You are quite right," he said. "Our friend is still there. What's to be done now, and what on earth is he waiting for?"
"He is going to see your mistress and myself depart," Dick said, "and he shall not be disappointed."

XX. — A PERFECT CONFIDENCE.

Dick walked into the drawing-room with a heart that was beating fast. The room was familiar to him as if he had seen it a hundred times. During that one brief visit the whole perfect picture had been photographed on his mind. Here were all the dainty ornaments, the pictures, the palms and the flowers everywhere. As before the whole atmosphere was redolent with the smell of

flowers.
At the piano Mary sat ringing some simple pathetic air to her own accompaniment. There was a slight smile on her beautiful face, the clear blue eyes seemed full of expression. Gently as Dick crept into the room, the girl heard him, and stopped instantly.
"It is Mr. Stevenson," she said quite naturally. "The gentleman who was so kind to my father the other night. I am so very glad to see you."
She came forward quite naturally as if she had sight to see like other people. Dick felt quite dazed for a moment and could say nothing whilst holding that little hand in his.
"Did you actually recollect my step!" he stammered.
"Oh, yes," Mary smiled. "I have a fine feeling for that kind of thing. One sense always increases as another is injured. I hope you have no bad news for me?"
"Why do you suggest that?" Dick asked. "Because your voice is not quite steady," Mary said. "And because nobody comes here. And my father has not yet returned. I hope he is not ill."
"Your father is perfectly well," Dick replied. "But he has sent me here. Miss Mary, he has taken me into his confidence."
"It is more than he has done for me," Mary said, with a sad little smile. "He is a good man; and I love him dearly, but there is a chapter of his life that I have not been permitted to read as yet. The dark secret that hangs over our lives."
"Is a secret from me also," Dick said. "More than once it has been necessary for you to leave a place hurriedly, and ask no questions. Do you call them to mind, Miss Mary?"
"Twice—once in Paris and once in San Francisco. There is a Nemesis somewhere that dogs us, and we have to fly. But I thought that was all over. Is it coming again?"
"My dear young lady, it has come to-night. Your father has sent you a message by me. You are to come with me and ask no questions. The danger is very much alive again. If it falls it will bring ruin upon many people concerned. You are not afraid?"
The girl shivered and turned a little pale. The blue eyes had grown very pathetic. She gave a longing look about the room as if she could see all the familiar objects before her.
"You do not hesitate to trust me?" Dick asked.
A little white hand crept along Dick's sleeve and rested in his fingers. The touch thrilled him and brought the colour into his face. The action was so pretty, so full of confidence.
"I trust you implicitly," the girl said. "You are kind and honorable, my father says, and he knows. And in your voice there is a ring that I like; a ring of feeling and sincerity. It will be a great sorrow to me to leave the place where I know everything, but my father knows best. Where are we going?"

"We are going to a place called Shepherd's Spring, at Stanmere."
Mary's face flushed. She pressed Dick's hand suddenly.
"I know it," she said. "Oh, I shall be on familiar ground there. I might have known that even in the bitterest trouble my father would not forget me. I shall be able to walk there and to feel that I know exactly where I am. And the people there?"
"Are my sister and myself. It is a very strange thing, Miss Mary, but when you gave me that photograph by mistake my sister recognised it. She was at school with you—Molly Stevenson."
A little cry of delight came from Mary.
"My dear girl," she said. "I was called Mary Gay there because that was because my father came into his money and changed his name. And so I am going to stay with Molly! If my father is well, I shall be entirely happy at Stanmere."
"Your father is perfectly well and will come to no harm. You can make your mind quite easy as to that. And it all rests with yourself."
Once more the little hand pressed Dick's fingers.
"You may rely upon me. I am sore afflicted, but you will not find me lacking in courage. Only tell me what I am to do."
"You are to go up to your maid and get her to pack a small valise for you that you can carry under your cloak. You are to put on a somewhat elaborate evening dress with a certain amount of jewels—diamonds for choice—say a brooch. The rest of your wardrobe can come later on, so long as you have enough for the present. Then you will come down dressed and cloaked as if you were going to a party. After that you will go down to a carriage that I am getting from a good livery stable close by. In the street you will drop your diamond star and find out the loss at once. I shall not pretend to see it, and you will point out that it is in the gutter, where I shall take care to kick it. It is a lovely starlight night, so when we get outside you are to point out the fact to me, especially noticing Charles's Wain. Also, you are to have a fleecy, cloudy thing to hide your face. If you could manage to assume another voice, say rather a mincing and affected voice—"
"Oh, I can do that easily," Mary cried. "The girls at school used to say that I could take off all the mistresses to perfection. How will this do? 'What a lovely night, Dick!' I know your name is Dick, because your sister used to speak of you. 'What a glorious night! Look at Charles's Wain.' Will that do?"
"Splendidly!" Dick cried. "As we get into the carriage you had better turn round and remind me that my tie is not on straight. Shall I ring the bell for you?"
A quarter of an hour later and Dick was arrayed in one of Mr. Spencer's dress suits. The fit was none too good, but a long overcoat hid all imperfections, and it was dark outside. At the head of the stairs Mary stood, a lovely picture in

white satin and diamonds.
"I hope I shall do," she said, shyly. "I have plenty of beautiful dresses that I seldom wear. Do you think that I shall pass the watchful eye that waits for us?"
Dick was absolutely certain of it. He stood with a deep admiration for a few minutes. If only Mary could see! Surely hers was the most beautiful face in the world. Kant, standing in the background, coughed with discretion.
"Our man's still there, sir," he said. "And the carriage is at the door. We are doing a wrong thing, both of us, but good may come of it, and it won't be for long."
Dick drew Mary's arm through his own, with an injunction to touch him lightly. She passed down the stairs and into the street quite blithely. She looked from one side to the other. Then her gaze went upwards and she broke into raptures on the beauty of the night. It sounded like somebody entirely different to Dick as he listened in great admiration. The falling of the diamond brooch and the detection of it by Mary were both perfect.
"And do you know, my dear Dick," she said sweetly, "your white tie is under your ear? Those new patent fasteners of yours are quite useless."
The door of the brougham was banged to and an address in Gloucester Place given by Kant, who stood back with a rigid forefinger to his forehead. Mary laughed aloud.
"It is like an adventure," she said. "Did I do that well—Dick?"
"Magnificently!" Dick said with emotion. The pair of eyes that gleamed malevolently out of the darkness were puzzled yet satisfied, and not a little angry. "And if you would always call me Dick—"
"In future I shall. I am very lonely, Dick, and I have few friends. And if you would be good and kind to me, be a brother to me—"
Dick caught the little hand held out to him, and pressed it to his lips.
"Always!" he said. "I will never forget you. I will see for you and fight for you. But as to being a brother, why, you see—"
Dick stopped abruptly. He was confused and nervous, but on the whole the happiest man in England to-night.

XXI. — UNDER THE STARS.

Small wonder that Dick's heart beat high within him. There had been time for day-dreams lately, lying on the heather with the golden meadows leading down to Camelot, a brief idyll after those grinding weary years. The breadth, the beauty, the purple flash of a swallow wheeling in the blue, all filled Dick with a pure delight. He was a young man, strong and sanguine, and he had the artistic temperament.
Small wonder, then, that he should dream and glow and weave his romances

with a central figure, blue-eyed, fair, and sightless. When the means was won Dick would marry Mary, always providing that she would have him, a possible factor that chilled the ardent Richard occasionally.

Mary had been the central figure in so many romances, but never in one quite so thrilling as the present reality. He was going to have beautiful blind Mary under his own roof for the time being—an idyll amongst the roses, a poem in honey-suckle. Dick was a happy man to-night.

The carriage drove on until the lamps grew far between and hedges took the place of houses. Then came the sweet fragrance of dew-washed grass, a full round moon crept like a shield into the sky.

"Are we going to drive all the way?" Mary asked. She had been strangely silent, though her face was calm and untroubled.

"Every inch of it," Dick replied. "On the whole it is more prudent to do so. It is such a glorious night."

"I felt it," Mary said. "I have a kind of instinct in such things. Cool and still and dewy with a brilliant moon overhead. If you say I an wrong, I shall be very disappointed, Dick."

She turned towards him with a wistful little smile that had something pathetic in it. She seemed to be conscious of the spot where Dick was sitting, for she laid her hand on his.

"You are perfectly right," he said, eagerly. "How clever you are!"

Mary smiled again as she patted Dick's fingers. All her life she had seen nothing of men with the exception of her father, and all men were like him in her sight. What in another girl would have been boldness seemed quite natural in her case.

"I like the touch of your hand, Dick," she said. "So strong and firm and kind. You and I are going to be good friends. Is there anyone you love, Dick."

"Molly," said Dick; "and, well, I am going to be very fond of you, Mary."

It cost him an effort not to say more. It really was a lovely night, and the thrill in his voice was testimony to his feelings. There was a smell of wild thyme on the dewy air. And the touch of those white fingers was thrilling. On the whole it was quite time to give the conversation a more prosaic turn.

"We have not so very far to go, now," Dick said. "We are on the top of Longmead, and I can see the lights of Stanmere in the valley."

There came a strange gleam into the sightless blue eyes.

"Dear old Stanmere," Mary whispered. "I was very happy there. It was all vague and mysterious, that coming and going of mine, but I was really happy there. All the same, Dick, you must keep me away from Stanmere."

"Tell me all about it," Dick asked.

"I—I cannot. There is a secret. It is not my secret. Lady Stanmere—"

"No, no!" Dick said. "Don't think I am prying. We will talk of something else."

He was just a shade disappointed. He had asked too much. With her quick intuition Mary guessed his feelings.

"Don't be hurt," she said. "You are so good and kind, and we are going to be such good friends. Dick, I think you would do anything for me?"

"Anything in the wide world," Dick said, with the largeness of romantic youth. "If you could only realise what I would do for you!"

There was another pressure from the slim fingers.

"Some day it will all come out; some day the truth will be known, and my father's character vindicated. But don't talk of Stanmere, Dick, for the mere thought of it fills me with remorse. And keep me from the house, though if you put me down upon the heath I could find my way there, blind as I am."

"Only one question," Dick urged. "You lived at Shepherds Spring once?"

"Yes. We had a kind of holiday there. My father furnished it for me much the same as the house in Cambria square is furnished. It was a lovely time. Dick, you come from Stanmere. Did you ever known my—Lady Stanmere's sons?"

Dick replied that he had not had the dubious pleasure.

They were much older than himself, and he had been a child when they left home. There had been a lot of trouble and anxiety over those boys, he understood.

"I suppose so," Mary said sadly. "And yet my father says the wild boys often make good men. Are we very near, Dick?"

"Near enough to see the lights of Shepherd's Spring," Dick said, cheerfully. "And there is Molly in the doorway wondering what has become of me. Let us pay off our driver here and take her by surprise."

Molly was peering anxiously into the darkness. She seemed to be utterly puzzled. Once in the light of the hall her face cleared.

"Dick," she cried. "Dick, what does it mean? Little Mary Gay—I mean to say —Spencer. My dear, my dear, I am so glad to see you."

The delight was genuine and spontaneous. Just for a moment, Dick longed to be a girl so that he might have taken Mary in his arms and kissed her. Here, too, was a new phase of the dream of happiness—Mary under his own roof and being fussed over and made much of by his own sister! Mary was moving about the house as if she had never known a deep affliction, her face was glowing with delight.

"You are not to help me at all," she cried. "Positively, I decline to have any assistance. On the whole I am a great deal more at home here than you are. And what a dear, delightful old Molly it is! You are positively dying with curiosity to know how I got here, and not one question on the subject have you asked yet."

"I shall take it out of Dick when you are in bed," Molly said. "For the present, I am only too delighted to see you near me once more. And if Dick is going to make a great name out of a romance he has all the materials at his fingers' ends here. What a charming heroine you will make to be sure, Mary."

Dick blushed ingenuously. The colour was reflected in Mary's cheeks.
"You mean Dick and myself," she said. "Dick is strong and tall, and good and true. But whoever heard of a blind princess?"
Molly laughed as she kissed the pretty wistful face.
"Dick is a very original genius, my dear," she said, demurely. "And I am sure that your affliction will lend a charm to the story."
Dick effected to be suddenly busy and avoided Molly's mischievous glance. But he knew now that there would never be anyone else for him. It was an hour later before Molly came to him and aroused him from his dream.
"Mary is tucked up in bed, fast asleep," she said. "Prince, prince, how did you come to fly away with your princess like this? Tell me at once or I shall expire from sheer curiosity. Go on at once."
For the next hour Dick had an interested listener.

XXII. — HALCYON.

The cup of happiness seemed full, but there was room for more in the golden measure. It came the next morning in the form of a telegram from Spencer. He hinted vaguely that for the present the danger was averted, and congratulated Dick upon his brilliant success of the previous evening. He was to stay down at Stanmere for the present and see that nothing happened there. He was supposed to be away on business for the proprietor of the Record.
"Something is going to happen to me presently," Dick said, with a delighted grin as he handed the telegram to Molly. "I am given a holiday, I have the most delightful weather, and the companionship of the most delightful girl in the world."
"Two delightful girls," Molly said, severely. "My dear boy, you are in danger of forgetting your manners. But seriously, Dick, you will have to be careful. You have hit upon a most delightful and mysterious romance, you have found a charming heroine, but after all, Mr. Spencer is a man of business. If you had really given your heart to Mary—"
"The mischief is done," Dick said with a fine glow on his face. "I fell in love with Mary the first time I saw her. It was all done in a moment. When I came home that evening with those violets in my buttonhole, I had made my choice. Come what may, I shall never love another woman."
"And when Mr. Spencer comes to know, as he must—"
"Oh, he shall be told. I am not going to sail under any false colours. But there is is plenty of time for that. Molly, doesn't it strike you that I am talking like a conceited ass all this time?"
Molly laughed. Perhaps the conversation was a trifle premature. When Mary came down to breakfast, brother and sister were planning an excursion for the day. It was a sin to stay indoors such weather as this.

"The watchword is the Warren," Molly said. "We shall take our luncheon with us; also out tea. If I could only find a spirit-kettle—"
"In the store-room you will find everything, luncheon-basket included," Mary interrupted. "I recollect those picnics in the old days. Let us go to the Warren by all means. Once put me down there and I shall know where I am. It is so good to feel that you are not utterly useless. In this house I can do everything for myself. Now, am I not very neat, seeing that my maid is not with me?"
She looked very charming and simple in her white dress. She was facing towards the sun and speaking of certain points in the landscape here and there, when suddenly she paused.
"There is somebody coming up to the house," she said. "I can hear a strange footstep. I hope it is nobody come to see you on business, Dick. I will go into the drawing-room and play till you have got rid of him."
Dick could see nothing and hear nothing. Presently a step came outside, and the sound of a cheerful whistle, very much out of tune.
"Greigstein!" Dick exclaimed, in great annoyance. "There seems to be no getting away from that ubiquitous German. Well, there is one thing pretty certain—he must be got rid of."
Dick raised his voice angrily, and Molly lifted a hand of warning. It was too late. Through the open window Greigstein had heard everything.
He stepped coolly through the long French window, still whistling his air out of tune.
"I am not to be got rid of!" he said, coolly. "I am your Paul Pry, the limpet that clings to the affliction of my friends, Dick and Miss Molly. Behold I come down to see you; I say to myself they will be glad to see me, but now I am de trop. It is sad, but je suis, je reste."
Dick laughed with the air of a man who grudgingly admits the humour of the situation. It was very difficult to be hard with Greigstein.
"You have visitors," he said, wagging his head to the melody from the drawing-room; "stately visitors, who are far too good for humble tutors."
"We are not snobs, whatever else we may be," Dick laughed. "On the whole, Molly, we had better make the best of a bad business and take Greigstein along. And if you see anything out of the common to-day, Greigstein, you are to be silent."
"My tongue shall be dumb," Greigstein cried. "I swear to you—"
He paused and stood looking open-mouthed towards the doorway. Mary stood there smiling, and asking if she might be admitted. She came forward, Greigstein still standing there like a man who beholds some wonderful and unexpected vision. The next moment he had turned his face away, but not before he had caught the queer expression in Dick's eyes.
"Our friend, Miss Mary Spencer," Dick said, with a certain solemn savageness. "This is Mr. or, rather, Herr Greigstein. Mary, Miss Spencer, is

blind, Greigstein."
Greigstein murmured something that it was hard to catch. His usual self-possession had absolutely deserted him. He looked like a man who was in a waking dream. Never before had Dick see him silent for so long.
Long after they had started on their excursion, Greigstein had still remained in his dreamy condition. Dick watched him with the incident of the photograph still in his mind. Puzzled and bewildered as Greigstein evidently was, he was not more puzzled than Dick. The two men glanced at one another with a certain veiled antagonism. They were on the Warren now, with the fair stretch of the country at their feet. Molly was getting the luncheon ready, and Mary was rendering her some little service in so doing.
"You have seen Miss Spencer before?" Dick asked.
"There you are greatly mistaken," Greigstein said, presently. "We have never met before."
"Perhaps you will tell me that you have never heard of her?"
"No. Because that would not be true. But I shall be discreet and silent as yourself, for I have need to be."
Dick was silent for a moment. It had occurred to him that Greigstein was playing the spy in some way; he had come down with the idea that he might see Mary Spencer. But this view was not to be entertained seeing that the sight of Mary had filled Greigstein with such genuine amazement. There was no acting here.
"You are an enigma to me," Dick said. "You are the hem of a secret that is concealed from me. But I have trusted you and been your friend. That you know something of this mystery I feel certain. And you play me false—"
"Stop," Greigstein cried. His face had grown stern and hard as Dick's. "You are going too far. I pledge you my word that I am acting for the best. Years ago I brought great sorrow on a noble house. I am one of those unfortunates who mean well. I have tried to atone for my error, and, between ourselves, my dear Dick, I have made matters worse. One word in your ear—keep Miss Mary out of Lady Stanmere's way."
A moment later and Greigstein was laughing and talking gaily again. The stern, hard man had become a child once more, he was full of infinite resources and amazing stories. Mary sat on the grass, a happy smile on her lips. She looked upwards presently as a flashing white cloud trailed over the sun.
"I hope it is not going to grow dull," she said. "I always feel the sunshine so."
Greigstein turned from the luncheon basket that he was unpacking. He turned a keen glance on the speaker. Then he crossed over to her, and in a perfect semblance of the professional manner drew down one of her eyelids. Mary winced a little.
"I'm sorry," Greigstein said. "What effect has that upon you?"

"Most strange," Mary murmured. "I seemed to see something dim and rugged. A figure in a mist. But it was gone directly."
Greigstein nodded. With his head on one side he regarded Mary as if she had been a new variety of butterfly. It was a long time before he spoke again.

XXIII. — A RAY OF HOPE.

Greigstein had disappeared in his erratic fashion. In was nearly tea time when he came back with the casual information that he had been down to Stanmere to send a telegram, and that he had decided to accept Molly's invitation to stay the night.
"Not that you have yet given me the invitation," he said, in the most inconsequent manner, "but it was sure to come. And when we get back to the house I propose to make an experiment or two on your eyes, Miss Mary. I know something about the science."
Mary shook her head. She had seen more than one physician who had given her no hope. She had schooled herself to recognise the inevitable.
"I had a long illness," she said, "and gradually my sight failed me. As I grew well and strong they hoped that my sight would return."
Greigstein muttered something about paralysis of the optic nerve. It seemed hard to to look at those clear blue eyes and believe that they were sightless.
"You speak like Von Wrangel," Dick said.
"Ah, if he were only alive," Mary cried. "They say he was a perfect marvel as far as the sight was concerned. I was going to him when he disappeared. My father said he got mixed up in some mad Bohemian conspiracy, and had to fly for his life. He was shot by a spy. It was a sad ending for so brilliant and valuable a life."
"Did you ever ever meet him?" Molly asked.
Greigstein was lying on his hack with his face turned skywards.
"As a matter of fact, I knew him very well," he said. "A clever man with a large amount of quicksilver in his veins. The desire to do something rash was his ruin. He never lost an opportunity of that kind. He would say to himself, 'my friend here is a magnificent opportunity of making a fool of yourself.' And straightway he did it."
"I believe you disliked him," Molly cried, "or you would not be so bitter."
"I never met a man I liked more," Greigstein said, with a certain dryness. "Still, it may be that it was all for the best. For years I was that man's closest friend and his bitterest enemy. But, I may say without egotism, that he taught me as much about the human eye as he knew himself."
Dick looked anxiously at the speaker. If he was going to try any experiment with those lovely blue eyes he would have to interfere. Sightless as those eyes were, their beauty remained. But already, in his mercurial way, Greigstein had

changed the subject.

Tea came presently, the long shadows were lying across the moorland, the last butterfly had fluttered into the bracken, and Molly reluctantly suggested a move.

"A pity such a day should come to an end," she said.

"But what a happy memory," Mary cried. "You and Dick have opened a new world to me. I used to think that I was perfectly happy in Cambria Square, with my flowers and piano, but it will never be quite the same again. Perhaps it is this lovely air that makes one feel so gay. Dick, please, give me your arm, I am delightfully tired."

They were back at Shepherd's Spring at last. Greigstein nodded approval as he saw a neat-looking package in the hall. He could do nothing till the morning-room was chartered and half filled with queer-looking instruments and tubes of strange shapes. He was masterful and dictatorial at dinner. Once the meal was over he took Mary into the morning-room.

"Now, I am going to make my experiments," he said. "Dick, I give you my word there is not going to be anything wrong. See here," He touched a kind of electric torch, and a crimson glow suffused the room, then another, then another, and there came a beautiful blend of glowing colors.

"It is no longer dark," Mary cried. "The room feels as if it were flooded with moonlight. There is a suggestion of purple somewhere."

Greigstein manipulated his lights, first in one hue and then in another. All the time the dominant note of color was purple. Whenever this came uppermost Mary seemed in some strange way to be aware of the fact. Greigstein tried again and again with similar result. He was quiet, almost saturnine, now, with a grim fighting look in his eyes. It was as if something had roused his anger. Outside the house he paced up and down long after Mary and her hostess had retired. Dick could hear the tramp of those footsteps and the muttered tones as Greigstein talked to himself. The versatile, volatile little butterfly hunter seemed to be entirely gone.

He came back to the house presently, and began to smoke in silence.

Gradually the dark mood turned from him and he began to smile once more.

"Wrangel could cure that girl," he said, suddenly.

"If he happened to be alive," Dick said, sententiously.

"If he happened to be alive!—quite so. And I told you this afternoon, that he was not dead at all. Dick, do you recollect the meeting with Lady Stanmere in the summer-house?"

Dick nodded. It was hopeless to try and follow Greigstein's mental wanderings.

"Do you recollect what she called me?"

"Let me see," Dick mused. "I recollect noticing that was not the same name.

She called you Wrangel, Von Wrangel. Good heaven! Why, you are—"
"Von Wrangel, only I am still to be known as Greigstein. Someday I will tell you how I came to get into this dreadful mess. But I am Von Wrangel, and Lady Stanmere is my aunt. And now you know why I sent that telegram, and why I made those experiments."
Dick paced up and down in great agitation. He hardly dared to ask the question that was on the tip of his tongue.
"And you think," he said, "you really think—"
Greigstein lighted a cigar coolly.
"It is no matter for speculation at all," he said. "I deceive no patient, and I make no mistakes. Your beautiful sweetheart is going to see once more."

XXIV. — ANXIOUS MOMENTS.

Kant stood watching the carriage drive down the square with the air of a man who has discharged his duty and has earned his realisation. He regarded the sky somewhat critically, and gave to the hall-keeper his studied opinion that there would be rain before long. At the same time he was looking keenly for the figure that he knew was concealed not far off. Presently a dark shadow stole out from under the shadow of the trees opposite, and Kant followed cautiously. He satisfied himself that at length the coast was clear.
"A very near thing," he muttered. He wiped a gentle moisture his forehead. "I'm getting a bit too old to enjoy this business of sitting on a volcano. What a nerve that young gentleman has got, to be sure. You may say what you like, but education has its advantages. But sooner or later the whole truth must come out."
It was some half an hour later before Spencer came home. He crept up the stairs like a man who is on the verge of paralysis. The grey pallor of his face, the blue tinge of his lips, startled Kant. He poured a little brandy into a glass and handed it to his master.
"I dare not," Spencer groaned. "I am absolutely shattered, and the spirit would make a man of me, but I dare not. With nerves like mine, once I took to that kind of thing, I should be a lost man. Take the accursed stuff away, I tell you."
Kant complied in his noiseless way. The flash of anger encouraged him. Spencer was not so far gone as his appearance denoted. Gradually the grey pallor left his face, the horrid twitching of his nostrils ceased. A gleam of interest came into his eyes.
"That is a clever young man, Kant," he said, with a feeble smile. He rubbed his thin hands nervously together. "A very clever young man. I knew he would manage it."
"Well, he did, sir," Kant said, respectfully. "Walked in here as if the place was his own and ordered me about in a manner that—that—"

"I should never dare to imitate, Kant. Go on."
"Well, sir, we servants have our feelings the same as other people. I didn't know what to do. There he sat, smoking your cigars and grinning all over his face, ready to stay and wait for you till day-light if necessary. And Miss Mary playing the piano, a few feet away, all the time. I assure you, sir, a Turkish bath was nothing to it. Then that young gentleman came."
Kant proceeded to go into details. Spencer smiled approvingly.
"A very clever fellow," he said, "a very clever young fellow, indeed."
"Ay, and an ambitious one, too," Kant said shrewdly. "A young gentleman who would hold himself to be as good as anybody. And if he happened to fall in love with the daughter of a millionaire its little he'd care for the millionaire if the young lady was willing."
The faint suggestion of a smile faded from Spencer's face. Kant was a privileged servant and deep in his master's secrets. His speech was a gross impertinence, but Spencer failed to notice it. With his own selfish ends in view, he had never taken into consideration what might be the result of the romantic side of the adventure.
"You are talking nonsense," he said, "and impudent nonsense at that. Mr. Stevenson is a gentleman, and is under certain obligations to me. Let me have a few months longer and my life's work will be done. Then nothing can make any difference. But if anything happened now, if the truth should come to light. . . . I dare not think of it. This is the shadow that follows me night and day, the haunting dread that never leaves me. And now there are two of them. . . . Heaven grant that I do not break down before my work is finished. Perhaps I have done wrong."
"I am certain of it, sir," Kant replied. "Mr. Martlett."
"But I sent for him. He was out of town. There was hardly time to think. I wanted somebody who was young and strong and full of resource, and young Stevenson suddenly occurred to me. And you can't deny that he saved the situation."
"Perhaps to create another one, sir. And Stanmere of all places in the world!"
Spencer made a feeble, impatient gesture. "I tell you fate was too strong for me," he cried. "It always is too strong for one who has committed such a crime as mine. To-day, rich and respected, working for the resurrection of a noble house—to-morrow, a criminal in the dock with all my plans ruined, with more misery on innocent heads than before. The thought haunts me night and day, it causes me to wake in the night and tremble. To conceal one crime, I have committed another. And yet it is for the best."
"You would be best to go to bed," Kant said, practically.
"Yes, you are right. I feel so old to-night. I'll go to bed, Kant."
Spencer dragged himself to his feet wearily, a human wreck, a dotard in the last stage of decay. He was like a child in the hands of his servant. Presently he

closed his eyes wearily.
"I shall sleep to-night," he said. "To-morrow I shall be myself again. Do not forget to send round for Mr. Martlett the first thing in the morning."
Martlett came in due course, silent, self-contained, and rusty as ever. He found Spencer sitting at his breakfast, with little trace of last night's emotion upon him. He was calm and collected now, there was a touch of ruddy color in his cheeks. A calm presentment of a great philanthropist stood out before the lawyer. But the pupils of the eyes were dilated and the hands shook slightly.
"What's the matter now?" Martlett asked bluntly.
Spencer proceeded to explain. Martlett listened with absolute gravity. Whatever were the follies or the virtues of his clients, no gleam of his feelings was reflected on his parchment face. He listened to the very end without a sign.
"Well," Spencer said impatiently. "What is your opinion?"
"That Dick Stevenson is a very smart young man," Martlett said, drily. "Also that he has got you out of the frying-pan into the fire."
"I am afraid that I do not follow you."
"Because you don't want to. To begin with, you have landed Miss Mary—the poor blind child round whom such tremendous interests revolve—at Stanmere. Lady Stanmere—"
"Is the last person in the world who is likely to see Mary."
"Because she never leaves the house, because she is wrapped up in her troubles? Pshaw! Now, let me tell you something. A little time ago, Dick Stevenson and his sister were living in Pant-street. There they made the acquaintance of an erratic German who, for political and other reasons, was masquerading as a teacher of languages. He called himself Greigstein. I knew all about it, because he is a client of mine. Being so friendly with the young people, what more natural than that he should visit them in the country?"
"And see Mary, you mean. Why should he not? Stevenson is quite discreet."
"It matters little how discreet he is. I told you that the German aforesaid called himself Greigstein. When I tell you his real name is Von Wrangel—"
A queer choked cry came from Spencer.
"The last man in the world who ought to know," he said, hoarsely. "If he goes down to Stanmere he is certain to recognise the child. That reckless busy-body!"
"He's got exactly that," Martlett interrupted. "Von Wrangel is a man with many noble qualities, but he is terribly indiscreet. All his lifetime he has been a man who has allowed his heart to rule his head. But we need not go into that. The point is that Von Wrangel is on the verge of discovering the secret."
Spencer looked blankly at the speaker. "What is the best thing to be done?" he asked.
"The best thing under the circumstances is to leave matters to me," Martlett

said, drily. "I am as keen on seeing your plans through as you are yourself. And there is another point that you have lost sight of."

"Tell me what it is, do not spare me anything."

Martlett rubbed his hands together.

"Von Wrangel is a brilliant surgical operator," he said. "But for his political indiscretions and his outspoken tongue, by this time he might have been at the top of his profession. People have short memories, but Von Wrangel's operations on people with defective sight, or no sight at all, are still talked of with bated breath in certain circles. And Von Wrangel is romantic. Here is a lovely girl, here is a chance to exercise his skill. One of those magnetic touches of his, the prick of a lance and Mary sees once more."

Spencer made no reply for a moment. He stood staring at the speaker with dilated eyes. From deep red to pink, from pink to dull yellow and ashen grey his face gradually changed. His chest was heaving, and great drops stood on his forehead.

"I believe you are a fiend," he said, in a voice so low that it hardly reached Martlett's ears. "You sit there with no heart or feeling or bowels of compassion, and torture me like this! I had never thought of that—the idea had never occurred to me. If such were the case, I—I—"

He broke down and wiped his wet face. Something had shaken him terribly. Absolutely unmoved, Martlett took a huge pinch of snuff.

"I fancy I can understand," he said. "Very awkward position for you. But as to torturing you, that is also nonsense. It is my duty as your legal adviser to point out the risks you have to face. But if you are going to talk like a hysterical woman—"

"No, no," Spencer said, hastily. "I feel like a man struck by lightning. Here is a new and horrible suggestion that takes the manhood out of me, here is another crime, Martlett. I am on the verge of the greatest crime of them all."

Martlett rose and deposited his big snuff-box in his pocket.

"Wait," he said, "I may be wrong, of course. It does not follow that Von Wrangel may be in a position to—but I will see him, I will try and see him to-day."

Martlett walked out with his hands behind him, inscrutable and mysterious as ever, his back slightly bent, as if the weight of the family secrets was a little too much for him.

XXV. — LAWYER AND CLIENT.

The weight of the family secrets had pressed Martlett down so close to his desk that he had not looked up from it for the last three hours. So absorbed was he in a mass of figures that he had quite forgotten that Greigstein, otherwise Von Wrangel, had telegraphed asking for an interview at four o'clock, which had made up for the disappointment of an unsuccessful search after the erratic German on the day before. The stuffy atmosphere of the room was rendered none the less so by the presence of an oil lamp on the lawyer's desk. Even the most brilliant summer light seemed to get discouraged and refused to show in these dingy chambers after mid-day.

A clerk in rusty black stole in presently and laid a card on Martlett's table. He nodded gravely, and immediately Greigstein came in. He was in boisterous spirits and brought a refreshing atmosphere into that sad and stuffy room.

"Ever busy, my old spider," he cried. "Ough, when I come in here I find it hard to breathe. Is air a crime? or is it a crime against the majesty of the law to open a window? If ever I want to kill any of my specimens instantly, I shall bring them here."

"Sit, down, Von Wrangel," Martlett said, without a smile. "I tried to find you yesterday, therefore I was very pleased to get your telegram. Now, where were you yesterday?"

"Where was I? Guess, old fox. Give one of your shrewd guesses."

"I will. You were at Stanmere with my young friends, Dick and Molly Stevenson. You had a very pleasant day, and a tremendous surprise in the bargain. There you found the young lady whom we call Miss Mary, Lady Stanmere's missing relative. You have not met her before, but you recognised her from the amazing likeness to her mother."

Von Wrangel nodded. He was too astonished to say anything for the moment.

"You are to keep your knowledge to yourself," Martlett went on. "For instance, you are not to say a single word of her presence to Lady Stanmere."

"But the hint has already been given," Von Wrangel cried. "I got on the trail quite by accident. It was a photograph I saw at the lodgings of my young friend Dick. And when a further accident brought myself and Lady Stanmere together, I told her what I had seen."

Martlett permitted himself to indulge in the luxury of a groan. It was not often that he gave way to human weaknesses of that kind.

"I might have expected it," he said. "So, at the present moment Lady Stanmere is within a mile of our young friends the Stevensons, and knows that Dick can tell her what she requires."

"But why not? The poor lady is longing for her relative. I had done the family so much harm that I longed to bring back a little sunshine into that lonely life. And Mary's father is as much in the dark as anybody else. I have proved that."

Martlett's eyes twinkled for a moment. "We can leave him out," he said. "Mary's father—"

"Is one of the greatest rascals that pollute the face of the earth."

"Well, we won't argue that either. My dear Von Wrangel, if I could invent some charge that would lead to your being locked up for, say, twelve months, I would do it with the greatest possible pleasure. You are always complicating things and getting in the way. You are brave and have tenacity, as that business at Potsdam proved. But you are terribly indiscreet; I never knew a brilliant man so indiscreet before. If Mary finds her way back to Stanmere at this moment it will mean ruin to Stanmere and disgrace to the lady who rules it. To prevent it I would sacrifice my fortune, my practice—ay, I would mortgage my good name."

Two points of flame flashed from Martlett's eyes. His voice was raised, he crashed his fist down upon the table in a sudden spurt of fashion.

"I have put my foot in it again?" Von Wrangel asked, "and with the best intentions. That dear lady's eyes were so sad, I thought of the poor girl's mother."

"Whom you knew very well at one time?"

"Whom I loved," Von Wrangel said, with great intensity, "who was taken from me by a knave and a scoundrel by lies and fraud. If it was not for the girl—"

"But it is for her. To a certain extent I have taken you into my confidence, but I dare not go further, because an impulsive man like you is not to be trusted. Now listen to me. You want money?"

"I do. My telegram asked you to find me five hundred pounds at once."

"You shall have it. Mind you, I am not fool enough to try and bribe a man of your integrity. But you shall have it on one condition. In the first place, you are to do nothing, you are not to interfere in the matter in any shape or form."

"I promise that. It seems to me that I have done mischief enough."

"Ay, ay," Martlett said grimly. "If you only knew how much mischief, you would attach yourself to a sheet of cork as a specimen—of the biggest ass in Europe. But there is another thing. You are intimately acquainted with Stephen Stanmere Gay."

Von Wrangel nodded. There was a murderous gleam in his eyes.

"Yes, I see," Martlett went on. "We will not dwell upon that tender point. What I want to ask you is this: if we want to rid England of Master Richard's presence suddenly, can you show us any way of bringing that desirable consummation about?"

Von Wrangel laughed unpleasantly. His eyes gleamed again.

"You have come to the right place now," he said. "When the time comes you send to me the one word 'act' in the form of a telegram, and an hour or two later Richard Gay shall be flying, fearful of his life. I would hunt him from continent to continent like a mad dog. I would strike him down and rid the world of one of the worst."

Von Wrangel paused, and laughed with marvellously sudden change of manner.

"But enough of that, old fox," he cried, "You leave it to me. And now tell me, can I have that five hundred pounds that we were talking about this week!"

"Yes," Martlett said thoughtfully. "Come to me on Saturday."

XXVI. — LOST.

Like a wet sponge passed over a slate, all Dick's suspicions of Von Wrangel fell away. The mystery of the disguises and the sudden transformation to the brilliant polished man of the world were explained. Dick could smile at his own fears. It was flattering also to feel that he had made a friend of a man of such wide attainments. Von Wrangel read him like an open book.

"Now you will not mistrust me any longer," he said. "For the present I am a refugee, but the time is coming when I can take my place again. Deliberately I sacrificed my position to save a worthless rascal for the sake of his wife and family. But apart from that the fact remains that I am Von Wrangel, the greatest eye operator in the world."

He spoke so simply that there was no suggestion of egotism about him. In a drifting whirl of cigarette smoke he paced restlessly up and down the room.

"Look you," he went on, "there is a secret about that young lady, the whole of which even you don't know."

"But on which you might enlighten us," Dick suggested.

"To a certain extent, yes; we might help one another. But we won't do that, because we are both pledged to secrecy and are both gentlemen. Besides, there is a story that I tell to no one. It is only on the professional side that I look now. Mind you, much or little as I know, I have never met Miss Mary face to face before. Directly I looked into those beautiful pathetic blue eyes of hers all my old instincts were aroused. They are lovely eyes, and there is nothing wrong with them—as eyes. I need not bore you with scientific phrases. I could see at a glance that the pupils were uninjured. But on the other hand the optic nerve might have perished. If that had taken place no surgery in the world could cure her, though certain experiments with the filaments—"

Von Wrangel trailed off for an instant into details which Dick could not follow. The great scientist had fallen into a brown study and was talking to himself. The blue cigarette smoke was still like a cloud about his head.

"But I am forgetting myself," he went on presently. "If the optic nerve was not destroyed, there was hope. You recollect the cause of the mischief was a long illness. Miss Mary is well and strong again once more, and consequently—But I am wandering again. A remark or two made to-day caused me to try certain experiments. They were quite successful. I want certain instruments and one or two exceedingly expensive drugs before I begin the operation in earnest; and you and I are going to town to-morrow and procure them. My lawyer shall find the money, and then—"

"And then you are really hopeful?" Dick cried.

"It is no question of hope at all," Von Wrangel said, coolly. "In a week those beautiful eyes will see as well as yours or mine. But you are to say nothing about it. If anything went wrong, the disappointment would be too keen. But I

shall not fail."
Dick gazed at the speaker with frank admiration. He made no boast; he did not raise his voice; he spoke as a man who knows his power and the way to use it. And whilst he slept peacefully, he gave Dick a restless and uneasy night. The whole thing seemed too good to be true. It seemed to Dick that this was the one thing wanting to make his happiness complete.
He must tell somebody; it was impossible to keep so beautiful a secret to himself. When at breakfast time Von Wrangel alluded casually to a visit to London with Dick, Molly jumped, woman like, to the conclusion that it had something to do with Mary's eyes.
"And I believe you know all about it," she said to Dick as she drew him into the garden. "I believe that you have some good news, and that we are entertaining Von Wrangel in disguise."
"You'll guess a long time before you beat that," Dick cried. "My dear old girl, it is the most wonderful thing. Mary's sight is going to be restored, and I am off to London to get the necessary mysteries. Only, Mary is not to know. For the present, at any rate, Greigstein is Greigstein. He has no doubt whatever as to the success of the operation."
Molly listened in tearful delight. It was like a story from a fairy book. And there was just the fear that the operation might end in failure.
"It will be a fearful day for me," Molly gasped. "I am such a poor diplomatist. I shall have to stuff my handkerchief in my mouth for fear lest I should betray the secret. Think of the happiness before the poor child—think of the delight of her father. And to fancy that we have under our roof so distinguished a scientist as Von Wrangel!"
"And to think of the cheap way we occasionally treated him," said Dick, with a suggestion of colour in his cheeks. "Molly, don't you feel ashamed of yourself?"
It was late in the evening before Von Wrangel and Dick returned to Stanmere. The former hugged under his arm a precious parcel that he refused to confide to anybody. Contrary to his usual custom, he was short and snappy in his manner, and grew even to moody silence. The case was on his mind now to the exclusion of anything else, and would be till the operation was over. An allusion to butterflies on Dick's part was met with a snarl of contempt for men who waste valuable time upon such frivolity.
"There is Molly waiting at the gate," said Dick. "Why, what is the matter?"
Molly was pale, there were dark rings under her eyes. She looked miserably wretched and anxious, and the dust on her shoes showed that she had tramped far.
"It's Mary," she gasped. "She went out this afternoon. I had something to do. She said she could find her way anywhere, and so she seemed able to do. Her idea was to go on as far as the edge of the Warren and back. And she—she—"

"Has not come back at all?" Von Wrangel asked
"I went to look for her," Molly said, briefly. "She has not been in the Warren because the gate was locked. I called and called to her, and for the last two hours I have looked everywhere. Dick, the mystery of it frightens me. If harm has come to her—"
Molly could say no more. The picture of the poor blind girl wandering alone overcame her. Dick turned away with a groan of despair. Then he turned across the fields on a search that he knew in his heart of hearts was bound to end in failure.

XXVII. — MARY TAKES A WALK.

A brilliant sunshine lay over Stanmere, there were purple shadows on the woods behind. Mary stood there with the golden light on her face picturing the different points of the landscape, a series of views from memory. There was something pretty and tender about it, a touch of pathos, no less touching because there was no shadow of sadness about it.
"I can see it perfectly," she said. "The old beeches by the church porch and the golden cornland beyond. We must go there after we have had lunch."
But Molly had to decline regretfully. At any rate, she could not go out till after tea. Really, there was so much to do. But there was no reason why Mary should not walk up and down outside. She professed to know every inch of the ground, and, indeed, she moved from place to place with a certainty that relieved Molly's mind from anxiety.
"I am going as far as the edge of the Warren," Mary cried. "You need not have the smallest anxiety about me, Molly. Do let me go."
Molly had no objection to make. And really she was very busy. There was a great deal of unpacking that she wanted to have off her mind. And then there was another thing, the secret of the forthcoming operation. Every time she glanced at Mary and saw the pathetic patience of those blue eyes she felt a wild desire to speak. She felt that she really must tell Mary the good news. It seemed cruel to conceal it from her.
"Very well," she said cheerfully. "If you get into trouble call for me. But I am sure that you will be able to manage it all right."
Mary went off slowly down the path and into the road. There was no road in the proper sense of the word, but a broad grass track that led to the Warren on the one side and the broad expanse of the heath on the other. It seemed easy in the daytime, but many a faltering footstep had found disaster there on a dark winter's night.
But it was soft and elastic now and downhill. Mary wandered on filled with the sense of the delight of her new-found freedom. The feeling of helplessness had left her. She touched a bush here and there to satisfy herself where she

was, heedless of the fact that the shadows of the early September evening were creeping in. Her knowledge of the locality was all right, only her sense of time was at fault. It was getting a little late, Mary thought. The sun must have gone how, for the dim glow was no longer on her face. Perhaps she had better turn back. She must have been out for over an hour and she was getting a little tired. It would be as well to turn back.

Mary did so, utterly ignorant of the fact that it was nearly dark. Somebody rustled up to her side and a hand was slipped into her own. Mary smiled as she felt the hand to be that of a child.

"I'm afraid I'm lost," a fearless voice said. "We are staying at Brattle, and I came so far to look for white heather. I've got the heather, but which is the way home?"

It was a well-bred and nurtured little girl, as Mary could tell from her voice and the smoothness of her hand. Blind as she was, Mary could be useful here.

"We ought to be close to a clump of Scotch firs," she said. "Over to the left are they? My—my sight is not very good, so you must lead me there. From the firs the path is quite straight down to the church. Would you know your way then?"

The child was certain of it. She gave a little cry of delight when the firs were reached.

"How silly of me," she cried. "Why I could see my way before, only I got confused. I expect they will be rather anxious about me at home. Good-by."

The child skipped away. Mary smiled a little proudly to think how useful she had been, and then the smile faded as she had lost her track.

She would not cry out, she would try and find it. . . Surely it was getting very dark. And that path must lead to the house. Very few people came this way after dark, and perhaps—But somebody was coming. To Mary's quick ear it sounded like the step of a man. It was a swaggering step in a light boot; presumedly the passer-by was a gentleman.

"Can you put me on the upland path that leads to Shepherd's Spring?" Mary asked, with some little hesitation. "Or if you could tell me where I am now?"

"Under High Beeches, and going the wrong way," the stranger said. "Why, great heavens!"

The speaker paused, the artificial politeness of his tones changed to a slight Cockney accent. The man in the loud tweed suit stared with amazement into Mary's face. There was something about the last few words of his speech that struck the girl as familiar.

"I know you," she cried, "where have I heard you before? Oh, I know. You are Venner, the husband of my dear nurse Cecilia. What are you doing here?"

Venner muttered something—he was utterly taken by surprise. The uneasy swagger had gone, the exaggerated loudness of his grey suit had a touch of humor about it.

"Cecilia is here, and you have come to see her," Mary went on. "You have come to persecute her and worry her for money, as usual. I shall not permit it, Venner."

An uneasy grin came over Venner's face. Of course Mary was staying at Stanmere. There might be something to be made out of this discovery later on. It never occurred to the man that Mary might have been staying somewhere else and had lost her way.

"My wife came down here at Lady Stanmere's request," he said, with the uneasy grin still on his face. "I wanted to see her over some misunderstanding about a watch. You see, the watch was missing from her rooms; in fact, I took it by mistake. Being temporarily short of money, I disposed of the watch. It was unfortunate that my wife put the matter in the hands of the police. You quite understand, Miss Mary. If you could put in a good word for me—"

Mary understood enough. The rascal had stolen the watch and pawned it. Mary knew where she was now. She could catch the scent of the sweetbriar hedge that bordered the Stanmere grounds. She would go on till she came to the lodge and get someone to send for Nurse Cecilia and warn her. She turned and left Venner grinning uneasily behind her.

Cecilia must be warned of what had happened; she must let this fellow have his deserts. Probably Venner had stolen into her London rooms and carried off the watch, and Cecilia had informed the police without really knowing who the thief was. As a matter of fact, such was exactly the case. And Mary was quite alive to the character possessed by Horace Venner. Years ago before he married Cecilia, he had been a servant in the Stanmere household.

Yes, this must be the way. But really the sweetbriar hedge was longer than it used to be. It seemed to lead now right on to the lawn. Groping about with her hands Mary came in contact with a stone figure that seemed familiar to her. Unless she was greatly mistaken there should be a sweep of gravel path close here. Before the thought was framed Mary's feet pressed it.

She knew where she was now, close under the dining-room window at Stanmere. The poor girl was trembling from head to foot with fatigue and excitement. She had done a foolish thing, she might so easily have got Molly to send a few words of warning to Cecilia. But then Cecilia was in mortal fear of her husband.

But Mary must not enter Stanmere. She had never inquired the reason why she had been so mysteriously taken away from there, but her father had willed it, and everything that he did was was right in her eyes. She must try and find her way back to Shepherd's Spring.

Voices! Somebody was speaking somewhere, surely in the dining-room, the window of which must have been open. Mary listened eagerly, her heart beating fast with delight. For assuredly it was Cecilia who was talking. Cecilia would keep her secret and see her home. The truth about Venner could be told at the same time. Mary flung prudence to winds. She crept up to the window, which was wide open, and passed in without the slightest hesitation. She would see Cecilia and then—

And then there was a wild glad cry, a pair of arms were wound round Mary's neck, and a voice which was not Cecilia's was pouring endearment in her own ear, and Mary realised in a tired, misty fashion, that she was in the close embrace of Lady Stanmere.

XXVIII. — LADY STANMERE SEES A GHOST.

The beautiful decorous life was moving on slowly at Stanmere. There were no signs of poverty or anxiety there now; the trim lawns and flowers, the perfectly appointed gardens spoke of wealth. To the outsider with a sense of order and beauty it seemed impossible for trouble to touch Stanmere. Even the sleek servants seemed to be beyond the laws of sorrow.

But to the mistress of it all life was dull and monotonous. Like Lady Deadlock, life had no charm for her. Unlike Lady Dedlock, she loved her home and was never bored there. But it was a house of shadows all the same, a houseful of painful associations. It was here in this room that Stephen had defied his father, and by that door that he had quitted the house for ever, by the passage that Lord Stanmere had gone to his death. There was much to care for but nothing to love.

"If only Mary were back again," was the constant prayer going up from Lady Stanmere's heart. The girl had come into her life at the time when she sorely needed something to care for, and she had given the full wealth of her affection in return. And so suddenly Mary had been spirited away. Lady Stanmere had asked no questions, for there was nobody to answer them. The girl's father had taken her away and there was an end of the matter. The father might be dead by this time for all that Lady Stanmere knew to the contrary; but in any case the cloud was still over her life.

Mary had gone for ever; Lady Stanmere had made up her mind to that. And then Von Wrangel had come back with the news of the child. She could not be dead, because she had so recently been photographed; there was no question of her identity, because Von Wrangel had known and loved her mother—the mother that Lady Stanmere had never seen.

And here the child was—in some way connected with Richard and Molly Stevenson, the children of the late rector of Stanmere. It was very strange. And it was stranger still that Mr. Martlett had actually forbidden Lady Stanmere to follow up the clue, hinting at all kinds of evil consequences if Mary came under that roof again.

But she must find out something, if only to satisfy her curiosity. Mary might be close at hand for all she knew to the contrary. Lady Stanmere was thinking it all over as her maid was dressing for dinner. The weary process was finished at length, and Lady Stanmere was alone in the vast solitude of the drawing-room. The windows were open to the lawn; through one of them came presently a tall, dark-eyed woman in a nurse's dress.

"Cecilia!" Lady Stanmere cried. "What are you doing here!"

The woman stooped and raised one of the long slim hands to her lips. She sank into the chair with the air of one who has come at length to a haven of peace.

"I could not help it, my lady," she said. "You told me that whenever I wanted peace and rest I was to come down here. In the old days—"

"For the sake of the old days you are always welcome, Cecilia."

The dark eyes in the pale face filled with tears. Nurse Cecilia looked like a woman with a history. It was the class of face which is softened and beautified by sorrow.

"You are very good, my lady," she said. "My husband is about again. And he is seeking to make money out of some family secret. I can't quite guess what it is, but it has something to do with one of the—your sons. And he persecutes me; he declares that I shall come and live with him again."

"Always trouble here," Lady Stanmere said, sorrowfully. "It was a bad day for us when Venner came here; and his father was respectable, too! But he dare not follow you here."

"My lady, he dare follow me anywhere. I was tired and worn out, and I fled here to escape him. He found his way into my rooms and took a presentation watch from there. And I told the police, never guessing for a moment who the thief must be. If the police take him now, he will be sent to prison once more."

"Surely that would be better for all parties, Cecilia?"

"Oh, it would, my lady! If I hold my hand, he must be taken. But I cannot forget the old days; and if he sees me, I am certain to be weak—"

"And submit yourself to the old persecution. Cecilia, if that man comes here, I will tell the servants to flog him from the doorsteps. After all you have done for him, after the way he has lived on you, this kind of thing is intolerable. Keep out of his way, Cecilia, let the police do their work and get rid of him."

Nurse Cecilia wiped the tears from her dark eyes. She had not forgotten the old days when that rascal had been a passable husband to her. It was not for long, but the memory still remained.

"I ought to do it," she murmured; "for the sake of the family to whom I owe so much, I ought to do it. And there is more rascality afoot behind it. Venner has some hold on one of your boys, my lady; I don't know which, but I am certain it is one of them. If I do nothing now, much anxiety and misery may be spared. But if I see that man—"

"I tell you, it shall not be," Lady Stanmere cried. "You shall not see that man. You shall stay here as long as you like, Cecilia, and welcome. I was sorry to lose you. Indeed, I never could understand why you went at all."

"Pride," Cecilia murmured, "my pride drove me away. All the servants here knew my pitiful story from the time I came here as a child. But it is very good of you, my lady. I have had so much work and worry lately that I am quite broken down."

She stopped, unable to proceed. Lady Stanmere regarded her pitifully.

"Not another word," she said. "We will find you something to do. My silks are on the mantel-shelf in the dining-room—pray get them for me."

The dining-room was empty save for an elderly footman who was placing flowers on the table. He stood regarding the intruder with surprise.

"Well, well," he said, "and so you have come back again. You were foolish to leave. Put those few chrysanthemums right for me. What a rare hand at flowers you used to be! I've wasted a whole hour over those, and look at them."

A few deft touches and the flowers were transformed. Ceclia's heart was in her work.

"There!" she said, standing back to admire her handiwork, and heedless of the fact that the aged footman had left the room. "It only needed the dark ones to be pulled out a little, so that the white blossoms have full play. If I could do nothing else but this work—"

She paused as a light footstep struck her ear. She turned to see Mary in her white dress standing by the window. A cry of surprise and delight escaped her for she had known and loved the girl for years; she was something more than a sacred memory.

"Miss Mary!" she cried. "Miss Mary back again! Where did you come from? Where have you been? Oh, my dear, dear child! my sweet Miss Mary!"

In the decorous quietness of the house the cry rang out loud and clear. It reached Lady Stanmere, dreaming of old times by the side of the logwood fire. It came to her in a confused kind of way as if Cecilia's troubles had touched her brain and that she had lost her reason for the moment. Then there came a light laugh, light as thistledown.

The cry brought Lady Stanmere to her feet, her hands pressed to her heart. She knew that laugh at once; she had heard it a thousand times in her dreams. Was it possible that she, too, was suffering from some passing hallucination?

But there was that little laugh again, followed by voices. Somebody else was talking besides Cecilia. With shaking limbs, Lady Stanmere crept out into the vast gallery hall and crossed over to the dining-room. The voices were still ringing in her ears.

She looked in. There was Nurse Cecilia with her hands on the shoulders of a girl in white, a girl with a serenely beautiful face and a pair of large, pathetic, blue eyes. There could be no possible doubt—it was Mary in the flesh. She stood there smiling as if she had never been away from Stanmere at all.

"Now I must go," she was saying. "It seems very hard, but—"

"No no!" Lady Stanmere cried, "you must never go any more. My child my child, what power was it that induced you to leave us at all?"

XXIX. — ANOTHER VISITOR.

It was a long time before Mary could speak. She had done a foolish thing on the impulse of the moment. From the instant that she recognised Venner's voice, her prudence had been cast to the winds. Perhaps the fact that she had lost herself had rendered her a trifle hysterical.

But she had done wrong. She had no business to have troubled about Cecilia at all. And that man had made her a kind of tool on the chance of his not being able to obtain an interview with his wife. She had come to Stanmere knowing that her father would sternly disapprove; indeed, why had he taken her from Stanmere in that mysterious manner unless there had been grave reasons?

And yet what could she do? Lady Stanmere's broken cry had gone to her heart. It told how terribly she had missed the girl to whom she had given her love. Nor was it the time for explanation. She would stay a little time, despite the fact that Molly would be terribly anxious, and then, aided by Cecilia, she would steal away again. She had never expected to be trapped like this.

"You are going to stay here, now," Lady Stanmere murmured, with her arms about the girl's neck. "My dear child, I could never part with your again. Your father sent you back?"

"No, no," Mary said, in deep distress. "Dearest, I have no business here at all. I am here quite by accident. A little later and I will explain to you. But I am so dreadfully tired and hungry. If you will let me go to my own room with Cecilia to look after me—'"

"Oh! yes, yes. But you must not run away again. Your room is ready—it has always been kept ready for your return. There is a fire there at this moment, and all your toilette things are laid out. The dresses you left behind are in your wardrobe, for I knew you would return."

Lady Stanmere sat down on a big armchair and cried softly. Meanwhile Mary had hurried away. In her old room everything was ready and waiting. Cecilia closed the door.

"Now what does it all mean, Miss Mary?" she asked, eagerly. "Why did you go away? And how did you come back in this strange fashion?"

"But I have not come back at all," Mary explained, hurriedly. "I am here by the merest accident of chance. I lost my way near here and Venner—"

"Ah!" Cecilia drew a deep breath. "And you recognised him?"

"By his voice. He was down here looking for you. I guessed that, and he did not deny it. And then he told me a shameful story of a watch that he had stolen. On the impulse of the moment I came on here to find you. Cecilia, do you know anything of the mystery that surrounds me?"

"I can give a pretty good guess," Cecilia said.
"Well, I am to ask no questions. I leave it all to the wisdom of my father. When I went away from here I did so without demur, though it seemed cruel to my grandmother. Good as my father is, there is something that persecutes him and follows him from place to place. Can you guess what it is?"
"Ay," Cecilia said, with her eyes glowing. "I can guess, but I dare not say."
"Oh, I am not going to ask you. The old persecution followed us a day or two ago, and I had to leave London. I left it late at night, and in a most mysterious fashion. Again I asked no questions. I am with friends now that I love, and I am happy, but I was not to come here. Cecilia, you must get me back to those friends again."
Cecilia said nothing. Her eyes were gleaming wildly. She pressed her hand to her side as if there were some sharp physical pain there.
"I am the most miserable woman in the world," she cried. "You are asking me to deceive my benefactor, and, for your sake and others, I must do so. But not yet, give me time. You will dine with Lady Stanmere, and we shall see what we can do afterwards. Your friends must wait."
Mary gave in with a little sigh. Her adventures had dazed her a little, and she was very tired. Down below, dinner was served, and Lady Stanmere was waiting. Behind her chair was Goss, manfully struggling to preserve his air of indifference. The long elaborate meal proceeded almost in silence. Lady Stanmere was waiting for the time when she should be alone with Mary. She pushed her plate aside—her dinner was a mere matter of form.
Goss moved about in his own silent steady way. The presence of royalty would have failed to hurry him a pace. For once the decorous stillness and methodical slowness of the service irritated Lady Stanmere. She longed to be alone with Mary. From without the silence was suddenly broken, there was a harsh commanding voice that caused Mary to start and her hands to tremble. Contrary to all decorum, a footman fetched Goss out. He came back presently with a pencilled card that he laid by the side of his mistress. His face was a little pale and even his equanimity was shaken.
"Mr. Stephen is down below," the message ran; "says he must see you."
A queer strangled cry broke from Lady Stanmere. She hurried out at once, followed by Goss.
"Go and ask Cecilia to come this way," she whispered. "At once, please. Where is my son, Goss? Did you say that he was in the library? Strange how deaf I seem to have grown suddenly. Goss, on no account is Mr. Stephen to come in here. If necessary, force must be used. I am old and feeble, but I am not going to be treated like this any longer. I am going to have an explanation."
Lady Stanmere went on her way towards the library, and Goss hurriedly departed to fetch Nurse Cecilia. His face was white now, and he seemed to

have some difficulty in controlling his legs. He burst into the housekeeper's room where Cecilia was sewing.
"The devil has come back," he said. "He is in the library with my lady. And you are to go to the dining-room at once. Heaven knows what it all means."
Cecilia departed swiftly as a shadow. There was the noise of a hoarse blustering voice in the library. In the dining-room Mary sat pale and silent. Even there the hoarse voice carried.
"Cecilia," Mary cried, as she recognised the footstep. "What has happened? Something has gone wrong; and I can hear my father's voice."
"Surely not, my dear child."
"But I tell you that I can. It is my father, only he is hoarse and angry. I never heard him like that before, Cecilia. I am going to find out what it is all about."
Cecilia rose and locked the door. Her face was white, her eyes hard and stern.

XXX. — THE PRODIGAL.

Just for one moment Lady Stanmere faltered. She stood in the great hall with the dead and gone Stanmeres looking down upon her, soldiers and statesmen and clerics that Lely and Van Dyck and Reynolds and Romney had painted. There had been terribly wild blood in many of them, but no disgrace. It would have been easier to have faced the shade of any of them there than meet the degenerate man now waiting in the library.
Lady Stanmere stood there with her hand pressed to her heart, and a dryness in her throat. At any cost this disgrace must be averted. Stephen Gay had left home with the shadow of crime upon him, and he had never been back till to-night. What his record had been in the meantime, Lady Stanmere did not dare to think.
But he was her son; this wayward, handsome boy had sat at her knee and lover her in the golden days. It all passed before her eyes like a flash—the promising son, the small disgraces, and the gradual unfolding of those meaner qualities that the mother had in vain tried to hide from a stern father.
Twenty years. Nearly 20 years since she had seen Stephen last. Perhaps if she had been a little more severe! A stern-faced bishop after Holbein frowned at her from his frame, and one of Lely's beauties simpered. What were vain regrets now? For Stephen was in the library, a desperate man, or he would not have been here at all. With all the courage that she could command Lady Stanmere walked into the library and closed the door. The room was brilliantly lighted, for Stanmere had its own electric supply. In a spirit of bravado Stephen had switched on all the lamps. He stood in the centre of the room—the very picture of a hunted animal brought to bay. Under ordinary circumstances his suit of Harris tweed would have spoken eloquently enough of hard wear, uncertain habitation, and dubious company; but now it was torn

and soiled and stained as if he had come headlong across country with pursuit hard behind him.

His eyes gleamed, too, his hair was matted and dishevelled. He was still breathing very hard as if he had run far and fast. The handsome face scowled and then the hard lips quivered. A long scratch down the right cheek, the result of a bramble, did not add to his appearance. He stood there hard and defiant, as if uncertain of his welcome.

"Stephen," Lady Stanmere whispered. If the man had not been so utterly wrapped up in himself and his troubles he would have seen how pitifully the slim hands trembled. "Stephen!"

He laughed recklessly. He looked round at the handsome appointments of the room, the thick Persian carpet, the deep leather chairs, at a reflection of himself in the carved Florentine mirror opposite. How different everything might have been.

"Nothing changed," he said. "No alteration after twenty years. You wind the clock and the clock goes round, and there is an end of it. I might have been as respectably dull as Stanmere. I might have been sitting down in decent sables with Goss handing me my coffee. I should have ended by burning the old place down. And at—"

He broke off with a queer strangled sigh.

"Stephen," Lady Stanmere said, "you are in trouble?"

"Of course I am. I was born to be a trouble to myself and everybody connected with me. My dear mother, I am flying from the police."

"Oh, Stephen! My poor, headstrong boy."

"There, there," the man said, not unkindly. "I was a bitter grief to you in the old days, but I have kept myself out of the way. For twenty years I have not worried you."

Lady Stanmere sat down and folded her hands. There was a gentle patience about her that was almost sublime.

"There you are wrong, my boy," she said gently. "For twenty years, day and night, you have never once ceased to be a trouble to me, and till I go down to my grave you never will. It was here that your father and myself sat with yourself and Paul playing before the fire—"

"Don't, mother. I know what you are going to say. And here am I a nameless vagabond, and Paul, wherever he is, a smooth-faced ruffian far worse than I am. I have wronged many a man, but never one as Paul has wronged me. I have been hunting for him, and when we meet—"

Stephen Gay was talking to himself, he had entirely forgotten his surroundings. Lady Stanmere gave a little cry as she saw the expression of his face.

"Look at yourself in the glass," she whispered. "What do you see there? The features of a murderer. And you are speaking of your own brother."

Stephen laughed recklessly. The hard look faded from his eyes.
"We need not go into that," he said. "And Paul is safe for the present. Mother, I am penniless. I want you to let me have some money to get away with. Money was scarce enough in the old days, but I hear that things are different now. What does it mean?"
Lady Stanmere shook her head.
"I cannot tell," she said. "I have no head for business. I only know that after your father died the old money worries ceased. All the clamouring tradesmen were paid, and Stanmere is nearly free. Mr. Martlett has managed everything. If you want money you can have it—five hundred, a thousand, two thousand, if it will only save the disgrace."
"No, no. I want less than that. Can you let me have a hundred pounds in gold? Give me that and I shall find a way out."
Lady Stanmere nodded. The money was in the house ready to clear the housekeeping books at the end of the week. His hard, scratched face softened as he heard. Perhaps there was feeling in him somewhere.
"I swear to you that I would not have come could I have managed it otherwise," he said. "But for the first time in my life I am absolutely and entirely beaten. I have lived in mansions and in hovels, and I have been equally happy in both. For five years I was absolutely respectable and prosperous. But always with the fear of the past before my eyes. The vendetta never loses sight of me for long. Von Wrangel's sacrifice for me is vain."
"Von Wrangel is the curse of the house," Lady Stanmere cried. "He is of my own flesh and blood, but I wish he had never been born. But for him you—"
"Would always have been what I am. Make no mistake on that head, mother. If I had not gone in for the seamy side of foreign politics, I should have taken up something infinitely worse. I know that Von Wrangel dragged my father in, but he could not possibly foresee what was going to happen. Do you know why my poor father was found in the lake?"
"An accident," Lady Stanmere faltered. "The jury said—"
"The jury would say anything where a peer is concerned. My father committed suicide. You know that as well as I do. And why? Because he had discovered what I had done. There was a woman in the case; the poor creature who afterwards became my wife. It was not me she cared for, but Von Wrangel. And to part them I betrayed the Order to which we both belonged. There are many good lives being wasted in gaol to-day because of that dastardly act of mine. But those blue eyes drove me mad. I never stopped to think. And I betrayed the Order to the police."
Gay paced up and down as he was speaking. There was no shame about him; he might have been a criminal telling his story after his capture, when all was lost.
"Von Wrangel knew," he went on. "He did not kill me as he ought to have

done, but, for the sake of the woman he loved, for your sake, mother, he made it appear as if the whole thing was one of the queer headlong blunders of his own. He lost his position, he had to disappear. Do you mean to say that he has never told you this?"

"I am hearing it for the first time," Lady Stanmere said, wearily.

"Ah, he is a noble fellow. I am not so bad that I cannot admire nobility in others. But unhappily for me, there were members of the league who got at the truth; ruined men all of them. For years they have been hunting me all over the world. If my life had been a valuable one it would have been forfeited long ago. Being a useless vagabond I have escaped—till last night. Then I had to fight for existence. And as to the man I had to fight, I can't say whether he is dead or not."

"Stephen, you don't mean to say that—that—"

"Indeed I do. I had to be the hammer or the anvil, and naturally I preferred to be the hammer. How close the police are on my track now I cannot say, but they were very close this morning. I had expended my last sixpence; I was close to Stanmere, I lay in a ditch for two hours debating whether I should come here or not. It was a hard struggle, but when a man is penniless and hopeless, his resolution is apt to fail him. And that is all."

Lady Stanmere listened dully. The horror of the thing froze her. She must wake up presently and find the whole thing an evil dream. The intrusion of vulgar crime amongst all these refined surroundings seemed impossible. It seemed almost impossible to believe that this hunted, dirty scoundrel, with the scar on his face still bleeding, could be her son, the handsome, headstrong boy who had played soldiers in that very room not so many years before.

No, he must be some impostor who by chance had learnt by heart several dark pages from the family history. But, then, the voice was the voice of Jacob; a mother would not be deceived like that. And if Stephen Gay had not been so wrapped up in himself he would have noticed the change that a score of year's had produced.

"I thought that the cup was full," she murmured. "I thought that the cup was full. But one never knows the measure of one's grief. You must stay here to-night."

"Impossible!" Stephen cried. "I should not be safe. Give me the money and let me go, and—"

He paused as the door opened and Goss looked in. This butler's face was perfectly grave and composed, but he could not repress the agitation in his voice.

"Inspector Lawman to see you, my lady," he said. "He is in the morning-room."

Goss bowed and closed the door gently behind him. Stephen Gay looked about him eagerly.

"What did I tell you," he said hoarsely. "The hounds are nearer than I imagined. You must not see that man, mother; it would be fatal it you did. Is there anybody in the house you can trust, anybody who is familiar with our history?"
"Nurse Cecilia, Venner's wife," Lady Stanmere cried, eagerly. "I am not well enough to see anybody, which, indeed, is no more than the truth. I will fetch her."
Stephen Gay was alone for a moment. He looked round eagerly for some avenue of escape. He knew every trick and turn of the great house, though he had not seen the inside for a score of years. There was a doorway leading to an annexe terminating in a conservatory, which in its turn gave upon the smaller drawing-room. Once in the drawing-room it would be possible to dash across the terrace and so gain the haven of the wood. Beyond the wood was the manor and the moorside, where nobody could follow. There was a time when Stephen had known the secret paths by the bogs, but he had forgotten them.
"I'll see how the land lies," he muttered. "They might have made some changes since my time. Just as well to be on the safe side."
He crept cautiously into the annexe, and from thence into the drawing-room. It was soft with shaded lights and yet perfectly bright and clear. By the fireside sat Mary, in an altitude of rigid attention. She was quite alone, but she seemed to be listening to something. Stephen Gay staggered back with his hand to his head. He was like a man who has had a sudden shock. Then a hand came out from behind and dragged the dazed adventurer into the conservatory again. Mary half turned her head at the sound of the closing door.
"Cecilia," Stephen cried. "Cecilia Venner! What does it all—"
"Hush," Cecilia whispered. "Heavens, how near you were to spoiling everything. If you would not bring ruin upon us all, be silent."

XXXI. — "IF I COULD ONLY SEE."

Mary stood there trembling from head to foot with excitement. It had been a trying day with her, and her nerves were strung to their highest pitch.
"I am sure it was my father," she said. "He speaks now as if he were disturbed and angry, like he used to do years ago before the money came and we were prosperous. And there is something dreadfully wrong or he would never speak like that. I must go to him."
"I hear nothing but confused sounds," Cecilia said.
"That is because all your senses are alive," Mary replied. "What I lost in one way I gained in another. I cannot follow the words, but I am certain of my father's voice. Let me go to him."
"No," Cecilia said quietly. The white, worn face was very hard now, the dark eyes firm. "You are to stay here. It will all be explained presently."

"I must know now. I must, I tell you. You can't detain me by force."

"I can and will, Miss Mary. A rash step now and you will regret it all your life."

Mary yielded with a passionate sigh. The gentle nature could not combat firmness like this. And yet her heart was in wild revolt.

"If I could only see," she cried. "If I could only see, I might understand things better. But I seem to move in a dark world that is full of mysteries. Nobody seems to have any confidence in me. I am like a child who has a sweet popped in its mouth to prevent it asking questions. I am taken here and there and never am I to ask questions. If anybody cared for me—"

"Oh, dearest, there are many who love you. My dear, if you only knew how precious your life is, what tremendous interests revolve around you! Blind as you are, your power is tremendous. And surely, surely you can trust in me!"

"Can I trust in anybody?" Mary cried.

"Hush! Not so loud. You are saying cruel things. If you will only be guided by me!"

Mary's hands went out, feeling for those of her companion.

"I did not wish to be unkind," she said. "But it is dreadful sitting out here in the dark with all these strange things going on about me. It is not as if I was of any importance."

"But you are, dear," Cecilia said, gently. "You are of more importance than Stanmere itself. I am not supposed to know, but I found it all out long ago. And if you are indiscreet and let others find out, we shall all be ruined. Dear Miss Mary will you be guided by me?"

"My dear Cecilia, I will do anything that you ask."

"Then remain exactly where you are. Don't move till I come back. And if anybody comes into the room take no notice till you are spoken to."

Mary promised, in her simple, childish way. It was some time before she heard a step, and then it seemed to be behind her. She heard something that sounded like a stifled cry, and then the banging of the conservatory door. If only she could have seen what was going on behind her!

Stephen Gay stood amongst the flowers swaying to and fro like a drunken man. Nurse Cecilia seemed to have become transformed. The sad and weary look had left her face, she was alert and vigorous now. She turned defiantly to her companion.

"Well," she said, "have you any questions to ask?"

"A thousand," Stephen said hoarsely. "How did SHE get here?"

"That for the present will remain a secret. The fact remains that she is here. And if you want to ruin everything, to bring the house down about our ears and drive your mother into a pauper's grave, then throw prudence to the winds and go and speak to her."

"Mysterious and dramatic," Stephen sneered. "My brother—"

"Your brother is a thousand times a better man than you. He never won a wife by a dastardly lie and broke her heart afterwards. But we need not go into that. Come this way. I am going to see Inspector Lawman and put him off the track. I doubt if he comes for you at all, but your conscience is uneasy. However, it is best to be on the safe side. Go up to your father's room. You used to be wonderfully alike as regards figure. Get into a suit of dress clothes; make a respectable appearance for yourself. Then come down again and wait for me here."

"Always clever and full of resources," Stephen growled, admiringly. "So clever that I don't understand why you ever came to marry Venner."

"Women are strange creatures," Cecilia said coldly. "It is not so remarkable when one considers that you found a woman to marry you."

She walked off calm and neat across the hall. In the morning-room a slight, active-looking man was walking up and down the room impatiently.

"You asked to see Lady Stanmere," she said, "but I fancy I am the right person. When I tell you that my name is Cecilia Venner—"

"Exactly," Lawman interrupted. "In a measure I am down here in connection with the watch that was stolen from your rooms in London. We have traced the watch to a certain pawnbroker, who is able to identify the man. I am sorry to say—"

"You need not be in the least sorry. I am quite aware of what you are going to say. The thief you have in your mind is my husband. I might have known that before I placed the matter in the hands of Scotland Yard. Directly I did so I knew that I had done a foolish thing. If I could only go back now—"

"I am afraid that is impossible. Once a thing is in the hands of the police—"

"I am quite aware of that. If you have made any arrest—"

"Not up to the present. But we have traced your—the thief down here. We are perfectly aware that he is somewhere in the house. We are very loth to disturb Lady Stanmere, but we have a certain duty to perform."

"But there is no necessity to alarm the household," Cecilia cried eagerly. "If that man is here I shall find him. He shall be expelled from the place, and once outside your course is clear. And if you only knew what an effort it costs me to say so much—"

Inspector Lawman was outside again a few minutes later with a clear idea of his plans and the assurance that he had enlisted a clever woman on his side. But the clever woman's face had grown grey and worn again, all the strength seemed to have gone out of her limbs.

"Fortune favours me," she muttered, "but the price is heavy. So my husband is actually hiding in the house somewhere. I must betray him; it is a terrible thing to do, but my duty is clear. And there is no reason why Mr. Stephen should know that the police have not come for him—yet he must be got out of the house, too. If I had not come down here goodness only knows what might

have happened. But, on the other hand, Miss Mary would not have entered Stanmere, so that my presence is as much a curse as a blessing."
Cecilia stood in the corridor waiting patiently for Stephen Gay. He came at length, but so utterly transformed that it was almost impossible to believe that he was the same man. His ragged hair was shaved off, the dirty suit discarded. In his somewhat old-fashioned dress clothes and glossy linen he looked the presentment of a country gentleman, a little given to dissipation, perhaps, but quite to the manner born.
"A sufficiently passable disguise," he said, with a sinister smile.
"Admirable," Cecilia said. "I have got rid of the police for you—for the time being, never mind how. But you cannot stay here, Mr. Stephen. To-night, perhaps, it will be best for you to remain."
"As if I did not know that as well as you do. But for the present I am quite easy in my mind. You ask who I am. I am not Stephen Gay at all. Oh, you need not look at me in that curious way. I know a great deal more than you imagine."
Cecilia muttered something as if she had a difficulty in swallowing.
"You will do nothing," she said, presently, "you will ask no questions. As sure as you do, I will betray you. You have not been in the drawing-room?"
"Indeed I haven't."
"Nor are you to go there. Lady Stanmere has gone to her room. Oh! why did you come here at all, why did you not leave us alone as we were before you came?"
Gay laughed. There was a certain enjoyment in his reckless adventure. He was his own self again now.
"Have no fear," he said. "I have passed my word, and there is a look in your eyes that tells of a pretty temper when you are aroused. Ask Goss to see that there is a bed for me, and some whisky and cigars in the library. I'll be lord of acres for a few hours to-night."
The house grew quieter. Most of the lights had been out for some time, but still Stephen Gay sat there with a cigar in his mouth. Despite the respectability of his appearance, there was an expression on his face that was not good to see. He bit his cigar nervously; he had a curious, hunted expression in his eyes, like a dog that is always alert.
"Strange," he muttered, "I heard a sound somewhere. If those fellows think—"
The cautious step came nearer. Gay rose softly and switched off the light. A moment later and he pounced down upon something distinctly warm and human. The struggle was a short one, for the stranger made no fight at all. The sudden rush of light again dazzled his eyes.
"Venner," Gay said coolly. "Toujours Venner. As to your motives here there can be no two opinions. If things were not as they are I should hand you over to the police. For the sake of your wife I am going to quietly put you off the

premises."
"I didn't know," Venner gasped. "I didn't expect. But don't put me out to-night, sir. Let me stay here till it gets light and—"
"Did you hear me speak? If you don't go I'll throw you out of the window."
Venner fell back as the other rose. There was an ugly look in his eyes. The front door closed behind him, there was a rattle of bolts and bars. On his hands and knees Venner crawled away as if fearful of every shadow. He paused for breath behind a bush at length. He shook his fist savagely at the house.
"Very well," he muttered. "If it is to be me, it shall be you as well. If they take me they shall take you as well, you murderous spy. What's that?"
A light flashed out, holding the bush in the centre of a ring of dazzling flame.

XXXII. — A WHITED SEPULCHRE.

Dick caught the full significance of Molly's speech after a moment. A stinging reproach rose to his lips, but the whiteness and misery of Molly's face restrained him. Under ordinary circumstances there would have been no occasion for anxiety, but with the halo of romance that surrounded blind Mary from the first, Dick saw the shadow of crime here.
"How did it happen?" he asked as gently as possible.
"It all seemed so natural," Molly explained. "I was too busy this afternoon to go out. And really, I wanted to be alone, because I could hardly trust myself to keep the good news from Mary. She said she could walk as far as the Warren."
"Go down to the Warren alone!"
"Why not, Dick. She knew the way quite well. I watched her going down the path as steadily as I could have walked myself. Not very fast, perhaps, but she never seemed to hesitate. When tea-time came and she did not return—but I need not go into that. I have looked everywhere."
After all, there was little more to be said. Mary had utterly disappeared, leaving no trace behind her; it was not possible to believe that she had deliberately run away from her new friends. The trio by the garden gate looked furtively at each other, neither of them daring to suggest foul play.
"It would be as well, perhaps, to go into the matter," Von Wrangel said, "if I only knew the circumstances under which the young lady came here—"
"That is impossible," Dick said curtly. "It would be a betrayal of confidence."
"And I quite agree with what Dick says," Molly murmured.
"In that case your duty is plain, Dick," Wrangel went on. "The young lady has disappeared. She seems to be the central figure in a strange mystery; she comes down here to be out of the way of somebody, and it is fair to assume that somebody has found her. We cannot find that somebody till we know who he or she is. The young lady's guardian is most likely to know. Dick, you must go and see him at once and tell him what has happened."

Dick nodded gloomily. Obviously Mr. Spencer must know of this disaster without delay. If some enemy had spirited Mary away, Spencer would be most likely to know who that enemy was.

"I'd rather cut my right hand off," Dick said. "After all his kindness and goodness and the implicit way he trusted me, it seems dreadful to fail like this. Oh, I'll go, Molly. Perhaps our kind friend here may solve the problem."

Dick strode off down the road without another word. He would be in London again and at Cambria square a little after ten o'clock. The whole thing had been a terrible blow to him, the sudden change of circumstances had shaken even his steady nerves. Half an hour before he had covered the ground with a cheerful heart and the fairest dreams of the future.

There was London and the fierce lights of the electrics. As Dick neared his destination he found his heart beating faster and a certain dryness in the back of his throat. He would try the Record office first; possibly Mr. Spencer was there.

Yes, the proprietor of the paper was in his office alone. Dick wished guiltily that he had been at home, anywhere so that the evil hour might be postponed. Mr. Spencer was stooping over a pile of accounts as Dick entered. The kindly smile on that pleasant face vanished as he caught the haunting misery in the eyes of the young man.

"Shut the door," he said sternly. "Now tell me what has happened—quick."

There was command in his voice but fear in his eyes. He passed his hand across his forehead in a confused kind of way.

"It is Mary," Dick stammered. "She went for a little walk this afternoon and —"

"You mean that she went out alone?"

Dick explained. Mr. Spencer's head was turned away, his eyes shaded by his hand. For a little time he sat there quite still. Dick stood by miserably.

"If you only knew," he said; "if you could only tell how I—Give me another chance, sir. Really, I am not thinking about myself. It seems so cruelly hard—"

"It is cruelly hard, Dick. My dear boy, I am not going to blame you at all. I ought never to have sent Mary down there, the risk was too great. And yet I believe it is an axiom that the safest place to hide is where one is least liable to be looked for. You acted with such fertility of resource the other night that—"

"But Miss Mary must be found, sir," Dick urged. "Somebody must have spirited her away, and it seemed to me that you would be most likely to know, if not where she is, at least who is responsible for this outrage. If you will only tell me—"

"My boy, I know exactly where Mary is. She is at Stanmere."

Dick regarded the speaker with astonishment. Was he suffering now from one of his lapses of memory? But he spoke so calmly and deliberately that that was out of the question. He could not have been more assured if he had taken Mary

to Stanmere himself.
"Then you are quite easy in your mind, sir?" Dick asked.
Mr. Spencer laughed drearily. Then his mood changed, and he paced up and down with great agitation.
"I have not been easy in my mind for years," he cried. "I shall never be again. Long ago I committed a great crime. I had been reckless and wild in my youth, but I had done nothing that had disbanded me from the company of honest men. Then I fell. It was bad enough to have that crime on my mind, it was worse to be followed by a shadow that never left me. There was a scoundrel whose silence I had to buy. For years I bought it hard. Then I got rid of my incubus, and I began to grow rich. I set myself to do a certain thing, and I am within reach of attaining it. I became wealthy, respected; I almost forgot my shadow."
Spencer paused and wiped the moisture from his face.
"One day the shadow returned. It came at a time when it was vital that I should be free. There was a crisis in my affairs. I went to one of the cleverest men in England and told him how I stood. And he showed me a way out of the difficulty. It was so clever and daring and ingenius that I was almost afraid. There was an element of cruelty and deception about the plan, but I was desperate. I put it into execution, and it fell out with the greatest ease. I rid myself of my shadow, and the scheme of my life blossomed like a rose again."
"If it distresses you," Dick said, as Spencer paused, "I hope you won't—"
"It does not distress me at all; on the contrary, it does me good to open my heart to somebody. I got rid of my shadow, but that bold deceit of mine gave me another enemy. I have successfully evaded him for a long time, but I fear he has the best of me at last. If he has done so and Mary is at Stanmere, as I fear—"
"Could you not go down there and fetch her away?"
"Fetch her away! Go to Stanmere! I dare not. If Venner only guessed the truth! Oh, if you could only realise the enormity of a crime like mine! If we fail now I shall stand in the dock; honest men will turn from me. . . . And I shall be struck down without a word of warning. . . . Of course, if it had been anybody but Venner. . . . What was I saying?"
The speaker came back to himself with a start. His eyes were wild with a kind of delirium, his grey hair was tangled on his head.
"I had forgotten," he whispered. "My memory has failed me for a moment. Perhaps it is not quite too late. I tell you Mary is at Stanmere; I am certain of it. If she has learnt the truth, then the best thing I can do is to put a pistol to my head and end my unhappy life."
"Yours has been a good and noble life, sir," Dick said.
"Good, noble! I am a whited sepulchre. I am a wretch with blood upon my soul. And to forget it I have attempted a stupendous task. It seems strange, but

without Mary that task is impossible. Around that poor blind girl the most tremendous interests resolve. If you could only get her back for me; only let me have her again—"

"We can try, sir," Dick said eagerly. "Come along with me to-night. I am ready to do anything, and so, I'm sure, is Von Wrangel."

"Von Wrangel! What an extraordinary coil it all is, to be sure! What is that man to you?"

Dick explained hurriedly. He would have said more, only it had just struck him forcibly that Von Wrangel's proposed experiment on Mary's eyes was a gross piece of presumption without the consent of her father. All this had never occurred to Dick in the joy of the discovery that Mary might see again. The thought would not have occurred to Von Wrangel in any case, he was far too impulsive and headstrong for that. Dick looked down a little guiltily.

"Von Wrangel is a man with a high reputation," he said.

"Von Wrangel is one of the finest and most indiscreet men in Europe," Spencer said. "At the risk of still further confusing you, I may say at once that Von Wrangel must not see me. Under no circumstances must I come face to face with Von Wrangel. If I did so the secret of my life would be exposed, the whole story out. Get rid of him, boy; if Mary happily returns to you, make some excuse to get him out of the house."

Dick gave it up as hopeless. He had made more than one ingenious attempt to solve the tangle, but at every step it only got worse. Why was this man playing at hide-and-seek with all the world? Why did he receive strangers in semi-darkness; why were there certain people that he could not meet? And if Mary was at Stanmere, what on earth was the reason why her father could not fetch her away without all this mystery?

Spencer seemed to read his thoughts. He smiled at Dick sorrowfully.

"I am an enigma to you," he said. "I am an enigma to myself. You wonder why I don't go down to Stanmere. I might as well proclaim my crime in the open street. And yet I am going to speak; in a few months I shall tell the truth. . . . I am wandering again. Only, whatever you do, get Von Wrangel out of the house without delay."

"He may have solved the problem by this time," Dick said. "Come down with me to Shepherd's Spring. If you will not stay the night, there are plenty of very late trains. If we start now we can get to the cottage by 11 o'clock."

Mr. Spencer stepped in his restless, impatient stride.

"I'll come with you," he said. "Anything better than eating one's heart out here. If the blow is to fall, I should like it to fall swiftly and suddenly. Wait a moment."

From an inner room Spencer presently emerged with no traces of his recent agitation upon him. He looked his benevolent, kindly self, the effect heightened by the spectacles he had assumed. The thought of action seemed to

have lightened his fears.
"Now I am ready," he said. "Oh, no; I have no blame for you. I have done a thing that has been wrong from its very inception, and my sin is finding me out."
He spoke no more till Stanmere was reached, and then he pulled up his collar and drew down his hat as if to escape detection. Presently he held up his head more jauntily and stepped along with the air of a man who is thoroughly at home.
"How familiar it all seems," he murmured. "I remember when I was a boy taking a kite's nest out of those high trees yonder. There were three eggs in it, and—"
He paused again, and did not speak till the cottage was reached. The door stood hospitably open, and the hall lamplight streamed down the pathway. There was nobody inside, for the maid had gone to bed, and Von Wrangel, with Molly, was still, presumably, searching.
"It is quite safe for the present," Dick said. "Pray come in, sir."
Spencer stood for a moment with the air of a man who dreams. He crossed to the doorway and looked down upon Stanmere, where one or two lights twinkled. There was something very wistful in the expression of his face.
"A house of sorrows," he said, "sorrows that some day may be lifted. Dick, there is somebody coming up the road. And that voice sounds like Von Wrangel's. I am going inside. If it is absolutely necessary to declare my presence, pray do so, but only as a last resort. I am going to sit in the little alcove at the bottom of the garden."
He slipped away and disappeared into the night.

XXXIII. — A RUSSIAN CIGARETTE.

Von Wrangel stood deep in thought for a moment or two after Dick had gone.
There was before him a kind of adventure after his own heart. He was very nearly on the track of the secret, but there was one point that he had overlooked.
"We are going to find that young lady," he said, "and we are going to look for her at Stanmere. Miss Molly, do you know who your visitor is really? You don't? Well, I will tell you—a relative of Lady Stanmere's. Therefore, Stanmere is our hunting-ground."

"But in that case Mary would have let us know," Molly urged.
"Perhaps she did send a message, which for certain reasons was not delivered. There is a mystery here, and two scoundrels to deal with. On the whole, they are the worst scoundrels that I know. Do you feel brave enough to accompany me?"

"I feel desperate enough to do anything," Molly replied. "There are very few things I would not do to see Mary back again."
"Then we set out on our search immediately. Ostensibly, we are moth-hunting. You shall take the lantern. I have done a great deal of this sort of tracking in my time. Come along."
They passed along till they came to the spot where Molly had seen the last of the blind girl. The pathway was soft here, for there were many small springs in the heather; and Von Wrangel swept the surface with the powerful rays of his acetylene lamp. His keen, dark face lighted up presently.
"These are footprints," he said. "See, she turned aside for some purpose here, for the footprints do not return. Perhaps we shall find them again by the other track that leads down by side of the Warren. She couldn't have gone farther this way."
There were three parallel tracks leading by the side of the Warren, and over these Von Wrangel ranged with the quickness and silence of a hound. The lamp flashed here and there, till presently it stopped in a deep depression filled with clay.
"See here," Von Wrangel whispered. "Here are the footprints again. They trend downwards in the direction of Stanmere; and here are large footmarks, evidently those of a man. Obviously, Miss Mary paused here and asked her way. She must have remained for a minute or two talking, for you can see how the man shuffled about. No; there are no marks of a struggle or anything of that kind. The man passed upwards, for his prints get fainter as the road hardens again. Ah!"
With a little cry of triumph, Von Wrangel pounced upon a tiny cylinder of paper. It was merely the end of a cigarette, but the German eyed it as if he had found a great prize.
"Now, this tells me a good deal," he said. "This is the end of a Russian cigarette filled with very fine tobacco. You never see this in shops in the country; and, indeed, they are quite an acquired taste, like the French Caporal. I only know one man in England who smokes these cigarettes, and it is quite easy to account for his being near Stanmere. It was the same man we saw the night we were moth-hunting and met Lady Stanmere."
"But he could not account for Mary's disappearance," Molly cried.
"Possibly not," Von Wrangel muttered. "But he could account for the presence of somebody in the household that Miss Mary wanted to see. The man who smoked that cigarette is called Venner. He was once a servant at Stanmere."
"I recollect the name," Molly cried eagerly. "My father told me once of a servant of that name who had got into trouble. He married one of the maids at Stanmere."
"He did. Now it so happens that I know Mrs. Venner—or Nurse Cecilia, as she calls herself now—very well; indeed, she is down here now, and her husband

has evidently followed her. By chance Miss Mary met the man and asked him the way. It is long odds she knew the man and recognised his voice. Let us assume that she learnt from Venner that his wife was here. What more likely, as she knew the way once she got the proper track again, that she should conceive the idea of seeking out her old nurse? My dear young lady, we are getting along."

Molly smiled dubiously. As a piece of reasoning, the argument was not without flaw.

"We will go as far as the house," Von Wrangel went on. "With our specimen-case and our lantern we shall not attract any attention, more especially as the Warren is the happy hunting-ground for all kinds of entomologists. We will go through the Warren."

They plunged into the darkness of the woods, for there was a short cut for those who were familiar with the bypaths of that dense foliage. Von Wrangel was quite satisfied in his mind now where Mary was to be found. He was uneasy all the same, for he had not forgotten the sound rating he had received from Mr. Martlett for betraying to Lady Stanmere that he had come upon traces of blind Mary. Doubtless the lady in question had found Mary and refused to part with her again. She was a lonely woman, she was passionately fond of the girl, and she might even have stooped to deceit to retain her.

"There are other people hunting specimens here," Molly said. "Don't you see those lights? And what a funny way they have of speaking! They are gipsies —"

Von Wrangel extinguished his lantern hurriedly. He just touched Molly's lips as a sign to keep silent. Now that the lantern was out, the other lights in front shone out with added brilliancy. Behind them was a small caravan, and by the steps two men sat smoking. There was another lamp inside the caravan, and by its gleam it was possible to make out a man with his head bandaged up lying on a bed.

"Not a word," Von Wrangel whispered. "Be silent and say nothing. These are not gipsies; I only wish they were. They are here on quite another errand."

"They are very picturesque," Molly said. "If there is any danger—"

"No danger for you and me," Von Wrangel said; "but a terrible menace for somebody who is not far off. There is another inmate at Stanmere that I never expected to see there again."

Von Wrangel spoke in a low agitated whisper that had more horror in it than fear.

"More mystery," Molly whispered. "Who is it this time?"

"One of Lady Stanmere's sons, Stephen. He has not been at Stanmere for many years; he would not be there now unless he were hard pushed indeed. The presence of those men by the light yonder tells me all this as plainly as if they had put it in words. Stephen has been tracked down here, and they are waiting

take his life."
"How dreadful; how horrible! But why?"
"I cannot go into that now. The man's blood is on his own head. I did my best to save him after an act of the blackest treachery that one man has ever shown to another. It is not my fault that Stephen has to fly from place to place to save his life, knowing that it must be sacrificed in the end. I must see him to-night and warn him."
Von Wrangel said no more for the moment. One of the men standing in the circle of light tossed the end of his cigarette away and said something to his companion. Presently one of them could be seen tending the sick man and shaking up his pillows. A moment later all lights were out, including the one in the caravan, and the two men set off in opposite directions.
"They seem to know the ground very well," Molly said, when they were out of hearing.
"They are Black Foresters," Von Wrangel explained. "Woodcraft is second nature to them. Give them a few hours and they could find their way anywhere. And now you had better let me see you home. There is stern work here that is not for a girl, work that makes it impossible for me to go on with our original search to-night."
Von Wrangel spoke in his best and purest English now, a sign that he was deeply moved. Molly's heart was beating a little faster than usual, but she had no fear.
"I cannot go back," she said. "I will be discreet and silent, I may be of use to you. And if your life is in danger—"
"My own life is in no danger at all. I could drive those men away by saying two words. They would crawl at my feet and lick the dust from my shoes if I asked them. And then the danger would come back to-morrow for they are under an oath, and if they fail there are others to take their places. The only chance is to hoodwink them. How it is going to be done I don't know yet, but, I shall find a way. And if you really insist upon coming along—"
Von Wrangel shrugged his shoulders by way of protest. His life and the life of his companion were in no danger, but there might be a tragedy presently. They went along in silence until they came out into the road by the main avenue up to Stanmere.
Von Wrangel struck boldly into the grounds past the silent lodge, and from thence to the terrace. There was a light burning in the hall and another in the library, the window of which was open so that it was possible to catch the air.
"What reckless folly," Von Wrangel muttered. "Why does a man deliberately invite death like that? He must be here because nobody connected with the family is up at this time of night; Lady Stanmere never has any guests. Ah!"
The hall door opened, and two figures stood boldly outlined against the brilliant glare. One of the figures stood big and commanding, the other abject

and pleading. Finally the door was closed and the smaller figure was seen creeping along the grass like a worm.
"Stand here," Von Wrangel whispered. "I shall not be a moment. Where has that fellow gone? He seems to have vanished all in a moment."
"There he is, behind that laurel bush," Molly whispered.
Von Wrangel went forward quietly. Then his lantern flashed out on the startled features of the man who was crouching behind the bush.
"Venner," he said quietly. "Get up you rascal. You have nothing to fear from me as long as you tell the truth. Was that Mr. Stephen who put you out?"
"Ay," Venner growled, "it was; and if ever I get out of this he'll find it the very worst day's work he ever did in his life."

XXXIV. — VENNER IN LONDON.

The mean face looked uneasily into the ring of light made by the acetylene, then the expression of it changed a little. It began to dawn upon Venner that he was not in the hands of the police at all. In his first moment of despair and anger he was about to say something very much to the detriment of his late antagonist. In his own vernacular, he had regarded the game as being up.
But the man concealed behind that blazing line of flame knew him, which was a compliment he hardly expected from the police. And there was something familiar in the voice, too. There was a bare chance for Venner after all.
"I'll tell you anything," he whispered eagerly. "Only put that light out, sir. I don't mind saying that there is somebody looking for me."
"Somebody who wears a long blue coat with pewter buttons," Von Wrangel suggested, "and a bracelet round his wrist. Now get up, since I have to put the light out."
The brilliant line of flame snapped off suddenly, and for a few moments Venner could see nothing but dancing spots before his eyes. As the sense of sight came back he could see a small, active man standing before him.
"Name of Greigstein," Von Wrangel said tentatively.
Venner nodded. The name was quite familiar to him, and he had good reason to stand in considerable fear of the man who called himself Greigstein.
"I know you sir," he muttered. "I—I didn't expect—"
"Or hope to see me again. Now, you scoundrel, tell me the truth. Otherwise, you will do no mischief for a long time to come."
Von Wrangel's voice was hard and full of contempt. Venner wriggled in a fawning kind of way before the man who was so much smaller then himself.
"I'm doing no harm, sir," he said. "I swear I was doing no harm at Stanmere. I came down to see my wife. There was a little misunderstanding about a watch."
Von Wrangel smiled. He had a pretty good grip of the situation.

"And the police followed you down here," he said. "You were hiding in the house, and Mr. Stephen found you and put you out. Possibly—nay, most assuredly—you were going away with a certain amount of portable property in your possession. Was that right?"
Venner mumbled something in reply.
"Now, I want you to tell me exactly what happened," Von Wrangel went on. "Let me have chapter and verse, and don't forget anything. Who are present in the house at this moment besides Lady Stanmere and the servants?"
"My wife," Venner explained, "Mr. Stephen, and Miss Mary."
Von Wrangel had discovered everything that he wanted to know. From first to last all his deductions had been logically correct. Molly, standing motionless within shadow, listened with the deepest admiration.
"You saw Miss Mary this afternoon," Von Wrangel went on, "you met her by the Warren, and you put her back in the path again. And you took advantage of the opportunity to get her to put in a good word for you with your wife."
Venner gasped. Cleverness of this kind always appealed to him. It was the one attribute he longed for. With that he might have taken a high place among criminals, instead of being a poor, vulgar blackmailing rascal.
"I don't know how you do it, sir," he said, "but it's all true as gospel. And it isn't as if you could possibly have seen the young lady. If you'd only be clever enough to get me beyond the lodge gate I should admire you more than ever."
Von Wrangel smiled. That was precisely what he was going to do. Personally, he would have preferred to hand the fellow over to the police and get him out of the way for a time, but there was something pressing to be done, and here was the tool ready forged to his hand.
"Your lucky star is certainly a rising one to-night," he said. "Our greatest blessings often come in disguise. For instance, it was a blessing for you that Mr. Stephen kicked you out of the house. Otherwise you would assuredly have fallen into the hands of the police. Now you are going to escape them and take a message for me somewhere."
Venner was effusively grateful, so grateful that Von Wrangel felt a strong temptation to box his ears. He took from his pocket a small enamelled button, much like those so popular during the war fever, and handed it over to Venner.
"Now let me have a pencil and a scrap of paper," he said. "I write an address here that you are to put into your pocket. As soon as you are back in London, no matter what time of the day or night it is, go to the address on the paper and leave the button there. Give no message and ask no questions, and that is all I require. Have you any money?"
With a gleam of hope in his eyes Venner confessed that he had nothing. A moment later and his eager fingers were clenched upon a sovereign. There was a turn of Von Wrangel's wrist, and the long line of flame flashed out once more. Venner started in dismay.

"If you want to spoil everything, sir—" he began.
But Von Wrangel knew what he was doing. At the back of that flame it was impossible to see anything. The light flashed here and there, and the little German began to discuss eagerly on his favourite topic. He was nothing now beyond a gentleman engaged in moth-hunting. As he moved steadily on, talking to Molly all the time, Venner followed on his hands and knees. Presently a gruff voice gave a challenge out of the darkness.
"That is my friend Lawman!" Von Wrangel cried. "My friend who makes all the London squares possible at night for an enthusiastic entomologist. Are you hunting specimens, too?"
"Not your sort!" came a voice came out of the darkness. "I have reason to believe—"
"Always be cautious; reason to believe is always a good formula. You want a tall man in a grey suit, who is a ludicrous caricature of a gentleman? Between ourselves, my dear sir, you are not likely to find him. I have every reason to believe that the bird has flown. In your place I should try the road on the way to Formly. The man is not in the house!"
"You are quite sure of that, sir?" the officer asked eagerly.
"Absolutely! I saw him expelled just now with some violence. If I can help you—"
But the officer had gone. Gradually Von Wrangel worked down to the lodge gates, where there was a loose stone or two in the fence. He turned upon Venner.
"Now is your chance," he said. "Over you go. And remember what I told Inspector Lawman. Keep off the Formly road and you will be all right."
Venner needed no second bidding. He was over the wall and across the road in a minute. Von Wrangel turned to Molly with a sigh of relief.
"I am glad to be rid of that scoundrel," he said; "he poisons the air around him. Much as I should have liked to lay him by the heels I did not do so, because I had other uses for him. My message to London was urgent, and may result in averting a tragedy. And now, my dear young lady, we are going back to the house again. It may be that I shall want to do a little amateur burglary myself before very long."
They were back on the terrace in front of the house again presently. Only the library window was lighted up and still stood open. Suddenly a light flashed out in a bedroom, the casement was pushed open and a woman's face peered out.
"Look," Molly whispered; "it is Mary. Shall I call to her?"
Mary was gazing pensively out of the window as if she was taking in the darkness of the night. Von Wrangel watched her with his hand on Molly's arm.
"Better not," he suggested. "We know where she is, and that she is safe. To speak now might be to bring about the very thing that we want to avoid. If I

could only see to the bottom of the strange tangle and the reason for all this secrecy!"
The speaker paused and looked at Molly as if she had suddenly struck him. The expression in his eyes was that of a man who has made an amazing discovery—something that he ought to have seen long ago. He drew Molly a little further down the terrace. There was no longer a figure looking pensively out of the bedroom window.
"I am the greatest fool in the universe," Von Wrangel said. "I have had a thing simple as an alphabet before my eyes and I could not read it. Now that I have read it, I see my way to great things. Miss Molly, Dick has gone to see the parent, guardian, what you will, of the young lady upstairs. It is more than possible that this guardian will come back with Dick."
"More than likely," Molly agreed.
"Myself, I think that such a course is inevitable. Therefore I am going to tax your good nature. You are not afraid to go back to Shepherd's Spring alone?"
Molly smiled at the suggestion.
"You are a good and brave girl," Von Wrangel said, approvingly. "Go back home and wait till Dick and his friend come. If they have already arrived say that I require them here. The guardian will probably demur; he may say that he has the strongest possible reason for not seeing Von Wrangel at this particular moment. If he urges this, you may reply that I know it. Say, Von Wrangel has found you out!"
Molly nodded. She would have liked to ask questions, but it was neither the time nor place for that. She had only to carry out the instructions of a man who knew quite well what he was talking about.
"Very well," she said; "I will do what you say. And if he refuses this?"
"Then I shall most assuredly come and fetch him. My dear girl, if you only knew what great results depend upon the success of your mission!"
Von Wrangel said no more; and with a nod of her head, Molly went off towards the garden and entrance to Stanmere. It was very dark and still there, but she was not in the least afraid. She pushed on with a firm step and a resolution to succeed.

XXXV. — THE WRITING ON THE TABLET.

A welcome light streamed out from the cottage as Molly breasted the hill. She called to Dick as Spencer slipped down the garden, under the impression that she was not alone. Dick came out into the porch to meet her eagerly.
"You are very late," he said. "Have you got any news?"
Molly explained what had happened, breathlessly. From first to last Von Wrangel had made no kind of mistake; and, anyway, Mary was perfectly safe where she was. Molly looked round her as if expecting to see somebody; and

Dick smiled.
"Mr. Spencer is here," he said. "He thought he heard Von Wrangel's voice, and so he stepped down the garden into the arbor. He particularly doesn't want to see Von Wrangel."
"Which, I am afraid, he will have to do," Molly said, "seeing that I am sent back by our German friend especially to fetch him. Go and bring Mr. Spencer here."
Dick came back a minute later with Mr. Spencer dragging behind. The white anxious face lighted up as he saw Molly. He held her hand for a moment or two, and looked searchingly into her eyes. The pretty, kindly face pleased him.
"I am not blaming anyone for the disaster," he said. "Sooner or later something of the kind was bound to happen. But where is she?"
"Mary is quite safe," Molly explained. "She is at Stanmere. I have actually seen her. And, thanks to the wonderful astuteness of Von Wrangel, I know exactly how she got to Stanmere. If she had not had the ill fortune to meet Venner—"
"What?" Spencer asked, hoarsely. "What name did you say?"
All the haggard anxiety had come back to his face again. He fell back in a chair as if his limbs had suddenly failed him.
"That rascal at every turn," he said, speaking to himself. "And so near as that! But perhaps my fears are in vain. My dear young lady, will you please tell me everything from the beginning. Never has there been a narrative with a more attentive listener."

"It must have been a coincidence," Molly exclaimed. "Venner was here only to see his wife, who might have got him out of a serious trouble. He had concealed himself in the house, and Mr. Stephen found him. It was Mr. Stephen who put him out."
"And who is Mr. Stephen?" Spencer asked, with his hand to his head. "Really, I am getting afraid that one of my mental attacks is coming on. The worry of the evening has tried me terribly. Now, where have I heard the name of Stephen before?"
He rose from his chair and paced up and down the room with the pettishness of a man who has for the moment forgotten a name and a place. He tapped his forehead and muttered to himself. Then he paused, and a strange cry escaped him.
"Stephen," he said. "Oh, I know, I know, I know. Stephen in that house under the same roof as Mary! The thing is maddening, not to be endured. To think that Stephen should be there of all places in the world! Why did he go, and what does it mean?"
Apparently the speaker had forgotten where he was. He raved up and down the room until the touch of Molly's hand brought him to himself.

"My crime is going to find me out," he said. "After all these years the truth will be told. And my work is not yet finished. What can I do?"
"Come and see Von Wrangel," Molly said presently.
"My dear young lady, I cannot. I particularly desire not to see Von Wrangel. I don't want him to know the truth."
"But I am afraid he knows everything," Molly urged. "He sent me back to fetch you. He was talking to me quietly when suddenly he seemed to make some stupendous discovery. He said it was pretty certain that you would come down here with Dick, and he sent me back for you. If you declined to come, I was to say that he had found you out."
Spencer nodded with the air of a man who is beaten.
"After that I have no more to say," he murmured, "before long the whole world will have found me out. But Von Wrangel is a clever man, and he may find some way through the difficulty. On the other hand, he may be embarked upon one of his wild, visionary schemes that will make confusion worse confounded. Still, I will see him—anything is better than this maddening inaction."
He strode out into the porch resolutely enough. In a measure he reminded Dick of the hunted criminal who is caught at last and feels a kind of pleasure in the fact that the strain has vanished. They passed in silence by the Warren, and from thence into the grounds at Stanmere, where they waited. Von Wrangel was not to be seen, but there were voices coming from the direction of the library window.
"We had better stand here," Molly whispered. "Let us trust our friend implicitly. He will come to us if we only have patience."
Left to himself, Von Wrangel had not been idle. He carefully selected a cigarette from his case and lighted it. Just for a moment he stood as if getting an inspiration and enjoyment from his tobacco, and then he crossed the terrace and entered the library quietly. His step was so soft on the thick carpet that the occupant of the room had no notion of his presence.
Stephen sat on one chair with his feet on another enjoying his cigar to the full. It was a long time since he had sat in a room like this, dressed as a gentleman and surrounded by all the luxuries that the heart could desire.
There was a sense of soothing satisfaction about it all. Had he not been a reckless, headstrong individual, and a great rascal to boot, he might have spent the rest of his days here. Really there was something in a refined home after all. It was all so artistic and graceful; those electric lights blended so well with the surroundings. Stephen Gay was in the frame of mind when most people of his class wish that they had been better men.
Von Wrangel reached over and tapped him on the shoulder. He turned round with a sudden cry and a horrible grey pallor on his face for a moment.
"No way of getting rid of you," he said coolly. His teeth chattered still, and the

ashy hue was still on his lips. "Where did you come from?"
"My good Stephen, the reply is obvious. I came by the way of the window. You are as foolishly reckless as usual, I see. It might as well have been—somebody else."
Stephen Gay shuddered slightly. He was not a man of much imagination, but he seemed to see a little now in the suggestion of the darkness outside.
"Somebody else is far off," he said.
"On the contrary, somebody else is very close. It in not the slightest use for you to try and deceive me. If I ask you why you are here, you will tell me a lie. But I am not going to ask you, became I know why you are here perfectly well. You are at your last gasp; you were at the end of your resources and the danger was horribly close. I know perfectly well that you must have been hard pressed to come to Stanmere at all. You had to fight for your life—"
"I had. And I gave better than I got; I killed that man—"
"No, you didn't. He is much better than you anticipate."
Gay looked at the speaker uneasily. He seemed to know more than he cared to say.
"I am not going to tell you where I got my information from," Von Wrangel went on. "But you are in a greater danger than you imagine. If I get you out of that danger I shall be a much cleverer individual than I take myself for. Still, for the sake of the family and the old times, I am going to try—for the sake of the girl."
"I know nothing about the girl," Gay cried. "Before Heaven, nothing. She may be near to me, she may be at the far end of the world, for all I know. But when I free myself from the millstone about my neck, I am going to know."
Von Wrangel nodded. Not a muscle of his face moved. On the whole he was doing a most magnificent night's work.
"I fancy I shall be able to help you in that respect a little later on," he said. "But that must keep for the present. As a man once high in the profession that I once hoped to adorn—"
"You know where the girl is?" Gay cried.
Von Wrangel said nothing; he would have prevaricated, but Gay caught the expression of his face. There was a strange gleam in the latter's eyes as he turned away.
"No possibility of getting back her eye-sight?" he asked carelessly.
"Talk not to me of possibilities," Von Wrangel cried. The professional enthusiasm was on fire in no time, also his prudence was cast to the winds. He was for the moment that strange uncertain mixture that caused Martlett to distrust him. Up to a certain point nobody could exceed him in prudence and discretion, but touch his enthusiasm and he was a child.
"It is out of the question," Gay said, in the same careless tone.
"It shall be done," Von Wrangel said. "I tell you it shall be done. It shall come

as a secret, but those eyes shall be opened once more and—"

Von Wrangel paused. He would have bitten his tongue out for the indiscretion. For Gay was lying back in his chair given over to noiseless mirth. He wriggled and twisted about in a perfect ecstacy of pleasure. His sinister eyes were full of amusement.

"Ah, you are clever," he said, "you know everything. You are a statesman with the heart of a child, a born diplomat with the tongue of a woman. As a general you might be trusted either to win a great victory or invite the enemy to tea. Go on, my dear Von Wrangel, restore that girl's sight. To think of it, only to think of it!"

He rolled about again in the same fiendish glee. There was no real pleasure or emotion or gladness about him; his feelings were not touched in the least. Von Wrangel stepped towards him in a sudden outburst of rage.

"Bete!" he cried, "beast. Have you no feelings? Ah, it were far better if I left you to your fate."

Gay calmed down a little and wiped the tears from his eyes. There was something in the aspect of the other that silenced him.

"Have you really come to help me?" he asked.

"No," Von Wrangel said candidly, "I have not. You are only a pawn in the game, but if I can prevent the pawn from having his throat cut, for the sake of the family I shall be glad. I don't think you quite realise the full measure of your danger."

Gay waved his cigar contemptuously. He had not been in quite so easy and sanguine a frame of mind when he came down to Stanmere.

"You profess to know," he said. "I will be guided by you. Now, what is it to be? Something plain and straightforward, or a little theatrical? If you consider my feelings—"

"I don't consider you or your feelings in the slightest," Von Wrangel burst out furiously. "I can live here for a far better and nobler purpose than that. I am here to save the honour and good name,—ay, and the good fortune, too—of the house. I have been puzzled, but I am puzzled no longer. Ah, if I told you one thing that I know, you would be kneeling at my feet and imploring me to show you some way out. But I shall not tell you that unless I am driven to an extremity, unless you force me to make you a nerveless puppet in my hands."

"Always theatrical," Gay sneered. "Go on; what shall I do?"

Without retort Von Wrangel crossed the room and pulled up the blind, so that the full brilliancy of the electrics made it light and bright as day. Anyone standing outside could have seen everything that went on in the room.

"Go and stand there," Von Wrangel said. "Stand there for three minutes by the clock. Can you see anything to enlighten you?"

There was nothing but the black darkness behind the band of light.

XXXVI. — MORE BLIND THAN ONE.

Stephen Gay stood there with the brilliant light behind him, smiling in a way that expressed his contempt for the whole proceedings. The thing seemed so utterly false and theatrical. And in any case Stanmere was no setting for this kind of thing. The mysterious in connection with so fine a place was absurd. Nothing cheap or tawdry had ever existed there; the old walls and trim lawns protested against any suggestion of that kind.

And Lady Stanmere, placid and most gentle of women, was lying asleep upstairs in happy ignorance of all that was going on. Gay laughed.

"The setting is wrong," he said. "It should be a gaudy scene in a transpontine theatre."

"It is quite fitting," said Von Wrangel. "There are other houses, older and grander by far, where worse tragedies than these have taken place. And what could be more dramatic than the home-coming of the scoundrel of a son who broke his mother's heart and drove his father to a suicide's grave? In that respect, what is the matter with you?"

Gay was silent for a moment. He had a wholesome respect for Von Wrangel's tongue when it was once started.

"What have I to be afraid of?" he asked sullenly.

"That you best know yourself, but if I give you the succession to Stanmere you would not dare to cross the park to-night. I am doing my best to save your life, unworthy as you are. If you were not so utterly and hopelessly blind—"

Von Wrangel paused and stopped altogether. The unexpected had happened—a thing that threatened to upset his plans altogether, he had not calculated on anything like this. For Mary was in the room—Mary, still in her white dress, feeling her way delicately and deliberately into the room, her face anxious, eager and quivering. Just for a moment Von Wrangel's hand shot out as if he would have taken Gay by the throat and strangled him.

There was no time to think, to scheme anything now. A wild idea of taking the girl in his arms, of carrying her away before she could speak, was rejected. Then Gay half-turned to know the reason why Von Wrangel had broken off so abruptly.

His eyes fell on the white, silent figure before them. Like Von Wrangel, he said nothing; he was too overcome for words. There was a queer, dry, ugly smile on his face—an evil, vindictive triumph that was not lost on Von Wrangel. All the fierce, wild blood was boiling in the latter now; he met the shifting glance in Gay's eyes.

There all at once was one of the most dangerous and reckless conspirators in Europe. There was murder in Von Wrangel's eyes. With his finger to his lips he was exhorting Gay to silence, and with those flashing eyes telling him plainly it was more than his life's worth to speak. And if Gay was no coward, he knew the reputation that Von Wrangel had enjoyed in the old days. He shifted his ground moodily; he could afford to smile, to wait the turn of events. With those speaking eyes upon him he kept silence.

Mary advanced to the centre of the room. She looked white and distressed, and the blue eyes were more pathetic than usual.

"I could not sleep," she said. "I had no business to stay here; I ought to have gone back to my friends. Why don't you speak to me, Mr. Greigstein? I heard you talking as I came into the room. And there is somebody with you."

"Somebody else here?" Von Wrangel stammered.

"Oh, yes. I can FEEL somebody else. I don't understand it at all; I don't understand why you are here, but I daresay it is all right."

"A patient of mine," said Von Wrangel, very quietly and steadily; "a patient of mine. You see—"

"Oh, blind, like myself," Mary cried. "I heard you say so as I came in. Will you please say how sorry I am for him? It is dreadful to be like that."

"He is the blindest man in the world," said Von Wrangel, crossing the room as if to whisper to Mary, and yet keeping a glittering, basilisk eye on Gay all the time. "Nobody ever saw anybody so blind. But I am in hopes of curing him. As a matter of fact, I was reading a letter to him when you came in. It is a letter in cypher, and contains some of the strangest phrases you ever read. Now, what do you think of this sentence? 'The red-headed man is waiting outside. If you say any more now, you will only have yourself to blame if I leave you to yourself.'"

Every word was spoken slowly and with great distinctness. The effect of the words upon Gay was extraordinary. He dropped back in his chair with a queer choking cry on his lips. The beads had gathered like a heavy dew on his forehead. Every scrap of fight had gone out of him.

"Your friend is not well," Mary said, with the sweetest sympathy.

Her eyes were turned by a kind of instinct to the chair where Gay was all huddled and twisted. It was a strange scene—the perfectly-appointed room, the brilliant bath of shaded lights, the beautiful pathetic face of the girl, half-puzzled and full of sympathy, the grinning triumph on the face of Von Wrangel, and the abject misery on that of Gay.

"He has heart spasms," he said. "There is nothing like air for heart spasms. I will lead my friend into the open and place him on one of the garden seats. Then, Miss Mary, I will come back and have a few words with you. Your arm, my friend."

Gay rose from his seat. Not one word had been uttered, he seemed too docile for that. He followed, leaning on the arm of Von Wrangel as if he had grown suddenly old. He dropped down suddenly on a seat outside. Then he found his voice.

"You are lying to me," he said hoarsely. "You lied because fate placed such a chance in my hands, and you did not intend me to use it. You know the truth."

"I do not intend you to use it," Von Wrangel said coldly. "Yes, I know the truth. But I did not guess it till to-night, which shows how liable even the most wise of us are to err. But I am not lying to you. When did I ever lie deliberately to anybody?"

Gay conceded the point gracefully enough.

"The man you have most cause to dread is close by," Von Wrangel went on. "He has traced you to the house. I have done my best to save you. I have given up much to save the man who lied and tricked me out of the woman I loved, and who loved me—"

"Good heavens! You have found that out, too?"

"I know everything. But there is a certain society sworn to avenge traitors. What sort of a traitor you have been I need not say. If I had the men who are following you hard by the heels, others would spring up to take their place to-morrow. What are you going to do?"

Gay shivered miserably and kept silent.

"Precisely. You are at your wit's end. You have no plans. If you could get beyond the cordon you would be safe for a little time, perhaps for years. But the man whose hair is red is here, and you fear him more than anything in the world. Still, I can save you."

"If there is anybody who can do it you are the man," Gay muttered.

"I am going to try, not so much for your sake, as for others. You were going to do a cruel thing to-night; you were going to bring ruin and disgrace upon innocent people. But you read murder in my eyes, and you were afraid to speak. By all that I hold sacred, I would have killed you had you said one single syllable to that girl to-night."

Gay nodded. He knew that perfectly well.

"And she is going to save you," Von Wrangel went on. "She is going to snatch you out of the net, and if you say one word to her all will be lost. She will be by your side, but you are to remain silent. Her arm will be on yours, but, you shall not utter a sound. I shall not need, because I know now that you dare not speak."

"I will be discreet and silent," Gay said.

"Ah! So we understand one another. You remain here whilst I go back to that room. You are going to have another surprise presently—in fact, a night of surprises. Don't move till I return for you. You are safe where you are."

Von Wrangel stepped back into the library again. Mary stood there waiting with the pathetic patience peculiar to her misfortune. Her face was very white and miserable, but there was no suspicion there. She trusted everybody too implicitly for that.

"It is Mr. Greigstein," she said tentatively. "Now will you tell me what it all means? I am not going to ask why you are here, when only to-day you went to London with Dick—"

"I might ask why you are here," said Von Wrangel, "since I left you safe with friends whom your father had chosen to look after you. From the bottom of my heart I am sorry for you. I deeply regret the mystery that seems to surround you. If you had stayed where you were—"

"With all my heart I wish it," Mary said passionately. "But I met a man—a bad man,—who was going to do an evil thing, and I yielded to impulse. And then Lady Stanmere found me. Was she glad to see me? Well, that is a mild way to express her happiness. Mr. Greigstein, I am a poor blind girl, who sees nothing and who has to take all that is told her on trust. Why am I shifted about from place to place like a criminal flying from justice. Why should I not come down here, where I was so happy years ago? Is it fair that I should not be trusted? Is it just that I should be kept in the dark like this? If I cared for my father less —"

"Your father is one of the best men in the world," Von Wrangel hastened to reply. "But he has a heavy cross to bear, far heavier than you imagine. If you refuse to share it with him, all his efforts are in vain. If you elect to stay here, there is an end of everything."

Mary listened with tears in her eyes.

"I will not be wayward," she said; "but it is all so very hard to bear. I thought I would stay here for the night and get Cecilia to help me in the morning. But I could not sleep. I felt so guilty I came down here to try and find my way out. Then I could see that there were lights here, and I heard your voice. I ought to have been surprised, but latterly I am surprised at nothing. Now, what do you think I had better do?"

"Come with me a little way," Von Wrangel said promptly, "and have a little talk with Miss Molly, who is waiting outside to see you."

"And if I can explain to her," Mary said eagerly. "I can perhaps stay."

"To-night, at any rate," Von Wrangel said. "I can avert the danger so that you may remain for the present, and you shall hear your father say so. But, first of all, you will have to take a little walk and ask no questions. After that I can promise you a long spell of peace."

Mary was quite ready to do anything that she was asked now. If she could only satisfy her new friends that she had done no wrong, and please Lady Stanmere at the same time, she would be happy. And there was a deep note of sincerity and power in Von Wrangel's tones.

"Then come along," he said; "there is no time like the present."

He touched Mary's finger tips, and she laid her hand on his arm. A moment or two later, in the garden, she was talking eagerly to Molly and Dick. Von Wrangel had promptly drawn Spencer apart from the others. He led him up to the library windows. Somebody inside there was pacing up and down on the far side of the room. The footstep was muffled, but Spencer seemed to recognise it.

"Now listen to that," Von Wrangel said. "Paul, I have found you out. It was only to-night that the whole conspiracy came upon me like a flash. I know all the mystery now, and the reason for it. Your daughter is here, as you know. There is no reason she should not stay—if a certain person is out of the way. That certain person is here."

"Here!" Spencer stammered. "Under this very roof!"

"Yes, under this very roof. There! Keep calm. No cause for agitation. Listen!"

The muffled footsteps went up and down—the footsteps of Gay, who had returned to the library at a signal from Von Wrangel, as he passed with Mary on his arm.

"That's the step," Spencer gasped; "the step that has haunted me for years. I cannot stand it, Von Wrangel—take me away, for I am in danger of my life. I must go."

Von Wrangel grasped the speaker firmly by the arm.

"You are going," he said, "going with me into that room!"

XXXVII. — FACE TO FACE.

Spencer regarded his companion with a sort of frozen horror on his face. Go into that room, deliberately face the man he had been avoiding for years, wreck the whole fabric of his life!

"I cannot do it," he said hoarsely. "Oh, it is impossible! If you only knew—"

"My good Paul, I know a great deal more than you imagine. I have clipped the claws of the tiger—at least, others have done it for me. How long do you require to—"

"Give me a year's immunity and I care not what happens then."

"You shall have your year, and perhaps more. But it is in your hands to purchase that 12 months of freedom. The tiger is in great danger."

"But if he should happen to see Mary—"

"He HAS seen her. To-night face to face. But I found the means to silence his tongue, and he did not speak. And he has his own peril to occupy his mind to-night. You know what he did; you know that sooner or later the traitor must pay the penalty. Somewhere in the darkness, close by, the danger lies hidden. If you can get Stephen past that danger, and you can—"

"I! What have I to do with it?"

"Merely to help me. Merely to stand in a certain position and smoke a cigar for half an hour. The amazing likeness between you two—"

"I see," Spencer cried. "I begin to understand. And Stephen will have to fly. You are indiscreet sometimes, my dear Von Wrangel, but when you turn your mind to a thing you are marvellous. I am a great coward; my nerve is not what it used to be, but you inspire me. Lead the way; I am quite sure that you are going to save me."

Von Wrangel passed through the open window. Gay was still pacing up and down inside. The broad band of light showed up his white, agitated face. The expression changed altogether as he saw the man who followed Von Wrangel into the room.

"A pleasant and unexpected meeting," he said, "a gathering of the clan. How dare you come into my presence like this, you rascally thief? If you recognised our danger—"

"There is no danger," Von Wrangel said, with cold contempt. "You will have enough to save your own skin intact. And here is a method of safety. Accident has favoured you. A little time ago I asked you to stand in that light and smoke a cigar. You sneered at me. Well, you know now who was watching you all the time."

Gay shuddered, and his face grew perceptibly paler.

"I brought this gentleman here," Von Wrangel went on. "You have seen his face, but nobody else has. I want him to sit in that corner with his back to the light. Paul, I presume you dined before you came down here this evening? Good. Keep your overcoat on for the present. We shall need it for Stephen presently."

"What's going to happen?" Stephen asked sullenly.

"You are coming with Miss Mary and myself to the lodge gates," Von Wrangel explained. "You will wear your brother's overcoat, you will have the young lady on your arm as if she was seeing you off the place, and you will have me for your other companion. Then Paul will stand all the time at the window with a cigar in his lips. The likeness the amazing resemblance from a little way off—"

A shout of admiration broke from Gay.

"Admirable!" he cried. "I shall trick the assassins yet. And if they steal up and kill yonder thief, the whole thing will be complete. 'He who fights and runs away,' you know. And when I come back, look to yourself."

He turned threateningly upon Spencer. The latter said nothing, but stood with his eyes on the carpet. A strange smile came over Gay's face.

"But I am going to have another revenge," he said. "Von Wrangel forecasted it. The mere thought of it will keep me warm many a cold night. And you won't be able to avert it; the very man who calls himself your friend will bring it about."

Gay was shaking with secret mirth. Even in the midst of his danger he seemed incapable of thinking of anything else for the moment. Von Wrangel regarded him with a puzzled expression.

"Come along," he said impatiently; "there is no time to lose. Paul, will you take off your coat and hand it to Stephen? In the corner, please. That will do nicely. Now, Paul, will you be so good as to stand in the window and smoke a cigar? You must stand there, looking out into the night, till I come back. There is no danger as long as you don't leave the house. Meanwhile, Stephen and myself are going round by a back way. Come along."

Spencer stood there, apparently calmly looking into the night, and tranquilly smoking his cigar. As a matter of fact, his whole mind was in a confused whirl. He could make out the figure of Von Wrangel presently, and then he saw the German disappear, with something white by his side. He had left Gay in the thicket behind the house, and then he reappeared with Mary.

"Now let us hope this is the last of the mysteries," he said, as he drew the girl's arm through his. "You are to be discreet, and speak when you are spoken to. The other man—my patient—will be with us, but he will not say one word. You understand?"

Mary quite understood. She had not the remotest idea where she was now, but she felt quite safe with Von Wrangel. She was cognisant presently of a further footstep, and then her hand was transferred from Von Wrangel to the arm of somebody else. Something seemed to be flashing before her eyes. The German had his lamp out again; he was dilating upon his hobby. Though he chatted on in his most easy and inconsequent manner his face was deadly white, and he paused from time to time to wipe his forehead. At every bush he passed he took care to keep the dazzling light between it and the silent twain that he was piloting towards the road.

Looking back from the avenue it was possible to make out the dim outline of the figure smoking in the library window, and so far all had gone well. But there was a strain upon Von Wrangel that he was feeling terribly. It was only a few minutes now between his companion and safety, but the minutes dragged on like the hours of a dull day.

Above all, it was imperative to avoid anything that looked like haste. Von Wrangel stepped from place to place, flashing his lantern here and there, and chatting all the time. He was listening intently with all his ears. Mary was nervous and distraught, and made short replies to the many questions put to her; her companion was rigidly silent.

The roadway was reached at length, and the lodge gates passed. Von Wrangel shut up the slide of his lantern, and gave a deep sigh of relief. He bade Mary stand aside for a moment whilst he drew her reticent companion a little further down the road.

"It is all plain sailing now," he said. "Fortunately, you know the way. We have baffled those people, and you have got the start you require. If you require funds—"

"I don't. My mother supplied funds this morning."

"Very good. You had better go abroad. England is no place for you at present."

"And I shall be snugly out of the way," Gay said, bitterly. "Circumstances have been too strong for me to-night, or I should have upset the pretty scheme of friend Paul. But I am going to have my revenge. Oh, if I could only be here to

see it!"
He laughed again in the same noiseless manner, waving his hand to Von Wrangel, and plunged into the darkness, leaving the latter a little disgusted and puzzled.
"Well, he's gone, at any rate," the German muttered. "It ought to be all smooth for some time to come. A few years ago I should have enjoyed an adventure like this. As it is, my limbs shake as if I had an attack of ague."
Mary was standing there, white and patient. She sighed as Von Wrangel touched her.
"Did I play my part well?" she asked. "It seems to me that I'm doing nothing else just now but play patience. If I could only see, I might enjoy this. But it is dreadful to be in the dark like this. Tell me, are you satisfied?"
Von Wrangel was even more than satisfied.
"Now you can go back to bed with a clear conscience. Only when you get inside take care to fasten the window behind you. As to the rest, it is between your father and yourself. I have done my work, and I flatter myself that I have done it well. Now I am going to see you home by the side entrance, and atone for my act of burglary by restoring the lost property that Lady Stanmere values so much."
It was all over at length. Mary had crept back to her old familiar room with her mind in a whirl and a feeling of utter fatigue. And yet to a certain extent she had brought it all upon herself. Perhaps now she might be allowed to remain here; she might even be permitted to spend her time between Stanmere and Shepherd's spring. She might—
Down below the figure in evening dress was still smoking in the window. Dick and Molly were seated exactly where Von Wrangel had left them. The German came along presently, and passed to the far edge of the lawn with his lantern in his hand. He flashed it over a range of bushes, and as he did so he called gently for somebody to come out.
There emerged a dark-eyed man with a curious frizzy head of red hair. He stood blinking viciously in the path of flame.
"You know me?" said Von Wrangel. "You recognise my voice?"
"Le Baron," came the reply, "trust you to find us out. But it is useless, quite useless. We are not going to fail this time. He is yonder. And we wait and wait and wait, but never, never do we lose sight of that villain again."
"You are mistaken," Von Wrangel said. "I have got the right man away. You know the family; you have interested yourself in it as deeply as I have. That is not Stephen Gay yonder."
"So! Then who is it?"
"Surely a superfluous question. Have you forgotten the other man?"
The red-headed man smote his forehead passionately.
"A trick," he said. "Herr Baron, I cannot blame you—for the sake of the

family. For the time I am beaten, I am in despair. Such a magnificent ruse Herr Baron, I wish you good-night. But there are other cards to play before the game is finished."

XXXVIII. — AFTER THE STORM.

There was sunshine on the lake at Stanmere; the old house lay bathed in it. The deer were knee-deep in the bracken, the woods behind the house were one upward sheet of green silence. To view the picture from the road or the lake it would be the last scene chosen for a tragedy or a mystery that darkened so many lives. It was Tennyson's "haunt of ancient peace;" one thought of "moaning doves in immemorial elms," and the "murmur of innumerable bees,"—anything but human passions and human weaknesses.

And such it was a day or two after the strange events played there. The tourist passing by looked and admired, and perchance envied. Goss stood in the gateway bland and benign, the model of what a butler should be, the last man to connect with vulgar crime, and listened respectfully as my lady talked to him. There was a placid, contented look on Lady Stanmere's face, an expression of rest, that had not been there for years.

Below the terrace in the rose garden Mary was walking. There was a strange feeling upon her as if she had been asleep for a long time and was not yet fully awake. She had long given up as hopeless any idea of solving the mystery that surrounded her, but once back at Stanmere again all that seemed to have faded away. Perhaps she would be left altogether at peace now; her father would fetch her away when the time came. As to the rest, nothing mattered. She was to remain where she was for the present, Lady Stanmere told her.

Lady Stanmere, in her turn, asked no questions. She was quite as much a puppet in the hands of fate as any of them. She had greatly feared that Mary might be taken away again, but she made no effort to retain the girl. She might have asked a few questions from her son Stephen, but he had disappeared as mysteriously as he had come. She expected nothing from him, not even love or gratitude. His life was in danger and he had gone. He might have been dead by this time for all Lady Stanmere knew to the contrary. But, nothing mattered now, so long as she had Mary with her. She would go away and take the girl with her; they could hide somewhere, and—

But a letter from Martlett had saved all these desperate adventures. Martlett had to make a communication to her Ladyship which he was quite sure would meet with her approval. Circumstances had so fallen out that there was no reason why Miss Mary should not remain at Stanmere for the present; on the contrary, it was highly desirable that she should do so. There was nothing more than this—no details of any kind; but Lady Stanmere was satisfied.

And Mary had no objection to make. She loved Stanmere; she had known in the old days, and she could find her way anywhere. It was good to be in a place where she could SEE, especially a place so beautiful as Stanmere. She was not to be cut off from congenial society, and Lady Stanmere had no objection to the presence of Molly and Dick.

"I hope there will be no more changes and mysteries," Lady Stanmere said gently, as she and Mary walked up and down the rose garden together. "I shall be glad to have you always."

"Not more than I shall be to stay," Mary smiled. "Only I shall hope to see my father sometimes, but he can never come to Stanmere."

"I could never see why," Lady Stanmere said.

"I never asked," Mary went on. "I was told that if ever I found myself here again I was to ask no questions and answer none. Some day all this mystery is going to be cleared; but I know that whatever happens, my father is a good man."

Lady Stanmere sighed gently. She had the bitterest reasons for knowing that Mary was wrong, but this simple faith was not to be disturbed.

"He is a good father to you?" she asked.

"Oh, yes, yes. A long time ago he used to be harsh and angry, and I was a little afraid of him, and when the prosperity came he seemed to change altogether. Then there was even something different in his voice, and when he has mentioned you—"

Lady Stanmere hastened to change the subject; it was all very painful to her. She had not yet recovered from the shock of seeing Stephen again. She would have liked to have a walk after luncheon, but one of her nervous headaches prevented her.

Mary would sit and talk to her, but Lady Stanmere would not hear of anything of the kind. She would lie down with the blinds drawn, and, besides, Molly Stevenson and her brother were coming over in the afternoon.

"These heads of mine go as quickly as they come," she explained, and Mr. Martlett was coming down to dinner, and she must try and be ready to meet him.

"Go out into the sunshine and wait for your friends," she said, "and be sure that you give them some tea. Now, run along and leave an old woman to her thoughts."

Mary walked down by the rose garden and away by the lake. There came a step presently that brought a soft colour to her cheeks and made her heart beat a little faster, there was something suggestive about the flutter of her hands that the new-comer might have noticed.

"Dick," she cried, "Dick, you have come alone!"

"Because you can't hear Molly's footsteps," Dick laughed. "You are quite right; I left Molly just now in a beatific state of happiness. When we were having luncheon somebody came to the door. Molly cried out and rushed from the room. I rushed out to find her in the arms of a bronzed stranger with the regulation tawny moustache."

"Oh, I am so glad, Dick; Mr. Seymour has come home!"

"Tom Seymour came quite unexpectedly. Molly had not heard for two mails, and she was getting anxious. Seymour's idea was to give her a pleasant surprise, and from the expression on Molly's face he seemed to have succeeded."

Mary laughed, with a look of sympathy in her eyes.

"I am so glad," she said. "I am very fond of Molly. It must be nice to have a lover, to feel that one man cares for you more than all the world. If I were not blind—"

"What has that got to do with it?" Dick cried. "Why, he would love you all the more for that. Let me take you for a row on the lake. Molly will come over presently. It appears that Seymour has lost an uncle, or something of that kind, and his prospects are very bright in consequence. He says he is not going back to America any more."

They drifted about on the surface of the lake for some time, and then they returned to the rose garden again. It was warm there and still, and fragrant with the countless blossoms. Mary turned so that the sunlight came full on her face.

"I can almost see in a light like this," she said. "I wonder if ever I shall see again. If I could only see you at this moment, Dick!"

Dick started guiltily. He was looking into that quiet beautiful face with something more than liking in his eyes. He was thinking of Von Wrangel at that moment.

"I wish you could," he said. "I am not much to look at."

"That is nonsense," Mary said firmly. "Molly says you very good-looking. You have a kind face, Dick. If ever you cared for a girl—"

"I do care for a girl, Mary. I care for her very much, indeed."

The words came spontaneously. They were quite wrong, but it was warm and secluded in the rose garden, and the scent of the blossoms was breast high. The young novelist was carried away by his feelings. Mary's very helplessness appealed to him strongly.

"I hope she is a nice girl," Mary said; "a girl who is worthy of you. I should like to hear all about it. When you cannot see, such things interest you."

"I suppose it does make a difference," Dick murmured. "I suppose—I mean there would be no reason why anybody with your trouble should not fall in love with a man. Of course his looks—"

"Would not matter at all. I could judge of his actions and his voice, and the way that other people spoke of him. If he had a voice like yours, Dick!"

"That would be a recommendation, of course," Dick said, gravely.

Mary was looking at the sky in a quiet, speculative way.

"But it would never do," she said. "It would be wrong to tie a man to a helpless creature like myself. If he were ambitious I should stand in his way. I should be a burden to him. I might try my best, but I should ever be a burden to him. If you cared for me, Dick—"
"Mary, I do care for you. It was you I was thinking of just now. I am doing wrong I know, but I feel as if I must speak. You would be no burden to me, dearest. There is nothing I should like better in the world than to have you always by my side. The night I first saw you I fell in love on the spot. I knew that there was nobody else for me."
"And you would sacrifice your life," Mary said, gently.
"It would be no sacrifice at all," Dick cried, "but that is nothing. I love you, and I shall go on loving you always. I wish I could say more, but I could not think of any better words to express my feelings. Of course, I cannot expect you to care for me in the same way."
"But I do, Dick. I didn't know it a few minutes ago, but I do."
Her face was smiling, her eyes were dim with tears. She spoke in the simplest and most natural manner in the world. There seemed to be no reason why she should conceal her feelings. Dick loved her, which was the most wonderful and extraordinary thing in the world. The beautiful unseen hero of hers had picked her out of all the girls in the world as the one companion for him. Dick might have married anybody, of course. It never occurred to Mary that he was rather an ordinary type of young man with poor prospects, and those prospects entirely depending upon the caprice of the father of the girl he wished to marry. And he loved her and she loved him. Surely there was not such a romance as this since the world began!
Somebody was speaking to Mary, and somebody's arm was round her waist. The touch thrilled her. The world was no longer empty. And somebody was asking Mary if she really and truly loved him. She turned her beautiful, pathetic face to his.
"Kiss me Dick," she said, "and I will kiss you back again. Oh, my dear, you do not know how happy I am. To think that you could care for me!"
Dick protested that this was one of the most natural things in the world. The mystery was that she cared for HIM. It was very warm and secluded there, and the scent of the blossoms subtly fragrant.
"I almost feel as if I don't want to see your face," Mary said. "It seems more beautiful. And yet, for your sake, Dick, seeing you give so much and take so little—"
She paused with the suspicion of a break in her voice. This was a temptation greater than Dick could stand. He drew Mary's head down on his shoulder.
"I am going to tell you something," he said, "something that I cannot keep to myself any longer. A saint would fail with that pleading face looking into his. You know our friend who calls himself Greigstein, the man who made

experiments on your eyes. Do you know who he is?"
Mary shook her head. Dick could feel her trembling.
"No less a person than Von Wrangel," Dick went on. "The very man above all others that you wished to see. Mary, you are going to be cured. We have had it all out with Von Wrangel, and he has pledged his reputation on a cure."
Mary said nothing for a moment. The creamy whiteness of her cheeks gave way to a deadly pallor; the blood mounted to her face again. She was dazed—overcome for a moment. She had not dared to hope for this. In her most sanguine moments she had put the thought aside.
"I ought not to have told you so abruptly," Dick said.
"It did not matter," Mary whispered. "I was a little overcome, but I am all right now, Dick. Is it really possible that I am going to see again? The mere suggestion tells me all that I have lost; and I am going to be worthy of your love after all."
Her head fell on Dick's shoulder again, her face was hidden so that Dick alone was in full view of Lady Stanmere standing there in the archway leading to the garden. The grey figure stood motionless, the grey eyes were steady—whether with disappointment or anger Dick could not say; and Mary was crying quietly on his breast with only one thought uppermost in her mind.
She was going to see again and be worthy of this gracious lover.

XXXIX. — "IS THIS THING TRUE?"

A small party had gathered about the tea-table in Stanmere drawing-room. There was Molly, beaming with happiness, and looking shyly at a bronzed young man with a dark moustache and an expression on his face little less beatific than Molly's. Mary was quiet and thoughtful, with a look of perfect content in her eyes. Lady Stanmere was gentle and gracious, and Dick woefully ill at ease.
So far as Lady Stanmere's manner went, she might have been in blissful ignorance of that pretty little scene in the rose garden. Her headache had entirely gone; she was listening to some of Tom Seymour's American adventures with an air of interest. Dick was the only unhappy one of the party. Not that he was in the least ashamed of himself. In any case, Lady Stanmere must know in time, but Dick would have greatly preferred to have told her in his own way.
"I am going to take a turn on the terrace," Lady Stanmere said, presently. She removed a crumb from her grey silk dress carefully. "I am a little tired to-day, and so I need an arm to lean on. Dick, will you give me your arm for a few minutes?"
Dick responded that it would be a pleasure. If her were going to catch it he would like to get it over at once. There was a suspicion of colour on his face.

"Delighted," he murmured. "Shall I get a wrap for you?"
Lady Stanmere thought there was no necessity—she liked this kind of weather. Did Dick think that it was likely to last? And what a modest, manly young man Seymour was! Dick responded mechanically. He wondered when the storm was coming.
"Well, sir," Lady Stanmere said presently. "I am waiting for you to speak."
"And I was waiting for you to scold me," Dick said, "I throw myself entirely on your mercy, Lady Stanmere. It was a very wrong thing to do, but I have loved Mary ever since I first met her. And when I found that she cared for me —"
"I know, I know. I have been young myself, Dick. For my part, I can't see that there is so very much the matter. If I were to choose a husband for Mary, I should like one something after your style, Dick. And the fact that the poor girl is blind—"
"She may not remain so," Dick said, eagerly.
"So I gathered from what you were saying to the child," Lady Stanmere said, calmly. "It is one of my virtues or my misfortunes that I have very good ears. I heard what you said about Von Wrangel. Did he really go so far as to express a confident opinion?"
Dick explained. Lady Stanmere listened gravely.
"It is very strange," she said presently, "but Von Wrangel never occurred to me. True, he was not available at a time when—but we need not go into that. Of course, the whole thing has come as a great surprise to me. It would be a very happy day for me if Mary would once more be like the rest of us. I must get you to bring Von Wrangel to me."
Dick promised eagerly enough. He had very little else to think of for the moment. His attendance had been dispensed with at the Record office for the present, on the understanding that he was to come up at any time if his services were needed. He had carried out his last undertaking successfully, and this was a kind of reward for his pains.
"I will send Von Wrangel to you with pleasure," he said. "I ought not to have said anything to Mary, but when she looked at me in that pathetic way I really couldn't. . . . . . I know I ought not to have said anything to her at all. She is far above me. She is rich, or will be, and she has a father who—"
"Of that I know nothing," Lady Stanmere said, a little coldly. "I am as much in the dark as you are. But of one thing I am certain—any good honest man is a fit mate for the daughter of Mary's father. And if I have any influence—"
Lady Stanmere paused and began to talk of other matters. She had grown cold and hard for the moment. Evidently she was thinking only of Mary and her interests. But why did she speak thus of Mary's father, Dick wondered. He was a man evidently respected, and yet he might have been a felon from the way that Lady Stanmere referred to him.

"Your mother was one of my dearest friends," Lady Stanmere went on, after a long pause. "I knew you as a child, and now I meet you as a young man. It seems to me that Mary has made her own choice. There may be money, as you say, and there may be not. I am a mere puppet in these matters; I do not know how I stand myself. Mr. Martlett comes and he goes, and there is an end of it. But if ever I have anything to leave, that little will be Mary's. You are young and strong and resolute, Dick, and you will get on. I am rather glad that you are poor still, because you can't take Mary away from me for a long time. And that is the last word I have to say."
Dick went back to the house presently with a feeling that he had got off pretty cheaply. All the same the sense of mystery was still there. The more Dick thought of it the more puzzled he was. But that would no doubt solve itself in time, and he flattered himself that he had made himself almost necessary to the man who could make or mar his happiness.
In the drawing-room the group was added to by the presence of Mr. Martlett. He looked as rusty and as mysterious as usual, his clothes were dingy and his linen as clean as ever. He was laughing in his dry, silent fashion at some anecdote he had heard from Seymour. Presently, when the young people had drifted out into the sunshine again, he crossed over and took a seat by Lady Stanmere. He rubbed his dry hands together.
"Lady Stanmere, I have made a discovery," he said.
"We live in an atmosphere of them," Lady Stanmere replied. "Let us hope that it is one that will throw a little light in the darkness."
"On the contrary, it tends to confuse matters," Martlett said. "I have found out that Master Dick and Miss Mary are in love with one another."
"Indeed. Do you care for that kind of romance?"
"As a student of human nature, yes. Scraps of knowledge like this are always useful to us lawyers. I am sure they are in love with one another."
"Under the circumstances it is quite natural."
Martlett shot a shrewd sly glance at his companion.
"And they have found it out," he went on. "They have come to an understanding, my lady. And you know it as well as I do myself."
Lady Stanmere confessed that she was not in ignorance of the fact. But she had only recently made the discovery. She dropped her knitting silk, which Martlett picked up and handed to her with a grave courtesy that was all his own.
"And what do you propose to do about the matter," Martlett asked.
"I propose to do nothing," Lady Stanmere said coldly. "I suppose Mary will marry some day, and Dick Stevenson is really a very fine young fellow. In any case, I am quite sure that my advice would not be heeded. I am a mere figure-head here; you are good enough to tell me just as much as you please and no more. Really, I do not intend to interfere."

Martlett scraped his dry chin, thoughtfully.
"A blind wife would be a terrible incumbus to an ambitious young man," he said. "It is all very well at first when the bloom of the romance—"
"Mary will not be blind much longer, Mr. Martlett."
The lawyer started. It was not often that he allowed himself to betray surprise; but this time he was taken off his guard. He was just a little annoyed with himself, too.
"I should like to hear more of this," he said.
"It is quite simple," Lady Stanmere replied. "Von Wrangel has seen Mary, and he has given it as his decided opinion that an operation will be successful. And as you know Von Wrangel as well as I know him myself, I have no doubt he will tell you the same thing."
Martlett had no more to say on the point. He had come down to talk business of the estate. He had quite intended to stop the night there, but there was no necessity now. If he could have an early chop he had far rather get back to town again. His manner was a little hurried, and he was not quite so cold and watchful as usual.
It was still comparatively early when the lawyer reached London again. He did not go back to his chambers in Lincoln's Inn, but walked to Pant street, where he was so fortunate as to find Von Wrangel at home. The latter was trimming his lantern and had his specimen cases all about him.
"Ah, my mysterious friend," he cried. "Come and look at this chap. He is a moth. He lives on the trunks of decayed trees. Doesn't he look dry and leathery, and hasn't he got a cunning eye? I was going to call him the Martlett moth. Look at his eye."
"Put that rubbish away," Martlett said, calmly. "I have been to Stanmere. Lady Stanmere tells me that you can restore Miss Mary's eye-sight."
"So she's got to hear of that," Von Wrangel exclaimed. "On the whole, I would have preferred it to remain a secret for the present. I was going to operate—"
"Without the permission of the girl's natural guardian?"
Von Wrangel glanced at the speaker for a moment.
"Oh, you are a lawyer," he said. "I suppose you would make affidavits and file notices and look up all kinds of precedents and have counsel's opinion and all the rest of it. Mummy, with a piece of dry leather in place of a heart, what are you talking about? Wouldn't everybody be GLAD for that poor girl to get her eye-sight back? And do you suppose that I, Von Wrangel, am going to fail? Bah, you make me ill."
Martlett shrugged his shoulders. All this tirade affected him not at all.
"You propose to dispense with that formality?" he said.
"I propose to do as I like," Von Wrangel said. "Go out, you old mummy. Go away, or I'll get my moth to bite you. Allons!"
Martlett departed quite calmly and unruffled. "There's a nice thing," he

muttered. "To pose as a cruel ruffian who desires to keep a poor girl in the dark for the sake of. . . . . And am I as heartless as Von Wrangel says? All the same, this is a pretty kettle of fish altogether."

XL. — "NOT YET."

A decorous silence reigned in The Record office, for the hour of clanking presses was not yet. There were the green shades throwing little pools of light upon the tables where a dozen or so of pale-faced men worked feverishly. Here was one scoring rapidly with the pencil, another writing furiously, whilst a third was doing desperate things with a whole basketful of telegrams. The orderly hurry of it all seemed to please Spencer as he moved through the building on his way to his own room.

He looked straight, well set up, and pleased with himself this evening. The haggard look had gone from his eyes, his head was erect with the carriage of a man who not only dares great things, but generally accomplishes them.

The shades were on the tables in his own room, a pile of accounts with a parchment covered bank book or two gave a suggestion of wealth and importance. For a long time Spencer sat there pondering over his columns of figures. His mind was perfectly clear now, his brain was working rapidly.

"I fancy that will do," he muttered. "Another three months, and the thing will be successfully accomplished. But forty thousand pounds is a lot of money, and matters of this kind so easily go astray. If I only dared to show myself a little more freely, if I could be seen in the city the thing would be a certainty. And why not? One man is out of the way, and the other dare not show his face for fear of the police. I must risk it."

All the same, Spencer started slightly as a clerk came in with a message to the effect that there was a gentleman waiting down below to see the head of the firm. His nerves were not yet quite in such good order as he supposed.

"It's Mr. Martlett, sir," the clerk said. "I thought—"

"Why did you not say so before?" Spencer demanded, annoyed to find himself so easily disturbed. The room was so quiet and soothing. "Show him up at once."

Martlett came in in his own quiet manner. For once in a way he was in evening dress. He had been evidently dining somewhere and had left early, for it was barely nine o'clock. He drew up a chair to the table and took a pinch of snuff.

"You wanted to see me?" he said, tentatively. "It was the matter of that last mortgage."

"And the one that has caused me more trouble than all the others put together. If we can manage to pay that off, Martlett, my task will be accomplished. I have raised every penny I can on the paper and my property elsewhere; I have pinched and scraped. Of course 'The Record' is a fine income in itself, and

worth a lot of money to sell but I don't want to do that. What have you done in the matter?"
Martlett proceeded to explain. He had found a certain flaw in the signature to one of the old mortgages which had given the other side food for serious reflection.
"Of course they would like to foreclose now," he said. "They would make thousands by so doing. But if we fight them we gain time, and by the end of six months you will be in a position to find the money. It would be a pity to spoil it all now."
"A pity!" Spencer cried. "I have sunk half a million. I have built my scheme step by step; I have watched it expand before my eyes. It has been my penance, my life's atonement. And if I were to lose it now—"
He paused and wiped his face, for he was agitated and the room was warm. There was a wistful expression in his eyes, his lips were twitching. It was some little time before he spoke again. Martlett took snuff with great relish.
"We are not going to fail," he said. "If necessary, we will fight. Then there will be an order for the verification of signatures, and shall gain the time we require. Put yourself in the witness box for ten minutes and the thing is settled."
A peculiar spasm passed over Spencer's face. "I must," he said desperately. "I must if necessary. To-night I could face it; with those figures before me I could dare anything. If I were sure as to those two men."
"You are sure!" Martlett rasped out. "Thanks to Von Wrangel, you are certain. If you had gone a little more slowly into this business, we need not have sailed quite so close to the wind. Give me your instructions to act as I please over that unattested signature, and the thing is safe. I may have to call you as a witness."
"Anything you like," Spencer said. "I—I must."
He flung out his hands like a man who is prepared for anything. Long after Martlett had taken himself off with his snuff-box he sat staring with the mass of papers before him. He felt strung up and reckless enough for anything now, but would his nerves be as steady and as free in the morning? Could he go out into the street and meet one of two faces, and then carry on his resolution? A few years before such a thing might have been possible, but not now.
All being well, a few months hence nothing mattered. He would be able to speak then and clear himself in the eyes of those whose good opinion he valued. He had committed one crime, and, like many people in the same position, he had been forced to to commit another to hide the first.
And Martlett the immaculate Martlett, had suggested it.
Spencer was relieved and glad to find himself no longer alone. Dick Stevenson had come with head erect and eye shining. There was envy as well as admiration in Spencer's glance. He would have given up everything and

ventured anything to be young and strong like that again. His smile for the young man was quite fatherly.
"Nothing wrong this time?" he asked.
"No, indeed, sir," Dick said joyously; "quite to the contrary. I had to run up for something, and I thought I would come and let you know."
Spencer smiled again. Dick found himself wondering whether Mr. Spencer would be quite so amiable if he knew all that had happened. As a matter of fact Dick had come on purpose to tell him.
It was quite impossible for his engagement to Mary to be kept a secret. He grew a little more grave as the full weight of his responsibility came upon him.
"I should like to have a little talk with you, sir," he said. "I dare say I have done wrong, but really I could not help it. But I I think you ought to know."
Spencer motioned him to a chair. There was something frank and manly about Dick that made most people like him. His face was red, but he looked steadily at his companion.
"You see, I met your daughter under peculiar circumstances," he went on; "and from the very first we were drawn together. They say pity is akin to love. It seemed so strange that one so beautiful and with such beautiful eyes should be blind. I pictured what she might be if you—you were dead. And I felt that I should like nothing better than to be her protector, and she likes me."
"I am not in the least surprised at that," Mr. Spencer said, cordially.
"Indeed, that is very good of you, sir, and it gives me courage to proceed. We saw a great deal of one another, and I had some insight into your secret—not of my own seeking. And gradually it came about—well, sir, I let Mary know that I loved her, and I was surprised that she loved me in return. I daresay it was wrong, for Mary will be rich and I shall be very poor; and if you are very angry—"
Dick stopped breathless and confused. He had poured out his confession without stopping to think. He looked up almost fearfully at the man to whom he owed so much. But there was not the least suggestion of anger on Spencer's face.
"So it has come to this," he said. "It is very honorable of you to tell me; as a matter of fact, Mary will not be rich at all."
"So much the better, sir," Dick said boldly.
"Rash boy! Married happiness is not rendered any the less blissful because of money. Dick, you are a very ambitious young man."
"Or a very conceited one, sir," Dick said. "I don't quite know which."
"No, no; you have got the right stuff in you; and I like that square jaw of yours. But you have not sufficiently reflected over this business. There are reasons which you may know some day, that prevent my interfering with Mary in her choice of a husband. I feel quite sure she has chosen well; but have you thought what an incubus a blind wife may be?"

"I am ready to face that," Dick said boldly. His head was erect and his eyes shining now. "I asked Mary to be my wife with the fact before me. But she is not going to be blind."
"She is not going to be?—What do you mean?"
"I mean that Mary is going to see," Dick cried. "We have found the very man we most desired to see. He used to call himself Greigstein in the old Pant-street days, but I know him now as Von Wrangel. He has made a complete examination of Mary's eyes, and he says she will see. Lady Stanmere knows this too. It is the best news one man ever brought to another."
If it were so, then Spencer was most carefully disguising his feelings. There was no smile on his face, only a look of amazement and it might be a suggestion of fear. He ought to have been wildly, extravagantly, enthusiastically glad. As it was, he sat in his chair, listening to Dick, with a strange, cold, hard look on his face.
"You mean in the course of a long time," he said.
"Indeed I don't, sir," Dick went on, without noticing his companion's expression. "Von Wrangel has no doubts on the matter at all. He says that within a week Mary will see as well as you or I. He is going to operate at once."
"He is going to operate at once! When?"
"To-morrow night. He prefers night time because he uses strong electric light. And all the plant is ready at hand at Stanmere. Lady Stanmere telegraphed him to come down to-morrow. It is a terribly anxious time."
"I forbid the whole thing altogether."
A bucket of ice-cold water might have been suddenly poured over Dick by the way he started and shivered. The words were harsh and hard and grating.
"Forbid it, sir!" he gasped. "I—I don't understand. Do you actually mean to say—"
"My words were plain enough. Until I am thoroughly satisfied that. . . . Good Heavens! It will upset all my plans. . . I shall be a ruined man. . . . And this is how one crime leads to another. Put it off, my boy; get it postponed for a month, two months, and I will give you ten thousand pounds. I'll give you a partnership in the the paper. Manage it for me, only manage it. . ."
Spencer's voice had sunk to a whisper, his eyes were gleaming. A strange, cunning expression had come over his face. The man was completely transformed.
"This is an outrage," Dick exclaimed. "There is something wrong—your brain has suddenly given way. Two or three months! To deprive any creature of God's greatest blessing for one moment when the skill of a man can restore it! Why, if you suggested the temporary blinding of the vilest criminal on earth for three months the whole nation would rise up against you. And Mary! You are mad."

There was a thrill of horror in Dick's voice, he recoiled white and trembling before the man opposite. The stinging speech, the utter loathing and contempt, seemed to bring Spencer back to himself again.
"You don't know," he said hoarsely; "you can't tell how I am placed. And it has been so long that a little longer . . . and if the poor girl does not know."
"She does know," Dick said, sternly; "I told her. When she turned her face to mine and longed for sight I told her. The coldest and most callous man would have done so. And now you deliberately try and bribe me to—oh, you must be mad, mad!"
The last words rang through the room. The chief of 'The Record' actually cowered before the youngest and most recent member of his staff. He essayed to say something, but words failed him. He would have explained it all away, but he could not.
"Yes, I am mad," he said. "It comes on me suddenly. Perhaps your news has been too much for me. I am not the man I was. But it is dreadful, horrible. Go and leave me."
Without another word Dick turned and left the room.

XLI. — VON WRANGEL CAPTURES ANOTHER SPECIMEN.

About the same time of night Von Wrangel, in his shirt sleeves, was busy arranging his specimens in the little bed-sitting-room in Pant-street. He was on the best of terms with himself, for he had lately taken two fresh specimens, and in addition he had just had a telegram from Lady Stanmere asking him to go down to-morrow to perform Mary's operation. The telegram lay on the table, and Von Wrangel had used it to mix some precipitate powder on.
"This time to-morrow and that will be over," he said, sotto voce. "Under ordinary circumstances it would lead to fresh complications. But the tiger moth is hiding, and he can do no harm for the present, if the tiger moth had not been a fool he would have been flitting to a foreign shore by this time. I must find out and give him another warning. All the trouble I took at Stanmere the other night is not to be wasted; I spoil sport no longer. Come in."
The door opened and a little twisted man came in. He looked like one who had been badly broken up at some time in a railway accident—he had a big hump, and one shoulder was higher than the other. There was a long, bold red scar across his white face, but his eyes were wonderfully steady, and there was a certain suggestion of power about his shoulders.
"So you are here, Louis," Von Wrangel said. "You got my message?"
"I got the letter, Baron," Louis said in a husky whisper. His voice seemed as queer as his body. "And all day I have been looking for your man. I found him this morning, but he did not see me. The bird is too shy to come here, so I limed a twig for him. Behold, in the evening paper that they affect I put an

advertisement purporting to come from Milano. At nine o'clock to-night Hengel will be under the fourth elm tree on the walk by Regent's Park, nearest the Zoo. And if you happened to be there hunting butterflies you might see him."

The little man chuckled and winked one flaming red eye. Von Wrangel smiled.

"That was well done," he said, "especially as Hengel fancies that nobody but myself and Milano knows him to be in England. I will go and prospect for a new specimen presently. Regent's Park is not closed to me, indeed it is not closed to anybody who possesses the necessary agility to climb a railing. Ah, they are wise people these London police."

"The tiger moth has not flown away, Baron?"

"The tiger moth is a fool. He had his money, but he must needs stay for another night in London. Then he drinks too much, he plays too high, and his money is gone. He is hiding somewhere now, with his wings singed. I shall force Hengel to tell me where he is, so that I can repair those wings, for between ourselves, Louis, the tiger moth must be got away for a time."

"Let him perish," Louis grunted, with a sombre flash of the red eye.

"For the sake of the family which has suffered so much at my hands, I cannot. Go away, my dear Louis, and do not tempt me. There is a busy time ahead."

Louis took his queer twisted body away as silently as he had come. The easy smile faded from Von Wrangel's face; he had the air of one who has serious work before him. A little time after, and he was walking away in a north-west direction with a little box strapped to his back and a lantern in his hand. Regent's Park had been a happy hunting-ground for him for a long while, and, though the gates were closed and the police vigilant, Von Wrangel had no difficulty in getting access to the park. As a character he was well known to the police, who looked upon him as a harmless lunatic, who had somehow or other contrived to find a friend at court.

"You'll have it all to yourself to-night, sir," the policeman in the park suggested.

"Ah, so you think," Von Wrangel replied. "I tell you I see some queer specimens in these parks. If they were wise they would be thrown open all day and night and patrolled by the police. You think yonder place is empty! Bah! so empty that I always carry this."

He touched his hip pocket significantly. A moment later his lamp was flashing inside and he had given himself entirely up to the pursuit of his favourite hobby. He had plenty of time before it became necessary to work his way to the rendezvous.

He hunted along steadily for half-an-hour, placing more than one specimen in his box and enjoying himself immensely. He did not look in the least like a man who is out on a dangerous errand. He came presently to his destination; he fastened his box securely. From behind the line of light thrown by the

brilliant lantern he looked keenly and searchingly. A round object to the left of one of the trees caught his attention. He fixed the white rays upon it.
"Ah," he said. "There is the specimen I need. It is white, with a deep, fiery red hear, and it has long feelers. They reach from London to Berlin, and from Vienna to St. Petersburg. My moth is rarely seen, but he is the cause of great activity in others. The moth I see before me is only caught by stratagem. It has a great weakness for newspaper advertisements."
All this in a gay, rather loud voice, whilst the round object at the end of the line of light shuffled.
"I'll come out, Baron," a hoarse voice said. "In one way you are too clever for me. But you will not baffle me in the end. If I fail there are others."
"Come out and sit here in the light," Von Wrangel said, coolly.
The man with the fiery red hair emerged. He did not look in the least like a dangerous assassin. He might have been a better-class artisan, a workman who is fond of books. There are scores like him to be seen at any manufacturing town in Europe. He was just a little shy and retiring, and the eyes that were turned upon Von Wrangel were like those of a dog.
Yet the man was a fanatic. He had his creed, and stuck to it like a Hindoo might. He was not in the least blood-thirsty, but he had what he considered a duty to perform, and he would see it through to the end, though it cost him his own life to do so.
"What do you want, Baron," he asked.
"You know quite well what I want," Von Wrangel said. "I lured you here to meet me, knowing well that there was no other way. Hengel, you owe me something."
"I owe you everything, Baron. But for you I should have been tortured in gaol. You saved me from that. There is nothing I would not do for you."
"Quite wrong. There is one thing you would not do for me."
"Break my oath—no. I could not do that. There is not one of us who would do that for anybody. You spoilt our game at Stanmere because you, too, have sworn to do so. I have no feeling in the matter at all; I was only here to do my duty. I did not come when you tracked me the other night because sooner or later that man must die."
"And if I put the police on your track, and say—"
"What could you say?" Hengel said, with a shrug of his shoulders. "You could prove nothing. For a time the police would lock us up and then we should be released. Meanwhile, other men whom you know not would take up the mission. And you would fight better, Baron, with me. Better the devil you know than the devil you don't know, Herr Baron."
"Spoken like a wise man," Von Wrangel said. "I should be bringing about the very calamity that I am doing my best to avoid. I beat you the other night, but the tiger moth is a fool. He did not go away as I told him to do."

"What matters? We are certain to find him."
"Ah, well, you gave me a proverb just now, and I will give you another: 'He who fights and runs away, lives to fight another day'. Thus the tiger moth. You are going to tell me where he is, Hengel, so that I can give him funds and a further warning."
The he man with the red head smiled.
"That is not the game," he said. "But so sure are we, that I don't mind doing that, especially as you have taken all the trouble for nothing. Only a little time ago I was in the locality of the house where you have your chambers."
Von Wrangel smiled. He thought of Dick Swiveller and his rooms, where the mind might pass at pleasure through numerous and spacious saloons. He could not quite imagine what the man with the red hair was driving at.
"And yet did not favour me with a call," he said.
"Business before pleasure," Hengel said, grimly. "I was very near there, as I have been many times before. It was only a child looking in a shop window that stayed my hand. But I am not impatient; I know that the time will come."
Von Wrangel nodded. He knew perfectly well what the other meant.
"Look here," he said; "here is my collecting-box. I am hunting the tiger moth. Not that I love the creature, but for the sake of others. He is not here, but you know perfectly well where he is."
"As you say, I know perfectly well where he is, Baron."
"And you seem so sure of your ground. Therefore, as you are under such obligation to me, you are going to tell me where to find the tiger moth. For the sake of others whom I respect and love and admire, I am going to do my best to get the tiger moth out of the way. Come, let me know. Wipe out one of those obligations."
The man with the red hair was laughing quietly. Something seemed to amuse him. He stammered some apology as he saw the anger kindling in Von Wrangel's eyes.
"You take a great stick to kill so small a fly," he said. "All this pretty strategy is wasted. But you could not know that, and you have done very well indeed. Only if you had stopped at home and smoked your cigarette, you would have done still better. In any case, Baron, I would have given you the desired information, because it can make no difference in the long run. Still, I tell you frankly, because I do no violence to my orders. At the present moment the tiger moth is sitting waiting for you in your rooms in Pant-street."
A cry of astonishment came from Von Wrangel.
"You mean to say that you saw him enter?" he cried.
"Even so. Five minutes after you had gone. If I had known your errand, I would have taken the liberty of saving you all this trouble."
But Von Wrangel heard nothing of the other's politeness. He dropped his lantern and specimen case, and started to race across the park as fast as his

legs could carry him.

XLII. — ONE WAY OUT.

Von Wrangel ran on and on till the quietude of Regent's Park gave way to the well-lighted streets, and sundry policemen began to regard him with suspicion. There were other reasons why the German pulled up, not entirely unconnected with the fact that increasing years are not compatible with long-distance running.

A deep feeling of anger, too, filled Von Wrangel. There were vast interests at stake here, and according to all calculations Stephen Gay should have been out of England by this time. He was going to have a bad time of it presently.

But he had to be removed beyond reach of danger first. The mysterious power that was behind those who had sworn to have the traitor's life was not underrated by Von Wrangel. They were so calm, so certain, so assured of their ground. He had known them to wait patiently for years before they struck. He had fought hard in his time against this curse to progress and liberty, and he had given it up in vain.

Still there was always a chance. The chance lay in getting Stephen Gay away from Pant-street. The road might be apparently empty of spies, but the seeing eye would be there; and as sure as Gay left Pant-street in the ordinary way he was a lost man.

Von Wrangel came to a pause in Tottenham Court road. He stepped and looked into a pawnbroker's window to return breath and recover his scattered thoughts. Two flashing electric lights gleamed upon a miscellaneous collection of portable property that would have rejoiced the heart of Mr. Wemmick.

Here was a way out. Two or three hansom cabs creeping along the kerb were allowed to pass before Von Wrangel made his choice. Here was a cab-man who evidently drank, and consequently was none too prosperous and possibly none too scrupulous either. As he pulled up Von Wrangel mounted the step.

"Do you want to earn five pounds?" he asked, crisply.

The man with the cunning eyes nodded. It was fairly evident that the sum in question would purchase all the morality and conscience that remained to him.

"There's nothing wrong," Von Wrangel went on. "You have only to do as you are told. And I may want the loan of your cab for a few minutes. Stay where you are."

Von Wrangel dived into the pawnbroker's, to return in a few minutes followed by an assistant who carried a battered old portmanteau that his customer had just purchased. This being hauled on to the cab, Von Wrangel gave the direction of Pant-street. Once arrived there, the cab-man had orders to stay for a period that Von Wrangel calculated would not be more than twenty minutes altogether.

"I'll leave the portmanteau," he said. "I'll tell you what the next thing is. You are going to make money to-night easier than you have ever done in your life."
The cab-man nodded. Up to now there had been nothing calculated to bring about an endorsement of his license, and that was what he had to fear. Von Wrangel went up the stairs two steps at a time and burst into the room.
Hengel had not deceived him. Stephen Gay was there. At the sound of footsteps he had snatched up the poker and stood behind the table prepared to defend his life. All the swaggering insolence had gone from his face, the cheeks were mottled and soddened, a fact all the more prominent because of his trembling fear. He was a dead pasty white, his red eyes were full of terror.
"Get back," he cried. "You blood-thirsty ruffian, I'll—"
He dropped the poker and broke into a quavering laugh. Von Wrangel watched the twitching of his fingers with disgust. Here was a man whose nerves were entirely wrecked by the one thing beyond fear. There was a faint suggestion of spirits in the room. Gay laughed again and his eyes went down to the floor.
"What," Von Wrangel demanded sternly, "what are you doing here?"
Gay made no reply for the moment. He was trembling from head to foot with the reaction of his sudden fright. Von Wrangel glanced round the room searchingly. But apparently everything was just as he had left it, even to Lady Stanmere's telegram, with the precipitate powder still strewn upon it. It was impossible to suspect that Gay was here for any other reason than safety. The man was too horribly frightened to think of anything else.
"If you have such a thing as a drop of brandy," Gay suggested.
"Not a drop," Von Wrangel cried. "You are not sober now. You have been drinking heavily. I wouldn't have a brain and body like yours at this moment for all the money in the universe. Let me feel your pulse. Your nerves are all red-hot wires."
He drew down an eyelid of Gay's and examined the quickly expanding pupil.
"My friend, you are very nearly on the verge of delirium tremens," he said gravely. "It is hard to believe that you are the same man I piloted out of danger not so long ago. Where is all the money you had then?"
"Gone," Gay said sullenly. "All spent. I got to London quite safely. Then I decided to have one more royal night of it before I left London. I must have been mad, Von Wrangel. I began to drink and then I lost my head. And I got in some queer sort of gambling house. It's strange how a man of my temperament always drifts to this kind of place."
He maundered on and wept in a sudden fit of self-pity. Von Wrangel shook him passionately.
"None of that," he said, sternly. "I'll make you some coffee. How did you get here?"
"They found me out. I had a marvellous escape. The third time I had to jump into the Thames. Perhaps it was a pity that I ever came out again."

"Politeness forbids me to contradict you," Von Wrangel said, acidly.
"Ah, you can sneer. Then I had no more money to get anything, and my nerves gave out. The dogs were following me all the time. The mere presence of a child saved me just now when I was sitting in a state of collapse on a doorstep. I recollected the fact that I had been here before, and what is more to the point, I recollected the address. I tell you it was a near thing."
He broke down, and a fit of trembling came over him again. Von Wrangel brewed some coffee over a spirit lamp, and Gay drank greedily. A little color began to creep into his soddened face.
"Get me out of this," he said—"get me out this. I've got a little work to do to-morrow evening, and then I swear to you I will leave England."
Von Wrangel glanced uneasily at the telegram on the table. But Gay's dilated gaze had never for an instant turned in that direction.
"Get me out of this," Gay went on. "You've brains and imagination. Think! Those people are waiting for me outside. Only get me away."
"There is a back door to the house," Von Wrangel said, meaningly.
"What's the good of that? Do you suppose those brigands don't know it?"
"Very likely they do. When I came here for reasons of my own I was influenced in my choice of these desirable apartments by the presence of a back entrance. But you are not going that way. The other man disappears in that direction, and you go off in state. Do you think that you could manage to drive a hansom cab?"
Gay nodded. Country born and county bred, he knew all about a horse. Everybody who had ever had a pair of reins in his hand might drive a cab, especially in quiet streets at this time of night. He was eager to have the chance.
"Very well," Von Wrangel said. "You shall have your cab and £10 to boot. When you get away, and can write to me in safety, I will see that you have more. After then I wash my hands of you. If you get into another scrape you must find your own way out of it."
Gay gurgled something that sounded like gratitude. He was not going to be a fool any more. Von Wrangel stepped out of the house and called to the cab-man to bring in the portmanteau. The horse could stand for a moment. He certainly looked like that kind of horse.
The cab-man toiled up the stairs with the portmanteau on his shoulder. Without a word Von Wrangel laid five sovereigns, one after the other, on the table. The cab-man's eyes gleamed.
"Got to be earned first, governor?" he suggested.
"Why, yes. In the easiest way in the world. Give me your big overcoat, and your white top hat. I put them on this gentleman, who goes down to your cab and drives away. You need not be in the least afraid, for he has been used to horses all his life. He drives slowly, as if looking for a late fare, as far as, say,

Belt-street, which is a thoroughfare thoughtfully left in darkness out of consideration for the poverty of its inhabitants. There your cab waits for you. I will show you a back way out, and you can carry the jug as if you were an honest son of the toil going for your evening beer after a long day's work. Do you understand?"

The cab-man nodded. There was no great risk here, seeing that his cab and horse together was not worth much more than the fee he was being paid for this slight service.

"Right you are!" he exclaimed, as his hands clutched on the gold coins. "Lead the way, sir."

Von Wrangel came back presently. He avoided Gay's gratitude, and did not see the hand that the latter held out to him.

"It is perfectly safe," he said. "You have nothing to fear. So long as you are believed to be here, so long will your foes haunt the neighbourhood. And here is your money. If you like to remain in England after this, you must take the consequences."

It was perfectly safe. Gay sprang to the box and drove away with a flourish of his whip that had something professional about it. He smiled to himself as he passed two men lounging at the corner of the street, and blessed Von Wrangel's fertility of resource. He was free now, with money in his pocket, to turn his back upon England.

But not yet. There was something to do yet. There was a little revenge to take first. His heart grew lighter as he thought of it. Once he had got rid of the cab-man he would be free to put his plan into execution. And here was Belt-street.

The cab-man was unduly polite and sympathetic. He had made five pounds and a very nice-looking jug in a manner that could not possibly compromise him in the slightest. He had been in trouble himself, he hinted. He knew of some clean, cheap lodgings close by where no questions were asked, and where there were no less than three staircases.

Gay was glad to hear it. Cheap, obscure lodgings and no questions asked were just what he required. His nerve was coming back to him now, and he was desperately tired. The sight of half a sovereign was all that was required to provide him with fairly comfortable quarters. He put out his gas and falling across the bed with his clothes on dropped into a heavy sleep.

On the morrow he procured a razor and shaved himself. Then he proceeded to make certain changes in his personal appearance. The longing for strong drink was upon him, but he put that resolutely aside. Not yet; there would be plenty of time for that. He had his little revenge to take first. He laughed to himself as be thought of it; the big veins stood out on his forehead.

"I couldn't have invented anything like that," he muttered. "It's perfect. If I can duly prevent him from interfering. But I am not afraid of that. I'll go down and see it all. I won't touch him—I won't so much as lay a finger upon him. And he

will not go down till the evening train at 6.30, by which time it will be fairly dark. And then—"
Gay chuckled to himself again as he lighted a cigarette. For the rest of the day he lounged and ate and smoked. About six o'clock he paid his account and proceeded in the direction of Waterloo station. In the ticket office he waited. His eyes lighted up presently as a tall man with a soft hat over his eyes, came and asked for a first-class return to Stanmere.
Gay came forward after the other man had gone. He put down his money and asked for a third-class return. He found himself presently in the corner of a smoking carriage, where he sat deep in thought, till the train reached its destination.
"Pretty dark," he muttered, "but a moon presently. Now for it. I would not have missed this for all the money in England. And I'm safe here anyway."

XLIII. — ON THE TERRACE.

Mr. Spencer looked up again presently to find that Dick had gone—he had driven him away by his strange behaviour. What must the lad think of a man—a father—who deliberately objected to sight being restored to his only child? And what rational excuse could be made for delay?
Anyway, Dick must not be allowed to go away like this. He must be persuaded, he must be shown clearly that there was need for a postponement of the operation. A source of excuses rose to Spencer's mind, only to be rejected as absurd and inadequate.
Dick had left the building, and was striding in a white heat down Fleet-street, before his employer overtook him. He turned round as he heard his name spoken.
"My dear boy, you must not go off like that," Spencer said with a strange humility. That was not the tone usually adopted by millionaires even to favourite employees. "I want to have a long chat with you. Call a cab and we will go to Cambria square."
Prudence suggested a falling in with the suggestion. Not until Cambria square was reached was another word spoken. The place looked very empty and deserted without Mary. There was not a sign of her favourite flowers, even the violets had disappeared.
"I—I don't care for the smell," Spencer said, hesitating, as he noticed Dick's glance. "They have a very strange effect upon me. But for the sake of my child —"
The speaker paused as he caught the expression on Dick's face. The later had not yet learnt the art of disguising his feelings.
"It seems to me, sir," he said, "that your daughter—"
"Yes, yes. But you do not understand. Suppose that I am your father. You are

very fond of me; you regard me as one of the best men in the world. And you are blind. And when your sight comes back to you, you discover what I am. You find out my crime, you cannot help it. Do you suppose that you would care for me any longer?"

Dick tore the argument to tatters furiously. What sort of a child would he be who turned his back upon his father like that? On the contrary, he would care all the more for him. If we would overlook grave faults in the friends we loved, how much more would we do so in the case of blood relations.

"You do Mary an injustice," he cried. "If she found you out she would be sorry for you. Deep down in her heart would be a feeling of sympathy for the man who had suffered all these years in silence. I do not wish to try and penetrate your secret, sir—"

"I could not tell it. The story is unspeakable. But there is a deep, cruel deceit here. It was for a great and worthy end, but the deceit remains. Dick, I have never been so candid as this before. I tell you this thing must be postponed. Get Mary to wait, if only for a few weeks. I know that it sounds unmanly, inhuman, monstrous. Do it for my sake and Mary's, my dear lad. And you shall marry her, you shall be rich and prosperous, but do it."

Dick sat there silent and ashamed that for one moment he should have heeded the voice and temptation. He had had a hard struggle of it, he knew what grinding poverty meant. He looked round the perfectly-appointed room, the suggestion of wealth and luxury, all of which he might share with Mary for the rest of his life.

On the other hand he might lose it all, and slip back into the slough of despond again. A word from Spencer and it would be all over. And yet to keep that poor girl in the dark even for a few weeks longer! The cruelty of it!

"I couldn't do it, sir," he answered; "I couldn't."

"And if you refuse, have you reflected what it may mean?"

Dick sprung from his chair and strode towards the door with his head in the air.

"I have just done so," he said. "I can go down to the old grinding life again, but my conscience will be clear, and I shall sleep at night. But I shield not even the father when the daughter knows the truth. I think I had better go, sir."

Spencer motioned Dick back to his chair. Dick's speech was cutting and bitter, but for the life of him he could not summon up courage enough to resent it.

"I am a bad man," he said, as if speaking to himself. "At least I try not to be. Ever since I fell so low myself, I try to feel for the weaknesses of others. Dick, I had it in my heart just now to do you an evil thing. I was going to threaten you. But I see from your face that it would not be the slightest good. If you thought you were right you would go through with a thing to the bitter end. We will say no more about it. If you only knew what a criminal I am."

His head fell forward, his eyes were full of remorse. Dick watched him steadily. What a strange paradox of a man he was. And Spencer had nothing to say on the subject because a new idea had come to him. In any case, it was not a very creditable way out of the difficulty, but it was more creditable than trying to coerce Dick into using his influence with Mary.

"You are right and I am wrong," he went on. "You are a fine fellow, Dick, and you are going to make a son-in-law to be proud of. And Mary shall tell me all about it. There are reasons—grave reasons, but by no means shameful ones—why I cannot go to Stanmere. At the same time, I want to see my child for a few moments to-morrow evening, say a little before eight. If I am on the terrace, then you will try and get Mary to come and speak to me?"

Dick promised eagerly enough. Surely there could be no harm in that. Mary would see her father, and the mere sight of her beautiful face and pathetic eyes would take all his doubts away. Why, whatever crime he had committed and whatever discovery he might make would only induce Mary to cling more closely to her father than before.

"I am glad you are going to do this," Dick said, "I am glad I came here with you. On the face of it, it seemed such a terrible thing—"

"Yes, yes, I know it did. But if you only knew how cruelly I am placed! And sooner or later the whole truth is bound to come out. If a certain man discovered me now, and I could not have Mary by my side, all the work of years would be lost. And if she could see, would she be any longer by my side? That is the question that eternally tortures me."

Dick was certain of it, he had no doubts whatever. How anybody could look in Mary's face and think otherwise was beyond his comprehension. And yet Spencer's face was grave and troubled. It seemed strange that a man in his position should lean for support on the shoulders of a mere boy. He went off presently, wondering and longing for the time when the mystery might be made clear.

But Spencer's resolution was not so firm with the morning light. It was late in the afternoon before he despatched a telegram to Von Wrangel at Stanmere asking for an interview. A reply came back in due course to the effect that Von Wrangel had not yet arrived. Spencer groaned as he saw the message.

"I must face it through," he said. "I must tell the truth, or part of it, and rely upon the good nature of the child. Von Wrangel might have saved me. Why do I drive these things off to the last moment? Why do I prevaricate so? And why are my nerves in this pitiable plight? I do not smoke or drink, I do not unduly strain myself. And yet there comes a time when my heart turns to water and I am a nerveless, trembling coward!"

It was getting dusk before he braced himself to the effort of going to Stanmere. Even then Kant had to accompany him as far as the station. But it was near to the end of September now and getting quite dark. It was only under the shadow that Spencer felt anything like himself.

"I shall be back by the ten o'clock train, Kant," he said. "Better come and meet me. There has not been much sign of the foe lately, Kant."

Kant responded suitably. He could see that his employer was in a high state of nervousness. But once the train had started and the country reached, Spencer was himself again. The peaceful quietness, the bracing air, all had their effect on his nerves.

He walked along with the step of a man who is quite certain of his surroundings. He passed into the park by way of a little gate and thence across the grass to the terrace. It was quite dark now, and the lights gleamed in the windows. The stable clock struck half-past seven. Spencer had not long to wait now, and he was wondering what he was going to say. He was going to do something against which his conscience revolted. But he would not think of that yet.

He stood there like a thief in the night. Some of the blinds were not drawn yet; they were not down in the library, for instance. Somebody seemed to be very busy there. Spencer could make out a figure that looked like a nurse, and his heart beat a little faster. It was nurse Cecilia, of course, so that there was no great room for an effort of imagination there.

But there was Von Wrangel also, in his shirt sleeves. He had his grimmest professional air, and he did not look in the least like the volatile collector of butterflies now. There was some queer-looking apparatus and a very strong electric light rigged up to one of the standard lamps by a flexible cord. It seemed to Spencer that he was only just in time.

Then Dick came into the room and said a few words to Von Wrangel, who seemed to be displeased about something and irritably ordered him out. One of the drawing-room blinds was not quite down, and Spencer caught a glimpse of Mary and Lady Stanmere. He began to get impatient. Surely Dick had quite forgotten his promise; but the stable clock chimed again and it still wanted a quarter to eight. Spencer crept back from the window. A figure crossed the line of light. Spencer saw it, a queer little cry broke from him.

"Stephen," he gasped. "I thought that you. I—I—"

He could say no more. He put up his hand as if to protect himself from a blow. But the blow did not fall, and Stephen stood grimly before him.

"No, you don't," he whispered. "Come this way, so that we are hidden, safe from interruption. I know what you are here for and what you would do. This is my revenge, my little revenge, the thought of which is going to keep me warm on many a cold night. There will be an opening of eyes in more ways than one. You shall see what you shall see. Stir one step and I will kill you, thief and robber that you are. Look at the window yonder, and think what is going on. See, there she is, and her gallant lover by her side. Oh, this is great; it is glorious. And it all comes to me without my raising a finger. See into the library—"

Somebody stepped forward and pulled down the blinds.

XLIV. — SEYMOUR SEES A FACE.

Molly came down the path to the house with a great bunch of late roses in her hand. Her dainty little nose was buried in the dewy blossoms. She made a pretty picture as she stood there, a fact by no means lost on Tom Seymour, who stood watching from the porch. Molly's happiness just now was a wholesome thing to contemplate.

She had her lover back unexpectedly, and he was going to stay in England. There was no longer any necessity for him to go off to distant lands to seek a shadowy fortune. There was a house on the far side of the Warren that Seymour imagined would just suit him.

"Plenty of glass," he was telling Molly, "so that we shall be able to indulge our mutual hobby for flowers. And the conservatory is between the drawing-room and dining-room, so that it is possible to make a perfect promenade. The place has been kept in the pink of condition. I used to dream of a house like that under the stars."

Molly lifted a radiant face to her lover's.

"Didn't you like the life yonder, Tom?" she asked.

"Well, I did and I didn't. There was a murderous lot in San Francisco. And once or twice I came very low down there, very low down indeed. I didn't tell you that, little girl; because it would only have made you miserable. But I saw some queer company. You shall hear my friend and partner, old Maxwell, tell the story."

"Partner!" Molly laughed. "It sounds like a great business."

"No capital and no connection," said Tom. "Maxwell was lucky with the gold that pretty near cost him his life. But he was a man born to adventure. When he comes back from Paris we will get him down here. Now come and see the house."

Molly agreed, provided that they would be home by luncheon-time. She had promised to call and bring Mary back. Von Wrangel was coming down presently, and the operation was going to take place about 8 o'clock. There was nothing strange about the hour, as Tom seemed to imagine, seeing that Von Wrangel preferred to operate by a strong electric light in preference to the daytime. Mary was very nervous, and it was necessary to do something to distract her mind from the coming trouble.

"We'll manage to keep her alive this afternoon," Seymour said, cheerfully. "Meanwhile we'll go and make up our minds about that house. Dick is smoking moodily in the morning-room. What is the matter with him to-day?"

Molly explained. For the first time she told her lover all that she knew concerning Mary and the strange mystery that surrounded the poor blind girl.

Seymour listened with the deepest interest. He seemed to have heard something like it before.
"And so that man actually wanted to put off the operation," he said. "Why?"
"That is exactly what Dick cannot understand. He said Mr. Spencer was horribly frightened when he heard what was going on. Mind you, he doesn't want his own daughter to see again—at least, he did not want her to see for a long time. He threatened Dick, and then he tried to bribe him. It is the strangest mystery you ever heard of. Mr. Spencer knows all the family at Stanmere; he is quite intimate with the place, and yet in as many words he tells Dick he dare not show his face in the house. That is why he got Dick to promise to bring Mary outside to see him for a few minutes."
Tom admitted that the circumstances were peculiar.
"Perhaps the man had committed some crime," he said. "He has done something that he is afraid will be found out. Perhaps there is someone who is in a position to blackmail him. He seems a good man, on the whole."
"That is just it," Molly said eagerly. "He is a good man or he would not do good things, and Mary would not be so fond of him. And yet it looks as if he were about to behave now with the greatest and most deliberate cruelty."
Seymour frankly gave up the whole thing. With the cheery optimism of youth he was quite sure that everything would come right in the end. Dick would marry his employer's daughter, and subsequently become proprietor of The Record, after which he would go into Parliament, and he and Molly would be modest people by the side of Dick and his wife.
"Funny thing how small the world is," he said. "It was Maxwell who told me about the old house we are going to look at on the other side of the Warren. As a boy he used to live there. When he was in England seven years ago he visited his mother there."
"A queer old lady, who dabbled in speculation," Molly cried. "We used to see her sometimes. But she never encouraged visitors, and so she knew nobody. She used to dress like a Quaker. It was common gossip that she made it impossible for any of her family to live with her. I understand that she died a few weeks ago."
"Maxwell told me something of this," he said. "His mother liked to see her family sometimes, but not too often. The boys had their own rooms there, which were kept for them and never touched. There is little doubt that the poor old lady was quite mad."
"And there are some lovely things in the house," Molly said.
"Exquisite," Tom cried. "Everything is to be sold. There is much that is only lumber, but the old oak and the Chippendale and that class of furniture I shall make an offer for. Come along and see it for yourself. I've got the key in my pocket."
Molly passed from room to room with a feeling of pure delight. She could not

as yet quite grasp her own good fortune. A few days before she had been patiently waiting for her lover to make enough in foreign lands for her to join him. She had been prepared to rough it; she had looked forward to a life of hard work—no great trouble after the weary time in Pant-street. And here was Tom back, quite prosperous, and in a position to take a house such as Molly only permitted herself to dream about in romantic moments. She could imagine the lovely dining-room when she had filled it with flowers.
"Isn't it exquisite!" she said, rapturously. "That oak sideboard is a dream. Fancy it covered with old silver! And those chairs, Tom! Am I really going to be mistress of a place like this? That peep into the conservatory is a picture in itself. Let us go and ramble all over the house."
It was the same in most of the rooms. From the window there were glimpses of trim lawns and well-kept flower-beds, with a green fringe of trees beyond.
"Here is a plain enough room, at any rate," Tom said, presently. "Something severely military about it. This must have been my friend Maxwell's room, because I recognise so many of the framed portraits that he has on the walls. Five or six of these men I know well. If they could all tell their life-stories it would keep Dick going for some time."
Molly regarded the photographs with a new interest. These were the kind of men who went out to seek their fortunes, and took their lives in their hands in the doing of it. It was men of this class who had built up the British Empire. Molly regarded the grim, determined-looking faces with a look of admiration.
"So you know most of these men?" she said. "I suppose when Mr. Maxwell came on a flying visit home he left these here. Tom, who is that?"
Molly raised her voice as she spoke. She indicated a man with a fine-looking, open face and a fringe of beard that looked prematurely grey.
"I forget his name," Tom said. "I never met him in the flesh, but I know the face, because Maxwell had another copy of that photo in his rooms at 'Frisco. There is a story attached to it that Maxwell would not tell, though I got something of it through a scoundrel of a servant who should have been lynched if he'd had his rights. Why do you ask?"
Molly turned from the photographs to Tom.
"I asked," she said, quietly, "because that is our Mary's father, Mr. Spencer. You need not smile; I am quite certain of it. When I tell you that Mary has been in San Francisco you may be disposed to believe that I have not made a mistake."
But Tom could throw no further light on the mystery at all. On the subject of the origin of that photograph he could say nothing. Maxwell had been very reticent, and he was not at all the kind of man to gratify idle curiosity. The world was a small place, and there was no reason at all why this should not be a portrait of Mary's father. Maxwell would be back in England in a few days now, and then Molly might ask him for herself.

"Mary has been in San Francisco in recent years I know," Molly said thoughtfully. "They had to leave there hurriedly, like criminals. And I hardly think that your friend Mr. Maxwell was the pursuing Nemesis. At the same time, I fully believe that he could tell us the whole story—indeed, he may help us. If he were not attached to Mr. Spencer he would not have retained two of his photographs."

"Spoken like a wise little woman," Tom said cheerfully. "Meanwhile, let us think no more of the matter. And it's quite time to fetch Miss Mary."

Mary was quite ready for her friends. She looked happy and cheerful enough, but her hands were working restlessly, and there was a touch of heightened colour in her cheeks. Lady Stanmere regarded her anxiously. It was an anxious time altogether.

"Keep her thinking about something else," she said to Molly. "I know that the poor child was awake all night, because I had a bad night myself and heard her. Oh, my dear Molly, if only the next four-and-twenty hours were well over!"

Molly kissed the speaker affectionately.

"Herr Von Wrangel will not fail," she said. "He never does. And he would not have been so sanguine had he not felt certain as to the success of his operation. Is he here?"

But Von Wrangel had not come, nor had any news arrived of him. He was not going to bring a nurse down with him, as Cecilia was quite sufficient.

"Take Mary away and keep her out of doors," Lady Stanmere concluded. "I have not the youth and strength to dissemble my feelings. I cannot be gay. Keep Mary there, and don't bring her back before half-past seven. Anything to keep her mind off what is coming."

Mary had almost forgotten her anxieties by the time of her return to Stanmere. For once Dick had failed to carry the situation as he should have done. He was quiet and moody as he walked through the park in the gathering darkness, and Molly was left to make the conversation.

"I'll come and meet you presently," Tom said. "Meanwhile I'll smoke a cigar in the woods. I only wish that there was something for me to do."

In woodland paths and dark byways Tom Seymour was quite at home. He finished his cigar and then turned to make his way into the avenue leading up to Stanmere. He walked quietly with the instinct of a man who is accustomed to danger and to whom the snapping of a twig is a serious peril. As he skirted the lawn he became aware that he was no longer alone.

Two men were before him, two men face to face, and engaged in a bitter quarrel. The one was stern and resolute, the other obviously frightened, in fear of his life, in the last stage of terror.

Their heads were thrown up in strong relief by the lights gleaming from Stanmere. Seymour could catch words like 'revenge' and 'retaliation,' and the

note of deep satisfaction in the voice of one of the two men.
There was not going to be any serious mischief done. Tom's instinct told him that. The deep, satisfied ring in the voice of the assailant did not point to violence. It was the voice on one who has sought a blood-stained revenge, and who by accident has found the revenge accomplished for him in a far more satisfactory manner. Tom crept back softly.
As he did so he heard an unmistakable chuckle behind him. Somebody was watching the other two men and deriving great satisfaction from the fact. Tom stepped back further still. Behind the bowl of a tree he struck a match.
"My friend," he said, "I have lost my way. Can you tell me?"
"Don't know much about it myself," the other man stammered. "All I can say is—"
What it was Seymour never knew. The speaker broke off suddenly, looked into Tom's face redly glowing in the light of the match, and then raced off towards the house as if all the horrors of a sudden volcano were upon him.

XLV. — A FAILURE.

Von Wrangel came down to Stanmere in a frame of mind calculated to surprise any acquaintance who only knew the lighter side of his nature. It was not that he was afraid of failure or distrusted his powers in the least. He feared something quite different. There was the possibility that something might happen at the last moment to prevent the operation at all.
A telegram from Spencer was awaiting him. There was no great fear of Spencer appearing in person. And, if he did, Von Wrangel knew how to deal with the matter. But if Mary by any chance saw her father and he suggested a postponement of the operation, she would immediately fall in with his wishes. She had a gentle nature, but she could be firm, if Von Wrangel was any judge of faces.
"The most extraordinary complication," the little German muttered as he busied himself in his own room. "The man dare not interfere, and the only one who has a right to is far away by this time. And here is Lady Stanmere as much in the dark as anyone else. Nobody knows the truth but Martlett and myself, and I guessed it. I dare say I shall get myself into a fine mess when the business is finished, but I can't help that. As to the girl, she will behave like a brick. I shall be glad when the next hour is over."
Dinner was not thought of at Stanmere to-night. Even the servants' hall had nothing else to speak of but the forthcoming operation. In the dining-room Von Wrangel had a chop and a very small glass of claret and water. Lady Stanmere watched him with a pretence of eating that would not have deceived the smallest child.
"You are quite sure that you are ready," Lady Stanmere asked.

"My dear lady the question is superfluous," Von Wrangel said. "You have asked it at regular, not to say monotonous, intervals of ten minutes. Please try another. Ask me, for instance, if I have any doubt as to the success of the operation."
"Well, have you?" Lady Stanmere suggested innocently.
Von Wrangel rubbed his hair till it resembled a mop. He would be cool enough when the time came, but he was very nervous now.
"Not the slightest," he said. "I stake my reputation upon it. It is a moral certainty."
"And yet your hands are trembling worse than my own," Lady Stanmere murmured.
"Of course they are. That is eagerness to begin, the wild desire to be at work once more. And what do you suppose I have been doing all day? Why, I have performed two exactly similar operations like Miss Mary's, both with equal success. I go to one of the hospitals; I disclose my identity and ask for an operation; they welcome me with open arms. I am quite successful."
"Oh, I am glad to hear that. And yet your hand—"
"Never mind my hand. Look here. Suppose your eyes are affected. I take the pencil. So."
He took a pencil from the table and just touched the pupil of Lady Stanmere's eye. The touch was so firm, and yet so quick that she hardly blinked.
"There," he cried. "What do you think of that? No other hand in England could have done the same thing. But my patient should be here by this time. It is getting quite dark."
Von Wrangel fidgetted about restlessly; he had good reason for so doing. So long as Mary was under his personal supervision he felt master of the situation. But all through the business there had been the most irritating interruptions, the constant changing of the situation. Spencer was an unknown factor, who might come on the scene at any moment. Spencer would have prevented the operation. Von Wrangel knew why and what the reason was. But that made no difference to him. He had made up his mind in his headstrong way to go through with the thing, and not even a royal command would have changed him from the determination. It was all a matter of time. And Mary had not come back yet.
He met the little party presently on the terrace. He grasped Mary by the arm and hurried her into the house almost rudely. Von Wrangel in a temper was a new light to them. They had never seen anything of the kind in the little German before.
"Gently, gently," Dick expostulated. "If you are out of temper—"
"I am in the vilest rage in the world," Von Wrangel cried. "Say another word to me, you Dick, and I shall assault you violently. My patient ought to have been back long ago. Now that she is in the house she is entirely in my hands."

Dick drew the irate speaker a little on one side.
"Spencer is somewhere here," he whispered. "He can't come to the house, he says."
"Excellent!" Von Wrangel grunted. "He can't come to the house, which is capital. He knows what is going to take place because you told him. I daresay I should have told him myself under similar circumstances, but you were a fool all the same. And so the anxious father has crept down to have a few private words with the child before I begin, eh?"
"That's what I gather," Dick replied.
"Then he is not going to do anything of the kind. You can pursue what you call a policy of masterly inactivity, or you can go out and tell him, just as you please. The patient is mine now, and I am going to operate. I am not afraid of Spencer, for reasons that will be seen presently. And when those reasons are made plain, my young friend, you are going to get the surprise of your life. Go out and tell the man it is too late for him to see his daughter."
Dick hesitated. He had never seen Von Wrangel in this masterful mood before. At any rate he had made a promise, and it was his duty to tell Mr. Spencer that he was not in a position to keep it. He passed out on to the dark terrace. He could see nothing for a moment, and then the sound of voices fell on his ear. The blinds in the library were not yet down, and in a band of light two men were talking earnestly, the one protesting, the other fiercely angry.
Dick rubbed his eyes in astonishment. There were Spencer and the other man, like two people 'taken' on the same photographic film—Spencer and the man who had so maltreated him in Cambria Square on the eventful night of Dick's introduction to the mystery.
From the broad band of light falling on Spencer's face, it was evident that he was just as terribly frightened as he had been on the previous occasion. In a dull way his white face was turned upon his companion. Dick heard a few words as he crept away as silently as he had come. Evidently Spencer had not the slightest desire to see his daughter any more. The other man had defied him to do so. There was no violence going to be done, for the other man was too full of triumph for that.
Dick turned away with a deeper feeling of mystery than ever. Who was the other man? Even if he had solved that question he would have been as much in the dark as ever. Perhaps Von Wrangel would be able to throw some light on the subject.
But Von Wrangel had something else to do. He drove Dick from the library with contemptuous, not to say insulting words; he seemed only able to tolerate the presence of Nurse Cecilia just now. The latter was moving about the room setting things in order, a brilliant light lay on the table which had been affixed to one of the standard lamps by a long flex. An operating table had been improvised out of a long invalid chair.

Von Wrangel held a thin needle-like knife in his hand. The blade was nearly as fine as a hair and brittle as glass. He gave a gesture of impatience as he took the lance from its case.
"I ought to have three of those," he said. "But I find that two are broken. And they cost me eight pounds each in London to-day. They are the most perfect specimens of cutlery in the world, and now two of them are useless."
"Can you manage without them?" Cecilia asked.
"I can do with one, of course. But they are so delicate that an accident might spoil everything. If I laid them carelessly on a chair for instance. I shall have to operate on your eyes, too. They are red. Is it weakness or tears?"
"Tears," Cecilia said, half defiantly. "My husband has been here again, it is weakness, but there are times when I cannot help it. I ought not to mention it just now, but—"
"But I asked you a plain question. I shall know how to deal with that man presently. I hope you did not give him any money. Now, go and bring in the patient."
The thing had begun at length. Mary lay at full length on the couch with her face to the light. All Von Wrangel's irritation had vanished now; he was quiet and gentle, his hand steady and true as steel. He had his hand on the patient's pulse.
"That is right," he said. "You are not nervous now. All you have to do is to lie perfectly still, and I shall give you no more pain than a pin prick. Brave girl. Did you feel that?"
"Not more than a touch of a needle point," Mary whispered.
"And yet the thing is nearly half done. It looks so ridiculously easy, and yet the breadth of a hair makes all the difference. What's that?"
Von Wrangel started nervously, and the delicate lance fell on the carpet. The man's nerves and eyes and brain were strung to the highest tension; the noise of a cry, followed by a smashing of glass, as if a whole greenhouse had collapsed, threw him entirely off his balance. With a stifled exclamation he picked up his lance and showed it to Cecilia.
"I have forgotten something," he said, quietly. His face was as dark as night, there were beads on his forehead. "Come this way for a moment, nurse. Lie still, my patient."
He drew Cecilia hurriedly out. The sound of smashing glass echoed through the house. The expression on Von Wrangel's face was not good to see.
"I have partially failed," he said hoarsely. "One eye is a success, but it is useless without the help and sympathy of the other. Another moment and the thing would have been accomplished. For Heaven's sake tell your patient that I cannot go any further to-night, that we must wait a day two, that I am perfectly satisfied, anything to comfort her."
"I shall be able to manage it," Cecilia said quietly. "Perhaps to-morrow."

"Aye, to-morrow. And now to see what all that infernal din was about. And if anybody wants to know where I am, I had to go to London. To-morrow night at the same time nurse. And see that you don't mention it to a soul."

XLVI. — IN TROUBLE.

There are few things more pitiable than a scoundrel out of luck. He is the scorn of all God-fearing people; he may swagger and bully as much as he likes, but there is ever the consciousness of the gulf between himself and an honest man. All his cunning tricks and dodges have failed; his so-called friends have fallen upon him; the policemen as he slinks by mark him with a cold eye that makes a note as he passes.

For the moment Horace Venner had fallen very low indeed. He had to button his absurdly showy coat across his chest to conceal the want of a vest beneath. There was a dinginess about his linen that told its own tale of nights spent on open seats and toilettes performed mostly by the aid of his ten dirty fingers.

To add zest to existence the police were after him. He was perilously near to absolute starvation, his limbs shook oddly and his eyes were misty. And yet with all this struggle to keep body and soul together, Venner hugged to his breast a secret worth thousands. If he could only find the right man, he might be swaggering about in those blazing, blaring restaurants and served with the best by patient waiters. If he could only find that one man in London. He was like one who was starving in the desert and suddenly stumbles on a gold mine.

He had been very near that man more than once. On one occasion he thought he had found him, but he had only got a thrashing for his pains instead. It was maddening. There he was actually in want of a meal whilst those thousands—

He would go back to Stanmere. The police would not take the trouble to look for him there again. And his wife might be good for something. For the first time in his career Venner was reduced to the tricks of the road. He got a meal or two that way, and a shilling or two from a cynical philanthropist who was not in the least deceived by Venner's glib falsehood. If his wife would not give him a few pounds he would know the reason why.

But not again. Cecilia was quite firm. If Venner called upon Mr. Martlett he would be sent to Australia and his passage paid, with a few shillings for the voyage and a further ten pounds as his annuity, but not a penny would Cecilia part with. Venner urged and stormed and swore; he even threatened, but nothing seemed to shake the resolution on that pale, white face.

"I have finished with you," Cecilia said, quietly. "You will get nothing further out of me. Here are two shillings to pay your fare back to London. If you raise your hand to me again like that I will set the dogs on you."

Venner growled something, and so did the retriever dog by Cecilia's side. In the woman's purse were gold pieces that gleamed and glistened. They meant food and warmth and shelter and such vulgar dissipations as Venner's soul loved.

"You no longer care for me," he whined.

"Care for you!" Cecilia cried. "If I heard of your death to-day I should go down on my knees and thank God for His infinite mercy. Fool that I was to imagine that I could make a better man of you! There is contamination in all you touch. If you had never come to Stanmere as a body servant to the young men what misery might have been saved! You owe everything to the family at Stanmere, and yet if you could find the one to whom you owe the most you would try to ruin him. But he is beyond your reach."

Cecilia turned away with her skirts held high, as if fearful of contamination. She had never beaten her worthless husband quite so low as this before. He felt himself aggrieved, there were tears of maudlin self-pity in his eyes. He found a woodside public-house, where he ate a meal of sorts and talked like a landed proprietor, and at dusk made his way to the station. He had his pride still, and he had no fancy to be detected in Stanmere without a vest. And there was an hour to wait at the station. There was a train in from London first; it crept in presently, and Venner curiously watched the faces of the few passengers by the light of the two flickering oil lamps on the platform.

Venner's languid curiosity received a sudden stimulus. From a first-class carriage almost in front of him a tall, handsome man with a grey beard alighted. Hardly had he passed the barriers before another, identically like the first one, but more shabbily dressed, leapt from the train and followed his prototype into outer darkness.

Venner rubbed his eyes in amazement. He was trembling from head to foot with a sudden triumph; he felt almost physically sick with it. His head was spinning with the shock of a great discovery.

"It's my man," he muttered. "The first was my man; and I should have let him go, thinking it was Mr. Stephen, if Stephen himself hadn't popped out like that. I've been deceived, that's what's the matter with me; cruelly deceived. I see it all now."

He must have seen very brilliantly, for he had to press his hands to his eyes to shut out the dazzling vision. A porter with gruff sympathy asked if anything was the matter. Venner pulled himself together and staggered to his feet.

"Left my money behind me, and haven't any left for a ticket," he said. "I'll have to go back and return by the next train. Unless you could manage—"

"No," the porter said, shortly, "I couldn't."

Venner went off chuckling. His limbs were still shaky and uncertain, but he had forgotten his hunger and that insatiable thirst for liquid refreshment now. By mere accident he had found what he had been looking for for years. By a still greater chance he had penetrated the mystery that had puzzled him. He felt hot and indignant as he thought of the lost opportunities.

But he knew everything now. He knew that one of those men was following the other, and that the destination of the two was Stanmere. Well, he would follow in his turn. He might hear something useful. The prosperous one would stay at Stanmere; he would be certain to return by a later train, and Venner would follow. In his mind's eye he saw himself comfortably housed to-night, feasted upon game and champagne, with brandy and choice cigars to follow. To-morrow he would go to a tailor and hold up his head once more.

Yes, those two men were going to Stanmere right enough. One was dogging the other without a doubt, and Venner proceeded to dog the two. What could they be after, seeing that neither of them made any attempt to gain the house? Not that it mattered in the least to Venner so long as he did not lose sight of his quarry.

They were both in the grounds now, on the terrace, watching something that was going on in the house. Venner secreted himself behind a tree with his back to it. He wanted to be quite sure that there were not depths and complications yet that he had not been able to fathom. If he could only learn what those men were saying he would be safe.

He heard at length, enough and more than enough. There was no longer any doubt now as to which was his man. Venner knew everything in the light of recent experiences; he even gathered what was going to take place in the library at Stanmere.

"And so that is the way I was fooled," he muttered. "The very man I wanted has passed and repassed me when I was pretty nigh starving! It makes me almost weep to think of it all. All the time I might have been in West End chambers, with a man of my own and a private hansom and a good banking account behind me. But it was clever, and no mistake about that; very clever. And I'll bet that old fox Martlett was at the bottom of it."

Venner chuckled a little more loudly than was quite prudent. It seemed to him that he could hear a quiet footstep close by. Was it possible that the police—then a match flared out, and Venner caught sight of a face and a pair of dark eyes looking into his with a cool measure of surprise and an unmistakable recognition.

Venner's heart suddenly sank into his boots. Here was the whole fabric shattered like a cloud before a gale. Here, too, was a danger so great that the mere idea of facing it was out of the question. Venner put his head down and fled—fled in such terror that he had not the slightest idea where he was going. He could hear the flash of footsteps behind, and they were gaining upon him.

"What luck," he sobbed; "what cruel, cruel luck! Oh, Mr. Tom Seymour, if I was only on top of you in some quiet spot with a knife in my hand!"

Alas! for the immutability of human wishes; instead of this, Tom Seymour was close behind and running with the ease and speed of a trained athlete. On and on Venner struggled, sobbing and struggling for breath, something full of

dim luminous light rose before his tired eyes. There was a tremendous clash and clatter of falling glass, and the hunted man was on his back in a small conservatory with Seymour standing over him.
"Not much damage done," Seymour said, as he surveyed his fallen foe by the electric light. "A little cut about the face, but no more."
"I should like to know what this means, sir," a quiet, respectful voice asked.
Goss stood in the doorway, quiet, respectful and unruffled. He seemed to recognise Venner as one does undesirable vermin that is unfortunately impossible to be without.
"I have made a capture," Seymour said coolly. "I regret the damage, and I sincerely hope that Lady Stanmere has not been alarmed. I am staying with my friend, Mr. Stephenson, at Shepherd's Spring. If Herr Von Wrangel will step this way when he has a moment or two to spare I shall feel obliged. Meantime, you can leave this fellow to me. For the sake of the house, it will be better not to make a fuss. I think you understand me?"
"Perfectly," Goss said, quietly. "It shall be as you please; and if you can rid us permanently of that rascal you will be doing the house a great service."
Goss went off calmly, as if a catastrophe of this kind was quite in accordance with proprieties. He would have said himself that Mr. Seymour was a stranger to him, but that he always knew a gentleman when he saw one. Seymour looked at this sorry capture.
"Well, Venner," he said, "this is a bit of hard luck for you."
"It's cruel," Venner whined. "I fancied to-day wouldn't be bad, but it has been; and just when everything was turning out so rosy! It's very hard, Mr. Seymour, sir—very hard. If you wouldn't mind telling me, what are you going to do with me?"
"Well, it's not exactly my funeral, as we used to say out yonder. Take you to London and lay an information against you for robbery and fraud. By that means, you see, the police would hold you by the heels till the necessary papers arrived to support a more serious charge. After that I could safely leave you in the hands of my friend, Mr. Maxwell."
Venner stood there nervously grinding the palms of his hands together. They were wet and hot, and the grimy drops rolled off them. Something was working up and down in the man's throat with the regularity of a steam engine. He had the dazed blue look of the condemned criminal on his way to the scaffold. Venner was pretty nearly past all feeling now.
"If you would give me another chance, sir," he whispered.
"Not an inch! A real, full-blooded scoundrel I can do with. There is hope for him; indeed, I have known more than one resolve himself into a respectable member of society. But you are one of the pests of humanity. If you came into a million of money to-morrow you would be as great a rascal as ever. I am going to see you handed over to the police."

"When Mr. Maxwell comes back from America, sir—"
The door opened and Von Wrangel came in. He was still white and trembling with the passion caused by the failure of his operation. But there was just the flicker of a smile in his eye as he caught sight of Venner standing there.
"You seem to know this man, Mr. Seymour," said he. "So this is the secret of that din just now, the din that caused me to—but do you know him?"
"I know enough to hang him," Seymour said, crisply.
Von Wrangel's eyes glistened.
"Good!" he cried. "I am glad to hear it. Let him be hanged by all means. Only, if you would do the family a signal service, let the lawyer, Mr. Martlett, see him first. Afterwards, the interesting ceremony may proceed without delay. You will go up to London by the last train, and I shall come along. The night's work is not going to be so unsuccessful after all."

XLVII. — NOT QUITE A FAILURE AFTER ALL.

Von Wrangel had flung down his instrument in a passionate rage. He was occasionally given to childish fits of anger of that kind, as men with the artistic temperament often are. Not that he had absolutely failed; indeed, so far as he had gone, he had no reason to be dissatisfied with the result of his experiment.
But a sheer accident had deprived him of the chance of finishing it. Also he had positively promised Mary that she should see as well as anybody else again. And Von Wrangel shrank from giving pain outside the necessary pain that surrounds his profession.
How would Mary take it? he wondered. Under the circumstances of the case it was far better that she should be left to the tender care of Nurse Cecilia. Von Wrangel hurried out of the room, resolved to return presently when his presence would be more desirable.
Mary remained lying as she was for a few minutes. She had got herself well in hand now. She had been patient so many years that an hour or two made little difference. She wondered vaguely what that crash of glass meant, and why both doctor and nurse had hurried from the room. Cecilia came back presently outwardly calm, but greatly agitated and disappointed. Like Von Wrangel, she had set her heart upon the success of the operation.
"What does it all mean?" Mary asked.
"Possibly one of the cattle has strayed into the grounds and blundered into the conservatory," Cecilia said. "Goss seems to have taken the matter in hand. Miss Mary, I am afraid that we cannot go any further with the operation to-night."
"You don't mean to say," Mary faltered, "that—"
"Oh, no, no!" Cecilia cried. "The doctor was operating with some very delicate

instruments when the crash came, and he dropped it, and the point was broken, and he hasn't got another one. I have never seen a doctor in such a rage before."
A faint smile crossed Mary's lips.
"I can imagine Herr Von Wrangel," she said. "But it is all right if he is angry. If there was any chance of failure, he would be one of the first to show it. What shall you do?"
"I shall put a bandage over the eye that has been operated upon, and you are on no account to remove it. And if you are wise you will go straight to bed."
Mary complied with the suggestion in her sweet, uncomplaining way. She seemed tired and exhausted now, for the strain and suspense were a little greater than she had expected. Von Wrangel, with a queer bright alertness on his face, was waiting for Cecilia when she came down.
"What did you tell her?" he asked eagerly.
"I told her exactly the truth," Cecilia replied. "It seemed to me far best, and she is such a lovely patient. She was not in the least frightened or cast down, and she looks forward to the next time. If I did not do right, sir—"
"You did exactly right," Von Wrangel said. "You are a pearl among women. If it had not been for that most unfortunate business in the conservatory—but never mind that. I am going to town by the last train on most important business. I am going to open more sets of eyes than one. Let Lady Stanmere know that I shall be back at mid-day to-morrow, and don't say a word as to our next venture. Good-night."
Von Wrangel bustled off in his quick fashion, and was seen no more. But according to his promise, he came down the following day with the air of one who has accomplished great things. Lady Stanmere awaited him in the drawing-room.
"Where is the patient?" he demanded.
Lady Stanmere replied that the patient was in bed, and had no intention of getting up till dinner time. She had thought it best to keep the girl quiet, and even the young people from Shepherd's Spring had been denied admission. Von Wrangel rubbed his hands approvingly.
"That is right," he said. "Couldn't be better. I meant to operate again to-day, but my new lance has not come from the makers yet, so it must be to-morrow instead."
"WILL the next experiment be successful?" Lady Stanmere asked, with a steady look. "Are you sure?"
"There is no experiment," Von Wrangel said. "Would I EXPERIMENT on such a lovely pair of eyes as those? I tell you I am certain. But for that—that cow blundering into the conservatory and the breaking of my lance. But you will see what you will see to-morrow."
"I don't understand what happened," Lady Stanmere said.

"It was a simple accident. I had three of those lances. They are as fine as the hair of your head. Two of them got broken, and when the noise came I dropped the third and broke that. The place I had to touch was so minute that the most dainty instrument was required. For years I have tried to find that spot; nobody else has found it. There is the smallest contraction of the muscles from weakness; a touch, and the contraction has gone. But, my word, what a touch it requires! So there is the story of the operation, and why it failed. Lady Stanmere, I do not regret it."

Von Wrangel walked excitedly up and down the room, a fine contrast to the still grey figure patiently knitting. He seemed wildly excited about something.

"I shall bring back sight to those eyes," he said. "I shall bring back sight to other eyes too. The cloud is rolling away, the cloud is going. Ah, Ah!"

Lady Stanmere listened calmly. She was quite used to these outbursts from a man who would waste his time over a butterfly or cheerfully take over the administration of a kingdom. The man was ever sanguine, the doer of great things in a dream.

"Hadn't you better see your patient?" she suggested.

Von Wrangel came tumbling down to earth again.

"I will do so," he cried. "A practical idea of yours. A few hours and the condition of everything will be changed. Permit me to kiss your hand."

Von Wrangel went upstairs in the highest spirits. He found Mary propped up on bed with Cecilia reading to her. She heard his step and smiled as he came in. On the whole, the girl was taking her disappointment in a really beautiful manner.

"Now there is a patient for you," Von Wrangel cried. "The best in the world and a model to all others. Let me have a look at that one eye."

He removed the bandage as gently as a woman could have done. Then he spread out his hand close to the blue pupil and expanded his fingers.

"You imagine that you see something," he suggested.

"Is it imagination?" Mary asked. "I seemed to see in a dim kind of way, a long thin hand with some deep red freckles on the back, and there was a signet ring on the little finger with a purple stone in it. Now it has all gone again, but it was quite distinct."

Von Wrangel smiled as he replaced the bandage. There were red freckles on his hands and his little finger most certainly carried a signet with a purple stone.

"Quite right," he said in what he fondly imagined to be a professional voice. "It was my hand that you saw just now. Really, the thing has turned out better than I expected. But you are not to use that eye till the other has been operated upon, because that would be dangerous. What did I tell you? Ah, this is going to be a splendid case."

Mary lay back on the pillow crying quietly. Von Wrangel nodded approvingly.

Those gentle tears would do the girl good, and he had partially feared a more violent outburst. He drew the nurse gently from the room, his own eyes suspiciously moist.

"Leave her to herself," he said. "Leave her to herself as much as possible. A nature like hers does not need a lot of people fussing about her. She is quiet and devotional, and she has herself well in hand. Go in occasionally and ask her if she wants anything, but nothing more. That poor girl's thoughts are and will be too near Heaven for us to intrude upon them."

Cecilia nodded. She had no words for the moment.

"I am sure you are right," she contrived to say at length. "Oh, what a great doctor you are, Herr Von Wrangel, what a great doctor!"

"Great fool," the German growled. "If you only knew what a fool!"

But he had plumbed the depths of Mary's thoughts exactly. She desired nothing better than to be alone. She was very near Heaven at that moment. Her spirit seemed to be raised up and glorified. For hours she lay there thinking of the past and the future. Cecilia came in from time to time, but Mary wanted nothing. She was thinking of the delight of the beautiful world again, of what her father would say when she could look into his face once more.

They were dining downstairs and the house was very quiet. If her father could be near her now. . . . She seemed to hear his footsteps and his voice calling her. . . . With a strange dreamy impulse upon her she got out of bed and felt her way to the door. She was certain that she could hear somebody in the corridor, it sounded in her ears like her father's steps.

Just as she was she ventured into the corridor. She tripped over some hangings and clutched at the air for support. The bandage dropped from her eyes, and just for a moment she had a vision of the old corridor, the old pictures, the gleam of the electrics on oak and sliver, and a little way off a man in a grey suit, with a red tie and white spats over his patent leather boots. The broad forehead and the melancholy eyes, the grey beard, were familiar to her. It was her father, not the harsh-faced man that she used to know, but her father's face chastened by sorrow, and rendered soft, by the passing of time.

"Father!" Mary cried. "Father! you have come to me! Let me look—" The figure gave a cry and vanished. There was a murmur of voices in the hall, the rustle of Cecilia's skirts as she flew upstairs. Mary stood there in the white gown and with the fair hair over her shoulders, the bandage in her hand.

"How could you!" Cecilia cried, as she replaced the bandage, hurriedly. "How could you, Miss Mary! Come back to your room at once."

Mary followed without protest. She was crying quietly.

"I heard my father's step and his voice calling," she said. "And I saw him, Cecilia. I never knew what a noble face he had till now."

XLVIII. — RETALIATION.

Spencer stood there cowering fearfully, as if waiting for a blow. He seemed to have shrunk smaller, he looked greyer and prematurely aged. His attitude was that of the patient, despairing wife who knows what it is to feel the weight of her master's hand, and suffers uncomplainingly. The other man laughed with bitter contempt.

"Well, what do you think of yourself, my brother?" he asked.

Spencer said nothing. He looked up to the woods behind Stanmere, and then back the long facade of the house again. How many years, centuries ago, was it that he was a happy boy there? And the man by his side, the man whom he held in such dreadful fear, had shared his joys and sorrows. There was something unreal about the whole thing.

"I have done you no real harm," Spencer said at length. His eyes were turned now with a fascinated interest on the library window. "You have not suffered through me."

"That is a lie. Why palter in this way? I meant to have your life once. Mine was forfeit, and I said that yours should be, too. But there is a better revenge than that. If I killed you there would be an end of the matter, but my revenge is going to last as long as you last. Why did you come down to-night! Tell me that?"

"I came down to see Mary, and—and—"

"Prevent, this operation. Shall I tell you why?"

Silence on the part of Spencer. The respected philanthropist looked very small and mean now. A spectator would have picked out the other man as the better of the two.

"I found it all out by accident," Stephen went on. "I was in trouble—you know what trouble, it was partly my own fault, but that has nothing to do with it. I managed to get to our friend Von Wrangel's rooms, and there I saw a telegram. I knew that the girl was going to recover her sight, and I knew you would try and prevent it."

"No, no," Spencer cried. "Only to postpone it for a little time."

"And so on, ad infinitum. You know that you dare not permit it. I felt that you would come down here in this fashion, and I watched you. You haven't got that smart young fellow Dick Stevenson to help you this time. They seem to be busy over yonder. It is good to feel that by now that poor girl can see."

There was no feeling of sympathy in the words, nothing more than a certain savage satisfaction. Spencer could think of no personal justification. The other man shook him savagely.

"Do you hear?" he went on. "Oh, you need not be afraid for your cowardly life. I have better uses for you than that. The girl can see, my brother. She will see you, for instance. She is very fond of you; she regards you as a prince among men. And when she sees you with open eyes—"

"You are a fiend!" Spencer cried; "a perfect fiend. If you only knew—"

"Pshaw! I know more than you imagine—there's somebody listening. What was that?"
A kind of chuckle, ending in a cry of fear. Somebody dashed headlong across the terrace and past the line of light thrown by the windows, and immediately a second figure flashed along in hot pursuit of the first.
"If that is any game of yours," Stephen said, fiercely, "I'll take good care—"
"No, no," Spencer cried; "I swear I am as much in the dark as you are."
Stephen grunted something inarticulate. There was no doubting the evident sincerity of Spencer's words. He was looking towards the flying figures open-mouthed. Once more Stephen shook him savagely.
"You know something about it," he said.
"Only what I can guess. We were both being watched, watched by the last man in the world that I desired to meet. Now that he has seen us both together all my sacrifice will be in vain."
"Who on earth are you talking about?" Stephen demanded.
"Venner," Spencer replied. "That was Horace Venner."
"Your old valet and fidus Achates. So he has got hold of some scent and was blackmailing you. Or he would have done so if he had found you. I begin to see day-light. Hullo!"
Then came the sudden smash of glass and a frightened kind of cry from somewhere. With a feeling of curiosity Stephen Gay hurried forward. There were passions and emotions at play here, and that kind of thing appealed to him. Spencer was forgotten. He might have placed the darkness between himself and his antagonist.
But he could not leave here yet. He had been prevented from interfering, the precious moment had been lost, and by this time the finest operator in Europe had done his work, and done it well. Spencer must know before he returned to London.
From the second terror he could not escape now. Venner knew where he lived and the trick by which he had been deceived before. It was useless to fly home, seeing that that home was no longer sacred. And Venner was not far off. Venner had learnt something to-night that had been carefully and cunningly concealed from him for years.
The whole thing must came out now, the secret be revealed. But from the first that had always been inevitable. If only it could have been postponed for a few weeks longer! And what would Mary say when she knew everything?
A feeling of sullen despair had come over Spencer. Nothing seemed to matter now. Mechanically he followed in the footsteps of Stephen towards the house. He could see the broken glass of the conservatory, he could hear Venner's whining tones. Nobody could whine and fawn better than Venner when he pleased. The rascal had evidently met somebody that he was afraid of.
Then there came the quiet, staccato tones of Von Wrangel. There was no

suggestion of boyish triumph in his voice as there would have been had the operation been successful. Perhaps something had taken place to prevent it. With all his heart Spencer longed to know the truth. He had been hanging like a tramp about Stanmere when he had every right to be an honoured guest there. But he must satisfy himself. Stephen Gay came looming out of the darkness.

"Your luck again," he said savagely. "It has been a failure."

"You don't mean to say," Spencer gasped, "that—that—"

He paused, unable to proceed. His face was terribly agitated.

"I admit your affection for the child," Gay went on; "under ordinary circumstances nobody would be more glad for the poor girl to get back her sight again. The failure has been temporary. The man you have every cause to fear has brought it about. I have been in the house."

"You have been in the house?" Spencer asked in a dreary voice.

"Well, why not? I have been in the house; I have heard everything worth knowing. Von Wrangel failed in consequence of the breaking of a very delicate instrument he was using, and he had not another one in the house. Therefore the operation is postponed. The noise of that smashing glass disturbed our German friend; hence the trouble. It was Venner blundering into one of the conservatories."

Here was a respite. Spencer breathed more freely. Deep down in his heart he was execrating himself, but the fact remained that he was breathing more easily.

"Why did Venner do that?" he asked.

"That I can't tell you. The other fellow who was after him seems to be quite at home at Stanmere. By some means known to himself he has reduced Venner to a pitiable state of grovelling terror. But that part of the business does not interest me in the least. The fact remains that the operation is put off, and I don't mean to give you a chance to interfere. Come along."

Spencer found breath to ask where they were going. Gay laughed.

"We are going to London," he said. "For the present I have neither a local habitation nor a name. I am Mr. Nemo, and there are people literally thirsting for my blood. It sounds a little like a boy's penny novelette, but I know how horribly true it is. Under ordinary circumstances I should have left London by this time, but not now till I have seen this through. My dear brother, I crave your hospitality for a day or two."

"It—it is quite impossible," Spencer stammered.

"Not a bit if it. You have palatial quarters in Cambria Square, and I shall be safe there. They will never think of looking for me so near yourself. Kant will make me comfortable."

"Kant has gone for a few days' holiday."

"Well, that makes no difference. We shall be quite comfortable there. What!

you grudge a few days' shelter and food to your one and only brother? Come along."
The savage pleasantry of the words did not disguise the threat underlying them. With a weary sigh Spencer turned and followed. Across the park they went and out by the lodge gates without a word. It had been years since they were together before; perhaps they were thinking of the time when they had been friends and comrades, planning many a day's mischief, and dreaming nothing of the dark days to come. In the station they stood back from the feeble flare of the oil lamps, for neither desired to be recognised. As the train came in, three other passengers appeared. As they apparently had nothing to conceal, they stood where the lights fell upon them.
"The dark young man accompanied by Von Wrangel and Horace Venner," Gay muttered. "The first two very grim with a fighting look in their eyes, and Venner, looking like the caged criminal in a manner that would make his fortune on any stage. Did you ever see a more perfect picture of a man in custody?"
"They must not see us," Spencer said, anxiously.
But Von Wrangel and his companion were too intent upon the business in hand to care about anybody else. As soon as the train entered the station Venner was bundled into a third-class carriage, and the watchers followed a few coaches lower down. At Victoria a four-wheeled cab was called. In the press of passengers Gay got near enough to hear the address.
"They are going to Lincoln's Inn," he confided to Spencer. "Depend upon it that old fox Martlett is at the bottom of the business. I think we'd better have a cab, too. London streets after dark are dangerous to my health at present. Come along."
It was late when Cambria Square was reached and the servants had retired. Gay looked about him curiously as if the place was familiar to him. There was a queer, hard smile on his face as he turned from one object of art to another.
"You have done the thing very well," he said. "You are as artistic as the amateur who blacked himself all over to play Othello. So you have got about you all the lares and penates that belonged to me in the days of my meteoric prosperity? That was a happy thought."
There was bitter satire in the speech, an undercurrent of savageness that caused Spencer to wriggle and twist on his chair. He looked unspeakably small and humble now, and not in the least like a master of fortunes. He had no reply; there was nothing to be said, only to endure the silence.
"How long," he said at length, "how long—"
"Am I going to stay? With your fine hospitable instincts, that must be an exceedingly painful question to ask; but, of course, it was dictated by a desire for my welfare. To be perfectly candid, I don't know how long I shall stay. I shall be here till after that operation has been successfully performed. After

that I should dearly like to be present when you and Mary meet. But even so model a specimen of humanity as myself cannot have all the pleasure, so I shall forego that one with Christian resignation."
Stephen Gay rolled back in his chair, laughing silently. The abject misery of his brother's face amused him. If the man ever had a heart it had been cankered away long ago. He sat laughing there with his cheeks shaking and the tears in his eyes.
"Where is your boasted hospitality?" he cried. "I have not the least desire to eat your salt, not being partial to that class of diet; but I confess to a certain curiosity on the subject of your whisky and cigars. A delicate hint like that, my dear Paul—"

Spencer placed cigars and spirits on the table. He made no effort to control himself; his misery had got him down and was sitting on him. He had found an old man of the sea, and he wondered how long the incubus would be on his shoulders. Gay seemed to divine his thoughts, for he laughed once more in that unpleasant, silent manner.
"You had better ask Von Wrangel," he said. "I stay here till that is well over. And if you try and play me false I'll kill you. To think that a man who keeps whisky and cigars like this should be at heart so great a villain!"

XLIX. — THE FIRST BLOW.

Gay was making himself quite at home. There was no trouble about the servants. They had merely been informed that their master's brother had arrived unexpectedly, and there was an end of it. As to the secret of the household, Kant was the only one of the domestics who knew anything, and the striking resemblance between Gay and his unhappy host was too apparent to cause speculation.
There was no trouble about wardrobe, seeing that the brothers were so alike in figure as well as face. As Stephen appeared when he came down to breakfast the following morning he might have been fresh from the hands of a Bond street tailor. His grey lounge suit fitted him to perfection, his linen was glossy and immaculate, he approved of his host's razor.
"Wonderful what a difference clothes make," he said. "I feel an air of respectability that has not been set on me for years. I feel like a county magistrate. No coffee, thanks. A little brandy and soda-water. You looked shocked. But then you are a man of domestic virtues."
Spencer moved in his chair uneasily.
"What do you propose to do with yourself?" he asked.
"Je suis, je reste. For the rest nothing. I am safe here, which is more than I can say of the outer air, and so long as I have plenty to read and smoke, I am quite

content. For the next four and twenty hours I can suffer you out of my sight; after that I shall have to consider my position. If the counting-house requires attention, don't let me stand in the way."

Here was a respite at any rate. It might even be possible to go as far as Stanmere and see Mary. But that would be better done in the evening when the family were at dinner. In the first place it would be necessary to find Martlett and gather whether he knew anything of the mysterious events of the previous evening in which Venner had played so strange a part. There might just be a possibility of getting rid of that rascal altogether. Spencer's breath came a little faster as he dwelt upon the desirable circumstance. If only it might be!

At any rate, it looked as if Venner was safe for the present. He had evidently been more or less in custody the previous evening with captors who had no idea of losing him. In a frame of comparative curiosity Spencer went to Lincoln's Inn, but he was destined to hear nothing there beyond the fact that Mr. Martlett had gone to Paris.

A little disappointed, Spencer went back to Cambria Square. He must know a little more of what had taken place at Stanmere last night. A telegram to Dick Stevenson would bring that about. Then Spencer went back home and waited.

Dick came later in the afternoon. A heavy luncheon with more wine than was good for most people had left Gay cross and inclined to be quarrelsome. Finally he had fallen asleep on the sofa in the morning-room, where he looked like staying. What a handsome face it was still, Spencer thought, despite the marks of dissipation and hard living.

Dick's bright cheerful features were not without their effect on Spencer. Dick had a good deal to say, but he was a little guarded in his manner. He had not forgotten his last interview with his employer, and the recollection of it still rankled.

"Where is Von Wrangel?" Spencer asked.

"I haven't the remotest idea, sir," Dick replied. "All sorts of mysterious things seem to be continually happening at Stanmere, till one is almost bewildered. It is more than strange that wherever Mary goes these mysteries follow. And she is so gentle and patient, the last one in the world to be associated with violence. But there it is."

"But what has that to do with Von Wrangel?"

"I don't know, sir. Von Wrangel went away last night hurriedly with Tom Seymour who is engaged to my sister—and some fellow they picked up out of the conservatory. They were very mysterious, and I could get nothing out of them."

Mr. Spencer crossed one foot over the other and looked out of the window. He did not feel like meeting Dick's direct gaze at that moment.

"I am seriously annoyed with Von Wrangel," he said. "Of the sincerity of his motives there can be no question. But an operation like that should never have

been attempted without my sanction."
"I don't agree with you at all, sir," Dick said boldly. "You surely must remember—"
"I have the best of reasons for what I said, my dear Dick, if you only knew how I am situated. But we need not go into that again. Tell me what happened."
Dick explained. The operation was to be repeated again in a day or two, perhaps to-morrow. It all depended whether the new instrument would be in time or not. Spencer listened in a kind of benign satisfaction. He would be able to see Mary now and place his views before her. But there must be no delay, seeing that the operation had, after all, been partially successful, and delay might be dangerous.
And Mary was keeping to her bed; she desired to be more or less alone. It was a bit of a venture, but so long as the shadow of Venner was lifted, the path of adventure would be comparatively smooth. Besides, Spencer had Stanmere by the heart. He would steal down there about nine, so that he would be back at the office after ten and nobody be any the wiser.
"I dare say you will learn everything in time," he said, benignly. "My dear Dick, I am afraid that I have placed myself in a bad light before you. I am like a criminal who has had a heap of circumstantial evidence piled up against him. Then comes a prick of common sense and the whole case goes to the winds. If that operation is postponed it will not be dangerous—"
"It will be in embryo, Von Wrangel says," Dick replied.
"Ah!" There was no keeping the relief out of the speaker's voice. "In that case you need not be in any hurry. Dick, do you want to go?"
"I fancy I have told you everything, sir," Dick said, coldly.
"As you will," Spencer replied. He felt very mean and small just for the moment. "I shall require you this evening at the office just before ten."
Dick bowed himself out, glad to get away. His heart was not against his employer, and Spencer was seated with his head buried in his hands. He sat there until the shadows began to fall; a servant came in to lay the cloth for dinner. In the morning-room Stephen was stirring uneasily on the couch. He opened his eyes, red and bloodshot, and laughed.
"Where have you been?" he cried. "You dog, if you betray me I'll kill you."
His muddled senses had not come back to him yet. With a sudden passion Spencer stooped and shook him violently by the shoulders.
"Take care," he said, hoarsely; "take care. But we need not brawl in the presence of the servants. Go to your room and cool that hot head of yours. Dinner is nearly ready."
Gay lurched away. The dinner-bell rang but he did not appear. Spencer found him across his bed with a glass smelling of brandy by his side. He surveyed the huddled body with infinite contempt.

"To think what a pair of happy pure-hearted boys we used to be," he muttered. "And he has come to this, and I go about in fear of my life. Well, he shall lie there; he probably will lie there till morning. So much the better for me. I shall be able to go to Stanmere and back this evening, and nobody the wiser."
Spencer dined frugally, saying that his brother had gone to bed in consequence of a bad headache, and that he must not be disturbed. Then he threw a light dust coat over his grey morning dress, which he had not troubled to change, and drove to Victoria street.
Fortune favoured him. There was a train now and one back at three minutes to ten, which would give him the best part of an hour at Stanmere. He was on the road now with a sense of security upon him that he had not felt for years. He no longer looked for enemies behind every bush or saw the threatening danger in every shadow.
"A little time longer and it will all be over," he told himself. "There will be no more skulking along like a thief in the night. Was anybody situated like this before! Once let me get Venner out of the way and—"
His spirits rose at the thought. The lights of Stanmere were before him now. As he crept along the terrace he could see that it was the dinner hour. The windows of the library were open and Spencer stepped in. The hall was clear, too, so that he could make his way up the stairs. He knew perfectly well which room Mary was in. He could enter and say all he had to say and go. Really, the thing was most absurdly easy after all. Mary was—
He paused. Mary stood there in the corridor. She seemed to fall; she clapped her hands to her eyes and called out. It appeared as if she really could see. There was a rustling from the hall as Spencer sprang down the stairs and into the black throat of the night again by the way that he had come..... He stood there panting, sick and dizzy for the moment.
"It is to be," he gasped. "I can't fight against a fate like mine."
The presses were gathering up steam in the Record office, the chief of the great paper sat quietly in his office as if he had come down like any other respectable citizen straight after his dinner. There were no traces of a recent adventure about him. He was giving Dick some directions in his most clear and lucid manner.
"I fancy that is all," he said. "Well, what is it, Mr. Fisher?"
The editor came in with some copy in his hand. He looked annoyed and angry with somebody.
"The most astounding thing," he said. "Really, sir, you will have to get rid of Irvine. I am afraid he has been drinking again. He has just come in with a report that you, you, sir, have been nearly done to death in your own bedroom in Cambria Square. When I told him you were here he said that he had seen the body, that the police were already on the track of the would-be assassin."
"And it's the truth," a protesting voice in the doorway said. "If Mr. Spencer is

here—oh, Heavens, I'm mad. I'll never touch a drop of anything again. And yet I could swear—"
The reporter paused, and his own white face was reflected by the deadly pallor of Spencer's features. The latter turned to Dick helplessly.
"Dear lad," he whispered. "Try and think for me. It's one of my mental attacks. My mind has quite gone for a moment."

L. — FIXING THE TIME.

Spencer turned and looked from one to the other of the excited group in the most benign manner. It was quite clear that he was outside himself for the moment. It was equally true that the reporter Irvine was speaking from personal knowledge.
"It's real enough," he said, with a gasp. "I didn't know Mr. Spencer was here, so I was going to call upon him at Cambria Square. He helps me sometimes."
"Not worth mentioning, Irvine," Spencer said, coming back to himself with a start. The benign look had faded from his face, leaving a stony terror behind. "Well!"
"Well, sir, I heard one of the servants yell out something about murder. She was standing by a bedroom door, and I looked in. There was a commotion somewhere downstairs and a policeman came up. And there on the bed I saw —I saw—"
Irvine paused. Fisher jogged his elbow impatiently.
"I saw Mr. Spencer," the reporter gasped. "I would have sworn to him anywhere. And yet it can't be, because there is Mr. Spencer before me. . . . I can't make it out."
Dick stood there quietly waiting for his employer to speak.
Spencer's lips were twitching horribly, but no sound came from them.
"Can't you tell us anything, sir?" Dick urged.
"Better get back home," Spencer forced himself to say at last. "I fear, very much fear, that Irvine is not entirely wrong. I might have expected something like this?"
He pushed his way out of the office like a blind man, closely followed by Dick. He would have nobody else. Fisher and Irvine had their own work to do.
Out in Fleet street Spencer turned and placed himself entirely in Dick's hands.
"For Heaven's sake tell me what to do," he said. "I am absolutely dazed. Act for yourself. The truth can no longer be concealed."
Dick settled the matter by calling the first hansom that passed. They found a small knot of people excitedly discussing what they knew of the mystery in Cambria Square. Mr. Spencer, the great newspaper proprietor and philanthropist had been foully murdered in his bedroom by some miscreant who had succeeded in making his escape. It was fortunate that none of the

crowd recognised Spencer as he pushed through.
Two policemen in uniform and a plainclothes inspector had taken possession of the flat. They had got all they could out of the frightened servants when Spencer entered. He was still very pale and agitated, but he was himself now.
"And who may you be, sir?" the inspector asked. "Why, bless my soul, I—"
He paused, astonished, as well he might; making due allowance for physical changes, the inspector seemed to be speaking to the very man that he had left in extremis in the next room.
"I am Mr. Spencer," was the reply. "Can I do anything for you?"
"Indeed you can, sir. Will you please come this way? I daresay it will be quite simple when the matter is explained, but up to the present I am puzzled. I can make nothing of the servants, who seem to have lost their wits altogether."
Spencer, followed by Dick, entered the bedroom where the outrage had taken place. Stephen Gay lay on the bed there, his face turned upwards, and apparently dead. From the left breast a little red moisture oozed.
"Why, it's the man in the square," Dick cried, "it's the man who tried to kill you the night that you and I first met, sir."
The inspector started. He was getting to something definite at last. Dick realised his indiscretion. Goodness only knows what mischief he had done. But there lay the very man who played so strange a part in that night adventure in Cambria Square a few weeks ago.
"This man has been found thus in your rooms, sir," the inspector said. "Will you be good enough to tell us, in the first place, who he is?"
It was a long time before Spencer made any reply. His gaze slowly travelled round the room to the face of the dead man, and then slowly back again to the Inspector. He appeared to be pre-occupied. The policeman asked the question again sharply.
"He was my brother," Spencer said quietly. "You have only to look at the likeness to see that."
The Inspector nodded. So far the ground was clear enough. That the living and the dead were brothers, nobody could possibly doubt. But there was bad blood between them. The young man who had come in with Mr. Spencer seemed to know all about that.
"I think we had better sit down and talk it over, gentlemen," the Inspector suggested. "My name is Ridgway; I am sorry, but my duty is very plain. This gentleman here—thank you, sir—Mr. Stevenson, suggested just now that there was bad blood between the parties. He said something about the poor gentleman in the next room and an attempt to murder."
"I have no recollection of it," Spencer said, fervently.
Dick sat there moodily silent. But for his outburst that point would never have come to light. But he had been startled out of himself for the moment. And what Spencer said was quite correct. He had quite forgotten that eventful night

in the square. Dick recollected the strategy he had been compelled to use to find his employer's address. And when they met the next day in the Record office Mr. Spencer did not recognise him in the least.

"I am waiting for you to speak, sir," Ridgway said, pointedly.

"If you know anything, do not conceal it," Spencer said, in a shaking voice. "There has been misery enough already over the concealment of facts. Don't get yourself into trouble, Dick."

Dick told his story. Ridgway listened with critical interest, Spencer in blank astonishment. He was hearing all this for the first time. Not that he doubted the truth of it for a moment, for he was quite alive to his own mental lapses. Even now it was as if Dick were recalling some almost forgotten dream. Ridgway looked very grave.

"This is a very awkward business," he said. "If you like to say anything, Mr. Spencer, you may. On the whole, I should recommend that you consult your solicitor."

"In other words, you suspect me of the crime," Spencer said. "As I am absolutely innocent as a child, I have nothing to conceal. You want to know if there was bad blood between my brother and myself. In reply to that I may tell you I went in fear of my life. He gave me fair warning that he would kill me if he could. And at one time he would have kept his word."

"One moment, sir," Ridgway interrupted. "What do you mean by the expression 'at one time'?"

"I mean that my brother quite recently changed his mind. I don't mean that he changed his views or anything of that kind, but he made a discovery by means of which he could torture and frighten me in such a way that a threat of vengeance had no terrors by comparison. He found me out, and told me so quite callously. He was the kind of man to enjoy that kind of thing. He proposed to take up his quarters with me so that he could see the sport, as he called it, and I had to bow to his wishes."

"And this little scheme of revenge, sir?" Ridgway suggested.

"Is part of my secret, and has nothing to do with the case," Spencer said firmly. "For years I have been at work on a certain plan which is very near success. What it is, and what desperate expedient I had to resort to in order to bring it about will never be known to the public or yourself—which is much the same thing. That desperate expedient is the cause of the whole trouble. But I am going to say nothing about that. As to the rest, I am quite prepared to speak freely."

Ridgway shrugged his shoulders significantly.

"As you will," he said. "But all this mystery is slightly—"

"Harmful to myself. Quite so. Well, my brother came here yesterday. He was penniless and desperate, his only possession being a silver watch worth a few shillings—"

"I know that, sir. I shall have something to say about that watch presently. Go on—"

"I told the servants that my brother had come home unexpectedly from abroad. It was one of the little fictions that people use on these occasions. I found him in clothes. His stay, I gathered, was indefinite. He had breakfast and luncheon to-day, at which meal he had far too much wine. He went to dress for dinner, and, I presume, had some brandy in his room, for he was fast asleep on the bed. It was the last time I saw him alive. I had my own dinner and went out, and that is all I know."

"You had some sort of a quarrel, didn't you?" Ridgway asked. "Didn't you say to the deceased, or didn't he say to you, that he would kill you if you betrayed him?

"I believe there was something of the kind," Spencer admitted, thoughtfully. "My brother said that. I cut him short because the servants were within hearing. As soon as I dined I went out."

"Can you tell me what time you went out?"

"It was about half-past eight. I had a little private business to do that took me an hour or more, and then I took a cab as far as the Record office. I was not back at the house in the meantime, and I heard nothing of the affair until it was told me by one of my own reporters. If there is any chance of fixing the time of the murder—"

"That has been done for us," Ridgway interrupted. "The crime was committed at twenty-eight minutes past nine exactly. There is no doubt about that."

Spencer nodded. His mind was far away for the moment. At the hour mentioned by Ridgway with such positive assurance he was standing in the corridor at Stanmere, watching Mary in her white gown, and the gleam of her golden hair on her shoulders. Perhaps there was a way out of it yet, but the publicity could not be avoided now.

"How did you fix the time so exactly?" Dick asked.

Ridgway took a parcel carefully from his pocket. He opened it and laid on the table before him a silver watch that had apparently been damaged by some accident.

"Mr. Spencer was just saying that his brother had nothing in the world but a silver watch worth a few shillings," he said. "This is the watch. I took it out of the dead man's watch pocket to-night—the pocket on the left side over his heart. You can see where the assassin's knife shivered the glass and the cheap flimsy works on its way to the heart, so great was the force of the blow. I find that the watch is more or less fully wound, and appears to be in going order. The hands stopped at twenty-eight minutes past nine, which seems to me conclusive evidence as to the hour of the crime."

Then there was no more to be said on that point. Dick turned to Mr. Spencer.

"The Inspector is doing no more than his duty," he said. "At the same time it is

utterly ridiculous to imagine that Mr. Spencer had anything to do with the deed of violence. I am aware that he has admitted that there was bad blood between his brother and himself."
"I beg your pardon," Ridgway said significantly. "It was you who brought that out, sir."
"I suppose I did," Dick said, a little abashed. "But it would have been my plain duty to do so in any case. It seems to me that the watch is going to save us a great deal of trouble. Putting aside the absurd suggestion that a man would have lured his brother under his own roof to make away with him, we have the important question of time settled. Mr. Spencer, will you tell Inspector Ridgway where you were at about half-past nine to-night?"
Spencer looked up vaguely. His mind had gone wandering off in quite another direction. It was some little time before he caught the full significance of the question. At that very minute he had been at Stanmere. But there were reasons why he could not say so, reasons why he could not prove it. And in any case it did not make matters better for him.
"I was engaged on exceedingly private personal business," he said.
"But surely you can well prove an alibi," Dick cried, "it could not have been business of so private a nature that you could not bring witnesses to prove that."
Spencer shook his head in a kind of bland obstinacy.
"I can say nothing," he said. "My lips are sealed. I utterly decline to say more."
Inspector Ridgway picked up the watch and restored it to his pocket. He had no more questions to ask for the present. They would keep for the inquest to-morrow. Meanwhile he had locked and sealed up the room where the dead man lay. Dick waited for his companion to speak; perhaps Spencer would confide in him. But he sat there looking into the fire, and when Dick ventured to speak he bid him hastily to hold his tongue and go away.

LI. — AN EYE-WITNESS.

Von Wrangel came down to Stanmere by the early train with a fresh set of instruments in his pocket and the firm resolve that to-night should see his operation successfully through. He burst into the breakfast-room at Shepherd's Spring to find Molly having breakfast alone.
"Where is Dick?" he demanded. "Command the sluggard to leave his bed immediately."
Molly explained that Dick had not come back from London the previous night. Tom had gone off to town on some mysterious errand and Molly was left entirely alone.
"I am most melancholy," she said. "Actually I am reading the paper at breakfast, a thing that I never remember doing in my life before. You shall

take me for a walk presently, Baron. After that you shall go and cure Mary, and we shall live together happily ever after. Why, what is this?"

Molly put her untasted coffee down and stared at the paper with vivid interest. Von Wrangel watched her with a smile. Something to do with the fashions, he thought.

"Extraordinary!" Molly cried. "There has been a man murdered at the flat of Mr. Spencer in Cambria Square. At first it was thought it was Mr. Spencer himself, but it turns out to have been his brother. It appears that there is a most amazing likeness between them. Murdered in bed, Baron, and nobody knows who did it. When Mr. Spencer was out the assassin actually crept into the bedroom and—"

"Give it me," Von Wrangel said hoarsely. "Give it me. I—I beg your pardon, but this is really dreadful. Lady Stanmere must know of this."

"How can it interest her?" Molly asked.

"Because that dead man is her son Stephen, and Mr. Spencer, as you call him, is Paul Gay, Lord Stanmere. You would have found all this out in time, so there is no reason to conceal the truth any longer."

Molly murmured her astonishment. Things were growing bright very swiftly.

"Then the mysterious stranger in Cambria Square was Mr. Spencer's own brother," she cried. "But you know nothing of that, so I had better tell you Dick's strange adventure....... Now you understand. But why did Stephen Gay have such a deadly hatred of his brother?"

"For one thing, because he fancied Paul had betrayed him to some enemies of his. But there is another reason that I cannot tell you yet. If Dick tells the story of that amazing meeting in Cambria Square to the police, as he is bound to do, there will be trouble for Paul Spencer. It will be pretty sure to connect him with the crime."

"But he could not possibly have done anything so dreadful!"

"Of course not. How these two men came to be under the same roof baffles me. It is quite the strangest part of a strange story. If necessary, I shall have to speak."

"Baron," Molly cried. "I believe you could say something of the mystery. There is a look in your eyes—"

"Of course I could. I know the actual criminal. Do you recollect that night when we saw those strange men in the Warren? They were members of a secret society and they were after Stephen Gay. He had betrayed the cause they had belonged to most dishonourably. For years they have been seeking him. More than once I saved his life, but he was so desperate and reckless. I might have saved him now had he only followed my instructions. But these men were untiring as they were remorseless. They had their work to do, and they went about it in a fashion all their own."

"But if you had put the police upon their track—"

"Quite useless. You see I knew these men, and that gave me an advantage. If I had scattered them, their places would have been taken by others not personally familiar to me, and my task would have been doubled. Well, they have got the best of me, and the vendetta is ended."

"It is very dreadful for Lady Stanmere," Molly said sadly.

Von Wrangel, in his innermost heart, was not so sure of that. Lady Stanmere knew that the blow must fall some time; the sword had been hanging over her head for years. She was sitting in the drawing-room over her everlasting knitting as Von Wrangel came in. She gave one glance at him and her hands fell in her lap.

"Tell me all about it," she said. "I see that it has happened at last."

"I shall never make a diplomatist," Von Wrangel murmured. "My dear lady, you know how deeply I feel for you. And yet, and yet, it was inevitable. I have brought a paper over so that you may read for yourself. There is an extraordinary complication here."

Lady Stanmere felt for her glasses with trembling hands, but outwardly she was quite calm. This was but another drop in the full measure or her sorrows, but Mary was left. It was her balm of consolation. She read the whole long report with a seeming calm that aroused Von Wrangel's admiration.

"It is an extraordinary case altogether," Lady Stanmere said, alter a long pause. "Of course the Mr. Spencer is my son Paul. I deemed him to be dead long ago. I began to imagine that he was a kind of guardian, but really my head is quite confused. What manner of man is Paul?"

"He is rich and respected," Von Wrangel explained. "My dear lady, there is a complication here that even you have no knowledge of as yet. Perhaps, on the whole, I had better leave the proper person to tell you. But it is pretty sure that Paul will be accused of his brother's murder."

"But that in too horrible," Lady Stanmere cried. "We know better."

"Of course we do, and I shall be able to explain if necessary. Still, if there are no traces to be found of Hengel and the rest, my story will be regarded with suspicion and ridicule. And the worst of the whole thing is, we cannot avoid the scandal that has for so long hung over this house. If Paul is charged by the police, the whole thing must come out."

Lady Stanmere bowed her head wearily.

"If it must, it must," she said. "The wild blood in the race is bound to assert itself. I have carried so many sorrows that one more makes no difference. Still, it is good to know that one of my boys, at any rate, has come back to the path of honour again."

"Paul was never more than wild and headstrong," Von Wrangel said, thoughtfully. "And his father turned him out of the house, you remember. You are going to be proud of him yet. When he comes back to you—"

"He will never come back to me. After all these years—oh! it is impossible.

Von Wrangel, the matter must be concealed from Mary for the present."
Von Wrangel was of the same opinion. He wondered what Mary would think when the whole truth came to be told, as told it must be before long.
"She will be brave enough," he said. "And yet there is a thing here as obvious as the dazzling conjuring tricks when once they are explained. As to the other matter, you may simply leave it in my hands. I should very much like to see my patient."
Mary was having her breakfast in her room and would be down presently. She came after a time very quiet and subdued, but with a pleasant smile on her face that was good to see. Von Wrangel crossed over and gave her an encouraging pat on the shoulder.
"You are a marvel of patience," he said. "Many patients would have given their nurses no end of trouble. But there are only a few hours more to wait. And when you can see—"
"My dear, kind doctor," Mary said quietly. "I can see now."
She made the remark in an even tone of voice, with just a touch of gladness in it. Lady Stanmere had folded up her knitting and crept quietly from the room. Just for an instant Von Wrangel had glared uneasily at his patient, but there was no cause for alarm.
"What do you mean by that?" he asked. "Speak freely; we are quite alone."
"Yes, I heard my grandmother leave the room. It was last night as I lay in bed with nobody near. I wanted to be alone you see, because my thoughts were pleasant and I liked to have them all to myself. It was about dinner-time, and I fancied I heard my father calling to me. I got out of bed and went into the corridor. I fell over something and the bandage slipped from my eyes. And then I saw the corridor quite plainly with the eye that you have operated upon, and I saw my father looking the same, and yet so different from the time when last I had seen him. He seemed so good and so noble, and his eyes were shining; the old fear was gone from his face. . . . And then I cried out, and he vanished, and others came, and I said nothing for fear it was fancy. But it was not fancy, I am sure that I was not dreaming."
There was a queer, tense expression on Von Wrangel's face.
"How was your father dressed?" he asked eagerly.
"In a grey suit, with a red tie," Mary said promptly. "But what struck me was the wonderful change in him; he was softened and improved. If only I had not called out!"
"Had you any idea what time it was?"
"Well, yes. The chimes of the big corridor clock struck the quarter after nine just before I heard the voice calling to me. I recollect that distinctly."
Von Wrangel nodded. All this coincided with what he had hoped for and expected. And Paul Spencer often dressed in grey, with a red tie. The little German's expression changed to a look of pain, a dread of giving pain to

others.
"I am going to test you," he said, "and test you again in the presence of credible witnesses. Now, let me remove the bandage from the eye that has been under my care for a few moments. You are to look at the table and tell me what you see there. It is only to be for an instant."
He removed the bandage, and replaced it after the lapse of a few moments. Mary smiled.
"Flowers," she said. "A great bunch of flowers, of early chrysanthemums, and a few letters and some coloured silks plaited into a kind of skein. And there is old Williams trimming the lawn. What do you think of that?"
"I think it is wonderful," Von Wrangel said unsteadily. "Let me try again. Now, once more. Now."
They tried again and again with every kind of success. Finally Von Wrangel replaced the bandage for good and all. His fingers trembled slightly.
"We will repeat that this afternoon," he said. "And now, my dear young lady, I am going to ask you a great favour. Would you mind my not finishing my operation for a few days. It may seem strange to you, but the mere fact of the postponement may be the means of conferring a lasting benefit upon one who is very dear to you."
Mary hesitated, but only for a moment. Then she smiled.
"More mystery," she said, "and yet more mystery. My dear, good, kind doctor, I would make any sacrifice for those I love."

LII. — SCOTCHED.

Three candles in a silver branch sufficed to make a spot of light in the dingy sitting-room where Martlett spent his evenings. Half buried in an armchair, he was poring over some old black-letter manuscript, the text of which puzzled him. Next to his delight in finding things out, Martlett most liked to be puzzled.
He had been digging at intricate cases until he was as rusty as a village sexton, and yet, after all these years of delving and burrowing into the old manuscripts and old deeds, the keenness of his clear eyes was not dimmed in the slightest. He was beaten for the moment now; he placed the book on his knee to think the matter out.
A servant as old and dried up as himself came in with the information that somebody had come to see him on pressing business. Before he could frame an excuse Von Wrangel came in, followed by Seymour. There was a slight frown on Martlett's face.
"No use looking like that," Von Wrangel said. "You can put your black-letters up for to-night, you old fox. What have we here? An hour book by Elzar of 1594. A second impression."

"It isn't a second impression at all," Martlett said tartly. "Much you know about it. That is a first impression if ever I saw one. I picked it up in Drury Lane Court, and I wouldn't take a hundred pounds for it at this moment."
"There is no border on the title page," Von Wrangel retorted.
The argument waxed warm. Seymour coughed suggestively. Von Wrangel came to earth again.
"Some day I will show you," he said. "Meanwhile to business. Being so fine a business man myself, I should be ashamed to be led away. This is my friend Mr. Seymour—Mr. Martlett, the eminent lawyer. Do you see the candelabra, Seymour. It has the first James letter and the London hallmark, and a millionaire collector offered Martlett two thousand pounds for it. Ah, there are worse things than being an old family lawyer."
"Infinitely worse," Martlett said dryly. "To have an uncontrollable tongue, for instance."
"True," said Von Wrangel, not in the least, annoyed. "Now let us to our muttons. I have caught a specimen to-night, Martlett. Attracted by the light, he flew into the small conservatory at Stanmere. My young friend here can identify him. In other words, I have Horace Venner by the heels, and Seymour says he knows enough to hang him."
Martlett nodded. He had forgotten all about his black-letters by this time.
"You have met the man before?" he asked.
"Certainly," Seymour explained. "I found him outside the terrace at Stanmere to-night. I was waiting for my friends the Stevensons, and I struck a light for my cigarette. That fellow, for some reason or another, was hiding close by. I saw his face clearly as he saw mine. He bolted with sheer terror, and I after him. I caught him in the small conservatory."
"At the moment I was conducting my operation," Von Wrangel struck in. "The noise quite startled me, and I partially failed."
"No serious damage, I hope?" Martlett asked, with unusual eagerness.
"Not at all. I do not fail. It is all a matter of time. I have to wait for another instrument, and the thing is done. Go on, my young friend."
"I came face to face with that man," Seymour resumed. "There could be no possible disguise any longer. I could hang that fellow."
"You could prove a murder against him?" Martlett asked.
"Assuredly, given time and the aid of the San Francisco police. I kept my man there until I could send for Von Wrangel; I told him what I have told you, and he seems to think that you would be glad of this information."
Martlett winked once or twice swiftly. His eyes were gleaming with an eager light. Von Wrangel was regarding him curiously.
"But why do you suggest that I could use this information?" he asked.
"Because I know everything, old fox," Von Wrangel cried. "I discovered it for myself. Talk about being blind, why there is nobody blinder than myself. What

was Paul Spencer, otherwise Paul Gay, so fearful of besides being in the power of someone who knew some shameful secret of his? And who might that blackmailer be better than his old valet, the rascal Venner? And how to hoodwink Venner? Oh, it was a great plan, old fox, and reflected great credit on you. Stephen was out of the way."
"I beg your pardon," Martlett said stiffly. "It was no suggestion of mine."
"Of course not. All you could do was to show its possibility. And when your client said he had half a mind to try it, you gravely warned him of the risks. I understand."
A ghost of a smile hovered round Martlett's lips for a moment.
"All this is beside the point," he said. "We will admit, for the sake of argument, that my client, Paul Spencer, or Gay, as you please, desired to keep Venner at arm's length. He may or may not have adopted a neat and ingenious plan to do so. At any rate, we want to stop that fellow's mouth. If you can show us a way to do so, we shall be exceedingly grateful."
"I am here for that purpose," Seymour said quietly.
"Good! Where is the interesting specimen alluded to?"
"At present he is locked up on your confidential clerk's office," Von Wrangel said. "He cannot possibly get out of the window, which is a skylight, and the door is lined with iron. Besides, I don't think that the fellow would do so if he could, he is in such a pitiable state of collapse. I have told my young friend, Seymour, certain points of the case, and he tells me he is in a position to keep Venner's mouth shut for all time."
"I am quite certain of it," Seymour said. "But I am going to ask you one question, Mr. Martlett. Was that little indiscretion of your client's connected with San Francisco?"
Martlett wriggled uneasily on his chair. All this was very irregular to the strictly trained legal mind that specially abhors anything in the way of leading questions. Von Wrangel burst out impetuously. His was no game of judicial chess to be played out over a course of sittings.
"Come out of the hole, old fox," he cried; "come out of the hole. You are going to be astonished presently. We can't scotch this snake unless you help us a bit. Was it San Francisco?"
"It was," Martlett admitted. "But really, gentlemen, I must protest—"
"Against the betraying of a client's confidence, eh?" Von Wrangel laughed.
"There was a quarrel over some accounts, and revolvers were produced. The man on the other side was a notorious bully, and, moreover, had a bad repute. He got the worst of that encounter, and was shot by Paul Gay, who left him for dead in his tent. Is that a fact?"
Martlett nodded as if the information had been extracted from him like a tooth by an unskilful dentist. It was very irregular indeed.
"I think I had better take up the case here," Seymour said. "There had been a

great deal of violence in San Francisco for some time owing to some very bitter strikes and the like. It was a time when every man had to look to himself. If Gay had not shot down Miller, Miller would have killed him. There was a third partner, who was away at the time—a man named Maxwell."

Martlett nodded again. This was decidedly interesting.

"Maxwell was a great friend of Gay. The vigilance committee was after Gay, who fled with the crime of murder on his soul. Miller was dead, and a bit of gold dust he had about him had been stolen. This is the secret Venner holds, and upon which he would have traded heavily, only your ingenious plan—whatever it was—prevented him. Venner had not long been discharged from the employ of Mr. Paul Gay, and he wanted revenge. Then began the game of hide-and-seek, which has not finished yet. Correct me if I am wrong."

"I deny nothing," Martlett said, still cautiously. "Let us assume that everything is correct. But you have not shown me yet how to get Venner out of the way."

"I am coming to that part presently," Seymour went on. "I want my friend Maxwell, for whom I worked some years, to be present. Maxwell is in Paris at the Invalides hotel. If he were here now he would absolutely rehabilitate the character of your client."

"You mean that he might find some loophole for escape? Perhaps the American laws—"

"Laws have nothing to do with it," Seymour said, with some sign of impatience. "Maxwell will be able to prove that your client has absolutely nothing to fear. I can go further than that, and say that your client is absolutely innocent. If Maxwell were here—"

Martlett rose to his feet excitedly.

"I have not another word of protest to make," he said. "You have been right from the first, and I am wrong. But you must not lose sight of Venner. It is imperative that that rascal should be kept safe. There are interests at stake here far greater than you imagine. If I could see Mr. Maxwell, am I at liberty to repeat all that you have said?"

"Why not?" Seymour asked. "The story must be made public some time."

"Then I go to Paris in the morning," Martlett declared. "I will go and see your friend Maxwell, and I hope to induce him to return with me to England. My dear sir, it is impossible to over-estimate the importance of what you have told me to-night. I have not been quite so wise over the business as I had imagined."

"The same as the black-letter manuscript," Von Wrangel chuckled.

Martlett ignored the challenge. There was an air of excitement about him quite foreign to the man. He paced up and down the room scratching his dry chin and muttering to himself. Finally he came up standing and turned to Seymour.

"You have a very slippery man to deal with," he said. "If he gives you the go-by—"

"He won't," Seymour said coolly. "I shall know how to deal with him. I shall send him away to-night to the kennel where he lives with the absolute certainty that he will come to me when I whistle for him in the morning. I can hang the man; I can hold that in terror over him. We have Venner quite safe. It was only to please Von Wrangel that we went through the farce of locking him up in your clerk's room."

"Then go and send him off," Von Wrangel suggested.

Seymour went off in the direction of the outer office. Venner was perched on a high stool, a picture of the most hopeless, abject misery. His white soddened face was quivering with terror; he had bitten his nails down in a grinding, mechanical way during the half-hour that had seemed to him a small eternity. He looked up fawningly in Seymour's face.

"What are you going to do with me?" he whined.

"For the present, nothing," Seymour replied. "You need not look so pleased. I am going to let you go on the condition that you come here every morning at 10 o'clock to report yourself and to see if your presence here is needed. If you serve us faithfully and well, I shall hold my hand. You did the world a service by ridding it of a scoundrel, so that I do not feel any trouble on the score of justice. But if you play me false, by nightfall everything shall be in the hands of the police. Now you can go."

Venner looked up with abject amazement. He did not seem to grasp the meaning of it all. He was free to depart without further questions being asked. These people meant to let him down easily. If he could only go straight and tell the truth for once!

"Do you mean to say that I am free to—to—" he stammered.

"That is exactly what I desire to convey to your intelligence. Go! Be off! Don't pollute the air that honest men breathe any longer. And if you fail to keep your part of the bond—"

Venner broke out into a torrent of protestations. By all that he held most sacred he would not do anything of the kind. He would do anything in the world that Mr. Seymour required. He crept out of the house and down the street in a curiously ill-balanced frame of mind. He looked like saving his rascally skin, but at the same time he saw that once glittering fortune disappearing into the future. He had built up the most extravagant plans on that.

"You have got rid of him?" Martlett asked.

Seymour explained carelessly what had happened. Venner was to report himself daily, and he had not the slightest doubt that he would not fail to do so. Martlett nodded, helped himself to a rarely-smoked second cigar, and plunged into the pages of Bradshaw.

LIII. — CAUSE CELÈBRE.

The Cambria Square murder was at once recognised as material for a great sensation. There had been more vulgar crimes and more mysterious ones, but there was here all the making of the kind of drama that the soul of the modern journalist loves.
In the first place Mr. Paul Spencer had been more or less a fascinating personage. He was supposed to have laid the nucleus of his fortune abroad; he had come back to England, where he was at once established as a great philanthropist of the best kind. He was the sort of man who did good by stealth, and blushed to find it fame. His peculiarities were dwelt upon—his passion for privacy, the fact that most people outside his own household were only allowed to see him in the semi-darkness, all were told in the newspaper tale. There was something strange about the man.
The poetic side was supplied by his absolute devotion to his blind daughter. Then again, there was the fact that he had a brother exactly like himself. Then came the still more startling discovery that Mr. Paul Spencer was really Mr. Paul Gay, or, in other words Lord Stanmere, the only remaining son of the eccentric peer of that name who had committed suicide after becoming entangled in some cheap political conspiracy inspired by a foreign league of patriots.
Why, therefore, had the man hidden his identity and lived at Cambria Square, when be might have taken possession of a splendid property and become a man of the country? People recalled to mind the fact that there had been a second Gay who had brought a good deal of scandal on the family name and had subsequently disappeared altogether.
Of course, the murdered man was the missing brother. People who had known the family long ago were hunted up by busy reporters, and forgotten facts dragged to light. The amazing resemblance between the brothers was commented on, and as a problem the mystery was solved. All the same, people waited for the inquest with breathless interest. The whole truth would have to come out then.
And Paul Spencer would have to drag himself out into the light of day. With the broad glare of publicity upon him, it was hopeless to expect to hide from Venner any longer. Everything would have to be laid bare, and the work of his life absolutely ruined.
Worst of all, he had nobody to fall back upon. Von Wrangel seemed to have disappeared upon one of his erratic, mysterious errands, and Martlett had gone to Paris leaving no word behind as to where he was to be found, or when he would come back to London again.
There was only Dick, and he had been subpoenaed to give evidence at the inquest, which would merely tend to make the police case against Spencer blacker still. Dick remained the night at Cambria Square, and did his best to keep up the drooping spirits of his companions.

But to the man of vivid imagination the anticipation of trouble is always greater than the realisation. At the end of the second day's examination Spencer felt as if the bitterness of death were past. In the light of his own evidence he only wondered why no warrant had been applied for his arrest. But the inquiry would be closed on the morrow, and then the blow would fall.
On the whole, the police would have been justified. There was a blood feud, or something like it, between the two brothers. Dick had seen part of the drama enacted, and his evidence told greatly against the man who, in the eye of the public, was already on his trial on the capital charge. Spencer had elected to give evidence, much against the wish of the coroner, and he only succeeded in making bad worse. There had been a long feud between the dead man and himself. His brother had come to Cambria Square, where he had not been invited. He had got possession of a certain secret, but what that secret was the witness declined to say. They had quarrelled in the flat and the witness had gone out soon after that. Pressed to say where he had been, he declined to make any statement. That was no business of anybody's but his own, and he refused to go any further. There was no pretence at an alibi. The conclusion came to by the listeners was that Spencer had never left the house at all.
He finished his evidence at last; he looked fearfully round the court as if he expected to meet the eye of Horace Venner; not that it much mattered, not that anything much mattered now. He only wanted to get home again. The scandal had come at last, but not at all in the way that it had been expected. Scandals seldom do.
The story was reaching far and wide. It had got down to Stanmere, where it was studied as eagerly in the servants' hall as it was in the drawing-room. Goss was the only one who did not seem in the least astonished. But he knew certain facts concealed from the rest of the domestic staff.
Lady Stanmere read the evidence with mixed feelings. It was a sorry ending to a sorry business. Not that she believed for one moment that one son of hers had the blood of another on his soul. Still, Lady Stanmere sorely needed advice at this moment. She telegraphed for Martlett, only to be told that he had gone to Paris. Even Von Wrangel would have been something at this juncture.
There was nobody but Mary, from whom the facts were carefully concealed, and Nurse Cecilia. The latter came down to the drawing-room with a copy of 'The Standard' in her hand.
"Have you read all this, my lady?" she asked.
Lady Stanmere had read every line of it in the Telegraph. She could not understand it at all. She was quite sure that Paul had nothing to do with the crime. One of those dreadful secret societies was at the bottom of it all. Cecilia listened with well disguised impatience.
"It is no time to speculate," she said, her eyes gleaming. "I have tried to look at this matter as if I were one of the people—one of the jury. Mr. Paul stands in a

terrible position. And everybody seems to have deserted him just at the moment when he needs friends. If you were to tell Miss Mary—"
"Not for worlds," Lady Stanmere cried. "A shock at the present moment might be serious. And—and she is all that I have to care for now. I try to be calm and contained, Cecilia, but if you only knew. If I could tell what to do—if I could make some sacrifice!"
The knitting fell from the trembling hands. Nurse Cecilia walked away to Mary's bedroom. She marvelled at the blindness that seemed to have fallen on everybody save Von Wrangel and herself. Mary was sitting by a table arranging flowers.
"Miss Mary," she said carelessly, "are you quite sure you were correct as to what you said about seeing your father the other night? After a long period of blindness—"
"But I was not blind, Cecilia," Mary smiled. "I saw my father distinctly. He looked better and nobler than he used to do, but I recognised him in that brief instant. And he was in trouble; it was easy to read that much from the expression of his face. I believe that he came here to have a few words with me in secret, only I was alarmed, and he ran away. There are reasons why he cannot come to Stanmere, as he has so often told me. But he was here that night."
"Did you tell this to Herr Von Wrangel?"
"Certainly I did. And he tested my sight to see if such a thing was possible. He proved to himself that it was. And then he said a curious thing. He asked me to postpone the operation for a day or two in the interests of one whom I loved. It sounded like more mystery, but I asked no questions. I consented. And now you know as much of the matter as I do."
Cecilia knew a great deal more, but it was not her cue to say so. She stayed on chatting for a few minutes, but she had not the least idea what she was talking about. Here was a way out of the difficulty at last, a way, perhaps, attended by further scandal, but sufficient to clear Paul Spencer of the terrible charge hanging over him.
But why had not Von Wrangel moved in the matter? He knew the facts of the case better than she did. And the little German doctor seemed to be as much indifferent to what was going on as did Mr. Martlett. A happy thought came to Cecilia.
She would go up and see Martlett; she would follow him to Paris if necessary. Anything was better than the maddening inaction, to one of her quick temperament. She would get Mr. Martlett's address from the office and take the night boat to Calais.
But there was no necessity to do that. As she reached Lincoln's Inn she saw Mr. Martlett going in the direction of his office, with his hands behind his back, and apparently in an unusually tranquil frame of mind. Cecilia grasped

him by the arm vigorously.
"Ah," he said, "Nurse Cecilia. You look disturbed. I am just back from Paris. What is wrong?"
Cecilia proceeded to explain, breathlessly.
"Presently, presently," Martlett said. "Yes, I see the force of your discovery. Come back to me in an hour. I have a most pressing engagement at present, which is not entirely disconnected with the family you have such a high regard for. It is all coming right, my dear woman."
Cecilia sat down in the Embankment gardens with a strange feeling of relief. Martlett was never a man who committed himself, and if he said that everything was coming right he spoke from accurate knowledge. Meanwhile, Martlett entered his office, where Paul Spencer was waiting for him. The lawyer shook hands with his client in the most matter-of-fact way.
"So you seem to have been getting yourself into a fine mess," he said, "but there is one clear way out of it, and if you don't take it, I shall have to take it for you. I have been in Paris on your business. I have been hearing some wonderfully interesting details as to the private life of Mr. James Miller. You recollect James Miller?"
A shade passed over the face of the listener.
"I have cause to," he said. "It was the one act that has darkened my life. Why rake that old matter up now, Martlett?"
"Because it is absolutely necessary to do so, my dear fellow. And who do you suppose supplied me with all the details of that picturesque scoundrel's career? Why one Maxwell—"
"Maxwell? You don't mean to say that he is in Europe?"
"He was in Paris yesterday, and he is in London to-day. To go still further, he is very near; in fact, he is at the present moment sitting in the office of my clerk, and he is looking forward to the pleasure of an interview with you."
Spencer rose from his seat and hurried to the door. He seemed to have forgotten himself for the moment, forgotten everything in the wild desire for flight. By main force Martlett dragged him back again into his seat.
"You fool," he said contemptuously. "You have absolutely nothing to fear."
"Nemesis," Gay cried. "Nemesis. It has come at last; it always was inevitable."

LIV. — CROSS PURPOSES.

Lady Stanmere waited with patient resignation to see what was going to happen next. Fortunately there were no callers to worry her with idle curiosity or well-meant sympathy. The chatelaine of Stanmere had been a recluse for many years, alone with her sorrows, and almost forgotten by the world. She had less need of the world than ever now.
Meanwhile, life seemed to move on there as smoothly as ever. It seemed

impossible to connect that house with all its quiet beauty with a sensational tragedy. The sun beat down on the piled-up woods and the trim lawns, the deer dozed in the bracken, the rose garden was still in full fragrance. Goss had some questions to answer and some curiosity to satisfy in the way of reporters, whom he fenced off with his best episcopal manner.

Still, Mr. Martlett kept away, and Von Wrangel seemed to avoid the place. It was the third day before the latter came at length. He was a little quiet and subdued, but not quite so quiet as Lady Stanmere, engaged on her everlasting knitting.

"So you have found out that I am in trouble?" she said.

She did not look up, her hands were working restlessly. Von Wrangel looked round the perfectly-appointed drawing-room. He could conceive nothing more placid and restful. It was the very place to get rid of nerves and brain worries of all kinds.

"I have been doing all I can for you," Von Wrangel said. "My dear lady, you are very angry with me."

"I have been better pleased with you, I confess," Lady Stanmere said, without looking up from her work. "I am in great trouble."

"And I am sorry for you from the bottom of my heart."

"I am in great trouble, and nobody came near me. Even Martlett seems to have vanished; and there are so many things to think of. My unhappy boy must be buried here. But I suppose nobody has thought of that."

But Von Wrangel had thought of everything. He had taken the liberty of making all the necessary arrangements, or he would have been at Stanmere before. He was deeply sorry for the unhappy grey lady, who was the mother of so many sorrows. Much grief had bowed her down, but she had reached the limit of resignation now, and only waited for the end.

"It is a dreadful thing," she went on. "Of course, I had expected something like this. My unhappy boy was predestined for a violent death."

"For which you hold me more or less responsible?"

"No; you were merely an instrument. I have lived in daily expectation of something of this kind; I felt that fate had the blow in store for me. But I never dreamt that fate would give the blow such a cruel twist as this. Not that Paul is guilty—"

"Paul is absolutely innocent," Von Wrangel exclaimed. "To-morrow the inquest will be finished, and I shall give my evidence. I shall be in a position to tell the police a thing or two. Those shadows have been dogging Stephen for years. The result was inevitable. The assassin managed to get into the room in Paul's absence, and the rest you can imagine. But I have a witness who will settle the matter for all time."

"And who may that be," Lady Stanmere asked. "Oh, I am interested. After all, Paul is my own flesh and blood. They tell me he has lived a good life for years, and that he is rich and respected. In that case, why did he not come down here? Why did he not come and see his mother, who would have welcomed him with open arms? Here is a beautiful property, one of the best and richest in the country. And Paul is Lord Stanmere, though he calls himself Paul Spencer. Can you account for all this unnecessary mystery?"

It was by no means an unnecessary mystery, as Von Wrangel might have explained. But he had done too much by his tongue already, and besides the secret was not to be told. He shifted his ground a little.

"It is all going to be cleared up in a few days," he said. "And then I think you will recognise the fact that the succession to Stanmere is in good hands."

Von Wrangel went away, leaving Lady Stanmere with a vague sense of comfort. At any rate, it was good to know that her surviving son's good name was cleared, and that the time was coming when he could step into his property without any stain upon his honour. But why had he not come down before, why had he kept out of the way all these years? True, Stephen had been the eldest son, so that Paul had till recently nothing to expect from Stanmere, and was of comparatively small importance. But then he seemed to have atoned for his early wildness years ago, he had grown rich and respectable and prosperous, and with all his faults he had always professed to be fond of his mother.

And yet since she had first heard of his return from America, five years ago, she had not had one line from him. Her heart stirred within her as she thought of it all. She had Mary, to whom she had given all her affection, but it would be good to walk up the aisle of Stanmere Church on the arm of a son who could look the whole world in the face.

Perhaps it was coming. And Von Wrangel had said nothing as to the completion of his operation on Mary's eyes. He had put it off more or less unexpectedly a day or two before, and had hurried to London.

But the thing was uppermost in Von Wrangel's mind as he went through the house looking for Nurse Cecilia. Mary was out somewhere with Molly Stephenson, who openly bewailed the strange defection of her lover. Dick was in town, where he expected to remain for the moment. Nurse Cecilia was in the garden reading a letter when Von Wrangel found her.

"What is the matter with you?" he asked in his quick way. "Are you glad or sorry? Your face says glad, and your eyes say sorry. What is it?"

Cecilia turned to the speaker with an unsteady smile on her lips.

"I don't know," she said. "Many clever men say they do not understand women. That is not so very wonderful when women can't understand themselves. I am an enigma to myself, for instance. I was trying to solve the riddle when you came up."

"Through the medium of that letter, I suppose?"

"Precisely. It is fresh from my husband. Now you and I know the secret of the mystery that has so long surrounded Stanmere. There is no occasion for mystery any longer, since Mr. Stephen is dead."
"Don't forget that your husband still remains."
"I am coming to that," Cecilia said. "To hoodwink my husband all this elaborate plot has been necessary. It was quite justified, because it succeeded admirably. But Horace Venner found it out at last, and he was going to make himself rich over it. I was glad that he made his discovery too late. His claws have been clipped; his guilty knowledge was a lie. He is utterly beaten, and he has given up the game in despair and is going abroad. And he wants me to join him."
Von Wrangel nodded. He knew a great deal more of the business than Cecilia imagined.
"And being a woman, you are hesitating?" he asked.
"Well, yes. You see I loved that man at one time. I knew he was not good, but I hoped to reform him. And I have not forgotten that time."
"Then forget it at once," Von Wrangel said, vehemently. "I don't want to give you pain, but Venner is a scoundrel in grain. He could not help it. I know the history of that man's life. It is bad from start to finish. He would never keep to the straight path. If you go with him you march hand in hand with misery to the grave. You are embarked on a noble career where you are doing good. Why abandon it? and if your husband is sincere let him show it. Let him come to you in two years' time and prove the value of his words."
Cecilia removed the traces of tears from her dark eyes.
"You are right," she said. "I had not thought of that. I will write to Horace. And in the meantime I have others to think of."
Von Wrangel nodded significantly. He was eager enough now.
"Miss Mary," he said, "you must go and find her. Whether Lady Stanmere likes it or not, she must come to London with me this evening."
"I suppose it is impossible to keep her out of it?" Cecilia asked.
"Of course it is. The man whom we will call Paul Spencer for the nonce is exceedingly obstinate. He will not say where he was on the night of the murder. He was down here, of course. We know that he came; Miss Mary saw him. But he does not know as yet that she really saw him, hence he deems it quite useless to mention the circumstance. Miss Mary will go into the witness-box, and after hearing what I have to say, there will be no further question as to Paul's innocence."
Cecilia was turning the thing thoughtfully over in her mind.
"I dare say," she said. "But why didn't you complete the operation and make the thing assured?"
"Ah, you do not appreciate the subtleties of the legal mind. I should be very severely cross-examined as to whether the poor girl could see or not. Then I

should have to admit that I left my operation unfinished at a point where it was dubious to say how successful I should be. There is no doubt in my mind, but then it is possible that I might have failed. If I HAD failed, then Miss Mary's evidence would have been absolutely useless. If she had gone into the witness box BLIND, her evidence would have been worthless. No jury would have believed that she SAW, just for the correct psychological moment. But by leaving her as she is, we can prove that she can see, and that there has been no tampering with her sight. Do you understand what I mean?"
Cecilia understood quite clearly. She appreciated the thoughtful way in which Von Wrangel worked the matter out. At first she had regarded the whole thing as one of his wild vagaries. On other people's business the man was superb. It was only when he came to manage his own that he usually made so dismal a failure of it.
"You are wonderful," Cecilia cried. "I should never have thought of that."
"Perhaps not. Anyway, Miss Mary can see enough for our purpose. And directly she has given her evidence we will finish the operation. Only a day or two longer and everything will be made clear. I am under a heavy debt to the house, and I am trying to repay it. If I had never come here at all how different things might have been!"
It was nearly tea-time before Mary came in, her hands full of wild flowers. She seemed to be happy and gay enough. She was glad to see Von Wrangel again. He lifted the bandage from her eyes and held a small object up before them.
"Can you see this?" he asked.
"Pretty plainly," Mary cried. "It is a small pearl handled pocketknife with a silver name-plate on it. Herr Baron, when are you going to give me my sight back again?"
"I shall be glad to hear that also," Lady Stanmere said, quietly.
"To-morrow," Von Wrangel explained; "some time to-morrow. It will take place in London, where I have borrowed the operating-room of a famous surgeon friend of mine. Lady Stanmere must spare you for a few hours. You are going back to London with me this evening."
"More mystery?" Mary cried. "Is there never to be an end of it?"
"Mary is not going to London," Lady Stanmere said. "I have quite decided upon that."
"The operation takes place in London to-morrow, and the mystery ends at the same time," Von Wrangel said, with a flash of his eyes. "Once for all, and the last time, I am going to assert myself. Miss Mary goes to London with me. Within four-and-twenty hours more those eyes will be clear to read this mystery, which shall be made plain to ordinary intelligence."
"But surely," Lady Stanmere expostulated, "Mary has no need—"
"Miss Mary has every need. No, I cannot explain. You must be content to take

my word for it. Let Nurse Cecilia make all arrangements."
Lady Stanmere resisted no longer. She had no power to fight against Von Wrangel.
"Very well," she said, helplessly. "But you must bring her back again. Von Wrangel, you will give me your word of honor to bring her back again?"
Von Wrangel bent over the still grey figure and whispered in her ear.
"I will give you my word as to that," he murmured. "I will bring Mary back to-morrow night; aye, and I will bring back Paul, Lord Stanmere, as well."

LV. — FREE!

Paul Spencer, Lord Stanmere, stood facing Martlett like a man in a dream. It seemed to him that the clouds had gathered from all sides to overwhelm him. So this man had been hunting him, too, and had at length found him. He could fight no longer.
"If I must, I must," he said. "I knew Maxwell years ago. His mother lived near Stanmere. We were great friends at one time. We exchanged photographs. I have them at home now. And he used to come to England occasionally to see that eccentric old mother of his and bring me news of Stanmere. But I killed a man who was his partner, you see."
"By your own showing Jim Miller was a scoundrel," Martlett observed.
"That made no difference. Maxwell was on the vigilance committee. I shot Miller in what was little less than a vulgar brawl, and I had to fly. As San Francisco was at that moment, my life would have paid the penalty had I stayed. Even now I am liable to be extradited and hanged. From that day to this I have seen nothing of Maxwell."
"Nevertheless, he has been looking for you everywhere," Martlett put in.
"I do not doubt it for a moment. Well, he has been successful at last. I will hide no longer. Call Maxwell in and get the painful ordeal over."
"I did not gather that it was going to be painful," Martlett said, dryly. "On the contrary, I gleaned quite a contrary opinion. I have a pleasant surprise for you."
"Impossible. I killed that man and Venner knows it. Maxwell might forgive me, but Venner will always use his knowledge. But for Venner—"
"But for Venner there would have been no trouble or complication at all. I know that quite as well as you do. But we are going to scotch that snake permanently. He will be here very soon, and you shall have the pleasure of kicking him out of the office yourself, with the pleasing knowledge that he is quite powerless for the future."
But Spencer was hardly listening. His mind had gone back into the past. Martlett was not a man who promised vain things as a rule, but he was entirely over-sanguine now. And the dull office with its dust and gloom and musty

paper was hardly the environment of a miracle. Martlett rang the bell and the door opened; a big man in a rough shooting suit walked in.
His round face was beaming with good humor, his eyes were full of pleasure. He strode up to the dazed Spencer and gripped him with a force that was real enough.
"So you have been frightening yourself with ghosts all these years," he said. "Running away from me and the ghost of my queer partner, Jim Miller! If I had known what a thorough-paced ruffian Miller was I should never have chummed in with him. But I didn't know until it was too late, and then I tried to get rid of him, and he knew it. I don't like failing."
"Oh, I succeed where you failed," Spencer said, bitterly.
"And you have been haunted by that rascal's ghost ever since, eh?"
"By that and by a nemesis in the form of my old servant Horace Venner. You remember the fellow that I had to get rid of out yonder. He came back upon me at a time when fortune was smiling her sweetest. And there was no way of getting rid of him."
Maxwell laughed and smote the speaker on the back heartily.
"I'm sorry," he said. "If you had only stayed a day or two longer, if you had only faced the music. Do you suppose we should have let you hang?"
"There was Denman, for instance. A good citizen who defended his life—"
"That was a mistake. You see we hadn't got matters quite in hand then. But you might have stayed a bit longer—long enough to find out."
"But I came back with my daughter," Spencer cried, eagerly. "I wanted to see you and explain. But Venner turned up there, of all places in the world, and I had to fly."
"It was unfortunate I did not see you," Maxwell replied. "If I had done so, my dear Paul, I should have hanged your nemesis for you. So he turned up at 'Frisco? Really, the audacity of the fellow is amazing. But my young friend Seymour has cut him close now."
"You mean that there is some charge hanging over his head?"
Maxwell laughed, and Martlett permitted himself to relax into a smile. Maxwell was smoking a cigar in the precincts of the office, a flagrant disregard of precedent and proprieties. But it was to be a red-letter day in the annals of the old family solicitor.
"I do," he said. "The evidence is very clear. When Venner comes down here I am going to charge him with the wilful murder of one Jim Miller in San Francisco on Saturday, August the fifteenth—"
"But I killed him myself," Spencer cried. "I shot him down. I saw him fall."
"All the same, you didn't kill him," Maxwell said, coolly. "Here is the man who did. Come, you rascal, tell us how you murdered James Miller?"
Venner had been pushed by somebody into the room. He advanced with the carneying smile and the servile tread of the well-trained servant who has been

caught in some flagrant dishonesty, and who hopes to work upon the good nature of his employer. He paused with a gasping cry, and would have turned and fled had not Seymour stood by, big and strong, in the doorway.

Venner dropped into a chair and wiped his wet face. He ground the palms of his hands together and feebly suggested that his heart was weak. The shock had turned him sick and dizzy. The big form of Maxwell floated in a mist before his eyes.

"This is a surprise," he gasped; "really a great surprise."

"I thought it would be," Seymour said, grimly. "I worked hard to make it so. I am extremely glad to find that you are not disappointed."

"A great surprise," Venner groaned feebly. "Mr. Maxwell, sir, I hope you are well; I hope—"

"You don't hope anything of the kind," Maxwell said. "If you could see the whole of us dead at your feet you would be glad. Get up off that chair; how dare you sit down in the presence of your betters! Get up at once and tell us your story."

Venner staggered to his feet. He passed his tongue over his dry lips.

"Certainly, sir," he whined. "May I ask for a little patience for an unfortunate valet who is not the man he was? As I was saying, gentlemen—But, really, I feel so queer that—I'm better now. Just as well for me to make a clean breast of it; I did kill Jim Miller."

He paused as if to give effect to his words.

"My master, Mr. Paul, had discharged me. I don't say I didn't deserve it; but the fact remains. A good deal of the early troubles would never have been if Mr. Paul had not seen me at all. I was a bad lot, gentlemen, as a boy, and I shall never be anything better."

A murmur of approval followed from the interested listeners.

"But, we need not go into that. I am making the confession because if I don't do so I shall have to stand my trial. To go back again. Usually I flatter myself that I tell really a good story, but I have had a great shock to-day. Where am I? Oh, at the beginning. Well, I was quite discredited and without money. I hung about Mr. Paul, and I watched him carefully. Then I discovered that there had been a quarrel between you two gentlemen and Jim Miller, and it seemed to me that I might be able to make something out of it, especially as Miller was going to get you both out of the way.

"He meant to force a fight on you, and he chose Mr. Paul first. Mr. Paul, sir, when you entered that hut you were a doomed man. It was fortunate for you that you were warned by a sudden blow, and that you got your gun out first. Then you fired; I watched you from behind the door. You imagined that you killed your man, as he fell like a stone covered in blood, but you did nothing of the kind. You bolted off without looking once behind you, and then you gave yourself into my power.

"Miller was not dead at all. He was stunned by a bullet that grazed his temple. I thought he was dead, and here my chance came in. There was money in that hut hidden under a floor board. I went to get it. As I was getting it Miller sat up and looked at me in a dazed kind of way. There was only one thing for it. I shot him through the head, and left with more money than ever I had in my pocket before, and that is saying a good deal. I was fairly comfortable in my mind, because the crime would be put on you."

"But only for a time," said Maxwell. "The bullets didn't tally, so that gave us a clue. A coolie gave us another, and by the time my friend Paul had fled for his life, we were hot upon the track of our interesting autobiographical visitor here. We had enough evidence to hang him ten times over. But he got away, as these fellows always do, and that's about the end of the story."

It all seemed so simple now that it was told, but at the same time something in the shape of a modern miracle had happened. Paul Spencer Gay, Lord Stanmere, had never killed Miller at all; he had been free to hold up his head amongst men all these years, and yet he had walked in the sackcloth and ashes of repentance. His lingers itched to be at the sanguine throat of Horace Venner.

"Go on, you scoundrel," he said. "You have a little more to tell."

"Not much, sir," Venner said, meekly. "You had got away and I had got away. I found that you were in London in a prosperous condition. There was another little chance for me. With my luck you were still firmly of the opinion that you had killed Miller. If I could only find you, what a good time I might have. And I did find you, only you eluded me and got away. And then you put up a deception that led me from the track altogether. I fancy that my wife knew when I came back to her, but she said nothing, and till I happened to see you and Mr. Spencer together that night at Stanmere I had not the slightest idea of the way in which the feather had been drawn over my eyes. Mr. Martlett—"

"Has nothing whatever to do with it," the lawyer said shortly. "Go on."

But there was no more to say. The whole thing had been exposed, the bubble pricked, the scoundrel wrecked. He hung about in his servile way as if waiting for something.

"Send him to Australia," Spencer said; "pay his passage and give him one hundred pounds to start with. The scoundrel doesn't deserve it, but for the sake of the wife—and if you ever come back again I shall set the police on your track as sure as you are alive. Go out."

Venner crept away with the carneying smile on his face. There was silence for a little while after he had gone.

"Now what is the next thing?" Spencer asked.

"After to-morrow," Martlett said, thoughtfully, "the next thing is to put the cover on the whole business and go down with me to Stanmere."

LVI. — CLEARED.

So there had been nothing to fear all those long years. Paul Spencer, Lord Stanmere, felt like a man who has found the surface after a long and hazardous dive. He was absolutely free to go where he liked without fear of that shadow before his eyes. He went off to his own house as soon as he had finished with Martlett. His present wish was to be alone.

He was alone now, even the faithful Kant was nowhere to be seen. He sat in the window of the morning-room smoking a cigar, a most unusual thing for him to do at this time of the day. But he wanted to enjoy the luxury of feeling like other men. He watched the people coming and going with a glad feeling of satisfaction that he was like them, comfortable and commonplace, and free to do as he pleased. He was sitting there when Kant came in.

The faithful servant glanced at him uneasily. All this was so contrary to the morbid prudence of the last few years. There was an air about the master of the house that Kant had not seen for many a day. He advanced to draw down the blind.

"Excuse me," he said, "you don't seem to be aware that—"

"I am not aware of anything beyond the fact that I am free," Spencer replied. "My good Kant, the miracle has happened. I am absolutely free."

"You don't mean to say that Venner is dead, sir?" Kant asked.

"To me, yes; to the world, unfortunately no. I have been flying from shadows, Kant. There is no blood on my soul. It was all a strange mistake. Perhaps I had better explain."

He proceeded to do so. Kant's inscrutable features gradually relaxed into a smile. After a time he became his grave self again.

"But what about the other little matter, sir?" he asked.

Spencer came down from the clouds. In the joy of his new-found freedom he had forgotten all about that. He still stood in a position of some peril.

"I shall be able to prove an alibi now," he said, thoughtfully.

"Because there is no reason why you should not explain your visit to Stanmere, sir. That is all very well in its way, sir, but it only makes more scandal. There is no need for the world to know anything about Miss Mary. Keep her out of it if you can, for you owe her a great deal. She must know, and Lady Stanmere must know, but a curious public need not. I am afraid that I am taking a great liberty, sir."

"You are not doing anything of the kind," Spencer replied. "You have been a wonderfully good and faithful servant to me, and I am not likely to forget it. I had better consult Mr. Martlett. In this matter I shall be guided by his opinion."

It was later in the afternoon when Spencer walked to Lincoln's Inn. It had been years since he leisurely strolled through London in broad day-light. The whole thing was a luxury that he enjoyed beyond measure. There were no lurking shadows now. Here was the place where Stephen had come out and attacked him; there was the spot where he had almost walked into Venner's arms one

November evening. But all these terrors had gone.
He walked into Martlett's office, tall, expanding, commanding of presence. Martlett smiled behind his hand as he noticed the change.
"It is a fine afternoon, my lord," he said, drily.
Spencer colored slightly. He perfectly understood Martlett's meaning.
"Don't call me that yet," he said, "and my poor brother only buried this morning, Martlett. I have been indulging in the luxury of my freedom. Kant reminds me that I am not yet out of the wood. At the inquest to-morrow I should like to make my position perfectly clear. I can say now where I was at the time of the murder."
"Which was at Stanmere, I presume?"
"Quite so. I went down there to see Mary, or, rather, on the off-chance of seeing her. To be perfectly candid, I wanted to persuade her to postpone that operation."
Martlett scraped his dry chin thoughtfully.
"I quite understand," he said. "You seem to have raised a certain amount of prejudice over this matter. Our young friend, Dick Stevenson, for instance—"
"Regards me as an unfeeling monster. It is not often that anyone has spoken to me as he did. But a day or two ago the thing seemed absolutely necessary."
"Well, get on. It is not necessary any longer. Miss Mary must at once—"
"Of course, of course. I desire nothing better than a speedy chance of putting myself right in everybody's eyes. And I am longing for a good time at Stanmere."
"Also you want to get the thing settled without any suggestion of scandal. Now tell me exactly what happened at Stanmere when you were there the other night."
Spencer proceeded to explain. Martlett smiled with the air of a man who sees his way.
"You saw Miss Mary!" he said. "She cried out and you had to vanish. There is no need to go into all this before the coroner. You saw the child and she saw you."
"But, my dear Martlett, consider that it was impossible—"
"I say she saw you,'" Martlett went on, doggedly. "There was a bandage over her eyes; I suppose you imagined that was a kind of preliminary operation performed by Von Wrangel. The bandage slipped off her eyes and she saw you as plainly as I see you now."
"Then the operation has been performed?"
"Partly! In a measure it was your bete noir, Venner, who prevented the success of the affair. I have all the facts from Von Wrangel. Perhaps I had better explain."
Spencer listened with the deepest interest. He was not astonished, for so many things had happened lately that he was past extremes in emotion.

"Miss Mary could identify you across a room," Martlett went on. "She shall come up and do so at the inquest. All she has to do is to say that she saw you in the corridor about the time of the murder, and there will be an end of the matter. Wear the same clothes and tie to-morrow that you wore that night. After what Miss Mary and Von Wrangel have to say there will be no question as to your—er—innocence. Now you had better come with me and settle the question of the last mortgage."

Von Wrangel stood giving his evidence quietly and coolly, knocking the last leaves of sensational romance out of what the papers called the Cambria Square mystery. There had been no blood feud between the two brothers beyond a quarrel which was entirely outside the premises of the court. Stephen Gay was a passionate man, and like most passionate men, was given to say a great deal more than he intended. He had assaulted his brother, it was true; but then every man who commits bodily violence is not necessarily a murderer at heart. Stephen Gay had been the victim of a political society.

"That is your opinion?" the coroner asked.

"It is my knowledge," Von Wrangel said, calmly. "I once belonged to the same society myself, but I am Baron Von Wrangel, once known as an eye specialist. Two nights before the murder the man who had a hand in the crime actually told me where I should find the dead man, and what was going to happen him."

A murmur of astonishment ran round the room. There was a sensation of quite another kind.

"And you gave no notice to the police?" the coroner asked, sternly.

"It was useless," Von Wrangel replied. "I was doing my best to get the dead man away. If I had told the police and the gang had been arrested, others would have sprung up immediately to take their place; I should not have known them, and consequently would have been placed at a great disadvantage in my endeavors to battle them. The police would have been powerless."

The coroner shook his head gravely. All this was quite contrary to constitutional practices. The police should have been informed without delay.

"I was of more use than all the police in in Europe," Von Wrangel went on. "I should have baffled these men if the deceased had followed my advice. He had betrayed his cause and his life was forfeit. My own life was forfeit at one time, though I lost everything for the cause—hence my assumed name and the humble nature of my lodging."

"Do I understand that you advocate this kind of violence?" the coroner asked.

"Quite the contrary," Von Wrangel said, coolly. "It cost me all I had to prevent it. I would have done much to save the life of Stephen Gay, but it was impossible. He was a marked man by half the secret societies of Europe. See how cleverly they managed it. They got into the house in Cambria Square, then committed that crime without leaving a trace behind. They will never be caught. I am willing to give the police the names and description of two of the gang, and I am ready to stake my reputation that the police will never arrest them. The authorities in Berlin knew all about Stephen Gay and the way that he betrayed the trust placed in him; they will tell you exactly what I am telling you now, and they will not hesitate to confirm my opinion. If I stay here all night I can say no more."

For a long time Von Wrangel stood there undergoing a shower of questions. But his calm assurance and firm conviction remained entirely unshaken. All the romance was going out of the case, it was only one of those vulgar political murders after all. When Von Wrangel stood down at length there was hardly a person in the room who would have held Paul Spencer responsible for the mystery now.

The latter stood up calm and resolute, and demanded to give evidence. He could tell the court now what he was for private reasons unable to tell them before. On the night of the murder he had gone down to Stanmere to see his daughter. Unfortunately he had not been able to have the interview that he desired, because his daughter had been partly under an operation for her eyes, but she had seen him in the corridor at the time mentioned and would testify to the fact.

"But is not your daughter blind?" the coroner asked.

"She was," Spencer replied. "But she has the sight of one eye. The operation was interrupted, but she can see for all practical purposes."

The coroner, as a matter of form, would like Miss Spencer to be called. Not that there was much doubt as to the case after the evidence of Baron Von Wrangel. Miss Spencer was outside the court with friends and was available at any moment, Martlett intimated.

Here was just an element of romance in the case after all. There was something pathetic in the partially blind girl coming forward to clear her own father. With a bandage over her eyes Mary was led forward. The sweet, patient face and the clear voice made a deep impression.

"I did not expect my father," Mary said. "I understood that he had not been told of the operation; at any rate, I hoped it would be a pleasant surprise for him. I was in bed the night my father came. I fancied that I heard him call to me and I went into the corridor. The bandage slipped from my eyes and I called out, suddenly. A moment later and my father was gone."

"Why should he have gone so hurriedly?" the coroner asked.

"That I cannot tell you," Mary said, quietly. "I believe there are reasons why my father does not care to be seen at Stanmere. But he was there at the time I speak of."

The coroner pressed the question. It was impossible to deny the credibility of the witness.

"How was your father dressed?" he asked.
"He had a grey frock suit and a red tie," Mary said. "If I may remove this bandage for a moment—"
Von Wrangel jumped up and performed the necessary office. In a misty kind of way Mary looked round the room and smiled finally at Spencer, whose face flushed uneasily.
"Just the same as he is dressed now," Mary cried, "only there was no pin in his scarf. It was a little past the hour when I—"
But there was no need to say any more. Almost as soon as the bandage was removed Von Wrangel had it back again. There were no more witnesses to call, and the coroner proceeded to put the case to the jury. He was a little hard upon Von Wrangel, but the German listened calmly enough to that and the verdict of wilful murder against some persons or person unknown.
Outside the court Mary found herself leaning on her father's arm.
"Where are we going now?" she asked.
"You are going back to Stanmere to-night," Spencer said. "Von Wrangel is anxious to finish his work. And I hope to join you to-morrow. The shadows are all falling away now, Mary."

LVII. — MARY SEES AT LAST.

Dick and Molly were having a bad time of it at the hands of Von Wrangel. The little German was all impatience to finish the work that he had already begun; he was cross and snappish in the cab which conveyed the party to the operating-room which had been loaned for the occasion. Nurse Cecilia was waiting there, but there would be no need for her services.
"And why you two people came along, goodness knows," Von Wrangel said, testily. "Go away and look at the shops. Go and find my friend Tom Seymour. Scold him him for neglecting you all this time, Miss Molly. Then come back in an hour's time and we will go back to Stanmere together. At present I am not what you call in the most seraphic mood."
"You are absolutely intolerable," Molly laughed, "and Mary has my deepest sympathy."
Mary smiled sweetly. She was the only one of the party who seemed absolutely at her ease. Cecilia stood by, quietly looking out of her pale face with dark mournful eyes. Von Wrangel hustled them up the steps without ceremony and closed the door behind them. Once he was in the operating room his manner changed entirely. He was the cool resolute doctor once more.
"Now then," he said, "it is only a matter of a few minutes. But I don't want those young people about me for a while. Nurse, will you hand me those cases?"
It was all over almost before Mary was aware that her eyes had been touched.

There was just a prick or two, a cold lotion on her face, and she was looking up at Von Wrangel, who stood there with a quiet smile of triumph and power on his face.
The blinds were all drawn, but it was quite possible to see there. Mary noted the pictures on the walls and a bunch of late primroses by her side. She could see the wrinkled green foliage and the yellow sheen on the blossoms.
"Oh, it is wonderful," she cried. "Wonderful. And it is going to last. Doctor, doctor, I am very much afraid that I am going to have a good cry."
"The best prescription for you in the world," Von Wrangel said, cheerfully. "Have a nice long, comfortable cry with Nurse Cecilia to help you whilst I go and smoke a cigarette. And, between ourselves, I feel that I have earned it. Afterwards you are to put on those smoked glasses. They are pretty hideous, but it will be only for a day or two."
Mary lay back for a long time crying quietly, with Cecilia stroking her hair and whispering soothing words in her ears. But these tears were tears of pure delight, and seemed to carry off what might have been a dangerous hysterical outburst. When the eyes had regained their tranquility again, Cecilia fitted on the smoked glasses and bade Mary look at herself.
"You must get used to your beauty yourself," she laughed. "What do you think of that?"
Mary declared it was the pleasantest sight she had ever seen in her life. Outside people were passing; there were horses and carriages and dogs that Mary regarded with a childish delight.
"And there is Molly," she cried. "I am sure it must be Molly. Yes, there is Von Wrangel talking to them—I am sure it is Von Wrangel. And one of those young men must be my dear Dick. Cecilia, is Dick the one with the fair moustache?"
"You have guessed it exactly, Miss Mary," Cecilia said.
"Oh, I am so glad. And he is quite as handsome as Molly said he was. Let us go out and meet them and get back to dear old Stanmere as soon as possible. We must walk to Victoria. I could not think of riding on such a day as this."
They were all on the doorstep talking together. Dick had got hold of Mary and was looking down into her eyes. Von Wrangel was being vigorously thumped on the back by Seymour. The little doctor was a wild schoolboy once more. It seemed impossible to associate him with anything serious. It was a long time before Dick spoke.
"Oh, my dear," he said. "To think of it. My dear Mary!"
She returned the pressure of his hand. Then she laid her hand on his arm and together they turned along the street in that glorified walk.
"You talk and I will listen, Dick," Mary said. "If I say much I shall begin to cry again. No, I am not going to have a cab. I would not miss this walk for worlds. To see everything, to be like other people, to be able to look into your

face!"
She paused and swallowed down the lump that would come in her throat. Von Wrangel was laughing and chatting behind in his most inconsequent manner. It was like a fairy journey, the crowds, the bustling station, and then the green fields, the smiling landscape and the blue hills beyond. Mary sat drinking in its beauty with her hand closed in Dick's.
"How familiar it all seems," she said. "There is the lodge and old Betty standing in the gateway ready for a chat with anybody who comes along. Let us go in by the side gate, for I could not stand Betty just for the present. And there is my dear grandmother in the rose garden. Dick, let us go up to her and take her quite by surprise."
Lady Stanmere's surprise and joy were both complete. Mary could see her as well as she could see Mary. And so it was to continue now for all time.
"I shall see the light in those blue eyes of yours soon," Lady Stanmere said. "For the present I have only the joy of the recovery to think of. Von Wrangel, you have repaid everything, Mary's father—"
"Not a word," Von Wrangel whispered. "Say nothing about it, it is all coming right presently. Go into the arbour by the lake, gracious lady, and I will come to you presently. You have had one pleasant surprise to-day, and I hope you are strong enough to bear another."
"I have not had so many that they pall upon me," Lady Stanmere said, quietly. "Well, I shall be glad for a few minutes' peace and quietness. If you only knew how miserably anxious I have been. Von Wrangel, I have greatly misjudged you."
"Nothing of the kind," Von Wrangel protested. "I am not worthy of your kind consideration. I am going to keep those young people from you till dinner time. It seems unkind, perhaps, but you are going to be glad presently. Now, do go as far as the arbour."
Lady Stanmere walked along with joy in her heart and a sense of unsteadiness in her limbs. She would be glad to sit down for a little time.
But not alone, as she had expected. As she entered the arbour a tall figure in a grey suit arose and looked at her with wistful eyes. Lady Stanmere returned the glance with a drowsy kind of feeling upon her. Something that she had long lost had come back to her life again.
"Paul," she said unsteadily; "Stanmere, is it really you?"
She looked into the broad, open face again and could see no shadow of violence and passion there. She had pictured her lost boy to herself many times, but she had not hoped for this. For this man would have passed for something fine and wholesome and splendid everywhere. A true Gay, like his father; but with a grander air. Lady Stanmere held out her hands.
"You have come to stay, I hope?" she said, in trembling tones. "Paul, Paul!"
He stooped and kissed her reverently. There were tears in the eyes of both of

them. Stanmere led his mother to a seat and sat beside her with her hand in his.
"I shall realise it all presently," Lady Stanmere said. "But why have you been away so long? Why did you go at all, Paul?"
"I went because I quarrelled with my father. I am afraid that my father never understood either of us. He spoils us one day, and we are sternly punished for such faults the next. And both Stephen and myself were always passionate and headstrong."
Lady Stanmere sighed; she had reason to remember that.
"I declared that I would go and make my fortune," Stanmere went on. "I was not coming home until I could retrieve the family fortunes. After a time my dream looked like being realised, when a great misfortune happened to me. Presently I will tell you what that misfortune meant, and how it looked like preventing my accomplishing the task that I had cut out for myself. I had to stoop to deceit, and that deceit closed the doors of Stanmere to me."
"But I should always have been glad to see you, my boy."
"I know, I know. And I have often been nearer to you than you imagine. But we shall come to that presently. I dare not come here so long as I was practising that deceit. And thereby I did a cruel thing to you, for which I shall ask your forgiveness presently. It was a case where it seemed to me that the end justified the means. And all the time my project prospered. When my father died Stanmere was nearly out of my grasp. To-day it is perfectly cleared and a fine property."
"And you have done all this, Paul? You are the means of saving the dear old home."
"Yes; that much I can take credit for. I arranged it through Martlett. What means I had to take to do it, I shall explain later on. I hope to be forgiven, for I have done no real harm. My dear mother, will you be so good as to fetch Mary to me? I see her yonder with Von Wrangel. Bring her here, and let us not have anybody else for a few minutes."
Lady Stanmere came back with Mary presently. She could see Stanmere hidden in the glow of the little arbor, but he stepped into the light a minute later. Mary gave a little cry and then threw herself into his arms. Her happiness was complete.
"My own dear father!" she murmured. "My own dear, dear father! Baron Von Wrangel has performed the miracle, and I can see again. Oh, my dear father, how glad you must be!"
Lady Stanmere looked on as one who dreams. Stanmere was holding the girl away so that she could see fully into his face.
"Very near and yet so far from the truth," he said. "Look at me again."
Mary did so wonderingly. She seemed to be studying some puzzling picture.
"The same voice," she said, "the same tones, and yet so different." The puzzled expression left her face, her cheeks grew a little paler.

"What does it mean?" she whispered. "I don't understand what it all means. You are—you are? Why, you are not my father at all!"
Stanmere caught the girl's hands in his.
"I am your uncle Paul, Lord Stanmere," he said. "Let me be the father to you now that I have assumed to be for the last four years."

LVIII. — "EYES CLEARER GROWN."

Stanmere stood there with the girl's hands in his, watching for some signs of anger or disgust. But there was nothing but a certain puzzled expression, an eager curiosity.
"You mean that my father is dead?" she asked. "Please tell me. I am in the dark; there have been so many mysteries. And I see now that my grandmother is in mourning. If my father is dead—"
She paused unsteadily. Stanmere pressed her hands again.
"Your father is dead," he said, "he was killed in Cambria Square, where he was a guest under my roof. We had been on bad terms for years. And he—he died."
"Please tell me the worst," Mary said. "My father was murdered?"
"I am afraid so. It all seems strange yet. Perhaps my words may sound cold. Years ago my father and brother became involved in foreign politics. I fancy they went very far indeed. And there was trouble over some conspiracy—"
"My father betrayed his trust," Mary interrupted. There was just a suspicion of hardness in her speech. "I recollect that now. I did not understand it at the time, but I do now. It was some time before I had my illness, when things were going very well with us, and we lived at Stamford Hill. I was a little afraid of my father; he had outbursts of dangerous passion, and when we were poor we used to have a hard time with him. I recollect how good and patient my mother was. And then she died; I shall never forget my mother."
Mary paused for a moment. The other two exchanged glances. There was no reason to tell Mary yet how recently the tragedy had been enacted.
"A few days before I came back, or before I was sent to Stanmere four years ago, two men came to see my father. They were foreigners, and there was a great scene. I did not understand all they said, but I gathered that my father had done something shameful. When these men were gone I found him in a great state of agitation. He told me we must leave at once, because he dared not stay in England any longer. And when I asked why, there was a fearful outburst of anger that frightened me. After that I was ill, and Cecilia was nursing me. Then came my blindness. My father had been away. He crept back to the house one night and told me I might never see him again. I was to go to Stanmere, and if things took a turn for the better again he would send for me. And in the course of time he did send for me, the message saying I was to come with him at once and ask no questions. I was very happy at Stanmere,

but my duty was plain and I obeyed."
"It was I who sent for you," Stanmere said. "It was a desperate venture."
"But why did you do it?" Lady Stanmere cried. "Why did you so cruelly deceive me—"
"Mother, I am afraid I did not consider you at the time. My brother was an outcast, and his child was blind. She could not see the slight difference in our faces, and she would not recognise the equally slight difference in our voices."
"But I did," Mary said eagerly. "When I came back to you to Cambria Square I detected the difference at once. Your voice was softer than that of my father, except at times when you were excited or angry. And you treated me with a kindness and consideration that you had never before shown me. I tried to forget all I recollected of the past, and I succeeded. I thought that my father had become a better and a nobler man. You told me that you were prosperous, and that you had deemed it necessary to change your name to Spencer. All those late walks and the mystery with which you surrounded yourself did not arouse my suspicion, because as my real father had terrible enemies he would have done precisely the same thing. And yet at times I could not keep down the suspicion that you were somebody else."
"There was something you could not understand?" Stanmere said.
"There was something that made suspicion impossible," Mary said. "In Cambria Square I had exactly the same surroundings that I had at Notting Hill; my flowers, vases, pictures—everything. How could I entertain any lingering suspicion after that?"
"But why did you do it? Why did you do it?" Lady Stanmere asked again.
"I was coming to that presently," Stanmere said. "It had to be done; and, after all, the deceit harmed nobody. Mary, you and I have been all over the world together. You have trusted me implicitly—"
"And I have not been unrewarded," Mary said. "But for the mystery and the moving from place to place, they were happy years. I had everything that you could lavish upon me; you even gave me my old home. You have been more like a lover than a father all the time. That is why I asked no questions. I did exactly as I was told, though the thought of the way I left my dear grandmother has always been on my conscience. And I am afraid that I regretted my position at times."
"Nor more than was natural," Stanmere said. "And you little know what a tremendously powerful part you played in the drama. Without my blind girl I could have done nothing."
"If I am to be taken into your confidence," Lady Stanmere suggested, "I may perhaps be permitted to ask why I also should have been kept in the dark?"
"It was absolutely necessary, my dear mother," Stanmere replied. "I did not want Mary to see you. Suppose her father had died before; suppose you knew it and told Mary. She would naturally have asked, in that case, who I was.

Then the whole deceit would have been prematurely divulged, and all my plans ruined. There was just the chance after Mary knew how she had been deceived, that she would refuse to return to me. You wonder why I did this kind of thing. I will tell you in a word; I wanted to be mistaken for Stephen."

Lady Stanmere shook her head in a puzzled kind of way.

"You would not gain much by that," she suggested.

"Oh, yes, I would. I knew that Stephen was an outcast, flying from the vengeance that sooner or later must reach him. I learnt that he had sent his blind daughter down here. Stephen was out of the way, and his effects were to be sold by his creditors. I bought them. I was back in England then with the nucleus of a great fortune in my hands. But I had MY shadow dogging me, and I should never have carried out my plans if I had not baffled him. I bought up Stephen's effects, and decided to adopt his daughter. When my man fetched her she came, as she imagined, to her old home, or something like it. There was I, a speaking likeness of my poor unhappy brother Stephen, with my daughter by my side. The plan was a great success. The man who had meant to ruin my life was entirely taken in. He mistook me for Stephen grown rich and prosperous. I had only to avoid the broad light of the street and I was safe. For nearly three years my bete noir was hovering near me, and he never discovered the truth. And all that time I was steadily crowning the work that I had set myself to do."

Lady Stanmere was listening with great interest now. She looked up swiftly.

"But you stood to die by the hand that struck Stephen down," she said.

"No, I didn't. Those eyes were not deceived. Besides, they were following Stephen from place to place on the Continent, so I was safe in that direction. But all the time I had a great sorrow. I had committed murder; I had shot a man in California in cold blood, or something like it. The recollection of that crime haunted me day and night; I could not rid myself of the picture. And the man who was looking for me everywhere knew of my crime. Mother, can you guess who he was?"

"Horace Venner," Lady Stanmere said quietly. "The husband of poor, misguided Cecilia. It was a bad day when your father appointed that man to look after you two boys. I warned him, but he would not heed. He accompanied you when you last entered the house."

"Until I got rid of him out in San Francisco. There was no shaking off that man. He saw the crime that darkened all my life committed, and that is why he tried to get a chance to blackmail me in England. And all the time I had not committed that crime at all. I had merely stunned my man, and Venner himself came in and completed the tragedy. But I could not know that, and I went in fear of him. It has only been during the last few years that circumstances have proved too strong for Venner and forced a confession out of him. If I had only known—"

Stanmere paused for a moment. He had two interested listeners.

"I saw him in London and he saw me," he went on. "I managed to elude him. It was imperative just then that Venner should be blinded as to my identity. To be candid, it was Martlett who suggested a way to deceive the rascal. And this is how you came in, Mary. If you are angry—"

"I am not in the least angry," Mary said gently. "But I think that if you had told me in the first place I should have been quite ready to—"

"But we could not tell that," Stanmere went on eagerly. "Besides, you seemed so good and pure and incapable of playing a part. And your very innocence and simplicity made it so much easier. So long as you really took me for your father things could hardly go wrong. The scheme prospered, Venner was kept at bay, and I was growing rich. But there was one factor I did not reckon on."

"Mary recovering her sight, I suppose?" Lady Stanmere asked.

"No, I took her everywhere. I hunted for Von Wrangel, but after that affair in Berlin he seemed to have entirely disappeared. I had hoped some day for Mary to see again, but that is not the question. The part I had over-looked was the chance of Stephen turning up again."

"He did turn up and he found me out. Unfortunately he believed that I had a hand in putting his pursuers on his track. He would have killed me just then if he had had a chance. My nerves gave way entirely, and I was little better than a wreck. Fortunately for me, Stephen could not find out where I lived. If he had done so my plans would have been ruined. He found me at last through Venner, who had followed Stephen, thinking it was me. That wants a little thinking out, but it is quite plain. And Venner told Stephen he knew all about his little place in Cambria Square. Stephen tracked me; he followed me down here, where I had come to see Mary privately."

"But why privately?" Lady Stanmere asked.

"My dear mother, if I had done so openly you would have recognised me as your son Paul, and Mary would have known at once that I was not her father. Besides, I had a shameful purpose. I was going to try and get Mary to postpone the operation."

"Where was the need?" Mary asked.

Stanmere flushed a little uncomfortably.

"So that you should not see for a little time longer," he said. "I was half mad with terror, and the knowledge that all my plans were likely to fail. I did not dare to trust you or anybody. It was a cruel and disgraceful thing not to trust you. But there was danger all around, and it was for so short a time. Not that I did not suffer remorse and shame. I tried to get Dick on my side, but he spurned the suggestion with such words as I hope never to have applied to me again. I tried to frighten him, but I did not succeed. For those few hours I think I must have been mad."

"I came down here to see you, Mary, as I did the night we met in the corridor.

Stephen was there, and he guessed my errand. He knew of this operation, and it was his revenge. You would see once more, Mary. I had come to love you dearly, and when you knew the truth you would spurn me—"

"I shall love you all my life," Mary said gently. "There."

She stood up and kissed Stanmere on the cheek fondly. There was a pleased smile on his face.

"Then Stephen had to fly again. The danger was very real. When you found your way to Stanmere that night and subsequently took a walk with Von Wrangel, you had your hand on your father's arm. I stood in the window of the library personating him, so that his pursuers were entirely baffled. But we need not go into that at present. I only needed a few months longer before my work was complete. Then, by a fortunate accident, my character was cleared and I could face the world again. After that it did not matter how soon you learnt the truth, because there was no longer cause for concealment."

"But I went to London," Mary said; "I had to give some kind of evidence—"

"To save me from a charge of killing your father," Stanmere said. "I had better explain that."

Mary listened as the story was told. There was a deep sadness in her heart, but no tears in her eyes. For she had not loved her father in the old days; all that love had been transferred to the man who had been by her side in the dark and had uplifted and comforted her.

"So you forgive me?" Stanmere asked, at length.

"There is nothing to forgive," Mary said quietly. "I would have done all this for you, and more. But I should like to know what you were struggling so hard and running so great a risk for."

Stanmere looked round him across the lake to the hanging woods beyond.

"This," he said. "The restoration of the house of Stanmere."

LIX. — L'ENVOI.

Lady Stanmere pressed her hands together and gave a little cry.

"Now I begin to understand," she said. "For some years past I have been growing rich. One mortgage after another has been paid off through Mr. Martlett. He would tell me nothing, and I was fain to take the goods that the gods had provided. I had heard that you were in London, Paul, and that you were prosperous, and I didn't know Mary was with you. I actually thought she was with her father all the time, and so you have done this?"

"I have done all of it. It was the task I set myself to do directly I saw that I had a chance of fortune. I took Martlett into my confidence, and he managed the affair for me. When Venner came along and threatened to utterly ruin everything, it was he who devised the scheme in which Mary played so tremendous a part. Venner came near to upsetting everything, but nothing

matters now. And all this business of the operation came, and at a critical time when all that I had sunk might have been lost. There is one more sum of money necessary to be paid and Stanmere is free. I shall be the last Lord Stanmere, for I shall never marry again, but the properly will be a noble heritage some of these days for Mary and her children."
"I don't want to be a great heiress," Mary said quietly.
"Oh, yes, you do," Stanmere smiled. "Money is a precious thing in the proper hands. But you and Dick will learn how to appreciate it. You won't have much at first, and Dick will have to put all his energies into the 'Record,' which he shall have a share in presently."
"Then you are not going to stand in Dick's way?" Mary asked. "I was afraid that—"
"My dear, I have no right," Spencer said. "You are free to marry anybody you please. Between ourselves, I am quite delighted to find your choice falls on Dick. He loves you for yourself, and he would have loved you none the less for your condition. And but for Dick I should not be here at this moment. And now, let us both go back to our guests.'"
They crossed the terrace and entered the house. In the hall Goss was standing respectfully.
"Lord Stanmere has come home," Lady Stanmere said. "He proposes to remain here in future, Goss. I am sure you will be glad to see the master back again."
Goss forgot his dignity, and there were tears in his eyes as he took Stanmere's extended hand.
"I don't care what happens now," he said. "I've waited for this; I always knew it would come. I taught you to shoot, my lord, and I taught you to ride. I carried you in my arms before you could walk; and I always said to my lady that you would come back again some day. Thank God you have."
Von Wrangel, apparently sprung from nowhere, fortunately prevented any further weakness on the part of Goss, who averred that he had never behaved so shamefully before. From the corner of the dining-room Martlett was creeping, as musty and secretive as ever. The dry decorum broke down a little as Mary kissed him.
"So you are a maker of romance," she said. "I have been hearing all about your conspiracy, sir. I believe that you are a poet in disguise. If we searched your office we should find novels and plays and stories there. Mr. Martlett, I hope you feel thoroughly ashamed of yourself?"
Martlett permitted himself to indulge in the luxury of a chuckle.
"I beg your pardon," he said, in his driest fashion. "Nothing of the sort. I am an old-fashioned lawyer with a strong prejudice against the romantic and imaginative. I disclaim the scheme entirely. My client, Lord Stanmere, came to me in great trouble, and I merely advised him. He was good enough to

approve of my advice and applied it. I take no credit."
"And run no risks," Stanmere laughed.
Martlett took a pinch of snuff in a thoughtful manner.
"At the same time I don't mind making a confession," he said. "I have always taken a particularly warm interest in the fortunes of Stanmere; in fact, it has developed into a hobby of mine, like collecting postage stamps and other highly intellectual forms of science. If I had failed I should have been greatly annoyed—very much annoyed indeed. But we have not failed, though we came very near it. And I daresay in time you young people will forgive me."
They were a very happy party round the tea table in the drawing-room, though a little subdued, for the shadow of death was still close to the house. Stanmere drew Dick outside the window on to the terrace presently, under pretence of smoking a cigarette.
"Have you said anything to Mary yet?" he asked.
"My dear lord, as you have monopolized Mary ever since her return, it is perfectly obvious that I have done nothing of the kind," Dick smiled. "But you seem to understand each other."
A little of the old anxious look came into Stanmere's eyes.
"We have come to a perfect understanding," he said. "My dear Dick, you were right and I was wrong. I could have trusted Mary implicitly from the first. You perilled your position for her sake; you told me some home truths that I shall never forget."
"I am afraid that I was very rude," Dick said, with a fine color in his face.
"You told the truth, Dick; you spoke from your heart. And I was very nearly threatening you with poverty and trouble again if you did not fall in with my views. Thank God, I was spared that humiliation. But I was half mad at the time. Stanmere seemed to be slipping from my grasp. My mind was going. But all that had been changed, as probably Von Wrangel has told you."
"I fancy that I have heard everything," Dick replied.
Stanmere looked to the house with its grey worn front and away to the park and the woods beyond.
"I had set my heart on pulling through," he said. "As an atonement for all the follies of my youth, I resolved that Stanmere should be ours once again. When my father died it was a mere plank between my mother and the poorhouse. But step by step and stone by stone I won it back again. You can perhaps understand my feelings when I saw the ruins slipping through my fingers. But in a few weeks now it will all be mine. I shall never marry again, and by the time I die you will be, I hope, a man of ripe understanding, and you will be able to revive the old glories of the family and raise the old name again. It will be a noble heritage for Mary and your children."
Dick gasped. He had not expected anything like this.
"My dear lord," he stammered, "I could not possibly—"

"My dear boy, you can't help yourself. Mary is free to marry whom she pleases. At first you will have a small income and earn it. The Record will be yours some day; you shall have a share now. We will build out a few rooms at Shepherd's Spring, so that the place will be fitting for the future mistress of Stanmere. And I hope you will not be long before you are married. Before my time comes, I should like to hold in my arms a boy child, whom I could recognise as the future lord of these old acres."

Like the philosopher in the old story, Dick said nothing, for the simple reason that he had nothing to say. But he was eloquent enough presently, when he and Mary were alone together They wandered into the rose garden, which was one of Mary's favorite spots. And there, with Dick's arm about her, and her hand on his shoulder, she heard all the wonderful things that Dick had to tell.

"It reads like a wonderful romance," Mary said, after a long pause. "I have lost a father, and yet I feel that my father is still with me. How terribly he has been tried, Dick."

"He must he made much of," Dick said gravely. "He must be humored. For instance, he says he hopes it will not be long before we are married. We shall go to Shepherd's Spring for the present. My dearest girl, we really must not hurt Lord Stanmere by keeping him long waiting."

Mary smiled up into her lover's eyes. There was a deep flush on her face.

"Not just yet," she said. "We must wait six months. After that I am yours when you like to claim me, Dick. We have not known each other very long, but I fancy that we cared for each other from the first."

"I am sure that I did," Dick declared. "When I saw you standing there that eventful night with the light on your face, I vowed to myself that you were the one girl for me. And it must have been so, because otherwise we should never have been thrown together in that strange manner. And when I come to write my book I shall not lack material."

"An exciting situation," Mary said. "And that is all you want."

Dick stooped and kissed the red lips.

"Not quite all, sweetheart," he said. "Don't forget the heroine, lovely, amiable, charming and blind. What a pathetic figure? And love opens her eyes, and she sees again. Is it not wonderful! Could I have anything more perfect? My task will not be great, my darling, for it will contain the loveliest, daintiest, sweetest heroine that the world has ever seen."

THE END

Printed in the USA
CPSIA information can be obtained
at www.ICGtesting.com
LVHW061552290524
780938LV00008B/79